THE VERY PICTURE OF YOU

BANTAM BOOKS

NEW YORK

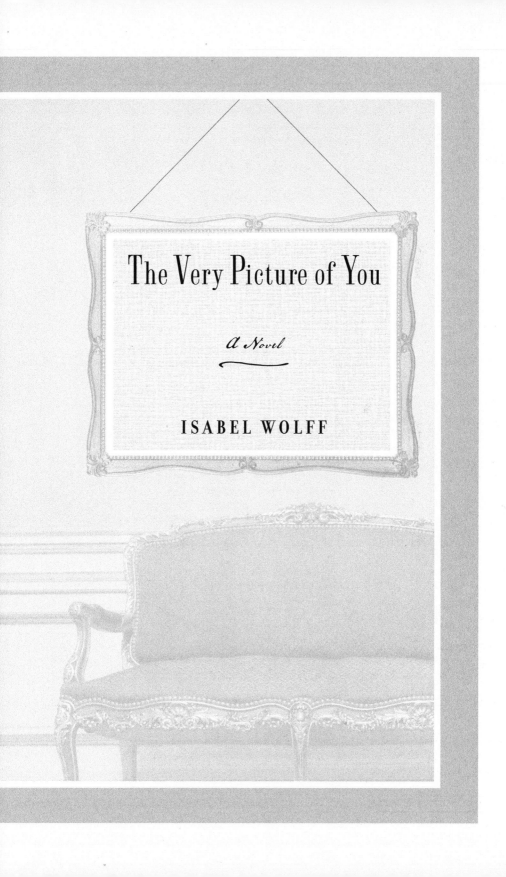

The Very Picture of You

A Novel

ISABEL WOLFF

Published in the United States by Bantam Books, an imprint of The Random House Publishing Group, a division of Random House, Inc., New York.

BANTAM BOOKS and the rooster colophon are registered trademarks of Random House, Inc.

Originally published in Great Britain in paperback by Harper, an imprint of HarperCollins Publishers, London, in 2011.

"Tears in Heaven," words and music by Eric Clapton and Will Jennings, copyright © 1992 by E.C. Music Ltd. and Blue Sky Rider Songs. Rondor Music (London) Limited. All rights for E.C. Music Ltd. administered by Unichapell Music Inc. All rights for Blue Sky Rider Songs administered by Irving Music, Inc. All rights in Germany administered by Rondor Musikverlag GmbH. International copyright secured. All rights reserved. Reprinted by permission of Hal Leonard Corporation. Used by permission of Music Sales Limited.

LIBRARY OF CONGRESS CATALOGING-IN-PUBLICATION DATA
Wolff, Isabel.
The very picture of you: a novel / Isabel Wolff.
p. cm.
ISBN 978-0-553-80784-4
eBook ISBN 978-0-440-42344-7
1. Women painters—Fiction. 2. Portrait painters—Fiction. I. Title.
PR6073.O355V47 2011
823'. 914—dc22   2011010439

Printed in the United States of America on acid-free paper

www.bantamdell.com

2 4 6 8 9 7 5 3 1

FIRST EDITION

Book design by Dana Leigh Blanchette
Title-page and interior photographs: © iStockphoto

For my parents-in-law,
Eva and John

Are we to paint what's on the face,
what's inside the face, or what's behind it?

PABLO PICASSO

THE VERY PICTURE OF YOU

Prologue

Richmond, England, July 23, 1986

"Ella . . . ? *El*-la?" My mother's voice floats up the stairs as I sit hunched over my sketchpad, my hand moving rapidly across the cartridge paper. "Where *are* you?" Gripping the pencil, I make the nose a little more defined, then shade in the eyebrows. "Could you *answer* me?" Now for the hair. Fringe? Swept back? I can't remember. "Gabri-*el*-la?" And I know I can't ask. "Are you in your room, darling?" I hear my mother's light, ascending tread and I stroke a soft fringe across the forehead, smudge it to add thickness, then swiftly darken the jaw. As I appraise the drawing I tell myself that it's a good likeness. At least I *think* it is. How can I know? His face is now so indistinct that perhaps I only ever saw it in a dream. I close my eyes, and it *isn't* a dream. I can see him. It's a bright day and I'm walking along and I can feel the warmth rising from the pavement and the sun on my face, and his big, dry hand enclosing mine. I can hear the *slap* of my sandals and the *click-clack* of my mother's heels and I can see her white skirt with its sprigs of red flowers.

He's smiling down at me. "Ready, Ella?" As his fingers tighten around mine, I feel a rush of happiness. "*Here* we go. One, two, three . . ." My tummy turns over as I'm lifted. "Wheeeeeee . . . !" they both sing as I sail through the air. "One, two, three—and *up* she goes! Wheeeeeeeeee . . . !" I hear them laugh as I land.

"More!" I stamp. "More! *More!*"

"Okay. Let's do a *big* one." He grips my hand again. "Ready, sweetie?"

"I rea-dee!"

"Right, then. One, two, three and . . . *u-u-u-u-u-p!*"

My head tips back and the blue dome of the sky swings above me, like a bell. But as I fall back to earth, I feel his fingers slip away, and when I turn and look for him, he's gone . . .

"*There* you are," Mum is saying from my bedroom doorway. As I glance up at her I slide my hand hastily over the sketch. "Would you go and play with Chloe? She's in the playhouse."

"I'm . . . doing something."

"Please, Ella."

"I'm too *old* for the playhouse—I'm eleven."

"I know, darling, but it would help me if you could entertain your little sister for a while, and she loves you to play with her . . ." My mother tucks a strand of white-blonde hair behind one ear, and I think how pale and fragile-looking she is, like porcelain. "And I'd rather you were outside on such a warm day." I will her to go back downstairs; instead, to my alarm, she is walking towards me, her eyes on the pad. I quickly flip the page over to a fresh sheet. "So you're drawing?" My mother's voice is, as usual, soft and low. "Can I see?" She holds out her hand.

"No . . . not now." I wish I'd torn out the sketch before she came in.

"You *never* show me your pictures. Let me have a look, Ella." She reaches for the pad.

"It's . . . private. Mum—*don't* . . ."

But she is already turning over the spiral-bound sheets. "What a *lovely* foxglove," she murmurs. "And these ivy leaves are perfect—so glossy; and that's an *excellent* one of the church. The stained glass must have been tricky but you've done it brilliantly." My mother shakes her head in wonderment, then gives me a smile; but as she turns to the next page her face clouds.

Through the open window I can hear a plane; its distant roar sounds like the tearing of paper.

"It's a study," I explain. "For a portrait." My pulse is racing.

"Well . . ." Mum nods. "It's . . . very good." Her hand trembles as she closes the notebook. "I had no idea that you could draw so well." She puts it back on the table. "You really . . . capture things," she adds quietly. A muscle at the corner of her mouth flexes but then she smiles again. "So . . ." She claps her hands. "*I'll* play with Chloe if you're busy, then we'll all watch the royal wedding. I've put the TV on so that we don't miss the start. You could draw Fergie's dress."

I shrug. "Maybe . . ."

"We'll have a sandwich lunch while we watch. Is cheese and ham okay?" I nod. "I *could* make coronation chicken—that would be *very* suitable, wouldn't it!" she adds with sudden gaiety. "I'll call you when it starts." She walks towards the door.

I take a deep breath. "So have I captured him?" My mother seems not to have heard me. "Does it look like him?" I try again. She stiffens visibly. The sound of the plane has dissolved now into silence. "Does my drawing look like my dad?"

I hear her inhale, then her slim shoulders sag and I suddenly see how expressive a person's back can be. "Yes, it does," she answers softly.

"Oh. Well . . ." I say as she turns to face me. "That's good. Especially as I don't really remember him anymore. And I don't even have a photo of him, do I?" I can hear sparrows squabbling in the flower beds. "*Are* there any photos, Mum?"

"No," she says evenly.

"But . . ." My heart is racing. "Why *not*?"

"Because . . . there just . . . aren't. I'm sorry, Ella. I know it's not easy. But . . ." She shrugs, as if she's as frustrated by this as I am. "I'm afraid that's just . . . how it *is*." She pauses for a moment, as if to satisfy herself that the conversation has ended. "Now, would you like tomato in your sandwich?"

"But you must have *some* photos of him?"

"Ella . . ." My mother's voice remains low, but then she rarely raises it. "I've already told you—I don't. I'm sorry, darling. Now I really *do* have to—"

"What about when you got married?" I imagine a white leather album with my parents smiling in every photo, my father darkly handsome in grey, my mother's veil floating around her china doll face.

She blinks, slowly. "I *did* have some photos, yes—but I don't have them anymore."

"But there must be others. I only need *one.*" I pick up my heart-shaped eraser and flex it between my thumb and forefinger. "I'd like to put his photo on the sideboard. There's that empty silver frame I could use."

Her cornflower blue eyes widen. "But . . . that simply wouldn't *do.*"

"Oh. Then I'll buy a frame of my own: I've got some pocket money—or I could make one, or you could give me one for my birthday."

"It's not the *frame,* Ella." My mother seems suddenly helpless. "I meant that I wouldn't *want* to have his photo on the sideboard. Or anywhere else, for that matter."

My heart is thudding. "Why *not*?"

"Because . . ." She throws up her hands. "Because he's not part of our *lives,* Ella, as you very well know—and he hasn't been for a long time so it would be confusing, especially for Chloe—he wasn't *her* father; and it wouldn't be very nice for Roy. And Roy's been so good to you," she hurries on. "*He's* been a father to you, hasn't he—a wonderful father."

"Yes—but he isn't my *real* one." My face has gone hot. "I've *got* a 'real' father, Mum, and his name is John, but I don't know where he is, or why I don't see him, and I don't know why you never ever *talk* about him." Her lips have become a thin line but I can't stop. "I haven't seen him since I was . . . I don't even know that. Was I three?"

My mother folds her slim arms and her gold bangle gently clinks against her watch. "You were almost five," she answers softly. "But you know, Ella, I'd say that the person who *does* the fathering *is* the father, and Roy does everything that any father *could* do, whereas . . . John . . . well . . ." She lets the sentence drift.

"But I'd still like a photo of him. I could keep it here, in my room, so that no-one else would have to see it—it would be just for me. Good," I add quickly. "So that's settled, then."

"Ella . . . I've already told you, I don't *have* any photos of him."

"Why *not*?"

She heaves a painful sigh. "They got . . . lost . . ." She glances out the window. ". . . when we moved down here." She returns her gaze to me. "Not everything came with us."

I stare at her. "But those photos *should* have come. It's mean," I add angrily. "It's *mean* that you didn't keep just one of them for me!" I am on my feet now, one hand on my chair, to steady myself against the clamour in my rib cage. "And why don't you *talk* about him? You never, *ever* talk about him!"

My mother's pale cheeks are suddenly pink—as if I'd brushed a swirl of rose madder onto each one. "It's . . . too . . . *difficult*, Ella."

"*Why?*" I try to swallow, but there's a knife in my throat. "All you ever say is that he's out of our lives and that it's better that way, and so I don't know what *happened* . . ." Tears of frustration sting my eyes. "Or why he left us . . ." My mother's features have blurred. "Or if I'll ever *see* him again." A tear spills onto my cheek. "So that's why—*that's* why I—" In a flash I'm on the floor, reaching under the bed, and dragging out my box. It has *Ravel* printed on it and Mum's best boots came in it. I get to my feet and place it on the bed. My mother looks at it, then, with an anxious glance at me, she sits down next to it and lifts off the lid . . .

The first drawing is a recent one, in pen and ink with white pastel on his nose, hair and cheekbones. I was pleased with it because I'd only just learned how to highlight properly. Then she takes out three pencil sketches of him that I'd done in the spring, in which, with careful cross-hatching, I'd managed to get depth and expressiveness into the eyes. Beneath that are ten or twelve older drawings in which the proportions are all wrong—his mouth too small or his brow too wide or the curve of the ear set too high. Then come five sketches in which there is no hint of any contouring, his face as flat and round as a plate. Now Mum lifts out several felt-tip images of my dad standing with her and me in front of a redbrick house with steps up to the dark green front door. Then come some bright poster colour paintings in each of which he's driving a big blue car. Now Mum lifts out a collage of him with pipe cleaners for limbs, mauve felt for his shirt and trousers and tufts of brown woollen hair that are crusted with glue. In the final few pictures Dad is barely more than a stick man. On these I have written, underneath, *dad,* but on one of them the first "d" is the wrong way round so that it says *bad.*

"So many," my mother murmurs. She returns the pictures to the box, then she reaches for my hand and I sit down next to her. "I should have told you," she says quietly. "But I didn't know how . . ."

"But . . . why didn't you? Tell me what?"

Her chin dimples with distress. "I was hoping to be able to leave it until you were older . . . but today . . . you've forced the issue." She presses her fingertips to her lips, staring at me, but somehow I know she's not seeing me. "All right, then," she whispers. Her hands drop to her lap and she takes a deep breath; and now, as the Wedding March thunders up to us from Westminster Abbey, she talks to me, at last, about my father. And as she tells me what he did I feel my world lurch, as though something big and heavy has just slammed into it . . .

We stay there for a time and I ask her some questions, which she answers. Then I ask her the same questions all over again. Then we go downstairs and I fetch Chloe in from the garden and we all sit in front of the TV and exclaim over Sarah Ferguson's billowing silk dress with its seventeen-foot, bee-embroidered train. And the next day I carry my box down to the kitchen and lift out the pictures. Then I thrust them all, deep, into the garbage pail.

One

"Sorry about this," the radio reporter, Clare, said to me early this evening as she fiddled with her small tape recorder. She tucked a hank of Titian red hair behind one ear. "I just need to check that the machine's recorded everything . . . there seems to be a gremlin . . ."

"Don't worry . . ." I stole an anxious glance at the clock. I'd need to leave soon.

"I really appreciate your time," Clare added as she lifted out the tiny cassette with perfectly manicured fingers. I try not to glance at my stained ones. "But with radio you need to record quite a lot."

"Of course." How old was she? I'd been unsure, as she was very made up. Thirty-five I now decided—my age. "I'm glad to be included," I added as she slotted the tape back in and snapped the machine shut.

"Well, I'd already heard of you, and then I read that piece about you in *The Times* last month . . ." I felt my stomach clench. "And I thought you'd be perfect for my programme—if I can just get this damn thing to *work* . . ." Through the makeup I could see Clare's cheeks flush as she stabbed at the buttons. *And when did you first re-alise that you were going to be a painter?* "Phew . . ." She clapped her hand to her chest. "It's still there." *I knew I wanted to be a painter from eight or nine . . .* She smiled. "I was worried that I'd erased it." *I simply drew and painted all the time . . .* Now, as she pressed FAST FORWARD, my voice became a Minnie Mouse squeak then slowed again to normal. *Painting's always been, in a way, my . . . solace.* "Great," she said as I scratched a blob of dried Prussian blue off my paint-stiffened apron. "We can go on." She glanced at her watch. "Can you spare another twenty minutes?"

My heart sank. She'd already been here for an hour and a half— most of which had been spent in idle chatter or in fussing with her tape recorder. But being in a Radio 4 documentary might lead to an-other commission, so I quelled my frustration. "That's fine."

She picked up her microphone then glanced around the studio. "This must be a nice place to work."

"It is . . . That's why I bought the house, because of this big attic. Plus the light's perfect—it faces northeast."

"And you have a glorious view!" Clare laughed. Through the two large dormer windows loomed the massive rust-coloured rotunda of Fulham's Imperial Gas Works. "Actually I like industrial archi-tecture," she added hastily, as if worried that she might have of-fended me.

"So do I—I think gas tanks have a kind of grandeur; and on the other side I've got the old Lots Road Power Station. So, no, it's not exactly green and pleasant but I like the area and there are lots of artists and designers around here, so I feel at home."

"It's a bit of a no-man's-land, though," Clare observed. "You have to come all the way down the King's Road to get here."

"True . . . but Fulham Broadway's not far. In any case, I usually cycle everywhere."

"That's brave of you. Anyway . . ." She riffled through her sheaf of notes on the low glass table. "Where were we?" I moved the pot of hyacinths aside to give her more room. "We'd started with your background," she said. "The Saturdays you spent as a teenager in the National Gallery copying old masters, the foundation course you did at the Slade; we'd talked about the painters you most admire— Rembrandt, Velázquez and Lucian Freud . . . I *adore* Lucian Freud." She gave a little shudder of appreciation. "So lovely and . . . *fleshy.*"

"Very fleshy," I agreed.

"Then we'd come to your big break with the BP Portrait Award four years ago—"

"I didn't win it," I interjected. "I was a runner-up. But they used my painting on the poster for the competition which led to several new commissions which meant that I could give up teaching and start painting full-time. So yes, that was a big step forward."

"And now the Duchess of Cornwall has put you right on the map!"

"I . . . guess she has. I was thrilled when the National Portrait Gallery asked me to paint her."

"And that's brought you some nice exposure." I flinched, but Clare prattled on, oblivious. "So have you had many famous sitters?"

I shook my head. "Most of them are 'ordinary' people who simply like the idea of having themselves or someone they love painted; the rest are either in public life in one way or another or have had a distinguished career which the portrait is intended to commemorate."

"So we're talking about the great and the good, then."

I shrugged. "You could call them that—professors and politicians, captains of industry, singers, conductors . . . a few actors."

Clare nodded at a small unframed painting hanging by the door. "I love that one of David Walliams—the way his face looms out of the darkness."

"That's not the finished portrait," I explained. "He has that of course. This is just the model I did to make sure that the close-up composition was going to work."

"It reminds me of Caravaggio," she mused. I wished she'd get *on* with it. "He looks a bit like Young Bacchus . . ."

"I'm sorry, Clare," I interjected. "But can we . . . ?" I nodded at the tape recorder.

"Oh—I keep chatting, don't I—let's crack on." She lifted her headphones onto her coppery bob then held the microphone towards me. "So . . ." She started the tape. "Why do you paint portraits, Ella, rather than, say, landscapes?"

"Well . . . landscape painting's very solitary," I answered carefully. "It's just you and the view. But with portraits you're with another human being and that's what's always fascinated me." Clare nodded and smiled for me to expand. "I feel excited when I look at a person for the very first time. When they sit in front of me I drink in everything I can about them. I study the colour and shape of their eyes, the line of their nose, the shade and texture of the skin, the outline of the mouth. I'm also registering how they *are,* physically."

"You mean their body language?"

"Yes. I'm looking at the way they tilt their head, and the way they smile; whether they look me in the eye, or keep glancing away; I'm looking at the way they fold their arms or cross their legs, or if they don't sit on the chair properly but perch forward on it or slouch down into it—because all that will tell me what I need to know about that person to be able to paint them truthfully."

"But—" A motorbike was roaring down the street. Clare waited for the noise to recede. "What does 'truthfully' mean—that the portrait looks like the person?"

"It ought to look like them." I rubbed a smear of chrome green off the palm of my hand. "But a good portrait should also reveal aspects of the sitter's character. It should capture both an outer and an *inner* likeness."

"You mean body and soul?"

"Yes . . . It should show the person, body and soul."

Clare glanced at her notes again. "Do you work from photographs?"

"No. I need to have the living person in front of me. I want to be able to look at them from every angle and to see the relationship between each part of their face. Above all I need to see the way the light bounces off their features, because that's what will give me the form and the proportions. Painting is all about seeing the light. So I paint only from life, and I ask for six two-hour sittings."

Clare's green eyes widened. "That's a big commitment—for you both."

"It is. But then, a portrait is a significant undertaking, in which the painter and sitter work together—there's a complicity to it—as though there's a pact between these two people."

She held the microphone a little closer. "And do your sitters open up to you?" I didn't reply. "I mean, there you are, on your own with them, for hours at a time. Do they confide in you?"

"Well . . ." I didn't like to say that my sitters confide the most extraordinary things. "They do sometimes talk about their marriages or their relationships," I answered carefully. "They'll even tell me about their tragedies, and their regrets. But I regard what happens during the sittings as not just confidential, but almost sacrosanct."

"So it's a bit like a Confessional, then," Clare suggested teasingly.

"In a way it *is*. A portrait sitting is a very special space. It has . . . an intimacy: painting another human being *is* an act of intimacy."

"So . . . have you ever fallen in love with any of your sitters?"

I smiled to hide the fact that I found the question intrusive. "I did once fall in love with a dachshund that someone wanted in the picture, but I've never fallen for a human sitter, no." I didn't add that as most of my male subjects were married they were in any case off-limits. I thought of the mess that Chloe had got herself into . . .

"Is there any kind of person you particularly enjoy painting?" Clare asked.

I paused while I considered the question. "I suppose I'm drawn to people who are a little bit dark—who haven't had happy-ever-after sort of lives. I like painting people who I sense are . . . complex."

"Why do you think that is?"

"I . . . find it more interesting to see the fight between the conflicting parts of someone's personality going on in the face." I glanced at the clock. It was half past six. I *had* to go. But . . . "Surely you have enough material now."

Clare nodded. "Yes, plenty." She lifted off her headphones, then smoothed down her glossy hair. "But could I have a quick look at your work?"

"Sure." I suppressed a sigh. "I'll get my portfolio."

As I fetched the big black folder from the other side of the studio Clare walked over to my big studio easel and studied the canvas standing on it. "Who's this?"

"That's my mother." I heaved the portfolio onto the table, then came and stood next to her. "She popped by this morning so I did a bit more. It's for her sixtieth birthday later this year."

"She's beautiful."

I studied my mother's round blue eyes with their large, exposed lids beneath perfectly arching eyebrows, at her sculpted cheekbones and her aquiline nose and at her left hand resting elegantly against her breastbone. Her skin was lined, but time had otherwise been kind. "It's almost finished."

Clare cocked her head to one side. "She has . . . poise."

"She was a ballet dancer."

"Ah." She nodded thoughtfully. "I remember now, it said so in that article about you." She looked at me. "And was she successful?"

"Yes—she was with English National Ballet then with the Northern Ballet Theatre in Manchester—this was in the seventies. That's her actually, on the wall, over there . . ."

Clare followed my gaze to a framed poster of a ballerina in a full-length white tutu and bridal veil. "Giselle," Clare murmured. "How lovely . . . It's such a touching story, isn't it—innocence betrayed . . ."

"It was my mother's favourite role—that was in '79. Sadly she had to retire just a few months later."

"Why?" Clare asked. "Because of having children?"

"No—I was nearly five by then. It was because she was injured."

"In rehearsal?"

I shook my head. "At home. She fell, and broke her ankle—very badly."

Clare's brow pleated in sympathy. "How terrible." She looked at the portrait again, as if seeking signs of that disappointment in my mother's face.

"It was hard . . ." I had a sudden memory of my mother sitting at the kitchen table in our old flat, her head in her hands. She used to stay like that for a long time.

"What did she do then?" I heard Clare ask.

"She decided that we'd move to London; once she'd recovered enough she began a new career as a ballet mistress." Clare looked at me enquiringly. "It's something that older or injured dancers often do. They work with a company, refreshing the choreography or rehearsing particular roles: my mother did it with the Festival Ballet for some years, then with Ballet Rambert."

"Does she still do that?"

"No—she's more or less retired. She teaches one day a week at the English National Ballet School, otherwise she mostly does charity work; in fact she's organised a big gala auction tonight for Save the Children, which is why I'm pushed for time, as I have to be there, but in here . . ." I went back to the table and opened the folder. ". . . are the photos of all my portraits. There are about fifty."

"So it's your Face Book," Clare said with a smile. She sat on the sofa again and began to browse the images. "*Fisherman* . . ." she murmured. "That one's on your website, isn't it? *Ursula Sleeping . . . Emma. Polly's Face* . . ." She gave me a puzzled look. "Why did you call this one *Polly's Face,* given that it's a portrait?"

"Oh, because Polly's my best friend—we've known each other since primary school; she's a hand-and-foot model and was jokingly complaining that no-one ever showed any interest in her face so I said I'd paint it."

"Ah . . ."

I pointed to the next image. "That's Baroness Hale—the first woman Law Lord; this is Sir Philip Watts, a former chairman of Shell."

Clare turned the page again. "And there's the Duchess of Cornwall. She looks rather humourous."

"She is, and that's the quality I most wanted people to see."

"And did the prince like it?"

I gave a shrug. "He seemed to. He said nice things about it when he came to the unveiling at the National Portrait Gallery last month."

Clare turned to the next photo. "And who's this girl with the cropped hair?"

"That's my sister, Chloe. She works for an ethical PR agency called PRoud, so anything to do with fair trade, green technology, organic food and farming—that kind of thing."

Clare nodded. "She's very like your mother."

"She is—she has her fair complexion and ballerina physique." *Whereas I am dark and sturdy,* I reflected balefully—*more Paula Rego than Degas.*

Clare peered at the painting. "But she looks so . . . sad—distressed almost."

I hesitated. "She was breaking up with someone—it was a difficult time; but she's fine now," I went on quickly. *Even if her new boyfriend's vile* I didn't add.

My phone was ringing. I answered it.

"Where *are* you?" Mum demanded softly. "It's ten to seven—nearly everyone's here."

"Oh, sorry, but I'm not quite finished." I glanced at Clare; she was still flicking through the portfolio.

"You said you'd come *early.*"

"I know—I'll be there in half an hour, promise." I hung up. "Clare, I'm afraid I have to go now . . ." I went to my worktable and dipped the brushes I'd been using in the jar of turps.

"Of course . . ." she said without looking up. "That's the singer Cecilia Bartoli." She turned to the final image. "And who's this friendly looking man with the bow tie?"

I pulled the brushes through a sheet of newspaper to squeeze out the paint. "That's my father."

"Your father?"

"Yes." I did my best to ignore the surprise in her voice. "Roy Graham. He's an orthopaedic surgeon—semi-retired." I went to the sink, aware of Clare's curious gaze on my back.

"But in *The Times*—"

"He plays a lot of golf . . ." I rubbed dishwashing liquid into the bristles. "At the Royal Mid-Surrey—it's not far from where they live, in Richmond."

"In *The Times* it said that—"

"He also plays bridge." I turned on the tap. "I've never played but people say it's really fun once you get into it." I rinsed and dried the brushes, then laid them on my worktable, ready for the next day. "Right . . ." I looked at Clare, willing her to leave.

She slipped the tape recorder and notes into her bag, then stood up. "I hope you don't mind my asking you this, Ella. But as it was in the newspaper, I assume you talk about it."

My fingers trembled as I screwed the top back on a tube of titanium white. "Talk about what?"

"Well . . . the article said that you were adopted when you were eight . . ." Heat spilled into my face. "And that your name was changed—"

"I don't know where they got that." I untied my apron. "Now I really *must*—"

"It said that your real father left when you were five."

By now my heart was battering against my rib cage. "My real father is Roy Graham," I said quietly. "And that's all there is to it." I hung my apron on its hook. "But thank you for coming." I opened the studio door. "If you could let yourself out . . ."

Clare gave me a puzzled smile. "Of course."

As soon as she'd gone I rubbed furiously at my paint-stained fingers with a turps-soaked rag, then quickly washed my face and tidied my hair. I put on some black trousers and my green velvet coat and was about to go and unlock my bike when I remembered that the front light on it was broken. I groaned. I'd have to get the bus, or a cab—whichever turned up first. At least Chelsea Old Town Hall wasn't far.

I ran up to the King's Road and got to the bus stop just as a number 11 was pulling up, its windows blocks of yellow in the gathering dusk.

As we trundled over the bridge I reflected bitterly on Clare's intrusiveness. Yet she'd only repeated what she'd read in *The Times*. I felt a burst of renewed fury that something so intensely private was now online . . .

"Would you *please* take that paragraph out before the article goes on the paper's website," I'd asked the reporter, Hamish Watt, when I'd tracked him down an hour or so after I'd first seen the article. I was gripping the phone so tightly that my knuckles were white. "I was horrified when I saw it—please *remove* it."

"No," he'd replied. "It's part of the story."

"But you didn't *ask* me about it," I'd protested. "When you interviewed me at the National Portrait Gallery last week you talked only about my work."

"Yes, but I already had some background about you—that your mother had been a dancer, for example. I also happened to know a bit about your family circumstances."

"How?"

There was a momentary hesitation. "I'm a journalist," he said, as though that were sufficient explanation.

"Please remove it," I'd implored him again.

"I can't," he'd insisted. "And you were perfectly happy to be interviewed, weren't you?"

"Yes," I agreed weakly. "But if I'd known what you were going to write I'd have refused. You said that the article would be about my painting, but a good third of it is very personal and I'm uncomfortable about that."

"Well, I'm sorry you're unhappy," he'd answered unctuously. "But as publicity is undoubtedly helpful to artists, I suggest you learn to take the rough with the smooth." With that, he'd hung up.

It would be on the Internet forever, I now thought dismally—for anyone to see. Anyone at all. The thought of it made me feel sick. I'd simply have to find a way to deal with it, I reflected as we passed the World's End pub.

My father is Roy Graham.

My father is Roy Graham and he's a wonderful father.

I've got a father, thank you. His name is Roy Graham . . .

To distract myself I thought about work. I was starting a new portrait in the morning. Then on Thursday a member of Parliament named Mike Johns was coming for his fourth sitting—there'd been quite a gap since the last one as he said he'd been too busy; and last week I'd had that enquiry about painting a Mrs. Carr. Her daughter, Sophia, had contacted me through my website and then had come to the studio to see my portraits "in the flesh," as she'd put it. Then there'd be the new commission from tonight—not that it was going to make me any money, I reflected regretfully as we passed Heal's. I stood up and pressed the bell.

I got off the bus, crossed the road and followed a knot of smartly dressed people up the steps of the Town Hall. I walked down the black and white tiled corridor, showed my invitation, then pushed on the doors of the main hall. Next to the entrance was a large sign: *Save the Children—Gala Auction.*

The ornate blue and ochre room was already crowded, the stertorous chatter almost drowning out the string trio that was valiantly playing away on one side of the stage. Aproned waiters circulated with trays of canapés and drinks. The air was thick with perfume.

I picked up a programme and skimmed the introduction. *Five million children at risk in Malawi . . . hunger in Kenya . . . continuing crisis in Zimbabwe . . . in desperate need of help . . .* Then came the list of lots—twenty of which were in the silent auction, while the ten "star" lots were to be auctioned live. These included a week in a

Venetian palazzo, a luxury break at the Ritz, tickets for the first night
of *Swan Lake* at Covent Garden with Carlos Acosta, a shopping trip to
Harvey Nichols with Gok Wan, a dinner party for eight cooked by
Gordon Ramsay and an evening dress by Maria Grachvogel. There
was an electric guitar signed by Paul McCartney and a Chelsea FC
shirt signed by the current squad. The final lot was *A portrait commission by Gabriella Graham, kindly donated by the artist.* As I looked
at the crowd I wondered who I'd end up painting.

Suddenly I spotted Roy, waving. He walked towards me. "Ella-
Bella!" He placed a paternal kiss on my cheek.

Damn Clare, I thought. *Here* was my father.

"Hello, Roy." I nodded at his daffodil-dotted bow tie. "Nice
neckwear. Haven't seen that one before, have I?"

"It's new—thought I'd christen it tonight in honour of spring.
Now, *you* need some fizz . . ." He glanced around for a waiter.

"I'd love some. It's been a long day."

Roy snagged a glass of champagne and handed it to me with an
appraising glance. "So how's our Number One girl?"

I smiled at the familiar, affectionate nickname. "I'm fine,
thanks. Sorry I'm late."

"Your mum was getting *slightly* twitchy—but then, this is a big
event. Ah, here she comes . . ."

My mother was gliding through the crowd towards us, her slender frame swathed in amethyst chiffon, her ash blonde hair swept
into a perfect French pleat.

She held out her arms to me. "*El*-la." Her tone suggested a re-
proach rather than a greeting. "I'd almost given *up* on you, darling."
As she kissed me I inhaled the familiar scent of her Fracas. "Now, I
need you to be on hand to talk to people about the portrait commission. We've put the easel over there, look, in the presentation area,
and I've made you a label so that people will know who you are." She
opened her mauve satin clutch, took out a laminated name badge
and had already pinned it to my lapel before I could protest about
the mark it might leave on the velvet. "I'm hoping the portrait will

fetch a high price. We're aiming to raise seventy-five thousand pounds tonight."

"Well, fingers crossed." I adjusted the badge. "But you've certainly got some great items."

"And *all* donated," she said wonderingly. "We haven't had to buy anything. Everyone's been *so* generous."

"Only because you're so persuasive," Roy told her. "I often think you could persuade the rain not to fall, Sue, I really do."

Mum gave him an indulgent smile. "I'm simply focussed, determined and well organised. I know how I want things to *be.*"

"You're formidable," Roy said amiably, "in both the English *and* the French meaning of that word." He raised his glass. "Here's to you, Sue—and to a successful event."

I sipped my champagne, then nodded at the empty podium. "So who's wielding the gavel?"

Mum adjusted her pashmina. "Tim Spiers. He's ex-Christie's and brilliant at cajoling people into parting with their cash—having said that, I've still instructed the waiters to keep topping up the glasses."

Roy laughed. "That's right, get the punters drunk."

"No, just in a *good mood,*" Mum corrected him. "Then they're much more, well, biddable," she concluded wryly. "But if things are a bit slow . . ."—she lowered her voice—". . . then I'd like *us* to do a little strategic bidding."

My heart sank. "I'd rather not."

Mum gave me one of her "disappointed" looks. "It's just to get things going—you wouldn't have to *buy* anything, Ella."

"But . . . if no-one outbids me, I *might*. These are expensive lots, Mum, and I've a huge mortgage—it's too risky."

"She's donating a portrait," said Roy. "That's more than enough." *Exactly*, I thought crossly. "*I'll* do some bidding, Sue," he added. "Up to a limit though."

Mum laid her palm on his cheek—a typical gesture. "*Thank* you. I'm sure Chloe will bid too."

I glanced at the crowd. "Where *is* Chloe?"

"She's on her way," Roy replied. "With Nate."

A groan escaped me.

Mum shook her head. "I don't know *why* you have to be like that, Ella. Nate's delightful."

"Really?" I sipped my champagne again. "Can't say I'd noticed."

"You hardly know him," she retorted quietly.

"That's true. I've only met him once." But that one time had been more than enough. It had been at a drinks party that Chloe had given last November . . .

"Any special reason for having it?" I'd asked her over the phone after I'd opened the elegant invitation.

"It's because I haven't had a party for so long—I've neglected my friends. It's also because I'm feeling a lot more cheerful at the moment, *because* . . ." She drew in her breath. "Oh, Ella, I've met someone."

Relief flooded through me. "That's *great*. So . . . what's he like?"

"He's thirty-six," she'd replied. "Tall with very short black hair, and lovely green eyes."

To my surprise I had to suppress a pang of envy. "He sounds gorgeous."

"He is—and he's *not* married."

"Well, that's good."

"Oh, and he's from New York. He's been in London a couple of years."

"And what does he do?"

"He's in private equity."

"So he can buy you dinner, then."

"Yes—but I like to pay for things too."

"So are you . . . an item?"

"*Sort of*—we've been on five dates. But he said he's looking forward to the party, so that's a good sign. I know you're going to *love* him," she added happily.

So a fortnight later I cycled over to Putney, through a veil of fog.

And I was locking up my bike outside Chloe's flat at the end of Askill Drive when I heard a taxi pull up just around the corner in Keswick Road. As the door clicked open I could hear the passenger talking on his mobile. Although he spoke softly his voice carried through the mist and darkness.

"I'm *sorry* but I can't," I heard him say. He was American. Realising that this could be Chloe's new man I found myself tuning in to his conversation. "I really *can't,*" he reiterated as the cab door slammed shut. "Because I've just gotten to Putney for a cocktail party, that's why . . ." So it *was* him. "No . . . I don't *want* to go." I felt myself stiffen. "But I'm here now, honey, and so . . . Just some girl," he added as the cab drove away. "No, no . . . she's nothing special." By now my face was aflame. "I *can't* get out of it," he protested quietly. "Because I promised, that's why—and she's been going on and *on* about it." My hands shook as I unclipped my bike's front light. "Okay, honey—I'll come over later. Yes, that *is* a promise. No, I'll let myself in . . . You too, honey . . ."

I stood there, seething and filled with dismay, expecting the wretch to come round the corner and walk up Chloe's path; and I was just wondering what to do when I realised that he was going in the opposite direction, his footsteps snapping across the pavement then becoming fainter and fainter . . .

So it *wasn't* him. I exhaled with relief. I went up to Chloe's front door and rang the bell.

"Ella!" she exclaimed as she opened it. She looked lovely in a black crepe shift that used to be Mum's, with a short necklace of pearls. "I'm so glad you're the first," she said quickly. "I've just poured the champagne, but if you could give me a hand with the eats that would be . . ." I was aware of steps behind me as Chloe's gaze strayed over my shoulder. Her face lit up like a firework. "Nate!"

I turned to see a tall, well-dressed man coming up the path.

"Hi, Chloe." As I recognised his voice, my heart sank. "I just went completely the wrong way—I was halfway down Keswick Road before I realised. I shoulda used my GPS," he added with a laugh.

"Well, it *is* foggy," she responded gaily. I stepped past her into the house so that she wouldn't see my face. "It's *so* nice that you're here, Nate," I heard her say.

"Oh, I've been looking forward to it."

Chloe drew him inside; then, still holding his hand, she grabbed *mine* so that the three of us were suddenly linked, awkwardly, as we stood there in the hallway. "Ella," she said happily, "this is Nate." She turned to him. "Nate, this is my sister, Ella."

He was just as Chloe had described. He had very short dark hair that receded slightly above a high forehead, and eyes that were a pure, mossy green. He had a sensuous mouth with a tiny indentation at each corner, and a long straight nose that had a slender bridge, as though someone had pinched it.

"Great to meet you, Ella." He was clearly unaware that I'd over-heard his conversation. I gave him a frigid smile and saw those un-expectedly green eyes register the slight. "Erm . . ." He nodded at my head. "That's a nice helmet you've got there."

"Oh." I'd been too distracted to remove it. I unclipped it while Chloe relieved Nate of his coat.

She folded it over her arm. "I'll just put this on my bed." She put her hand on the banister. "But have a glass of champagne, Nate—the kitchen's through there. Ella will show you."

"No—I . . . need to come up too." As I glanced at him, I tried not to show my contempt, but his puzzled expression showed that I'd failed. I followed Chloe upstairs.

We crossed the landing and went into Chloe's bedroom. She half closed the door, then put her finger to her lips. "So what do you *think*?" She laid Nate's charcoal cashmere coat on her bed then turned back to me eagerly. "Isn't he attractive?"

I took off my cycling jacket. "He is."

"And he's really . . . *decent.* I think I've landed on my feet."

I fought the urge to tell my sister that she'd almost certainly landed flat on her face.

I put my jacket and helmet down, then moved to the gilded wall mirror. I opened my bag. "So how did you meet him?" My hand shook as I pulled a comb through my fog-dampened hair.

Chloe came and stood next to me. "Playing tennis." As she checked her own appearance I was momentarily distracted by the physical difference between us—Chloe with the alabaster paleness of our mother, me with my olive skin, brown hair and dark eyes. "Do you remember telling me that I should try to go out more—maybe play tennis?" I nodded. "Well, I took your advice, and booked some lessons at the Harbour Club." Chloe licked her ring finger, then ran it over her left eyebrow. "Nate was on the court next door; and I had to retrieve my ball from behind his baseline a few times . . ."

I dropped the comb back in my bag. "Really?"

"So of course I said sorry. Then I saw him in the café afterwards and I apologised again . . ."

I snapped my bag shut.

"Then we had a coffee—and that's how it started. So I have *you* to thank," she added happily. My heart sank. "It's still early days, but he's keen."

I looked at her. "How do you know?"

"Well . . . because he calls me a lot and because . . ." She gave me a puzzled smile. "Why do you ask?"

It was on the tip of my tongue to tell Chloe that Nate was, in fact, a disingenuous, two-timing creep. But then, reflected behind us on the wall, I saw my portrait of her, her face so thin, and almost rigid with distress; her blue eyes blazing with pain and regret.

"Why do you ask?" she repeated.

As I looked at Chloe's happy, hopeful expression I knew I couldn't tell her. "No reason." I exhaled. "I was just . . . wondering."

"*Ella?*" Chloe was peering at me. "Are you okay?"

"I'm . . . fine. Actually, a van ran the lights by the bridge and nearly knocked me off my bike. I'm still feeling shaken," I lied.

"I *knew* something was up. I *wish* you didn't cycle—and in fog like this it's crazy. You've *got* to be careful."

I laid my hand on Chloe's arm. "So have you, darling."

"What do you mean?" She gave a little laugh. "I don't cycle."

I shook my head. "I mean be careful . . ." I tapped the left side of my chest. *"Here."*

"Oh." She sighed. "I see. Don't worry, Ella. I'm not about to make another . . . well, mistake, if that's what you're thinking. Nate's free of complications, thank God." I repressed a groan. "But he'll be wondering what we're doing . . ." She opened the door. "Let's go— I want you to get to know him."

That was the last thing I wanted to do, not least because I didn't think I'd be able to hide my hostility; and I was just wondering how I could get out of this impossible situation when the bell rang, so I said I'd do door duty, then I offered to heat up the canapés, then I went round with a tray of drinks, by which time Chloe's flat was heaving, and in this way I managed to avoid Nate for the rest of the evening. As I left, pleading an early start the next day, I glanced at him as he chatted to someone in the sitting room. I hoped that his romance with Chloe wouldn't last. Having overheard what I had, it didn't seem likely. The man was clearly a jerk.

So I was dismayed when Chloe phoned me three days later to say that Nate was taking her to Paris for a weekend in early December. Then just before Christmas they had a dinner party at his flat; Chloe wanted me to be there but I said I was busy. In January they invited me to the theatre with them but I made some excuse. Then last month Mum asked all of us to Sunday lunch; I told her and Chloe I'd be away.

"What a shame," Chloe had said. "That's three times you've been unable to meet up with us, Ella. Nate will think you don't like him," she added with a good-natured laugh.

"Oh, that's not true," I lied . . .

"Well, *I* like Nate," Mum said above the pre-auction chatter. "He's attractive and charming." Her voice dropped to a near whisper.

"And we should all just be thankful that he makes Chloe so happy after . . ." Her mouth had become a thin line.

"Max," supplied Roy helpfully.

I nodded. "Max *was* a bit of a mistake."

"Max was a *disaster,*" Mum hissed. "I told Chloe," she went on quietly. "I told her that it would *never* work out and I was *right.* These situations bring nothing but heartbreak," she added with sudden bitterness, and I knew that she was thinking of her own heartbreak three decades ago.

"Anyway, Chloe's *fine* now," Roy reminded us evenly. "So let's change the subject, shall we? We're at a *party.*"

"Of course," Mum murmured, collecting herself. "And I really must circulate. Roy, would you go and see how the silent auction's going? Ella, you need to go and stand next to the easel, and do make the portrait commission sound *enticing,* won't you? I want to get the highest possible price for every item."

"Sure," I responded wearily. I hated having to do a hard sell—even for a good cause. I made my way through the crowd.

The easel was standing between two long tables on which the information about all the star lots was displayed. The Maria Grachvogel gown was draped onto a silver mannequin next to a life-size cutout of Gordon Ramsay. On a green baize-covered screen were pinned large photos of the Venetian palazzo and of the Ritz and next to these was a Royal Opera House poster for *Swan Lake* flanked by two pendant pairs of pink ballet shoes. The guitar was mounted on a stand, and next to it the Chelsea FC shirt with its graffiti of famous signatures.

As I stood beside the portrait, a dark-haired woman in a turquoise dress approached me. She glanced at my name badge. "So you're the artist." I nodded. The woman gazed at the painting. "And who's she?"

"My friend Polly. She's lent the painting to us tonight as an example of my work."

"I've always wanted to have my portrait done," the woman said.

"But when I was young and pretty I didn't have the money and now that I *do* have the money I feel it's too late."

"You're still pretty," I pointed out. "And it's never too late—I paint people who are in their seventies and eighties." I sipped my champagne. "So are you thinking of bidding for it?"

She nibbled her lower lip. "I'm not sure. How long does the process take?" I explained. "Two hours is a long time to be sitting still."

"We have a break for coffee and a leg stretch. It's really not too arduous."

"Do you flatter people?" she asked anxiously. "I hope you do, because look . . ."—she pinched the wedge of flesh beneath her chin, holding it daintily, like a tidbit. "Would you be able to do something about *this*?"

I answered carefully. "My portraits are truthful. But at the same time I want my sitters to be happy; so I'd paint you from the most flattering angle—and I'd do some sketches first to make sure you liked the composition."

"Well . . ." She cocked her head as she scrutinised Polly's portrait again. "I'm going to have a think about it—but thanks."

As she walked away, another woman came up to me. She gave me an earnest smile. "I'm definitely going to bid for this. I *love* your style—realistic but with an edge."

"Thank you." I allowed myself to bask in the compliment for a moment. "And who would you want me to paint? Would it be you?"

"No," she replied. "It would be my father. You see, we never had his portrait painted."

"Uh-huh."

"And now we regret it." My heart sank as I realised what was coming. "He died last year," the woman went on. "But we've got lots of photos, so you could do it from those."

I shook my head. "I'm afraid I don't do posthumous portraits."

"Oh." The woman looked affronted. "Why not?"

"Because to me a portrait is all about pinning down the essence of a living person. His or her *vitality*."

"Oh," she said again, crestfallen. "I see." She hesitated. "Would you perhaps make an exception?"

"No, I'm afraid I wouldn't. I'm sorry," I added impotently.

"Well . . ." She shrugged, but I could see the irritation in her eyes. "Then I guess that's that."

As the woman walked away I saw my mother go up the flight of steps at the side of the stage. She waited for the string trio to finish the Mozart sonata they were playing, then she went to the podium and tapped the mike. The hubbub subsided as she smiled at the crowd and in her soft, low voice, thanked us all for coming, exhorting us to be generous. As she reminded everyone that our bids would save children's lives, the annoyance that I'd been feeling with her was replaced by a sudden rush of pride. Now she expressed her gratitude to the donors and to her fellow committee members before introducing Tim Spiers, who took her place as she gracefully exited stage left.

He leaned an arm on the podium, peering at us benignly over his half-moon glasses. "We have some *wonderful* lots on offer tonight— and remember, there's no buyer's premium to pay which makes everything *very* affordable. So without further ado, let's start with the week at the *fabulous* Palazzo Barbarigo-Minotto in Venice . . ."

An appreciative murmur arose as a photo of the palazzo was projected onto the huge screens that had been placed on either side of the stage. "The palazzo overlooks the Grand Canal," Spiers explained as the slide-show image changed to an interior. "It's one of Venice's most splendid palazzos and has a stunning *piano nobile*, as you can see . . . It sleeps eight, is fully staffed—and in high season, a week's stay there costs ten thousand pounds. I'm now going to open the bidding at an *incredibly* low *three* thousand pounds." He affected astonishment. "For a mere *three* thousand pounds, ladies and gentlemen, *you* could spend a week at one of Venice's most glorious private palaces—the experience of a lifetime. So do I hear three thousand?" His eyes raked the room. "Three thousand pounds— anyone? Ah, *thank* you, sir. And three thousand five hundred . . . and four thousand . . . thank you—at the back there . . . five thousand . . ."

As the bidding proceeded a girl in her early twenties approached and looked at the portrait of Polly. "She's very pretty," she whispered.

I gazed at Polly's heart-shaped face, framed by a helmet of rose gold hair. "She is."

"Do I hear six thousand?" we heard.

"What if you have to paint someone who's plain?" the girl asked. "Or ugly, even? Is that difficult?"

"It's actually easier than painting someone who's conventionally attractive," I answered softly, "because the features are more interesting."

"Seven thousand now—do I hear seven *thousand* pounds? Come *on,* everyone!"

The girl sipped her champagne. "And what happens if you don't *like* the person you're painting—could you still paint them then?"

"Yes," I whispered. "Though I don't suppose I'd enjoy the sittings much." Suddenly I noticed the doors swing open and there was Chloe, in her vintage red trench coat, and behind her, Nate. "Fortunately, I've never had a sitter I disliked."

"Going once," we heard the auctioneer say. "At eight thousand pounds. Going twice . . ." His eyes raked the room, then, with a flick of his wrist, he tapped the podium. "*Sold* to the man in the gray suit there!" I glanced over at Mum. She looked reasonably happy with the result. "On to lot two now," said Spiers. "An evening gown by Maria Grachvogel, who designs dresses for some of the world's most glamourous women—Cate Blanchett for example, and Angelina Jolie. Whoever wins this lot will receive a personal consultation and fitting with Maria Grachvogel herself. I'm going to start the bidding at a *very* modest five hundred pounds. *Thank* you, madam—the lady in pale blue there—and seven hundred and fifty?" He scrutinised us all. "Seven hundred and fifty pounds is still a bargain—thank you, sir. Do I hear one thousand now?" He pointed to a woman in lime green who'd raised her hand. "It's with you, madam. At one thousand two hundred and fifty? Yes . . . and one thousand five hundred . . . thank you. Will anyone give me two thousand?"

I glanced to my right. Chloe was making her way around the room, leading Nate by the hand.

I know you're going to love him, Ella . . .

She'd been wrong about that. I loathed the man. Suddenly she spotted Roy and waved.

"Is that two thousand pounds there?" The auctioneer was pointing at Chloe. "The young woman at the back in the scarlet raincoat?"

Chloe froze; with a stricken expression she shook her head, mouthed *Sorry* at Spiers, then she looked at Nate with horrified amusement.

"So *still* at one thousand five hundred, then—but *do* I hear two thousand?" There was a pause, then I saw my mother raise her hand. "Thank you, Sue," the auctioneer said. "The bid's with our organiser Sue Graham now, at two *thousand* pounds." Mum's face was taut with tension. "Will anyone give me two thousand two hundred? *Thank* you—the lady in the pink dress." Mum's features relaxed as she was outbid. "So at two thousand two hundred pounds . . . going once . . . twice *and* . . ." The gavel landed with a *crack*. "*Sold* to the lovely lady in pink here—well done, everyone," he added jovially. "On we go to lot three."

As the bidding for the weekend at the Ritz got under way I watched Chloe greet Mum and Roy. Mum smiled warmly at Nate, then as Chloe leaned closer to say something to her she clapped her hands in delight and turned and whispered in Roy's ear. I wondered what they were talking about.

"So for three thousand pounds now . . ." Tim Spiers was saying. "A weekend at the Ritz in one of their Deluxe Suites—what a *treat.* Thank you, sir—it's with the man with the red tie there. Going once . . . twice . . . *and* . . ." He rapped the podium. "Sold! You have got yourself a bargain," Spiers said amiably to the man. "If you'd like to go to the registration desk to arrange payment, thank you. Now to the dinner party for eight, cooked by Gordon Ramsay himself—*well* worth all the shouting and swearing. Let's start with a *very* modest eight hundred pounds—which includes wine, incidentally . . ."

The sound of the auction faded as I grimly observed Chloe and Nate. Chloe seemed to do most of the talking while Nate just nodded now and again, absorbing her words rather than responding to them. I saw him look at his phone and wondered if the woman he'd promised to meet that night was still in his life.

"Now for the portrait," I heard the auctioneer say, and as my picture of Polly was projected onto the screens he indicated me with a sweep of his hand. "Ladies and gentlemen, Gabriella Graham is an outstanding young artist." I felt a warmth suffuse my cheeks. "You've probably seen media coverage of the marvelous painting she did of the Duchess of Cornwall, which was commissioned by the National Portrait Gallery for its primary collection of notable figures. Now you too have the chance to be immortalised by Ella. So I'm going to open the bidding with a *pitifully* low—*two thousand pounds.* Do I hear two thousand?" Spiers's eyes swept across the room. "No? Well, let me tell you that Ella's portraits usually command between six and twelve thousand pounds, depending on the size and composition. So who'll give me a trifling *two* thousand? Thank you, madam!" He beamed at the woman in the turquoise dress who'd spoken to me earlier. "And two thousand five hundred?" I heard Spiers coax. "Just two and a half thousand—anyone?" He gave us an indulgent smile. "Come *on,* folks," he said jovially, "let's see some bidding now! *Thank* you, Sue." My mother's hand had gone up. "So it's with Sue Graham now at two thousand, five hundred pounds . . . and three thousand—the lady in turquoise again. Who'll offer me *four* thousand?" That was a big jump. "Four thousand pounds?" There was silence. "*No* takers?" he said with mock incredulity. I felt a pang of disappointment tinged with embarrassment that no-one thought it worth that much. Suddenly Spiers's face lit up. "*Thank* you, young lady!" He grinned. "I hope you *mean* it this time!"

I followed his gaze. To my surprise, I saw that this remark had been directed at Chloe, who was nodding enthusiastically. So she was bidding in order to help Mum. "Do I hear four thousand five hundred now?" Spiers demanded. "Yes, madam." The woman in turquoise had come back in. "And who will give me five thousand pounds for the chance to be painted by Ella Graham—you'll be getting not just a portrait, but an heirloom. *Thank* you! And it's the young woman in the red raincoat again." I stared at Chloe—why was she still bidding? "It's with you at five thousand pounds now. And five thousand, five hundred?" I held my breath. "Yes? Now it's back with the lady in turquoise." Chloe was off the hook—thank God. "So at five thousand, five hundred pounds—to the lady in the turquoise dress there—going once . . . twice . . . and—SIX thousand!" Spiers beamed at Chloe, then held out his right hand to her. "The bid's back with the lady in the red raincoat, at six *thousand* pounds now! Any advance on six k?" This was *crazy*. Chloe couldn't spare six thousand—she probably didn't *have* six thousand. Now I felt furious with Mum for asking her to bid. "So at six thousand pounds—still with the young lady in red there," Spiers said. "Going once . . . twice . . ." He looked enquiringly at the woman in the turquoise dress but to my dismay she shook her head. The gavel landed with a *crack*, like a gun firing. "SOLD!"

I expected Chloe to look appalled; instead, to my bewilderment, she looked thrilled. She made her way through the crowd towards me, leaving Nate with Mum and Roy.

"So what do you think?" She was beaming.

"What do I think? I think it's *insane*. Why didn't you stop when you had the chance?"

"I didn't *want* to," she protested. "I decided I was going to get it— and I did!"

I gaped at her. "Chloe, how much champagne have you had?"

She laughed. "I had some at lunchtime, but I'm not drunk. Why do you assume I am?"

"Because you've just paid six thousand pounds for something you could have had for *free,* that's why. Whatever were you *thinking*?"

"Well . . . today I was made a director of Proud, with a thirty per cent pay rise." So *that* was what Mum had been looking so thrilled about. "And I've just had a tax rebate—plus I want to support the charity."

"That's very generous of you," I told her. "But it was at five and a half grand, which was already a good price, plus I've *done* a portrait of you, remember?"

"Of course I do—don't be silly, Ella—but the point is—"

I suddenly realised. "You want me to do it again." I thought of how distressed Chloe had been at the time. She'd broken up with Max shortly after I'd started it. I'd urged her to wait, but she'd re- fused. She'd insisted that she *wanted* me to paint her in that state, so she would never forget how much she'd felt for him. "You know, Chloe," I said, "it probably *would* be good to do another portrait of you now that—"

"Ella," she interrupted. "That's *not* why I bid. Because it isn't me you're going to paint."

"No?"

"It's Nate."

This couldn't be happening to me. Now he was at her side. I gave him a frozen smile. "Um . . . apparently it's you I'm to paint, Nate."

He looked at Chloe in confusion.

"Yes, you," she confirmed happily.

"Oh . . . Well . . ." He was clearly as dismayed as I was. "I don't know whether I *want* Ella to paint me. In fact, I *don't* want her to— I mean, I don't want *anyone* to paint me." He shook his head. "Chloe, it's *not* my kinda thing, so I'm going to have to say thanks—it's *very* sweet—but no thanks."

Chloe gave him a teasing smile. "I'm sorry, but you're not allowed

to refuse, because the portrait's to be a present from me to you—
a very special one."

"His birthday present?" I asked her.

"No." She smiled delightedly. "His *wedding* present." She slipped
her arm through Nate's. "We're *engaged*!"

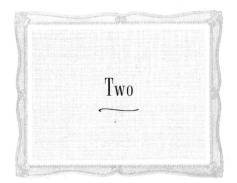

Two

"I will be keeping the sittings to a *minimum*," I said to Polly the following morning as we sat together in her bedroom overlooking Parsons Green. I'd taken her portrait, carefully bubble-wrapped, back to her flat. "I am *not* relishing the prospect of spending twelve hours with that creep in order to paint his face—or rather, his *two* faces. I'll paint him as Janus," I threatened darkly.

Polly's nail file paused in mid-stroke. "So I take it you still don't like him?"

I shuddered. "I thoroughly *dis*like him—and I don't trust him. I told you how he behaved before her party."

"Hmm." Polly scrutinised the tip of her left index finger then began filing it again, the rasp of the emery board masking the drone of morning traffic.

"He was very disparaging about Chloe—plus it was obvious that he was already in a relationship with the woman he was on the phone with. So for those two *very* good reasons I despise him, Pol."

"Fair enough . . . although, let's assume he *was* in a relationship with this other woman . . ."

"He was."

"But at that stage he hadn't known Chloe long—so maybe he was just hedging his bets." She shrugged. "Lots of men do that."

"It's still a despicable way to act." I would not be swayed.

"Or it *could* be that he was only *pretending* he wasn't keen on Chloe in order to protect the other woman's feelings." Polly blew on her fingertips. "I'd hardly condemn him for that."

"But if he'd wanted to protect the other woman's feelings then he shouldn't have told her about Chloe's party at all. He should have lied."

Polly looked up. "Now you're saying you don't trust him because he didn't lie?"

"Yes. *No.* But . . . what if that other woman's still on the scene?"

She began to file her thumbnail. "As he and Chloe are engaged, I doubt it."

"But it's not that long ago, so she could be—and he's clearly duplicitous. I don't want Chloe having her heart broken again. It was bad enough last time."

Polly reached for the tub of hand crème on her bedside table. "Ella, how old is Chloe now?"

"She's . . . nearly twenty-nine."

"Exactly—*oh* . . ." She grimaced as she tried to twist off the lid. "Open this for me, would you?" She leaned forward and handed me the pot. "I daren't snag a nail—I'm working tomorrow."

"What's the job?" I asked as I unscrewed it.

"A day's shoot for a feature film. My hands are going to double for Keira Knightley's—I have to put them up to her face, like this." Polly held her palms to her cheeks. "I'll be kneeling behind her and won't be able to see so I hope I don't stick my fingers up her nose. I did that to Liz Hurley once. It was embarrassing."

"I can imagine." I handed Polly the opened tub.

She scooped out a blob of crème and dabbed it on her knuckles. "Chloe's got to make her *own* mistakes."

"Of course: the trouble is, she makes such *bad* ones—like getting involved with a married man. The first thing she knew about Max was that he was someone else's husband."

"Remind me how she met him?"

"Chloe and I went into Waterstone's on the King's Road; we saw that Sylvia Shaw was signing copies of her new book, and as Chloe had liked her first two, we decided to stay. While she was queuing to have her copy signed, she struck up a conversation with this man— I could see right away that she really liked him—who said that he was Sylvia Shaw's husband. So that's how it started—*right* under his wife's nose."

"And his wife never found out?"

"No. Chloe said that she was too absorbed in her writing to notice. But Chloe was crazy about him. Do you remember the state she got herself in when it finally ended?" Polly nodded grimly. "She lost twenty pounds. And what she did to her hair?"

"It was a bit . . . severe."

"It was *savage.* She looked as though she'd been in some . . . war."

Polly stroked crème onto her right hand. "That was a year and a half ago," she pointed out. "Chloe's on an even keel again now."

"I hope so—but she's always been fragile. She's not like Mum, who has this core of *steel.*"

"That's ballerinas for you," Polly said simply. "They have to learn to dance through the agony, don't they, whether they've got a broken toenail or a broken heart. *Damn* . . ." She peered at her left hand, then reached for the magnifying glass on the bedside table and examined it through that. "I've got a *freckle.* How did *that* happen?" she wailed. "I use SPF 50 on my hands all year round—my rear end gets more UV than they do. Where's my Fade-Out?" She rummaged desperately amongst all the hand crèmes, nail polishes and jars of cotton wool puffs on her dressing table. "I can't afford to have *any* blemishes," she muttered. She lifted up a framed photo of her daughter—my goddaughter—Lola. "*Here* it is . . ." She sat down on the bed, then tucked a hank of strawberry blonde hair behind her ear as she held out another pot for me to open. "I know you've always looked out for Chloe, Ella."

"Well, she's a lot younger than me, so yes . . . I have." I lifted off the lid and passed the pot to her.

"That's nice; but now you should . . . just let go." Polly looked at me. "As I've known you since we were six, I feel I can say that." She began to massage the skin lightener onto the offending brown mark. "Chloe's over Max enough now to be able to marry Nate—just be happy for her, Ella."

"I'd be *thrilled* if Nate was someone I liked." I groaned. "And *why* does she have to give him a portrait? If she wants to spend that much, then why can't she give him something normal, like a gold watch or . . . diamond cuff links or something?"

Polly squinted at her hand. "Why don't you paint them together?"

"I suggested that, but Chloe wants a picture of Nate on his own. She's going to give it to him the day before the wedding."

"Which will be when?"

"July third—which is also her birthday."

"Well, she's always wanted to be married before she was thirty."

"Yes. So perhaps *that* explains the quick engagement—as though anyone could care less what age a woman is when she gets married . . . or whether she gets married at all. I mean, I'm thirty-five and still single but I really don't . . ." I floundered.

"I'm thirty-five," said Polly, "and I'm divorced. It doesn't bother me—Lola has a good relationship with Ben and that's the key thing. He's being tricky about child support, though," she added wearily. "Lola's school fees are fifteen grand now with all the extras, so thank God my digits give me an income."

I considered Polly's hands with their long, slim fingers and gleaming nail beds. "They *are* lovely. Your thumbs are *fantastic.*"

"Oh, thanks. But it isn't just about looks—my hands can *act.* They can be sad or happy." She wiggled her fingers. "They can be *angry* . . ." She clenched her fists. "Or playful." She "walked" her fingers through the air. "They can be inquisitive . . ."—she turned up her palms—". . . or pleading." She clasped them in supplication. "The whole gamut really."

"There should be an Oscar category for it."

"There should. Anyway . . . they're done. Now it's time for my tootsies."

"Have they got a part in the film too?"

"No. But they've got a Birkenstock ad next week so I need to get them tip-top."

Polly kicked off her oversize sheepskin slippers and examined her slender, size six feet with their perfectly straight toes, shell-pink nails, elegantly high arches and smooth, rosy heels. Satisfied that there were no imperfections to attend to she put them in the waiting foot spa and switched it on.

"Ooh, that's nice," she crooned as the water bubbled. "So what does your mum think about Chloe's engagement?"

"She's elated. But then, she couldn't stand Max."

"Well, he *was* married. You could hardly expect her to have been crazy about him."

"True—but it went deeper than that. Mum only met Max once, but she seemed to loathe him, as though it was personal. But I'm sure that was because . . . well, you know the background."

Polly nodded. "I still remember when you told me. We were eleven."

The window was misted with condensation. I rubbed a patch clear. "I hadn't known it myself until then."

"That was a long time for your mother to keep it from you," Polly observed quietly.

I shrugged. "I don't hold it against her—she'd been terribly hurt. Having made a new life, I suppose she didn't want to remember the awful way in which her old one had ended."

Your father was involved with someone else, Ella. I knew about it, and it made me desperately unhappy—not least because I loved him so much. But one day I saw him with this . . . other woman; I came across them

together, and it was a terrible shock. I begged him not to leave us, but he
abandoned us and went far, far away . . .

"Do you think about him?" I heard Polly say.

"Hmm?"

She turned off the foot spa. "Do you think about him much? Your
father."

"No." I registered the surprise in her eyes. "Why would I when I
haven't seen him since I was not even five and can barely remember
him?"

One, two, three . . . up in the air she goes.

"You must have *some* memories."

Ready, sweetie? Don't let go, now!

I shook my head. "I used to, but they've gone." I glanced out of the
window at the children playing on the green below.

Again, Daddy! Again! Again!

Polly reached for the towel on the end of the bed and patted her
feet with it. "And where in Australia did he go?"

"I don't know—I only know that it was Western Australia. But
whether it was Perth or Fremantle or Rockingham or Broome, or
Geraldton or Esperance or Bunbury or Kalgoorlie, I've *no* idea, and
I'm not interested."

Polly was looking at me. "And he made *no* attempt to stay in
touch?"

I felt my lips compress. "It was as though we'd never existed."

"But . . . what if he wanted to find you?"

I sighed. "That would be hard—"

"Oh, it probably *would* be," Polly interjected. "But you know,
Ella, I've always thought that you should at least *try* to—"

I shook my head. "It would be hard for him to *do*—given that he
doesn't even know my surname."

"Oh." She looked deflated. "I see. Sorry—I thought you meant . . ."
She swung her legs off the bed. "I remember when your name was
changed. I remember Miss Drake telling us all in school one morning that you were Ella *Graham* now. It was a bit confusing."

"Yes. But it was so Chloe and I would be the same—and Roy had adopted me by then so I can understand why they did it."

I had a sharp memory of Mum cutting the old name tapes out of my school uniform and sewing in new ones, pulling up the thread with a vehement tug.

You're not Ella Sharp anymore . . .

Now I remembered Mandy Parks, who sat behind me, asking me endlessly *why* my name had been changed and where my *real* father was. When I tearfully told Mum, she said that Mandy was a nosy little girl and that I didn't have to answer her questions.

You're Ella Graham now, darling.

But—

And that's all there is to it . . .

"What if he got in touch," Polly tried again. "What would you do?"

I smeared the condensation on the window and turned away. "I'd do . . . nothing. I wouldn't even respond."

Polly narrowed her eyes. "Not even out of curiosity?"

I shrugged. "I'm *not* curious about him. I *was*—until Mum told me what he'd done; after that I stopped thinking about him. I have no idea whether he's even *alive.* He'd be sixty-six now, so perhaps he isn't alive anymore, perhaps he's . . . *not* . . ." I shivered. I looked out of the window again, scrutinising the people below as though I imagined I might spot him amongst them.

"It's sad," I heard Polly say.

"I suppose it is. But if your father had behaved like mine, you'd feel the same."

"I don't know *how* I'd feel," she said quietly.

"Plus I wouldn't want to upset Mum."

"*Would* it still upset her—after so long?"

"I know it would, because she *never* mentions him—he broke her heart. I'm sure that's why she had it in for Max, because his affair reminded her of my father's betrayal."

"And . . . was she angry with Chloe too?"

I returned my gaze to Polly. "For seeing a married man, you mean?" She nodded. "There were big arguments about it . . ." I cast my mind back. "Mum simply wanted to protect Chloe from getting hurt. She kept telling her that Max would never leave his wife—and she was right; so Chloe finally took Mum's advice and ended it. And now Chloe's with Nate," I grumbled. "I hope *he's* not going to cause her any grief, but I've got the awful feeling he is."

"So when did they decide to tie the knot?" Polly put her slippers on again then stood up.

"Yesterday, over lunch. They went to Quaglino's to celebrate her promotion and came out engaged. They told Mum and Roy at the auction. Mum's so thrilled she's offered to plan it all for them."

"She hasn't got long, then. Only . . . what? Three and a half months."

"True, but she has a tremendous talent for arranging things—it's probably all the choreography she's done." I glanced at my watch. "Yikes! I must go—I've got to get to Barnes for a sitting."

"I love Barnes," Polly said. "I'd move there if I could afford it. So who are you painting?" she asked as we went onto the landing.

"A Frenchwoman who's married to a Brit. He's commissioned me to paint her for her fortieth. She doesn't want to come to the studio, so I have to go there. He sounds quite a bit older—but he kept telling me how beautiful she is: I could hardly get him off the phone."

Polly emitted a sigh of deep longing. "I'd love to have someone appreciate *me* like that."

"Any progress in that area?" I asked as we went downstairs.

"I liked the photographer at the Toilet Duck shoot last week. He took my card—not that he's phoned," she added balefully as I opened the closet and got out my parka. "What about you?"

I thrust my arms into the sleeves. "Zilch—apart from a bit of flirting at the framers." I looked at the bare patch of wall where Polly's portrait usually hung. "Shall I hang you up again before I go?"

"Please—I daren't do *anything* practical until the shoot's over; the tiniest scratch and I'll lose the job; there's two grand at stake and I'm short of cash."

I pulled the bubble wrap off the painting. "Me too."

"But you seem to be busy."

I lifted the portrait onto its hook. "Not busy enough—and my mortgage is *huge.*" I straightened the bottom of the frame. "Perhaps I could offer to paint the chairman of my mortgage company in return for a year off the payments."

"Maybe one of Camilla Parker-Bowles's friends will commission you."

I picked up my bag and slung it over my shoulder. "That would be great. I've just joined the Royal Society of Portrait Painters so I'm on *their* website—and I've got a Facebook page now . . ."

"That's good. Then there's that piece in *The Times.* I *know* you didn't like it," Polly soothed, "but it's great publicity and it's online now. So . . ." She opened the door. ". . . who knows *what* might come out of it?"

I felt my heart flutter. "Who knows . . . ?"

There was a sharp wind blowing as I walked home so I pulled up my hood and shoved my hands into my pockets. As I cut across Eel Brook Common, with its bright stripe of daffodils, my phone bleated.

"*El*-la?" My mother sounded elated. "I've just had the final figures from last night. We raised *eighty* thousand pounds—five thousand more than our target, and a record for the Richmond branch of the charity."

"That's wonderful, Mum—congratulations."

"So I just wanted to thank you again for the portrait." I resisted the urge to say that had I known who the sitter was to be, I wouldn't have been so generous. "But *how* funny that you're going to paint Nate."

"Yes . . . extremely amusing."

"It'll give you an opportunity to get to *know* him before the wedding. I've just booked the church, by the way."

"Mum, they've been engaged less than twenty-four hours."

"I know—but July third's *not* that far off! So I phoned the vicar at St. Matthias first thing and by some *miracle* the two p.m. slot for that day had become free—apparently the groom got cold feet."

"Oh, dear."

There was a bewildered silence. "No, not 'oh, dear,' Ella—'oh, *great*'! I didn't think we'd find *any* churches in the area free at such short notice, let alone our own."

"And where's the reception going to be?"

"At home. We'll come out of the church, then stroll down the lane to the house through a cloud of moon daisies."

"There aren't any moon daisies in the lane, Mum."

"No—but there will be, because I'm going to plant some. Now, we'll need a large marquee," she prattled on. "Eighty feet by thirty feet, minimum: the garden's *just* big enough—I paced it out this morning; I think we should have the 'traditional' style, not the 'frame'—it's *so* much more attractive—and I'll probably use the caterers from last night although I'll get a couple of other quotes . . ."

"You've got the bit between your teeth, then."

"I *have*—but most weddings are at least a year in the making: I've got less than four months to plan Chloe's!"

"Doesn't she want to do any of it herself?"

"No—she's going to be extremely busy at work now that she's been promoted, and if I take care of the details she can enjoy the run-up to her big day without all the stress. She'll make the major decisions of course, but I'll do all the legwork."

"Can *I* do anything?" I volunteered rashly.

"No—thanks, darling. Although . . . actually, there is *one* thing. Chloe's thinking about having a vintage wedding dress. Could you give her a hand on that front? I don't even know who sells them."

"Sure. Steinberg and Tolkein's gone now, isn't it, but there's

Circa, or Dolly Diamond, and I think there's a good one down in Blackheath—or hang on, what about . . . ?"

"Yes?"

"Well . . ." I bit my lip. "What about *yours*?"

"But . . . Roy and I got married in a register office, Ella. I wore a pale blue silk trouser suit."

"I know, but what about when you got married . . . before?" During the silence that followed I tried to imagine what my mother wore when she married my father in the early 1970s. A sweet, pin-tucked dress perhaps, Laura Ashley–style, with a white velvet choker . . . or maybe something flowingly Bohemian by Ossie Clark. "It would probably fit Chloe," I persisted. "But . . . maybe you didn't keep it," I added weakly as the silence continued. Why *would* she have, I realised, when she hadn't even kept the wedding photos? I had a sudden vision of the dress billowing out of a dustbin. "Sorry," I said, as she still didn't respond. "Obviously not a good idea—forget I suggested it."

"I have to go," Mum said smoothly. "There's a beep in my ear— I think it's Big Top Tents. We'll speak again soon, darling."

As she ended the call I marvelled at my mother's ability to blank things that she doesn't want to talk about. I'll steer a conversation away from a no-go area, but my mother simply pretends that the conversation isn't happening.

When I got home I booked my minicab to Barnes then quickly packed up my paints, palette and my portable box easel. I took three new canvases out of the rack, unhooked my apron and put everything by the front door.

While I waited for the car I went to my computer and checked my emails. There was one from Mike Johns, MP, confirming his sitting for nine o'clock on Thursday morning—his first in two months. I was looking forward to seeing him, as he's always great fun. There was some financial spam, which I deleted, and a weekly update on the number of visits to my official Facebook page. The last message was from Mrs. Carr's daughter, confirming that the first sitting with her mother would be on Monday, at Mrs. Carr's flat in Notting Hill.

Hearing a beep from outside I lifted the slats of the Venetian blind and saw a red Volvo from Fulham Cars pulling up. I gathered my things and went out.

"I've driven you before, haven't I?" the driver asked as he put my things in the boot.

I got in the back. "That's right. I use your firm quite a bit."

"So you can't drive?"

"I can. But I don't have a car."

As we drove up Waterford Road we passed The Wedding Shop. Seeing the china and cut glass in its windows I wondered if Chloe and Nate would have a wedding list. I wondered how many guests they'd have. I speculated about where they'd go on honeymoon; but that only made me think about the woman that Nate had called "honey." I wondered what had happened to her in the intervening five months. Now I tried to guess where he and Chloe would live—at her place, or at his flat in Earl's Court? It suddenly struck me that they might move to New York, a prospect that only made me feel more depressed.

"Shame," I heard the driver say as we idled at the lights at Fulham Broadway.

"I'm sorry?" I asked, startled.

"It's a shame." He nodded to our right.

"Yes," I said softly.

The railings at the junction were festooned with flowers. There were perhaps twenty bouquets tied to them, their cellophane icy in the sunlight. Some were fresh but most looked limp and lifeless, their ribbons drifting in the breeze.

"Poor kid," he murmured.

Secured to the top part of the railings was a large, laminated photo of a very pretty woman, a little younger than me, with short, blonde hair and a radiant smile. *Grace,* it said beneath.

"The flowers keep coming," I observed quietly.

The driver nodded. "I come past here a lot—there's always new ones." Today there was also a big teddy bear on a bike; it was wearing blue cycling shorts, a silver helmet and a sensible Hi-Vis sash.

Two months later and the large yellow sign was still there.

Witness Appeal. Fatal Accident, Jan 20, 06.15. Can You Help?

"So they still don't know what happened?"

"No," replied the driver. "It happened very early—in the dark. One of our guys said he saw a black BMW drive off, fast, but he didn't get the number and the CCTV wasn't working properly—typical; though the police are trying to enhance the footage." He shook his head again. "It's a shame." The lights changed and we drove away.

The rest of our journey passed in silence, apart from the stilted commands of the sat-nav as it coaxed us over Hammersmith Bridge towards Barnes.

Mrs. Burke lived halfway down Castlenau, in one of the imposing Victorian houses that line the road. The cab swung through the lion-topped gateposts then the driver got out and opened the boot.

He handed me the easel. "You paint *me* one day?"

I smiled. "Maybe I will."

I rang the bell. The door was opened by a grey-haired woman who told me that she was the housekeeper.

"Mrs. Burke will be down shortly," she said as I stepped inside. The hall was large and square, with a limestone floor and architectural prints in black and gold frames. On the sideboard was a big stone jug filled with branches of early cherry blossoms.

The housekeeper asked me to wait in the study. It had floor-to-ceiling bookshelves, an antique Chesterfield that gleamed like a conker, and a massive mahogany desk on which several family photos in silver frames were arranged. I looked at them. There were two of Mrs. Burke, a few of her son from babyhood to teens, and three of her with a man I assumed was her husband—a patrician-looking gentleman with a proud, proprietorial expression. He was at least a decade older than his wife. She had large grey eyes, a long, perfectly straight nose and a curtain of dark hair that fell in waves from a high forehead. She *was* beautiful. I began to make imaginary marks on the canvas to define her cheeks and jawline.

The appointment had been for eleven, but by twenty past I was still waiting. I went into the hall to try to find out what was happening. Hearing a creak on the stairs I looked up, to see Mrs. Burke coming down. She was slim and petite, and wore a pink silk shirt-waister that was cinched in by a very wide black patent-leather belt. I felt a flash of annoyance that she didn't seem to be in any hurry.

"I'm sorry to keep you waiting," she said flatly as she reached the bottom step. "I was on the phone. So . . ." She gave me a restrained smile. "You're here to paint me."

"Yes," I said, taken aback by her clear lack of enthusiasm. "Your husband said it's to celebrate your birthday."

"It is." She sighed heavily. "If hitting 'the big Four O' is a cause for 'celebration.' "

"Forty's still young."

"Is it?" she asked wearily. "I only know that it's when life is supposed to *begin*. So . . ." She drew her breath through her teeth. "We'd better get on with it, then." You'd have thought she was steeling herself for root canal treatment.

"Mrs. Burke—"

"Please." She held up a hand. "Celine."

"Celine, we can't start until you've chosen the canvas. I've brought along three . . ." I nodded at them, propped against the skirting board. "If you know where the portrait's going to hang, that'll help you decide."

She stared at them. "I haven't the faintest idea." She turned to me. "My husband's sprung this on me—I would *never* have thought of having myself painted."

"Well . . . it's a nice thing to have. And it'll be treasured for generations. Think of the *Mona Lisa*," I added cheerfully.

Celine gave a Gallic shrug, then pointed to the smallest canvas. "That one is more than big enough."

"Good. Now we need to choose the background—somewhere you'll feel relaxed and comfortable."

She blew out her cheeks. "In the drawing room, then, I suppose. This way . . ."

I followed her across the hall into a large yellow-papered room with a cream carpet. French windows opened onto a long, walled garden, at the end of which a huge red camellia was in extravagant flower.

I glanced around the room. "This will be wonderful. The colour's very appealing, and the light's lovely."

On our left was an antique Knole sofa in emerald green damask. The sides were very high, almost straight, and were secured to the back with thickly twisted gold cord. Celine sat on the left-hand side of it, then smoothed her dress over her knees. "I shall sit here . . ."

I studied her for a moment. "I'm sorry, but that won't look right."

Her face clouded. "You said I should feel comfortable—this *is.*"

"But the high sides make you look . . . boxed in."

"Oh." She turned to look at them. "I see. Yes . . . I am, as you say, boxed in. That is perfectly true. So where *should* I sit?"

"Perhaps here . . . ?" I ignored the petulance in her tone. To the left of the fireplace was a mahogany chair with ornately carved arms and a red velvet seat. I nodded towards it. Celine sat, and I moved back a few feet to appraise the composition. "If you could just turn this way," I suggested. "And lift your chin *just* a little? Now look at me . . ."

She shook her head. "Who would have thought that sitting could be such hard work?"

"Well, it's a collaborative process in which we're both aiming to get the best possible portrait of you." Celine shrugged as though this was a matter of sublime indifference to her. I held up my hands, framing her head and shoulders between my thumbs and forefingers. "It's going to be great," I said happily. "Now we just have to decide what you're going to wear."

Her face fell. "I'm going to wear *this.*" She indicated her outfit.

"It's lovely," I said carefully. "But it won't work."

"Why not?"

"Because the belt's so big and shiny that it will dominate the picture. If you could wear something a little plainer . . ."

"Are you saying I have to change?"

"Well . . . it would be better if you did, yes." She exhaled irritably. "Could I help you choose? That's what I usually do when I paint people in their homes."

"I see," she snapped. "So *you* control the whole show."

I bit my lip. "I don't mean to be controlling," I said quietly. "But the choice of outfit is very important because it affects the composition so much—I did explain that to your husband."

"Oh." Celine was rubbing her fingertips together, impatiently, as if sifting flour. "He forgot to tell me—he's away this week. All right," she said grudgingly, standing. "You'd better come."

I followed her across the room and up the stairs into the master bedroom, the far wall of which was taken up by a huge fitted wardrobe. Celine slid open the middle section then stood there, staring helplessly at the garments. "I don't know *what* to wear."

"Could I look?"

She nodded. As I began to pull out a few things her mobile phone rang. She looked at the screen, answered in French, then left the room, talking rapidly. It was more than ten minutes until she returned.

Struggling to hide my irritation I held up a pale green linen suit. "This would look quite lovely."

"I no longer wear that."

"*Would* you—just for the portrait?"

She pursed her mouth. "No. I wouldn't. I don't like myself in it."

"O-kay . . . then, what about this?" I showed her an oyster satin dress by Christian Dior.

She shook her head. "It's not a good fit." Now she began pulling things out herself: "Not that," she muttered. "No . . . not that either . . . this is horrible . . . that's much too small . . . this is *so* uncomfortable . . ." Why did she keep all these things if she didn't even like them? She turned to me. "*Can't* I wear what I'm wearing?"

I began to count to ten in my head. "The belt will wreck the composition," I reiterated quietly. "It will draw all the attention away from your face. And it's not really flattering," I added, then instantly regretted it.

Celine's face had darkened. "Are you saying I look *fat*?"

"No, no," I replied as she studied her reflection in the cheval mirror. "You're very slim. And you're really attractive," I added impotently. "Your husband said so and he was right."

I'd hoped this last remark might mollify her, but to my surprise her expression hardened. "I adore this belt. It's Prada," she added as though I could have cared less whether she'd got it in Walmart.

I was struggling to maintain my composure. "It won't look . . . good," I tried again. "It'll just be a big block of black."

"Well . . ." Celine folded her arms. "I'm going to wear it and that's all there is to it."

I was about to pretend that I needed the loo so that I could take five minutes to calm myself down—or quite possibly cry—when Celine's mobile rang again. She left the room and had another long, intense-sounding conversation, which drifted across the landing in snatches.

"*Oui, chéri . . . je veux te voir aussi . . . bientôt, chéri.*"

By now I'd decided to admit defeat and was just working out how best to minimise the monstrous belt when Celine returned. To my surprise her mood seemed to have lightened. Now she went to the far end of the wardrobe and took out a simple linen shift in powder blue, holding it against her.

"What about this?"

I could have wept with relief. "That will look *amazing.*"

The next morning, as I waited for Mike Johns to arrive for his sitting, I looked at Celine's portrait—so far no more than a few preliminary marks in yellow ochre. She was the trickiest sitter I'd ever had—obstructive, unreasonable and entirely lacking in enthusiasm.

Her attitude struck me as bizarre. Most people give themselves up to the sittings, recognising that to be painted is a special thing, if not a privilege. But for Celine it was clearly not something to be enjoyed, but endured. Why, I wondered.

One time I had to paint a successful businessman whose company had commissioned his portrait for their boardroom. During the sittings he kept glancing at his watch, as though to let me know that he was an extremely busy and important man whose time was very precious. But when I at last started to paint Celine she'd told me that she didn't work, and that now that her son was at boarding school she led a "leisured" sort of life. So her negativity can't have been because she didn't have enough time for the portrait.

Thank God for Mike Johns, I thought. A big bear of a man, he was always genial, cooperative and expressive—the perfect sitter. As I took out his canvas I was pleased to see that even in the painting's semi-finished state, his amiability and warmth shone through.

Mike's portrait had been commissioned by his constituency to mark his fifteenth anniversary as their MP: he'd been elected quite young, at only twenty-six. He'd told me that he wanted to get the painting done well before the run-up to the general election began in earnest: so we'd had two sittings before Christmas, then the third early in the new year. We'd scheduled another for January 22, but Mike had cancelled it abruptly the night before. In an oddly incoherent email he wrote that he'd be in touch again "in due course," but I'd heard nothing from him in the intervening two months. I was surprised not least because he lived nearby, just on the other side of Fulham Broadway, so it would have been easy for him to pop in for the sittings. Then last week he'd messaged me to ask if we could continue. I was glad, partially because it would mean I'd get the other half of my fee, but mostly because I genuinely liked him and looked forward to our sessions.

We'd arranged for Mike to come early so that the sitting wouldn't eat into his working day. At five past eight the bell rang and I ran downstairs, smiling.

As I opened the door, however, I stifled a gasp. In the nine weeks since I'd last seen him, Mike must have lost thirty pounds.

"You're looking trim," I remarked as he stepped inside. "Been pounding the treadmill?" Yet I already knew, from his noticeably subdued air, that his weight loss must be due to some kind of stress.

"I *have* shed a few pounds," he replied vaguely. "A good thing too," he added with a stab at his usual bonhomie. But his strained demeanour gave him away. He was friendly, but there was a new sadness about him—an air of tragedy almost, I realised with surprise as I registered the dead look in his eyes. "Sorry about the early start," he said as we went up to the studio.

"I don't mind at all," I replied. "We can do all the remaining sessions at this time, if you like."

Mike nodded, then took off his jacket and put it on the sofa. He sat in the oak armchair that I use for sittings. "Back in the hot seat, then," he said with forced joviality.

The morning light was sharp so I lowered the blinds on the Velux windows to soften it. As I set Mike's canvas on the easel I realised that I was going to have to adjust the portrait. His torso was much slimmer, his face and neck thinner. The collar of his shirt visibly gaped. His hands looked less fleshy as he clasped them in his lap. He fiddled with his wedding ring which was clearly loose.

I scraped a pebble of dried paint off the palette then squeezed some new colour out of the tubes, enjoying as I always did the rich oily scent of the linseed.

"I forgot to wear the blue jumper," Mike told me. "I'm sorry—it slipped my mind."

"Don't worry." I mixed the colour with a palette knife, then picked up a fine brush. "I'll be working on your face today, but if you could wear it next time, that would be great."

Now I looked at Mike, and began to paint; I looked at him again, then painted a little more. And so it went on, just looking and painting, looking and painting.

Mike usually chatted away, but today he was virtually silent. He directed his gaze towards me but avoided eye contact. His mouth and jaw were tight. Aware that I must have noticed the change in him, he clumsily confided that he was "a bit strung out" with all the extra work he was doing in preparation for the general election.

I wondered if he was worried that he might lose his seat; but I knew that he had a huge majority and was very popular with his constituents.

I shaded a slight hollow into his left cheek. "Have you been away?" I asked, wondering if that was why he'd been unable to sit for me lately.

He nodded. "I went to Bonn last month on a cross-party trip."

I cleaned the brush in the pot of turps. "What was that for?"

"We were looking at their tram system."

"Of course—you're on the transport committee, aren't you?" I dipped the brush in the cobalt to make the flesh tone around his jaw a bit greyer. "I know you've done a lot to try and protect cyclists, putting in extra bike lanes and cycle super-highways, so more power to your elbow—it's not easy on two wheels in this city."

Mike nodded, then glanced away. As he seemed reluctant to talk about work I asked him about his wife, a successful publisher in her late thirties.

He shifted on the chair. "Sarah's fine. She's incredibly busy though—as usual."

I dipped the brush in the turps. "I saw a photo of her in the business pages the other day—I can't remember what the story was but she looked terribly glamourous."

"She's just bought Delphi Press—to add to her empire." Mike's smile was slightly bitter. Now I remembered him confiding that his wife's career was all-consuming. Maybe she didn't want children and he did: or maybe they couldn't have them and it was getting to him. Maybe, God forbid, he was ill.

Suddenly he heaved a sigh so deep, it was almost a groan.

I lowered my brush. "Mike, are you okay? I hope you don't mind my asking, but you seem a bit—"

"I'm fine," he answered brusquely. He cleared his throat. "As I say, I'm just a bit stressed . . . with polling day looming . . . and it's particularly tense this time."

"Of course. Would you like to have a coffee break now—if you're tired?" He shook his head. "Well . . . shall we just listen to the radio, then?" Gratefully, he nodded. So I found my paint-spattered transistor radio and switched it on.

Ra-di-o Two . . . It's ten to nine. And if you've just joined us, you're listening to me, Kenny Bruce, taking you through the morning . . . Eric Clapton's on tour—he'll be playing the o2 next week, then he'll be in Birmingham and Leeds . . .

The doorbell rang. As I ran downstairs I heard a gentle guitar introduction, then Clapton's voice.

Would you know my name
If I saw you in heaven
Will it be the same
If I saw you in heaven . . .

I opened the door. It was the postman with the new bank card I'd been expecting. As I signed for it Clapton's sad ballad continued to drift down the stairs.

Would you hold my hand
If I saw you in heaven

I went back up to the studio. "Sorry about that." I went to my desk and put the letter in a drawer.

I must be strong, and carry on
'Cause I know I don't belong
Here in heaven . . .

I returned to the easel, picked up my brush then looked at Mike . . .

> . . . *don't belong*
> *Here in heaven.*

He was crying.

I turned the radio off. "Let's stop," I murmured after a moment. "You're . . . upset."

"No. No." He dashed his tears away. "I'm fine—and the picture needs to be finished." He swallowed. "I'd like to continue."

"Are you sure?"

He nodded, then raised his head to resume the pose, and we continued in silence for another fifteen minutes or so, at the end of which Mike stood up. I expected him to come look at the painting, as he usually does; but he just picked up his jacket and went out of the studio with a distracted air.

I followed him downstairs. "So just two more sittings now." I opened the front door. "Is the same time next week okay for you?" I couldn't help but be worried about him; he seemed so devastated.

"That'll be fine," he said absently. "See you then, Ella."

"Yes. See you then, Mike."

I watched him walk to his car. As I stood there, he lifted his hand, and gave me a bleak smile. Then he got in his black BMW and drove away.

Three

"Ella?" said Chloe over the phone three days later. "I need to ask you something."

"If it's that you want me to be a bridesmaid, the answer's no."

"Oh . . ." She sounded disappointed. "Why not?"

"Because I'm nearly seven years older and two stone heavier than you are—that's why. I don't fancy being a troll to your fairy."

"How about maid of honour, then?"

"No. See answer above."

"Actually, that wasn't what I was going to ask you—Nate has a five-year-old niece who's going to do the honours."

"That sounds perfect. So what did you want to ask?" My heart ached, because I knew.

"I'd just like to set up the first sitting with Nate. I was half expecting you to get in touch about it."

"Sorry, I've been working flat out," I lied.

"Can we fix up some times now?"

"Sure," I replied breezily.

I rummaged on the table for my calendar and found it under this month's *Modern Painters*. I scribbled in the first date she suggested.

"So where are you going to paint him? His flat's near yours, if you want to paint him there."

"No—he'll have to come to me." Given the way I felt about Nate, I preferred him to be on my territory.

"That's eleven a.m. next Friday, then," said Chloe. "Good Friday."

"So it is. I'll get some hot cross buns in for the break."

As I tossed the calendar back on the table I remembered the girl at the auction asking me if I could paint someone I didn't like. I was about to find out.

"Nate will be a good sitter," I heard Chloe say.

"I hope so." I sighed. "I've had some tricky ones lately."

"Really?"

I wasn't going to tell her about Mike—I felt a growing concern for him. What might have happened to trouble him so much?

"How are your sitters being tricky?" my sister persisted. I described Celine's behaviour. "How odd," said Chloe. "It's as though she's trying to sabotage the portrait."

"Exactly. And when we finally started, she took two *more* calls, then went to the door and spoke to her builder for twenty minutes. The woman's a nightmare."

"Well, Nate will be very good, I promise. He's not that keen on it all either, as you know. But at least he'll behave well during the sittings."

"In that case we should be able to get away with five rather than the usual six." The thought cheered me. "Or even four."

"Please don't cut corners," I heard Chloe say. "I've paid a lot for this portrait, Ella. I want it to be . . . wonderful."

"Of course you do." I felt a wave of shame. This was so important to her, and I wanted her to be happy. "Don't worry, I'll do a good job, in at least six sittings—*more* if they're needed," I added recklessly.

"And please make it truthful, not just attractive. I want the portrait to *reveal* something about Nate."

"It will," I assured her, then wondered *what*—that he was cynical
and untrustworthy, probably. Convinced that my negativity about
him would show, I now regretted the commission deeply and
wished I could get out of it. I fiddled with a paintbrush. "By the way,
I saw the announcement in *The Times*." Seeing it in black and white
had depressed me.

Mr. Nathan Roberto Rossi to Miss Chloe Susan Graham

Chloe snorted. "Mum also put it in the *Telegraph, The Independent
and The Guardian*! I told her that was over the top but she said she
'didn't want anyone to miss it.' " I suppressed a groan. I immediately suspected that what Mum really intended was for *Max* not to
miss it.

"She is *amazing*," Chloe went on. "She's already booked the
church, the photographer, the video man, the caterers, the florist
and the marquee—or Raj tent, rather. She now says that a Moghul
pavillion's the most elegant way to dine under canvas."

"Is it going to be a sit-down affair, then?"

"Yes. I told Mum that finger food would be fine, but she insists we
do it 'properly,' with a traditional, waitered wedding breakfast—
poor Dad! He keeps joking that it's a good thing he's an orthopaedic
surgeon, as he knows where to get more arms and legs."

I laughed. "And Mum said you wanted a vintage wedding dress."

"If I can find one that's perfect for me, yes."

While Chloe chatted about her preferred style I went to my computer and, with the phone still clamped to my ear, found three spe-
cialist websites. I clicked on the first, the Vintage Wedding Dress
Company.

"There's a wonderful fifties dress here," I said to her. "Guipure
lace top with a billowy silk skirt—it's called 'Gina.' " I gave Chloe the
name of the site so that she could find it. "There's also a thirties one

called 'Greta'—see it? That column of ivory satin—but it's got a very low back."

"Oh, yes . . . It's lovely, but I'm not sure I want to show that much flesh."

"That sixties one would suit you—Jackie: it's a twelve though, so you'd have to have it altered, which might ruin it."

"I can't see it. Hang on a moment . . ."

While I waited for Chloe to find it I clicked on my emails. There were three new ones, including a request for my bank account details, an advert for "bedding bargains" from "Dreamz" and some offers from Toptable. I deleted them all.

"*Here's* a gorgeous dress!" Chloe exclaimed. "It's called 'Giselle.' "

I navigated back to the site. The dress was ballerina style: dense layers of silk tulle below a fitted satin bodice spangled with sequins. "It *is* gorgeous. You'll look just like Mum in her dancing days."

"It's beautiful," Chloe breathed. "And I know it would suit me—*but* . . ." She was making little clicking noises. "It might be inauspicious to wear a wedding dress called 'Giselle,' don't you think?"

"Oh . . . because she has such bad luck in the husband department, you mean?"

"Exactly—Albrecht's such a cad, two-timing the poor girl like that. I hope Nate isn't going to do that to *me*," she snorted. "Otherwise I might have to kill myself, like Giselle does."

"Don't be silly," I scolded faintly. "After all, he's asked you to marry him."

"That's . . . true. Anyway, if you see any really great dresses, let me know."

"Sure. But I'd better go, Chloe—I've got a sitting."

"And I've got some press packs to check—I'll tell Nate that he's got a date with you on Friday."

A date with Nate, I thought dismally as I hung up.

I ordered a cab then began to get my things together for the sitting with Mrs. Carr. Her daughter had already specified the size of canvas, so I took one out, checked that it was properly stretched, then put my canvas bag and easel by the door. I was just getting my coat when the phone rang.

"Ella? This is Alison from the Royal Society of Portrait Painters. Remember, we spoke before Christmas—when you were first elected?"

"Of course I do. Hi."

"I've just had an enquiry about you."

"Really?" My spirits lifted at the thought of a possible commission. Through the window I could see the cab pulling up.

"It's slightly unusual in that it's for a posthumous portrait—"

My euphoria evaporated. "I'm afraid I don't do them. I find the idea of them too sad, and technically they're difficult . . ."

"Oh, I didn't realise that you felt like that—I'll make a note. Some of our members do them but we'll put on your page that you don't—not that these requests arise all that often, but it's good to know your position. Anyway, I'm sure there'll be other enquiries about you before long."

"Fingers crossed . . ."

"So I'll be in touch again sometime."

"Great. Erm . . . Alison, do you mind if I ask you . . . ?"

"Yes?"

"Just out of curiosity, who was it from? This enquiry?"

"It was from the family of a girl who was knocked off her bike and killed." I felt goose bumps stipple my arms. "It happened about two months ago," Alison went on. "At Fulham Broadway. In fact, there's been a bit about it in the press because the police still don't know what caused the accident—or rather, who."

I thought of what my driver had said, about the black BMW just speeding away. "I live near there," I said quietly. "I've seen where it happened . . ."

"There'll be a memorial service in September, and the girl's parents have decided to commission a portrait of her for it."

"Grace. Her name was Grace."

"That's right. She was a primary school teacher. It's very sad. Her family realise that any painting's going to take time, so her uncle called me to discuss it. He said that they'd been looking at our artists and had particularly liked your work."

"I see . . ."

"In fact, they're very keen for you to do it."

"Ah."

"But of course I'll tell him that you can't—"

"No . . . I mean, yes. Tell him that . . ."

"That you paint only from life?" Alison suggested.

"Yes . . . But please say I'm very sorry."

"I will."

From outside I heard the beeping of the cab's horn so I said goodbye, locked up, then went out to the car. It was the red Volvo again; the driver loaded up my easel and canvas while I climbed into the back.

He sat behind the wheel, then looked at me in the mirror. "Where to this time?"

I gave him the address and we set off.

"So who are you painting today?" he asked as we drove through Earl's Court.

"An elderly lady."

"Lots of wrinkles, then," he said with a laugh.

"Yes—and lots of character. I like painting old people. I love looking at paintings of old people too." I thought of Rembrandt's tender and dignified portraits of the elderly.

"You're going to paint me one day—don't forget, now!"

"Don't worry. I won't." Why not? He had an interesting, craggy sort of face.

Mrs. Carr's flat was in a mansion block on a narrow street close to Notting Hill Gate. I paid the driver, got out of the cab, then he brought me my easel and my canvas bag. To my left was an antiques shop, and to the right a primary school. I could hear children's voices and the sound of a ball being kicked about and laughter. I pressed the bell for flat 9 and after a moment heard Mrs. Carr's daughter, Sophia, over the intercom.

"Hi, Ella." The door buzzed and I opened it. "Take the lift to the third floor."

The interior of the Edwardian building was cold, its walls still clad in the original art nouveau tiles in a fluid pattern of green and maroon. I stepped into the antiquated-looking lift and rattled up to the third floor, where it stopped with a sonorous *clunk*. As I pulled back the grille I could see Sophia waiting for me at the very end of a dimly lit corridor. In her mid-fifties, she was dressed youthfully in jeans and a brown suede jacket, her fair hair pulled back into a ponytail.

As I walked towards her she looked at the equipment. "That's a lot to lug about." She stepped forward. "Let me help you."

"Thanks. It's not heavy," I assured her as she took the easel. "Just a bit awkward."

"It's nice to see you again. Thanks for coming to us," she added as I followed her inside. She shut the door. "It makes it so much easier for my mother."

"It's really not a problem." I didn't add that I like painting people in their own homes: it gives me important insights into who they are—their taste, how much comfort they like and the degree of tidi-ness that they choose to live in. I can detect, from the number of family photographs, how sentimental they are and, if there are invi-tations to be seen, how social. All this gives me a head start on my subjects before painting even begins.

"Mum's in the sitting room," Sophia told me. "I'll introduce you, then leave you two to it while I do a bit of shopping for her."

I followed Sophia down the hallway.

The sitting room was large and light, with two green wingback chairs, a lemon yellow chaise longue and a cream-coloured sofa. A green and yellow Persian rug covered most of the darkly varnished parquet floor.

Mrs. Carr was standing by the far window. She was tall and very slim, but slightly stooped, and she leaned on a stick. Her hair was tinted a pale caramel colour and was set in soft layered waves. In profile her nose was Roman, and her eyes, when she turned to look at me, were a remarkable dark blue, almost navy.

Sophia put the easel down. "Mummy?" She'd raised her voice. "This is Ella."

"Hello, Mrs. Carr." I stepped forward and extended a hand.

She took it in her left one. Her fingers felt as cool and smooth as vellum. As she smiled, her face creased into dozens of little lines and folds. "How nice to meet you."

Sophia took my parka. "Can I get you a cup of coffee, Ella?"

"Oh, no thanks."

"What about *you*, Mummy? Do you want some coffee?" Mrs. Carr shook her head then went over to the sofa and sat, leaning her stick against the arm.

Sophia waved to her. "I'll be back around four, then—*four*, Mummy! *Ok-ay?*"

"That's fine, darling. No need to shout . . ." As we heard Sophia's retreating steps Mrs. Carr looked at me, then shrugged. "She thinks I'm deaf," she said wonderingly. The front door slammed, creating a slight reverberation.

I took a closer look at the room. One wall was lined with books; the others bore an assortment of prints and paintings that hung, in attractive chaos, from the picture rail. I opened my bag. "Have you lived here long, Mrs. Carr?"

She held up her hand. "Please call me Iris—we'll be spending quite a lot of time together, after all."

"I will, then—thanks."

"But to answer your question—fifteen years. I moved here after my husband died. We'd lived not far away, in Holland Street. The house was too big and too sad for me on my own; but I wanted to stay in this area, as I have many friends here."

I opened up the easel. "And you have two daughters, don't you?"

Iris nodded. "My younger one, Mary, lives in Sussex. Sophia's just down the road in Brook Green. This portrait was their idea—rather a nice one, I think."

"And have you ever been painted before?"

Iris hesitated. "Yes. A long time ago . . ." She half closed her eyes as if revisiting the memory. "But . . . the girls insisted that they wanted a new picture of me. I did wonder whether I wanted to be painted at this age, with all my lines and wrinkles—but I have to accept the fact that my face is now an *old* face."

"It's also a beautiful one."

She smiled. "You're being kind."

"Not really—it's true." I knew that Iris and I were going to get on well. "So . . . I'll prepare everything then." I got out the paints and my palette. I tied on my apron and spread a dustsheet around the easel. "And did you have a career, Iris?" Her eyes were really the most extraordinary color. I couldn't wait to paint them.

"Ralph was in the Foreign Office, so *that* was my career, being a diplomat's wife—dutifully flying the flag in various parts of the globe."

"Sounds fascinating. And where did you live?"

"In Yugoslavia, Egypt and Iran—this was before the revolution—and in India and Chile. Our last posting was in Paris, which was lovely." As Iris talked I studied her face, seeing how it moved, and where the light fell.

I got out my pad and a stump of charcoal. "It sounds like a wonderful life."

"It was—in most ways."

I sat in the wingback chair nearest Iris, looked at her, and began to make rapid marks: "I'm just doing a preliminary sketch." The charcoal squeaked across the paper. "And do you come from a diplomatic background yourself?"

"No. My stepfather was in the City. So are you going to paint me sitting here?"

"Yes." I lowered the sketchpad. "If you're happy there."

"I'm perfectly happy. And is the light satisfactory?"

"It's lovely." I glanced at the window, through which I could see the dome of the Coronet Cinema and behind it a patch of pale sky. "There's a lot of high cloud, which is good because it eliminates strong shadows." I carried on drawing, then turned the pad round to show Iris what I'd done. "I'm going to paint you like this, as a seated half figure, in a three-quarters position."

She peered at it. "And will my hands be in the picture?"

"Yes."

"In that case I'll wear one or two rings."

"Please do—I love painting jewellery." I wiped a smudge of charcoal off my thumb.

"And what about my clothes?" Iris asked. "Sophia told me that you like to have some say in what your sitters wear."

"I do—if they don't object." I thought of Celine.

"I don't object in the slightest."

"You're very helpful," I said gratefully.

Iris looked puzzled. "Why shouldn't I be? You're going to deliver me up to *posterity*—the least I can do is to cooperate. My daughters say that your portraits are so vibrant that one almost expects the people in them to climb out of the frames."

"Thank you. That's a lovely compliment."

"But *I've* not yet seen one myself."

"Ah." I should have brought some photos of them with me. "Do you have a computer, Iris?" She shook her head. "Wait—I have an idea."

I got out my phone, went to "Gallery," then touched one of the thumbnail images. I handed the phone to Iris.

She brought it close to her eyes, then nodded appreciatively. "That's Simon Rattle."

I nodded. "The Berlin Philharmonic commissioned it last year—I went there for a week and painted him every day in between rehearsals. He was a good, patient sitter."

"I'll try to be the same."

I took the phone from Iris, touched another image, then handed it back to her. "And this is P. D. James."

"So it is . . . I see what my daughters mean—there's such *life* to your work."

As Mrs. Carr gave me back my phone I noticed that I had new emails. I touched the in-box and saw a flyer from the Victoria and Albert Museum and a message from Chloe. At that moment a new email arrived—one that had been forwarded automatically from my website. I felt a tingle of excitement because it was likely to be an enquiry; I could see a bit of the first line, *Dear Ella, my . . .* but resisted the temptation to open it, as I didn't want to risk annoying Iris— I was here to paint her, not read my messages.

"So now we'll decide what I'm to wear," Iris said. "Please come."

Reaching for her cane, she pushed herself to her feet.

I followed her down the corridor into her bedroom, a lovely room with pale blue chintz curtains and a blue candlewick bedspread. Along one wall was a big, Art Deco wardrobe. As Iris opened the doors, a faint scent of lavender mingled with camphor drifted out.

"Can I help you get things out?" I asked her.

"No . . . I can manage. Thank you." Iris leaned her cane against the wall, then, with slightly shaky hands, took out a pink, lightly patterned dress and a blue tweed suit. She laid them gently on the bed. "What about these?"

I looked at the garments, then at Iris. "Either would look good. But . . . the suit, I think."

She smiled. "I hoped you'd say that. Ralph bought it for me in Harrods on a home leave one time—he couldn't really afford it, but he saw how much I liked it and he wanted me to have it."

"It's perfect. So what jewellery will you wear?"

"Just a lapis lazuli necklace and my engagement ring."

Iris went to her dressing table and lifted the lid of an ornately carved sandalwood box. As she did so, I glanced round the room, curious. There was a gilded mirror on one wall, flanked by a pair of small alpine paintings. Over the bed was a silk wall hanging of a crested crane. A blue Persian glass vase stood in the window, casting a rich cobalt shadow onto the sill.

"Would you kindly get my cane?" I heard Iris say. "It's against the wall there by the wardrobe."

As I did so I noticed another painting, one hanging next to her bed. It was of two little girls playing in a park. They were throwing a red ball to each other while a small dog darted at their feet in a blur of brown fur. On a bench close by, a woman in a white apron sat knitting.

"What a lovely picture," I exclaimed.

Iris turned round. "Yes . . . that painting is very special. In fact, it's priceless," she added quietly.

"It's certainly very fine." I handed Iris her cane, then looked at the painting again. "Is it an heirloom?"

She hesitated. "I bought it in an antiques shop in 1960, for ten shillings and sixpence."

I turned to her. "So you just . . . liked it."

Iris was still gazing at it. "Oh, it was much more than 'liked.' I was drawn to it—*guided* to it, I sometimes think."

I waited for her to elaborate but she didn't say any more. "Well," I said after a moment, trying to disguise my curiosity, "it's easy to understand why you fell in love with it. It's beautifully composed and has so much—I was going to say charm, but what I really mean is *feeling*."

Iris nodded. "There's a lot of feeling there. Yes."

"The woman on the bench must be the girls' nanny."

"That's right."

"She seems absorbed in her knitting, but she's actually looking at the artist, covertly, which gives it a kind of edge. It looks like it's from the 1930s. I wonder where it was painted . . ."

"In St. James's Park, near the lake."

I studied the silvery-grey water shining in the background. "Well, it's lovely. It must lift your spirits, just looking at it."

"On the contrary," Iris murmured. "It makes me feel sad." She lowered herself onto the bed. "But I need to change, so if you could give me a few moments . . ."

"Of course."

As I went back to the sitting room I wondered why the painting would have that effect on Iris. As I put the canvas on the easel I reflected that we all see different things in works of art; yet the scene was, objectively, a happy one. So why did it make her sad?

While I was preparing the palette, Polly phoned. I answered.

"He's *called* me," she declared excitedly.

"Who has?"

"Jason—from the Toilet Duck shoot; he's *just* called and asked me to have lunch with him on Saturday."

"Great," I whispered. "But I can't chat—I'm in a sitting."

"Oops, sorry! I'll leave you to it."

As I pressed the End Call button I looked at the envelope icon and was about to open the email from my website when I heard Iris's footsteps.

"So . . ." She was standing in the doorway. The suit fitted her perfectly and brought out that extraordinary blue of her eyes; she'd put on some powder and a touch of pink lipstick.

"You look lovely, Iris." I put my phone back in my bag.

"Thank you. So now we can start."

Iris sat on the sofa, smoothed down her skirt, then turned towards me. As I looked at her, I felt the frisson I always feel when I begin a new portrait. We were silent for a while, the brush scraping softly across the canvas as I began to block in the main shapes with an ochre wash.

Then Iris shifted her position.

"Are you comfortable enough?" I asked her, concerned.

"I *am*—though I confess I feel a little self-conscious."

"Oh, that's normal," I assured her. "A portrait sitting's quite a strange experience—for both parties—because there's this sudden relationship. I mean, we've only just met, but here I am, openly gawping at you; you've got to admit, it's a pretty unnatural first encounter."

Iris smiled. "I'm sure I'll soon get used to your . . . scrutiny. But wouldn't you rather be painting someone young?"

I shook my head. "I prefer painting older people. It's much more interesting. I love seeing a whole life delineated on a face, with all that experience and insight and . . ."

"Regret?" Iris suggested quietly.

"Yes, that's usually there too. It would be strange if it wasn't."

"So . . . do your sitters ever get upset? At the experience and insight and regret that you capture?"

My brush stopped. "They do—especially the older ones because as they sit there they're looking back on their lives. Sometimes people cry." I thought of Mike. Again I wondered what had happened to make him so unhappy.

"Well, I shall try *not* to," Iris promised.

I smiled. "It doesn't matter if you do. I'm going to paint *you*, Iris, in all your humanity, as you *are*—or as I see you at least."

"You have to be perceptive, then, to do what you do."

"That's true. And I couldn't even *try* to do this if I didn't believe that I was. Portrait painters need to be able to detect things about the sitter—to work out who that person *is*."

We continued in silence.

"And do you ever paint yourself?"

My brush stopped in mid-stroke. "No."

Surprise flickered across Iris's beautiful features. "I thought portrait artists usually do self-portraits."

You're Ella Graham now . . .

"Well . . . I don't—not for years now."

And that's all there is to it . . .

"I'd love to hear more about your time abroad, Iris. You must have met some remarkable people."

"I did," she said warmly. "They weren't just people, they were *personalities*. Let me see . . . Whose names can I drop? We met Tito, and Indira Ghandi—I have a photo of Sophia, aged five, sitting on her lap. I also met Nasser—the year before Suez; I danced with him at an embassy ball. In Chile we met Salvador Allende; Ralph and I liked him enormously and were outraged at what the Americans did to help overthrow him—though we could never say so openly. Discretion is a frustrating, if necessary, aspect of diplomatic life."

"What was your favourite posting?"

Iris smiled. "Iran. We were there in the mid-1970s—it was paradisally beautiful and I have wonderful memories of our time there."

"But presumably your daughters went to boarding school?"

She nodded. "In Dorset. They weren't able to join us for every holiday, so that was hard. Their guardian was very good, but we hated being separated from our two girls."

There was another silence, broken only by the dull rumble of traffic in Kensington Church Street.

"Iris . . . I hope you don't mind my asking you, but the picture in your bedroom . . ."

She shifted slightly. "Yes?"

"You said it made you feel sad. I can't help wondering why—as it's such a happy scene."

Iris didn't at first reply, and for a few moments I wondered whether she *wasn't*, in fact, slightly deaf; I was considering whether to ask her again when she exhaled, painfully. "That picture makes me feel sad, Ella, because there is a sad story attached to it—one I learned a few years after I bought it." Her voice trembled. "Perhaps I'll tell you . . ."

I suddenly felt like I'd been crass. "You don't have to, Iris—I didn't mean to pry; I was just surprised by your remark, that's all."

"That's perfectly understandable. It *is*, on the surface, a happy scene. Two little girls playing in a park . . ." She paused, then looked at me. "I *will* tell you the story, Ella—because you're an artist and I believe you'll understand." *Understand what?* I wondered. What could the sad story behind that exquisite painting be? It now occurred to me that the girls might not have survived the war—or perhaps something awful had happened to the nanny. Now I wasn't sure that I *wanted* to hear the story, but Iris was beginning.

"I bought the painting in May 1960," she told me. "We were in Yugoslavia then—our first posting; but I'd come home with Sophia, who was then three, to have my second child, Mary. There were good hospitals in Belgrade, but I decided to have the baby in London so that my mother could help me. Also, she was widowed by then and I wanted to take the opportunity to spend some time with her; so I went to stay with her for three months."

I looked at Iris, and drew in the curve of her right cheek.

"My mother's house was in Bayswater. She'd spent most of her married life in Mayfair but, as I say, my stepfather lost everything after the war." I wondered again about Iris's own father. "The week before the baby was due I took Sophia out in her push-chair. We had an ice cream in Whiteleys then walked slowly up Westbourne Grove; I was just passing a small antiques shop when I glanced in the window and saw that painting. I remember stopping dead and just staring at it: I was completely smitten with it—as you have been today. Sophia squawked at me to go on, so I did. But I couldn't get the picture out of my mind. So a few minutes later I turned back quite impulsively and went inside.

"The man who owned the shop told me that the painting had come in the week before. It had been brought in with some other things by a woman who'd found it in her late brother's attic—she'd been clearing his house. She wasn't sure who it was by, as it was unsigned, but on the back of the canvas was the year it was painted, 1934. Anyway, I bought it, and I remember feeling as I carried it home what I can only describe as a kind of *relief*.

"I showed it to my mother and she looked at it closely, but said nothing. I felt hurt by her lack of enthusiasm, but assumed that it was because she felt I'd been extravagant. I volunteered that it *was* a lot of money, but added that I'd simply 'had to have it.' Then I hung it in my room.

"The following week Mary was born, and I stayed with my mother for another two months. She was very helpful, yet seemed sad, despite the birth of the new baby; but I guessed it was because she knew I'd soon be going back to Yugoslavia with her grandchildren and that it would be a long time before she saw us again."

"Did you have any siblings?"

"Yes—an older sister, Agnes, who lived in Kent. Anyway, before I went back to Belgrade I put the painting in storage with all the other things that Ralph and I had stored."

"Could you lift your head a little, Iris? I'm just marking out your brow. That's better. So . . . what happened then?"

Iris folded her hands in her lap. "In 1963 we returned to London for a two-year stint before our next foreign posting. We were glad to be back, the only sadness being that my mother had died a few months before. I think she knew that she might not see me again, because her last letters to me had been full of sorrow—she wrote that she hadn't been a good mother in some critical ways; she said she had so much to regret. I simply thought that the distance between us had made her feel vulnerable; so I wrote back saying that she'd been a very loving and caring mother, which, in most ways, she had . . ."

She brushed a speck off her skirt. "Anyway, Ralph and I had returned at last to our house in Clapham—it had been rented while we were away. I remember the day our things came out of storage and Sophia and Mary, who were by then six and three, delightedly helping us unpack the crates. Eventually we came to the china and glass, then to the few pictures we possessed, and there, wrapped in some old pages of the *Daily Express,* was my painting. I was *so* glad to see it again . . ."

Iris paused for a moment. Then she continued.

"This was the first time Ralph had seen it, although I'd told him about it of course. As he looked at it he said that it was clearly very good and added that he'd ask our neighbour Hugh, who worked at Sotheby's, to take a look at it. A few days later Hugh came round, and he said that the reason it was unsigned was because it was probably a model for a larger work. He was almost sure that it was by Guy Lennox, who had been a successful portraitist in the twenties and thirties. Ralph asked Hugh about its possible value and I remember feeling alarmed because I knew that I could never part with it—especially as I was now mother of two little girls myself. And this made me feel that *that* was what had first drawn me to the picture; when I was pregnant I was *sure* that I was going to have another daughter—and I did. Anyway, I was very relieved to hear Hugh say that the picture wouldn't be worth a huge amount, because Lennox was simply a good figurative artist, painting portraits to commission. I was about to put the girls to bed when he added that his uncle had known Guy Lennox well; he remembered him saying that Lennox had had a sad life.

"Really?"

"Hugh said that he could find out more about Lennox if I was interested, which I was. So he showed his uncle the painting on a visit to him in Hampshire not long afterwards. When Hugh brought the painting back a month later he confirmed that it *was* by Guy Lennox, whose life story he now knew. He told us that Lennox was born in 1900, had fought in the First World War, but had been badly gassed at Passchendaele and was sent back. While recuperating he'd taught himself to paint; he then went to the Camberwell College of Arts for two years—which is where he met Hugh's uncle. Lennox had decided to specialise in portraits and so in 1922 he went to study portraiture at the Heatherly's School of Fine Art in Chelsea. I'm sure you know it."

"Yes—very well; I used to teach at Heatherly's."

"While he was there Guy fell desperately in love with one of the models—a beautiful girl called Edith Roche. His parents tried to discourage the relationship but in 1924 Guy and Edith were married at the Chelsea Old Town Hall. In 1927 they had a baby girl, followed fifteen months later by another. By this time Guy was becoming successful, fashionable, even. He was much in demand, painting anyone who was 'anyone'—literary and political figures, and members of the aristocracy. He became a Royal Academician, and was able to buy a house in Glebe Place with its own studio. His life seemed gilded—until the day he was commissioned to paint a man named Peter Loden . . ." She fell silent.

"So . . . who was Peter Loden?" I asked after a few moments. I was entranced.

Iris blinked, as if surfacing from some dream. "He was an oil trader," she replied. "He was very rich—he'd laid the first pipeline to Romania. He had a huge house just off Park Lane; it was quite magnificent," she added absently.

"How old was he?"

"Thirty-eight—still a bachelor, and quite a ladies' man. In May 1929, Peter Loden won a Conservative seat in the general election and, to celebrate, he asked Guy Lennox to paint his portrait. He liked the painting so much that he decided to hold an official unveiling for it. So in October of that year he held a lavish party, to which he invited *le tout monde*. He also invited Lennox—and his wife—and when Peter Loden met Edith . . ."

"Ah . . ."

"He was infatuated with her beauty, and she was flattered to have the attentions of such a rich and powerful man. Soon everyone knew that Edith Lennox was involved with Peter Loden; worse, Guy had to keep on working with Loden's social crowd, knowing that the society figures he painted were gossiping behind his back about his wife."

"How horrible for him!"

Iris nodded. "It must have been agonising. And it was to have a devastating effect on his life, because within three months Edith had sued Guy for divorce. You'd think that she and Loden had done him enough harm," Iris added wearily. "But then it all became truly heartbreaking for that poor man because—"

Iris looked up. The front door was being opened, there was a grunt as it was banged shut, then footsteps, and now here was Sophia, clutching four bulging green carrier bags, her face pink with exertion.

"I'm pooped!" She smiled at us benignly. "I carried this lot back from Ken High Street. Still, the exercise is good for me." Laughing, she nodded at the easel. "So how are you two getting along?"

"Oh . . . fine," Iris replied. She glanced at her watch. "But you're early, Sophia. It's only a quarter to four."

"I know, but I'd got everything you needed—except the Parma ham: there was *no Parma ham*, Mum—so I thought I'd head back. Don't let me disturb you. I'll put all this away." She disappeared and now we heard cupboards being opened and shut.

Iris gave me a rueful smile. "Well . . . I guess this is a good moment for us to stop."

I nodded reluctantly, then clipped the canvas into the canvas carrier. "I'll see you next time, Iris." I collapsed the legs of the easel.

"It will have to be after Easter," she replied. "I'm staying with Mary that week." I got my calendar out of my bag.

As we were making a date Sophia came back. "Will you need me to be here again?" she asked. "I can be, if you want."

"That's kind, darling," Iris answered. "But now that Ella and I know each other we can just carry on from where we've left off."

I nodded. Sophia handed me my coat and I put it on. "I've enjoyed the sitting, Iris."

"I have too," she told me. "*Very* much. So until next time . . ."

I smiled my goodbye, then picked everything up.

Sophia held the door open for me. "Can I give you a hand?" she asked good-naturedly.

"I'll be fine, thanks." I hitched my canvas bag a little higher onto my shoulder. "Bye, Sophia . . ."

"Bye, Ella." The door shut behind me.

I clanked down in the lift then went out onto Kensington Church Street and hailed a cab. As I sat in the back my mind was full of Guy Lennox and the beautiful, impetuous Edith, and Peter Loden, and the two little girls, the nanny and the dog: they felt almost as real to me as if I'd known them myself. Soon we were passing Glebe Place and I craned my neck to look down it, wondering which house Lennox had lived in.

Suddenly the driver's intercom came on. "Did you say Umbria Place, miss?"

"Yes—it's next to the Gasworks."

"I know it—we'll be there in three minutes if the traffic keeps moving."

I rummaged in my bag for my wallet. Seeing my phone I remembered the unread email from my website. So I went to the in-box and opened it, and as I began to read, the story of Guy Lennox evaporated, and a jolt ran through me.

Dear Ella, my name is John Sharp . . .

Four

On the morning of Good Friday I prepared for my first sitting with
Nate. I got out the canvas, which I'd primed with a cream emulsion
base a few days before. I cleaned the brushes and laid them neatly on
my worktable. I put the oak chair in place and, behind it, the folding
screen that I sometimes use as a background. I mixed some burnt
sienna with turps to make the thin wash. Then, with still half an
hour before Nate was due, I got out my mother's portrait; I needed to
look at it. And to think about the email which I'd now read so many
times it felt seared on my brain.

Dear Ella, my name is John Sharp, and I am your father.

I shook my head. "I've got a father, thanks."

I hope you'll forgive me for contacting you . . .

"Shouldn't that be for *not* contacting me?" I asked tartly.

It must be a bit of a shock.

"It is!"

. . . but I came across an interview with you on The Times *website.*

I exhaled, sharply. "Just what I'd dreaded." I silently cursed the journalist Hamish Watt.

There was a link to it from The Western Australian, *and when I saw your face I knew at once who you were.*

"No," I murmured. "You have no *idea* who I am."

I recognised in your strong, dark features my own, and your story fitted with the life we shared so many years ago.

"So many," I echoed bitterly.

And though I have no right to say that I feel proud of you, I do . . .

"Well, it isn't mutual . . ."

Ella, I'm going to be in London the last week of May.

Resentment scorched through my veins. I went to my desk, picked up my mobile and opened the message.

I would so much like to meet you . . .

"Oh, God . . ."

I've always wanted to try to explain . . .

"Explain *what*?" I demanded. "That in 1979 you deserted your wife and child? I don't *need* that explained—I can remember it."

Now I looked at my painting of Mum and remembered her sitting at the kitchen table in our old flat, crying softly, while I sat next to her, helpless with fright and concern. I remembered drawing a picture of my father, desperate to cheer her up. And I remembered thinking that if I drew him well—so that it really *looked* like him—then perhaps, by some magic, he'd come back to us.

Ella, I've always felt very guilty about what happened.

"About what you *did,* you mean."

I'd like to try to make amends . . .

I went to OPTIONS then to DELETE MESSAGE?

. . . if it's not too late to do so.

I hesitated for a few moments, then pressed YES. My father's words vanished.

With a shaking hand I put my phone away.

Drrrrrrrrnnnnnnnng.

Nate had arrived—exactly on time. I breathed deeply to steady my nerves, then walked slowly downstairs and opened the door.

Relief flooded through me as I saw Chloe standing beside him.

"I know I said I *wouldn't* come"—she stepped inside—"but I'm going shopping with Mum at Peter Jones—we want to look at their wedding stationery—so I thought I'd just pop in on my way." She peered at me. "Are you all right, Ella? You look a bit . . . tense."

"I'm fine," I said tightly.

Chloe turned to Nate, who remained standing, awkwardly, in the doorway. "Come *in,* darling!" With palpable reluctance, he did. He was wearing jeans and a green cashmere sweater that had a collar, with dark brown suede shoes. As I looked at him a current of antagonism flashed between us.

I wrested my features into a pleasant expression. "Hello, Nate."

He gave me a wary smile. "Hi."

"The studio's on the top floor," Chloe explained, climbing the stairs. "Ella lives under the shop—don't you, Ella?"

"That's right," I said as Nate followed her up the open-tread staircase. We passed the bathroom, then the spare room, then my room, through the open door of which the wrought-iron bedstead was visible—I quickly pulled the door shut. Then we went up the last flight and into the studio.

Nate looked around in surprise.

"You wouldn't think there'd be this much space up here, would you?" Chloe said, delighted.

"No," he answered.

"I mean, the house doesn't look like much from outside—sorry, Ella." Chloe gave me an embarrassed smile.

I shrugged. "It's true. But it's got a steeply pitched roof, which makes for this big, high attic."

Chloe went over to the chair, put her hand on the back of it, then smiled at Nate. "All you have to do is sit here looking handsome—not hard in your case," she added with a laugh.

Nate rolled his eyes. "For how long?"

I unhooked my apron. "Two hours."

He grimaced.

"It'll *fly* by," Chloe told him with a reassuring smile. "You two can chat."

"Or not," I said as I put on my apron. "It's up to you. You can be quiet if you want—or I can put the radio on; if you want to bring an iPod, that's fine." It would be my preferred option, I decided—then I wouldn't have to talk to him.

"You *should* chat," Chloe said. She looked from me to Nate. "I mean, you hardly know each other—you've only met, what, three times?"

"Twice," Nate and I said simultaneously. We glanced awkwardly at each other, then looked away.

Chloe had crossed the room and was picking up my portfolio. She staggered back to us with it. "Have a look at Ella's portraits." She set it down on the table with a *thump*, and Nate sat on the sofa and obediently began to look through the images while Chloe sat next to him, occasionally explaining who the sitters were. "That's Simon Rattle, that's Roy of course . . ." Nate turned to the final page. "And that's me!"

"I know." He smiled indulgently. "I've seen the original often enough." I pushed away the unwelcome image of him in Chloe's bedroom. "I still can't understand why you'd want to have yourself painted in this state, though."

Chloe shrugged. "That was in the middle of the boyfriend trouble I mentioned—all water under the bridge now," she added airily. I suddenly wondered how much she'd told Nate about Max. "But as Ella had started the picture we thought we'd just . . . carry on. Isn't that right, Ella?"

I looked at her. "Erm . . . yes." Chloe could hardly tell Nate the truth—that the portrait was for her a record of the deep and painful attachment she'd had for his predecessor. "Anyway . . ." She threw her arms around him. "Thank God I met *you*!"

As she planted a kiss on Nate's cheek I saw his gaze stray to the portrait of Mum. "That's good," he remarked quietly.

Chloe turned to look at it. "It is, isn't it? You can see Mum's inner strength and her self-discipline and her . . . What's the word I'm looking for, Ella?"

Pain, I thought. Her pain. The wound she'd sheltered for so long was visible in her eyes, and in the slightly hard set of her mouth—it was visible even in her pose. On the surface it was the pose of a ballerina taking a curtain call, her left hand spread elegantly across her chest. But it was also a defensive gesture—she was shielding her heart.

I knew now that I was right not to have told her about my father's email. It would have been cruel to stir up such painful emotions. And it was quite unnecessary, given that I wasn't going to meet him.

"*Resolve,*" Chloe concluded, oblivious to my thoughts. She pointed to the *Giselle* poster. "That's Mum too. That was two years before I was born," she explained to Nate, "but Ella saw her in it, didn't you?"

"I did." I suddenly remembered sitting in the front row, utterly mesmerized by my mother's arabesques and her graceful jetés; she was so light that at times she seemed to be poised in mid-air, her slender limbs extending into infinity. Now I suddenly recalled my father sitting next to me, gazing at her, his profile bathed in the light from the stage: when Mum grabbed Albrecht's sword then fell down dead he held my hand tightly and whispered that she was "just pretending." And when we went backstage afterwards Mum was still in her long tutu and veil, and she threw her arms round my father and stood up on her pointes and kissed him, and they were both laughing and I was laughing too because my parents were happy and loved each other so much. But within a few weeks my father had gone . . .

"I *wish* I'd seen Mum dance," I heard Chloe say. "But her career was over by the time I was born."

Nate looked at her. "You mentioned she was injured."

Chloe nodded. "She fell, breaking her ankle—I'm not sure where it happened. Do you know, Ella?"

"No—I did once ask her, but she didn't want to talk about it." I knew only that it had happened more or less when my father left. So within a short space of time both her marriage and her career had ended abruptly, and in great pain.

"And that's how Mum met my dad," Chloe was saying to Nate. "He was the surgeon who did the second operation on her ankle a few months after her accident. He managed to make it a lot better than it had been, but he had to tell her that the injury had been career-ending."

"How heartbreaking for her." Nate's eyes were on the portrait.

"It was," said Chloe. "Though at least she got *him* out of it—he was completely smitten, wasn't he, Ella?" I nodded. "Mum often says that he was her silver lining." She glanced at the blue ceramic clock on the wall behind me. "I'd better go—she's a stickler for punctuality; in fact, she's a stickler for *everything*." She blew Nate a kiss. "See you later, darling."

He gave her a crooked smile. *"Ciao."*

"Chloe," I said as she turned to go. "Will you want to see the portrait while I'm working on it?"

She made a clicking noise with her tongue while she considered the question. "No," she decided. "I think I'd rather see it when it's finished, to have that wonderful sense of . . . *revelation*." She gave us a cheery wave and was gone.

We heard her light descending tread then the sound of the front door being opened, then slammed shut. The house fell silent . . .

I put the portrait of Mum back in the rack, then lifted Nate's blank, primed canvas onto the easel.

"So . . ." My pulse was racing. "Let's make a start . . ."

I nodded at the chair and Nate went and sat in it, gingerly, as though he feared it might be booby-trapped. He crossed his legs, then folded his arms. Then he uncrossed his legs. After a moment, he crossed them again.

"Erm . . . if you could sit in a slightly more relaxed way, Nate," I suggested.

"Oh." He uncrossed his legs. "Like that?"

"Yes . . . and if you could maybe put your hands on your knees." His hands were large and sinewy, I noticed, with strong fingers. "Now lift your head . . . and look this way . . ." I heard him exhale as if already exasperated. "That's great . . . in *fact* . . ." I felt that sudden, familiar frisson as I decided on the composition. "I'm going to paint you looking straight out of the canvas. It's not something I do very often but your features are strong enough, and I think it'll look powerful." Nate nodded uncertainly. "So you'll need to look right *at* me." As Nate's gaze fell on me I felt a shiver of awkwardness; but this was quickly dispelled by my growing excitement at the possibilities of the portrait. "That's great. Now I'm just going to stare at you, if that's okay . . ."

Nate nodded apprehensively, but I decided to ignore his discomfiture. I was too focused on the task at hand. I took in the shape of his head, the square of light that fell on his brow and the almost bluish shine to his hair; I studied the planes of his cheeks and the different textures of his skin. There were two short lines above his nose, like a number eleven; and a small round scar, like a watermark, on the right side of his brow. His eyes, I realised, weren't so much a mossy

green as dark sage, with flecks of gold. Now I stared at him from either side, examining the angle of his jaw, the swell of his mouth and
the long slender triangle of his nose.

Then I went back to the easel, dipped my brush in the wash and,
still looking at him, drew it across the canvas.

I worked in silence—aware only of the shapes flowing beneath
the tip of my brush and the sound of Nate's breathing. The runnel
between his lip and nose was very clearly defined. I was seized by the
bewildering urge to place my fingertip in it.

As I loaded the brush again I heard a deep sigh.

I looked up. "Are you okay?"

"Well . . ."

"Do you need a cushion?"

"No. I'm . . . fine." I turned back to the canvas and kept painting
for a minute or two, then the chair creaked. "Are you sure you can't
do this from a photograph?" I heard him ask.

"I *could*—but it wouldn't make for a good portrait."

"Why not?"

I ignored the edge in his tone. "Because a photo is only a
snapshot of a single moment," I said. It was an explantion I had
given many times. "But a portrait represents an accumulation of
moments—*all* the moments of the sitter's life. So although it might
look like you, it wouldn't show who you *are,* which is what I'll be trying to do."

"I see," he said grimly.

I worked for three or four minutes; then I heard another pained
sigh and the chair creaked again.

I lowered my brush. "You do seem a bit . . . uncomfortable,
Nate."

"I *am.*"

"Then let me get you a cushion."

"No, thanks. My discomfort isn't physical." His meaning lay between us, like a grenade.

"Sitting for a portrait isn't easy," I said defensively. After all, this whole thing wasn't my idea. "It's . . . an odd situation; there's often a . . . tension."

"There is," Nate agreed darkly. "Especially if the sitter feels that the artist doesn't like him."

My brush stopped mid-stroke. "I don't know what you mean."

"I think you do," he countered. "Because you haven't exactly been . . . *simpatico.*" He shrugged. "Maybe you think I'm not good enough for your sister."

"No, that's not—" I faltered. "I mean . . . Chloe's obviously happy with you, which is all that matters."

"In fact, you've been pretty hostile, right from the start."

I wiped a little splash of cerulean blue off the corner of the canvas. "You know, Nate, I really don't think this conversation is very helpful—especially as we have to spend another eleven and a half hours in each other's company."

"It's *because* we have to spend another eleven and a half hours in each other's company that I think it *is* helpful," Nate shot back. "You say you're going to show who I *am* in this portrait."

"Yes," I said weakly.

"I'm not happy about that—given your obvious negativity toward me."

I silently cursed Chloe for landing me with a commission that wasn't just awkward—it was becoming downright unbearable.

"You've clearly got a problem with me," Nate said. "I don't know why . . ."

I glared at him, astounded by his egotism. "Don't you?"

"No. I don't."

"Really?"

He gave me a challenging stare. "So you *do* have a problem with me. Do you mind telling me what it is?" I dipped the brush in the wash again, then turned back to the canvas. "If you're going to paint me, then I need to know," I heard him say. "And if you don't tell me, then I might just walk out and give Chloe the money for the wasted commission."

I put down my brush. "All right," I said, enraged. "I *will* tell you—as you've pushed me to it." A part of me was glad to be able to get it off my chest. So I told him about the night of the party. "You didn't see me," I explained, "because I was on the other side of Chloe's fence, locking my bike. But I heard you talking to someone—another woman—about Chloe. I didn't like what I heard—and yes, it's affected how I feel about you. *There,*" I concluded. "Now you know."

Nate was staring at me. "You listened to my private conversation?"

"No, because it *wasn't* private, given that you were having it on a mobile phone in the street. I couldn't help hearing it, and I wish I hadn't, because it was pretty upsetting."

"So . . . *what exactly* did you hear?"

"You said that you didn't want to go to Chloe's party, but that you felt you couldn't get out of it because she'd been going on and on about it—as though she'd pestered you."

"Well . . ." Nate turned up his palms. "She *did.* She must have phoned me ten times a day about it. It got to be pretty annoying."

I ignored this. "*Then* I heard you making arrangements to go and see this woman, who you kept calling 'honey,' later that night. That didn't exactly endear you to me either."

"Ah . . ."

"But what really stuck in my craw was the fact that you were *discussing* Chloe with this other woman—and in disparaging terms!" My face was suddenly burning with retrospective indignation. "You reassured her that Chloe was 'nothing special.' "

Nate was nodding slowly. "I remember this conversation now—and I *did* say that, yes."

The man was brazen! "So I heard *all* that," I raged, "then lo and behold, a few minutes later I see you greet Chloe warmly and tell her how much you've been looking forward to her party. At which point I knew that you were a cynical, disingenuous, hypocritical, *two-*faced, two-*timing* . . ."

"Creep?" suggested Nate helpfully.

"*Yes*. And to be frank, I hoped that Chloe wouldn't be seeing too much more of you, but now she's engaged to you and she's paid a lot of money for me to paint you, which for *her* sake is what I intend to do." My heart was pounding. "Now that I've answered your question, I suggest we get on with the sitting—if only to minimise the time that we have to spend together!"

I picked up my brush and began stabbing at the canvas with it.

"So you heard me talking to 'honey'?" Nate asked, after a moment.

I wiped the brush on a rag, accidentally smearing burnt sienna all over my fingers. "Yes. And I *don't* like men who date two women at a time—especially if one of the women is my sister."

"I see. You didn't *tell* Chloe any of this, did you?"

"No. Don't *worry*," I snapped. "Your secret is safe. I *was* tempted to tell her but couldn't bring myself to hurt her—so I didn't."

"Well, that's a shame," he said. "Because if you *had*, you would've found out from Chloe that the woman I call 'honey' is my first cousin."

I looked at him. "You appear to have an unhealthily close relationship with her."

"Her name is Honeysuckle. But everyone calls her 'Honey' or 'Hon.' "

My mouth had suddenly dried to the texture of felt. "But . . . you had keys to her place. You said that you were going to let yourself in, so it sounded as if she was your—"

"I *do* have keys," he interrupted. "Not to her 'place,' but to her office—our office—because Honey's also my boss. She's CEO of the firm I work for, Blake Investments, which was set up twenty years ago by her father, Ted Blake, who's married to my mom's younger sister, Alessandra."

I tried to swallow and failed. "I see . . ."

"And the reason *why* I was going to go and see Honey was because when I was on the way to your sister's, Honey called me on my cell to ask me to go back to the office—a problem had blown up with an acquisition we were handling. I didn't want to disappoint Chloe, so I told Honey I was going to a party but promised I'd go back to the office afterwards. I said I'd let myself in because the security guy leaves at eight—and that's what I did. I returned to the office at nine, and Honey and I worked until two in the morning and got the problem solved. Happy now?"

I felt my cheeks flush. "*No*—because you were *rude* about Chloe. You made out that it was a *chore* to have to go to her party."

"That's true—because although Honey's great, she can be very inquisitive. Chloe's party was none of her business."

"Okay. But you didn't have to tell her that Chloe was 'nothing special,' did you?"

"The minute Honey thinks I *am* seeing 'someone special'—as she invariably puts it—I never hear the end of it. Worse, she tells her mom, who then tells *mine,* and the next thing I know, *all* my sisters are phoning me, demanding information."

"So . . . how many sisters . . . have you got?"

"Five—all older."

"Oh." Now I vaguely remembered Chloe saying that Nate came from a big family.

"I'd only known Chloe a couple of months so I wasn't ready to talk about it to Honey."

"Well . . . this all sounds perfectly plausible, but—"

"It isn't just plausible, Ella," he interrupted firmly. "It's *true.* So on the basis of that one conversation you heard while you were eavesdropping, you decided that I was seeing another woman while dating Chloe, about whom I spoke *to* this other woman in disrespectful, if not downright contemptuous, terms. That's it, in a nutshell, isn't it?"

"Yes. That's how it *sounded,*" I added helplessly.

His green-gold eyes studied me. "The way it may have sounded was quite different from the way it *was.*"

"Well . . . I'm . . . glad to know that. And I'm . . . sorry . . ." I was floundering, "if I *have* been, yes, a bit cool with you."

"Cool?" Nate was shaking his head. "You were arctic, Ella."

"Okay, but that . . . coldness . . . was based on what I *now* understand to be a *misunderstanding*." My face was aflame. "But I am perfectly happy to accept that you are *not*—"

"A cynical, disingenuous, hypocritical, two-faced, two-timing creep?" Nate suggested pleasantly.

"Exactly."

"Well, I'm glad we've established *that*."

"Me too," I said sheepishly. I picked up my brush. "So *now* will you let me paint you?"

Nate unfolded his arms. Then he smiled at me. *"Yes."*

"So you got the wrong end of the stick?" Polly said on the Tuesday after Easter. We were having coffee in her small garden. As the sun was out she was wearing one of her many pairs of white cotton gloves.

"I *completely* got the wrong end." I cringed at the memory. "I feel awful."

"Don't—it's easy to see why you thought what you did." Polly nodded at the coffeepot. "Would you mind?"

"Oh, sure." I poured her a cup.

"Thanks. So what did you think of Nate after that?"

"Erm . . . Nice. Very. Yes."

Polly smiled. "That's great. He's going to be your brother-in-law after all, so it must be a relief to find that you like him." I tried to stifle the feeling that I'd been happier when I'd *disliked* him. "So—is he attractive?"

"He *is*. Definitely. I can't deny it."

She gave me a puzzled look. "Why would you want to?"

"Erm . . ." I filled my cup, spilling some on the little table. "No reason. He's, as I say . . . very attractive."

"Lucky Chloe," Polly sighed.

"Yes . . ."

"So what's his background?"

"Italian—his parents were from Florence but emigrated to New York in the early fifties."

Polly reached for the milk jug. "Why would anyone want to leave *Florence*?"

"That's what I asked him. He said it was because jobs were hard to come by, postwar. He was a surprise baby—his mother was forty-five when she had him; she's eighty-one now and a bit frail. Nate's father died ten years ago. He's got five older sisters—Maria, Livia, Valentina, Federica and . . . oh, yes, Simonetta."

"I see," said Polly slowly. "So why hasn't *he* got an Italian name?"

"Because he was named after the taxi driver who delivered him. He arrived three weeks early and his father, who worked for Steinway, was in Philadelphia at the time taking a new concert grand to the Academy of Music—not that he was a delivery man or anything, he was a master tuner, and a wonderful pianist himself apparently. He used to give *very* good recitals at a local church."

Polly was looking at me. "Really?"

"Oh, yes." I stirred my coffee. "Anyway, he was in Philadelphia," I went on, "and so Nate's mother, realising that the baby was coming, phoned for an ambulance but it didn't arrive. So she got in a cab but didn't make it as far as the hospital. Nate was born *in* the taxi, with the help of the driver, whose name was Nathan. So Mrs. Rossi promised that she'd name her son after him. The cabdriver came to Nate's baptism and gave him a pair of silver cuff links that Nate still wears. Isn't that sweet?"

Polly smiled. "Well . . . it sounds like you had a really good chat."

I laid the spoon in the saucer. "I was just trying to be extra friendly to make up for not having been terribly simpatico before."

"Simpatico?"

"Yes. What's the problem?"

"Nothing. It's just that you don't usually use that word."

"Don't I?" I sipped my coffee. "Anyway, Nate's five sisters have all long since had kids and they've been piling the pressure on him—

especially as his mother's getting on. He said they've been driving him crazy about it."

"What a pain."

"That's why he moved to London—to get away from his sisters."

"Poor chap. So they must be thrilled about Chloe, then."

"I guess they must be . . ."

"Has she met them?"

"Yes—she and Nate went to New York for a visit about a month ago."

"And are his family all coming over for the wedding?"

"I . . . don't know."

"You could ask Chloe."

"Yes . . . I could."

The idea of discussing Nate with Chloe made me flinch. It was only natural, I reminded myself, since I regard sittings as such private affairs: I don't like to talk about my sitters to anyone.

"So when are you seeing him next?"

"On Saturday morning. I'll get some croissants in for the break— we didn't have a break last time because we were talking so much and forgot; or maybe I'll get biscotti. What do you think?"

"What do I think about what?"

"Should I get croissants or biscotti? Biscotti," I decided before she could answer. "Or perhaps Florentines in honour of his origins—as long as he's not allergic to nuts," I added anxiously.

"Ella?" Polly put down her cup.

"What?"

"Well . . . you seem to have enjoyed the sitting with Nate."

I felt my skin prickle. "I *did* . . . because I was just . . . happy that we'd cleared the air. It *was* a relief, as you say. *So* . . ." I clapped my hands. "How was your date?"

"Well . . ." Polly heaved a weary sigh. "It *started* promisingly. I dropped Lola off at Ben's—they're in Wales until tomorrow, seeing his mum; then I went to Islington to meet Jason. We had lunch at Frederick's, during which we both talked about our work—he didn't know that I do feet as well as hands, and I told him about the Step by Step Pedicure Guide I'm doing for *Woman's Own,* and he seemed quite interested in that, and at the end of lunch he asked me if I'd like to go back to his place for coffee. I was feeling pretty mellow so I said yes, and as we strolled through Camden Passage he took my hand—"

"He didn't squeeze it, did he?"

"No, no—I told him to be careful. Anyway, I felt really happy and hopeful; so we went to his flat, which is in a converted warehouse at the top of Peter Street, but *then . . .*" She grimaced.

"His wife came back?"

"No—he's single. It was *weirder* than that. We went into his studio and he pulled me onto the sofa and I thought he was going to kiss me, which I wouldn't have minded—but instead, he asked me to take off my shoes. So I did. He gazed at my feet and said how beautiful they were, and he lifted them onto his lap and began to stroke them, which was nice, in a way, but *then . . .*"

"Oh, God—he tried to suck your toes!"

She pulled a face. "Not *quite.* He went out of the room and when he came back he was holding this pair of red patent-leather shoes with *eight-inch* heels, three-inch platforms with metal spikes on the sides, and black leather thonging right up to mid-high."

"So what did he want you to do—stand on him in them while he screamed for mercy?"

"No." Polly swallowed. "He just asked me to put them on, very slowly, and then lace them up, very *slowly . . .*"

"Uh-huh."

"While he filmed me."

"Oh."

Polly's eyes were like tea plates. "That's *all* he wanted—to film me putting on those horrendous shoes!"

"So . . . *did* you?" I was having trouble repressing my giggles.

"And risk getting bunions and fallen arches? No way! My feet are paying school fees. He *begged* me to do it but I refused."

"You'd have ended up on YouTube if you had."

"Exactly. Or he could have sold the footage—ha-ha—to some fetish site. Anyway, I put my Hush Puppies back on and left."

"So . . . a bit disappointing, then."

"It was. All I'd wanted was a cup of Nescafé and a cuddle." Polly rolled her eyes. "I get this *all* the time. The minute I tell a man I'm a foot model he goes all pervy on me. Anyway . . . so much for Mr. Toilet Duck."

"There'll be others, Pol."

"That's what worries me."

"No—your prince will come, bearing a nice comfy . . . glass slipper."

She glared at me. "I'd rather he came bearing a nice comfy Ugg; anyway, Cinderella's slippers weren't glass—that's a common misconception."

"Weren't they?"

"In the earliest French versions of the legend she wore '*pantoufles en vair*'—v, a, i, r,—which were slippers of squirrel fur; by the time Charles Perrault was reading these versions, that word was no longer in use, so it's believed that he assumed '*vair*' to be a mistranslation of '*verre*'—v, e, double r, e—and therefore made Cinderella's slippers, in *his* version, glass."

"I see. You're a mine of information on the foot front, Polly."

She shrugged. "You pick these things up if you're in toe business." She looked at me. "So . . . any other news?"

"No," I replied. "Wait . . . actually, *yes.*" For the first time, I told someone about my father's email.

Polly's hand flew to her chest. "Your father contacted you? Because of that piece in *The Times*?"

"Yes—which is *exactly* what I was worried about. *That's* why I tried to get that damn journalist to change it."

"I assumed it was because you thought it was too personal."

"I *did* think that; but my main worry was that if my father came across it he might get in touch—and now he *has.* Oh, Polly, I still don't know *how* Hamish Watt knew what he did. I never talk about it to anyone, nor does Chloe; and I know you wouldn't discuss it."

"Not in a million years."

"That wretched article is the reason for my father's email."

"Perhaps he was already looking for you."

I shook my head. "He said that *The Western Australian* had a profile of the Duchess of Cornwall, in which it mentioned my portrait of her and put a link to the interview with me in *The Times*. That's what prompted his message—a chance sighting of me online. But I've deleted it."

"*Ella . . .*" Polly's face was a mask of dismay.

"*Don't* look at me like that, Pol. I've had no contact with the man for three decades and I *don't* want it now—I've told you that."

"I feel sorry for him."

I put down my cup. "Why do you have to be on his side?"

"I'm *not*," she protested. "I'm on yours. But I just feel . . . well, you *know* what I feel, Ella."

"He said he'd like to 'make amends,' but what he really wants is to make himself feel better about what he did. Why should I help him with that?" I asked hotly.

"Because . . . you may deeply regret it in the future if you don't."

"I'll take that risk."

"And *maybe . . .*" Polly looked at me apprehensively. "Maybe there's another side to the story; maybe, somehow, it's not as bad as you think."

"No." I felt a rush of indignation. "It was an awful betrayal. My mother adored him—he was the love of her life. She said she did everything she could to make him happy and I believe her. But thirty years ago he deserted us, and we never heard of him again—until now."

"Okay. What he did was heartless." Polly's voice was earnest. "But he's going to be in *London*—perhaps even close by." I had an image of my father walking towards me. Would I recognise him? I didn't even have a photograph of him. I remembered that his hair was dark, like mine—it would be grey now, perhaps even white. He might not *have* much hair. He might be thinner than he was when I knew him, or heavier. His face might be very lined.

"Wouldn't it be good to *meet* him," Polly was saying. "If only once? Just to talk to him, and find a bit of . . . closure."

"I don't need 'closure,' thank you—I'm *fine.*"

"But there must be things you'd like to ask him."

"Oh, there *are.* I'd like to ask him why his marriage vows meant so little to him and how he could abandon my mother when she'd loved him so much; I'd like to ask him how he could bring himself to leave his only child, and why he didn't try to explain it to me, or say goodbye."

"So you didn't know that he was going?"

"No." I searched my memory. "He just stopped being around. I kept asking my mother where he was but she wouldn't answer—but then, she must have been in turmoil, not least because she'd just had her fall. Eventually my grandmother told me that I was going to have to be very brave, because my father had gone away and wouldn't be returning. I was convinced she was wrong. So I sat at the window of our flat on Moss Side and I watched for him. I sat there for weeks, but he didn't come. And I began to connect his leaving with my mother's accident, and I came to believe that my father must have left because Mum couldn't dance any more . . ."

"You told me you didn't remember much about your father, but you obviously do," Polly observed quietly.

I nodded. "And I've been remembering more and more since he got in touch."

One, two, three, up in the air . . . Why *was* that such a vivid memory? How could I remember it at *all,* given how young I would have been? And why did my mother's white and red skirt stand out in my mind?

Polly laid her hand on my arm. "I wish you'd see him, Ella."

"No. He's left it too late. He should have contacted me years ago."

"He didn't know where you *were.*"

"True—but he could have traced Mum. He could have made enquiries through English National Ballet or at the Northern Ballet Theatre. He could have put out all sorts of feelers. Okay, he wouldn't have known that she was no longer Sue Young—that was her maiden name and the name she danced under. But if he'd been determined enough he could have found her—and if he *had* done, he'd have found me."

"Well . . . maybe he *did* contact her."

"No, he didn't. I asked her that. There's been nothing from him all these years. Then one day he happens across my name online and with two clicks of the mouse he's in touch. It's been too *easy* for him, Polly—so it doesn't *mean* much."

"I can understand why you feel like that, but perhaps he felt he *couldn't* contact your mother after what he'd done."

"That *is* possible. Maybe he felt too ashamed—he *should* have done, especially as he left her with no money."

Polly's eyes widened. "Surely she got something, after they divorced."

"I don't think she did."

"Then she must've had a useless lawyer."

"Maybe, but wives didn't get such a good deal then—the law's changed."

"And was he well off?"

"I've no idea. He was an architect—whether successful or not, I don't know."

"So how long were your parents married?"

I shrugged. "Five or six years?"

"Surely he had to pay maintenance?"

"I haven't a clue. I do remember Mum swearing that she'd never take a penny from him after what he'd done; she was very bitter, and still is. So I'm not about to open a can of worms by telling her that he's been in touch with me, let alone that he's coming to London."

"Couldn't you see him, but not say anything to her?"

I hesitated. "I have wondered about that . . . but it's too big a thing to conceal, and telling her might be incredibly disruptive—it could spoil Chloe's wedding."

"Will you mention it to Chloe?"

"No—I can't take the chance that she'll tell Mum. Not that Chloe ever thinks about my father," I added. "As far as she's concerned Roy is my father: and that's another thing—I want to protect *his* feelings."

"But he'd be happy for you."

"No, he'd be upset."

"I think he'd understand. He'd support you," Polly went on. "I know he would. He loves you, Ella . . ."

Polly was taking this too far. I pushed my cup aside and stood up. "I'd better go, Pol. I've got stuff to do—canvases to prime, that kind of thing."

"Okay," she said wearily. "But there's a bit of time until your father comes and so . . ." She gave me a searching look. "I really hope you'll change your mind, Ella."

"I won't."

In any case, I *couldn't* change my mind, I reflected as I went to Barnes the next morning; I'd double-deleted my father's message. I had no record of him. He'd gone. As the cab swung into Celine's drive I decided to forget that he'd ever been in touch.

I paid the driver, rang the bell and the housekeeper let me in and once again asked me to wait in the study; I told her that I'd prefer to set everything up to save time. So she showed me into the drawing room and put down some dustsheets while I unfolded the easel and put the chair into position; then I mixed the yellow ochre wash, put the canvas out and waited. I glanced at the mantelpiece, on which, amongst the bits of antique silver, were a number of formal-looking invitations. On the glass coffee table was a copy of *Hello!* so I flicked through it. Amongst the ads I saw Clive Owen's face being stroked by Polly's hands; I'd know her fingers anywhere. As I turned to the next page I was surprised to find myself staring at a photo of Max. He had a champagne glass in his hand and was standing next to his wife, *best-selling crime writer Sylvia Shaw at the launch of her latest novel, "Dead Right."* Max looked more attractive than I remembered him— his face clean-shaven, his collar-length fair hair now short; but the photo did nothing for Sylvia, whose angular features seemed to jostle together, like a late Picasso. She'd be interesting to paint, I reflected.

"I'm sorry, I'm a bit late," I heard Celine say. I glanced up. She was *very* late, but at least she was wearing the pale blue dress. "I see you're all ready," she added pleasantly.

I resisted the temptation to tell her that I'd been ready for twenty minutes. I put the magazine back on the table then went over to the easel.

Celine sat in the chair, placed her bag at her feet, then turned towards me. "I was sitting like this, wasn't I?"

"You were." I picked up my brush. "But if you could just sit a little farther back . . . you're rather on the edge of your seat there; that's great." As I dipped my brush in the wash we heard the *ker-plink* of a text alert.

"Sorry," Celine muttered as she leaned down and reached into her bag. She fished out the phone, read the message and then, to my astonishment, began to text back. "I just *have* to reply . . ." she murmured as she thumbed away. "Almost done . . . *et . . . voilà!*" She put the phone back then resumed the pose.

I began to work. "I'm still doing the under-painting," I explained. "I'll start to build up the detail next week, using thicker and thicker paint each time until—oh . . ."

We'd heard the synthesised jingle of Celine's ring tone. She was rummaging in her bag.

"Celine—" I protested. But she'd taken the call.

"Oui?" She stood up. *"Oui, chéri, je t'entends . . ."* she said softly, furtively almost. *"Bien sûr, chéri . . ."* As she left the room I flung silent curses at her. I wished I could glue her rear end to the seat.

Ten minutes later she returned. She slotted her mobile back into her bag then sat down. "Okay." She placed her hands in her lap. *"Now* we can start."

"Great," I said brightly. I loaded the brush again, looked at Celine, and began to delineate the left side of her face. I'd been working for three minutes when we heard the doorbell ring.

Celine stood up. "I'd better get that."

"Surely your housekeeper—"

"She's at the top of the house—I don't want to derange her—inconvenience her, I mean."

"Celine—" I protested, but she was already halfway across the room. *You're "deranging" me,* I mouthed at her back. I heard her heels click across the hall then the door was opened. There now followed a long and animated conversation, in English, about . . . I strained to listen—the Church?

When Celine at last returned she blew out her lips in a dumb show of exasperation. "I'm sorry about that, but the Jehovah's Witnesses are *very* persistent."

I felt my jaw slacken. "You were talking to a Jehovah's Witness?"

"I was."

"For ten minutes?"

"Yes. I wanted to make it *quite* clear that they were wasting their time. I told them that they *mustn't* come here again. I don't think they will," she concluded with voluptuous satisfaction. "So . . ." She sat. "Shall we carry on?" I didn't reply. "I'd like to continue the sitting," she added with an air of dignified patience, as though I had kept *her* waiting.

I lowered my brush. "I *can't.*"

Celine stared at me. "Why not?"

"Because 'sitting' is the one thing you *won't* do. You keep getting *up,* Celine; you keep taking phone calls and *making* phone calls, and sending texts and going to the front door—this happened last time too. So I'm not going to continue until two things have happened—firstly, that you've turned off your phone . . ."

Her eyes widened. "I *must* have it on. It could be important."

"The sittings are important."

"The caller could take offence."

"*I* could take offence. In fact, I *am* taking offence—and, second thing, would you please *stay* in that chair. You're only allowed to leave it if the house is on fire."

Celine looked at me as though I'd slapped her. "*Don't* tell me what I can and can't do in my own home!"

I began to count to ten in my head. "Celine, if you don't give me your attention then I'm not going to be able to paint you." She shrugged as though she couldn't care less. "And I *want* to paint you— not least because your husband's already paid me quite a lot of money to do so."

"I didn't *ask* him to!" Celine's face colored. "I didn't *want* to be painted! I *don't* want to be!"

"Well . . ." She'd trumped me. "That's pretty obvious. But could you at least tell me why *not*?"

Her eyes blazed. "Oh, I don't know . . . I just feel . . ." She shrugged impotently, then shook her head.

I put down my brush. "Are you worried that the portrait won't flatter you?" She didn't answer. "You're extremely attractive, Celine, and that's how you're going to look, because I'll simply be painting what I see—a very beautiful woman."

"Of forty." She looked stricken. "I'm going to be *forty.*" For a moment I thought she was going to cry.

"Forty's not *old.*" Was *this* what it was all about? Some neurosis about her age? "You don't even *look* forty. You look younger than I do."

Celine peered at me. "How old *are* you?"

"Thirty-five."

"Are you married?"

"No."

"You have kids?" I shook my head. Celine looked at me sadly. "So you've never married or had children?"

I tried not to bridle at her air of sympathy. "I haven't, but I'm perfectly happy—there are many ways to live." Celine nodded slowly, her expression mournful. "But look, Celine, can we please talk about you? It would help if I knew *why* you don't want to be painted."

"I don't *know*. It's hard to explain . . . I just . . . can't . . . I don't . . ." She looked close to tears. Whatever the reason, she wasn't going to say.

"Being painted *isn't* easy," I offered. "For the painter the sitting's an absorbing, intense experience; but for the sitter it can be frustrating because they basically have to sit there staring at the same piece of wall. Is that why you seem so . . . *restless*?"

She blinked. "Yes. I find it a strain. Just sitting here . . . that's the reason. Exactly."

"Well, you'll find it a lot easier if we chat. But we can only do that if you ignore the front door. And if you turn off your phone."

"I *won't* turn it off . . ." She took the mobile out of her bag and began pressing buttons. My heart sank. "But I *will* put it on VOICE MAIL and VIBRATE." I closed my eyes in relief. "And I promise *not* to get up—unless I see flames."

"*Thank* you."

Celine placed the phone in her lap then resumed the pose. She seemed a little tense after our exchange so I began chatting to her, trying to build up some kind of rapport. I asked her which part of France she came from, and she told me that the family home was in Fontainebleau. Then I asked her what her husband did.

"He's now chairman of Sunrise Insurance. That's how we met: I wanted to work in London for a year or two—I had bilingual secretarial skills, so I got a job in the department that Victor was then running. We married when I was twenty-three; I had Philippe not long afterwards . . . and . . ." She shrugged. "Here I still am."

"You said Philippe's at boarding school. Does he enjoy it?"

"He loves it," she said flatly. "He was very keen to go, so he left his day school and went to Stowe to do his A-levels."

"So he's what—sixteen?"

"Just turned seventeen, and already *very* independent. He hardly comes home." Celine looked at me balefully. "The conveyor belt goes *so* fast. Yesterday I was pushing him down to Barnes Pond in his stroller to feed the ducks. Today he's a teenager with an iPod and a laptop; tomorrow he'll have a job and a flat; the day after that he'll have his own children and then . . . But you've never been married."

So you wouldn't know, her tone implied. I suppressed an irritated sigh. "That's right."

"But you have someone."

"No. My last relationship ended more than a year ago."

"Who was he?"

"A sculptor named David. He was quite a bit older than me."

"By how much?"

"Eleven years."

Celine nodded thoughtfully. "So *you* ended it?"

"Yes, though not because of that—it was because . . ."

"Because *what*?" It was as though my answer really mattered to her.

Although I wanted to avoid discussing my private life, I didn't wish to alienate Celine now that she was being cooperative. "I'd been with him for two years," I explained. "We got on well, but it just felt too, I don't know . . . too comfortable, too . . ."

"*Safe?*" she said shrewdly.

"Yes. He was very nice, but I wanted to feel . . . *more;* I may never find that, but at least I have hope."

"There's someone you like now."

I began to outline her bottom lip. "No. There isn't."

"There *is*," she insisted. "There's someone you're very attracted to—I can see it in your face." I felt my skin prickle. "I can sense it—I'm very intuitive."

"I'm sure you are." I smudged a line and had to redefine it. "But you're mistaken."

The rest of the sitting passed uneventfully. Celine's mobile buzzed a couple of times, but she just glanced at the screen. The doorbell rang again, but she let her housekeeper answer. She seemed to have resigned herself to the portrait at last.

At five past one we finished. Celine stood and came to see what I'd done.

"These are just the basic shapes," I explained as she looked at the canvas with its heavy geometric blocks of colour. "Next time I'll start to define your features." I clipped the portrait into the canvas carrier. "So . . ." I collapsed the easel. "Same time next week?"

"That'll be fine—do you have a taxi coming now?"

"Yes. I booked it for one-fifteen."

It arrived on the dot. I put my easel in the trunk; the canvas on the seat, beside me. Then I sat and looked out of the window as we drove over Hammersmith Bridge, the river glinting like sheet metal in the sunlight.

There's someone you like.

Celine was wrong. I wondered what colours I'd use to paint Nate's eyes . . .

I can see it in your face.

Cerulean blue with raw sienna . . .

I can sense it.

With a touch of yellow cadmium light.

The journey seemed to pass quickly—I looked at my emails as we sped along. There was one from Mum asking me whether, as I'd painted Cecilia Bartoli, I might approach her to sing at Chloe's wedding. I texted a one-word reply. *No!!!* There was an email from Clare, the radio journalist, with the date and time that her documentary was to be broadcast. As I scribbled it into my diary I became aware that the cab hadn't moved for a while.

"*What the eff?*" the driver said. I looked up. He was gripping the wheel, staring ahead. "Look at this!" We were close to Fulham Broadway; the traffic on our side of the road was at a complete standstill.

"Is there a football match on?" I asked him.

"No. There's a dead bus—up there, look; it's blocking both lanes."

We crawled towards the lights and, amid a cacophony of blaring horns, watched them go red then green then red again.

I got my wallet out of my bag. "I'll walk home from here. It's not far."

The driver turned his head. "Will you manage with all your stuff?"

"Yes, thanks." I passed him the fare. "It's not that heavy, just a bit awkward."

"Well, mind yourself as you get out."

So I picked up the portrait and quickly retrieved my easel and the canvas from the trunk; then I walked the hundred yards or so to the pedestrian crossing. The yellow sign urging any witnesses to come forward was still there, and there were more bouquets, one of them still with its price tag. As I pressed the button on the wait box I studied the photo of the woman who had been killed at this spot. It was the first time I'd seen it close up. Grace's face was alight with a kind of surprised happiness, as though she'd just been told some wonderful news. And now, beneath the photo, I saw a laminated note.

DEDICATED TO THE LIFE OF GRACE CLARKE

Beautiful, sparkling, funny, warm, happy, loyal, brave, strong, cyclist, determined, thoughtful, cool, snappy dresser, teacher, fizzing, unique, kind, reliable, Nutella, big heart, sensitive, friendly, sympathetic, bright, Lake District, energy, gardener, Three Peaks, Gracie, patient, children, green, Tic-Tacs, adventurer, open, mint tea, inspiring, sunny, caring, hugs, joyous, salsa, surfer, snowboarder, colleague, cousin, niece, aunt, sister, daughter, granddaughter, Miss Clarke, best friend in the world, our darling, loved by all.

At the periphery of my vision I had been aware of the green man on the walk sign, appearing then disappearing then appearing again with his jaunty emerald stride. Now I looked up, and saw that the red man was showing, but it didn't matter because the cars weren't moving. So I crossed the road, lost in thought.

I walked home, unlocked the front door, went to my desk, opened my address book, found the number I wanted and dialled. It rang three times.

"Royal Society of Portrait Painters—Alison speaking."

"Alison, it's Ella Graham here."

"Hi, Ella. What can I do for you today?"

"Well . . . you remember the commission that you phoned me about before Easter? The one for the portrait of the cyclist . . . Grace Clarke?"

"Of course I remember. I told the family that you didn't feel it was something you could do . . ."

"I *did* feel like that. But could you please tell them that I've changed my mind?"

Five

On Saturday morning I decided to give the studio a quick clean before Nate arrived. At half past nine the phone rang. I instantly knew it was him, phoning to cancel.

I picked up the handset. "Hello?"

"Ella?"

"Oh, *hi,* Pol. I'm so glad it's you." I clamped the phone to my shoulder and began vigorously wiping the table.

"You sound out of breath," she commented. "What are you doing?"

"I'm getting ready for Nate's second coming."

"His what?"

"His second *sitting,* I mean. Nate's coming for his second sitting, so I'm just . . . tidying up."

"I see . . . and what did you decide about the refreshments—biscotti or Florentines?"

"Hobnobs actually." I walloped the sofa cushions to get out the dust. "I wonder if he likes them."

"Ella, he's American—he probably doesn't know what a Hobnob *is.*"

"That's true." I put *John Singer Sargent: The Later Portraits* back on the shelf. "In that case I might be better off with chocolate digestives—or I've got some Penguins. Perhaps I should have made cupcakes." I glanced at the clock. "I *could* make some now—there's just time."

There was an odd silence. "Ella?" said Polly.

I chucked an empty paint tube into the bin. "Yes?"

"Ella . . . ?"

I picked some old sketches off the floor. "What?"

"Um . . . nothing." I heard her exhale. "It's nothing."

"Then, in that case, I'm going to go—I'm busy, Pol."

"*Wait!* I phoned you for a reason. Do you remember Mandy Parks?"

"I do." I began tidying the top of my worktable, putting the brushes into the pots. When did my life get so messy? "In fact, I was thinking about her just the other day. She was very annoying, with awful mousy hair, and pink glasses."

"Well, she's very attractive now, with long blonde hair and contact lenses."

"So . . . is that why you've phoned? To tell me that Mandy Parks's looks have improved since primary school?"

"No. I'm phoning because yesterday she friended me on Facebook and I've just read her profile; it says that she's a solicitor . . ."

"Jolly good . . ." I suddenly noticed that the windows were dirty. I went to the sink and rinsed a sponge.

". . . for a City law firm."

"Marvellous . . ."

"Specialising in commercial litigation . . ."

"*Super.*" I began to clean the glass.

"And that she's 'in a relationship' with Hamish Watt."

My hand stopped in mid-wipe. "The jerk who wrote about me?"

"Yes."

"Ah. So *that's* how he knew what he did." Through the window I could see a plane tracking across the blue vault, leaving a bright, snowy contrail. "Mandy was always asking me about my father, teasing me because he didn't come to our plays or games. I used to hate it. And now . . . this is weird, Polly, but I've just realised that in a funny roundabout sort of way, she's *reunited* me with him." I felt goose bumps rise up on my arms.

"Reunited?" Polly echoed. "Does that mean you've decided to—"

"No, no—it *doesn't.*" I heard a frustrated sigh. "Sorry, Polly, but can we please *close* the subject? There's nothing more to say. My father, after three decades of neglect, has decided to get in touch. *I've* decided not to respond. *The end.*"

There was silence for a moment. "Sorry, Ella . . . I didn't mean to be interfering."

"It's okay, Pol. I know you mean well—but now I'm going to draw a line under it. But thanks for telling me about Mandy. I always knew she had a big mouth." I glanced at the clock again. "I've only got an hour until Nate gets here, so I'm going to say *ciao.*"

"*Ciao?*" I heard her say as I hung up.

I finished tidying up, got the coffee things ready, then showered and dressed, did my hair, put on a little makeup and, with a few minutes to spare, went online to look at the news. Then, impulsively, I Googled *John Sharp, Architect, Australia.* Nothing came up, except a link to the Australian Architects' Association. I clicked on it, but his name wasn't there. Then, in an online architectural magazine, I found a reference to a John Sharp who, in 1986, had designed a school in Busselton. I guessed it was him, but as I could find no other references to anything he'd built I decided he hadn't designed in Australia for very long. And I was about to do a further search to find out what he *had* gone on to do when I remembered that I wasn't interested and stopped.

Instead, I went to my Facebook page. In the last week I'd acquired two more fans, one of them a boy whom I'd taught at Heatherly's.

He'd left a friendly message on my Wall, so I replied in kind, and all this set me thinking about Heatherly's, then about Guy Lennox, the painter who'd also studied there nearly a century ago; I thought about how Lennox had become enamored of someone he'd painted. I imagined him standing at his easel, gazing at Edith, falling more and more hopelessly in love with each stroke of his brush.

Drnnnnngggggg.

I started at the sound of the bell, then quickly checked my appearance in the mirror and ran downstairs.

I opened the door and there was Nate, smiling at me self-consciously, as though he was still amused by the idea that we had declared a truce. "Hi, Ella."

"Hi," I parroted back idiotically.

As Nate came in, he kissed me on the cheek—a gesture of peace, I assumed. He smelt deliciously of vetiver and lime.

"So . . . how did you get here?"

"I walked—it's only ten minutes. We're almost neighbours," he added as he took off his jacket.

"Let me take that. Oh, good—you remembered to wear the green sweater."

"Does that get me a gold star?"

"It does. It's a pain when my sitters forget to put on what they're being painted in."

Nate followed me upstairs. "So . . . how's your week been?"

"Not bad." I pulled the bedroom door shut. "Though it's felt a bit long, for some reason. Anyway . . ." We were in the light and space of the studio. "Here we are again." I tied on my apron, then nodded at the chair. "Get posing!"

He laughed. "Yes, sir!"

Nate sat down. I secured my hair with a yellow scrunchie, then picked up my palette. As he lifted his head and gazed at me, I felt a sudden voltage; I told myself that this was just an artistic frisson because I was excited about the portrait.

I stood behind the easel. "Here's looking at you, then."

I began to study Nate's face, the landscape of which was already so familiar that I could have painted him from memory. I looked at his nose, then his eyes—his lashes were very dark and his right lid was a little more exposed than his left; I studied his forehead and wondered how he'd got that small round scar. His hair was cut close to his head and grew down in front of his ears in a shape that tapered to a point, like the outline of India.

"I don't think I've ever been looked at quite so closely by *anyone*—not even my mom," Nate teased.

I held up a pencil and squinted at him as I measured the distance between his lower lip and his chin. "Well . . . that's my job. Basically I stare at people for a living."

"That must feel weird at times."

"It does." I put the pencil down and picked up a brush. "It makes me feel a bit predatory—like a stalker almost—especially when my sitters tell me that I've 'captured' them." I dipped the brush in the paint.

"I hope you'll capture me."

Nate had said it matter-of-factly, but I felt my face flush. "I'll try to," I faltered. "I mean . . . I just want my sitters to be happy."

"And are they?"

"If they're not, they're too nice to say."

"Do you ever stay in touch with them?"

"Yes—a few have become friends."

"So you've painted them into your life."

I smiled at the idea then reflected that Nate was already in my life. He's going to be my brother-in-law, I reminded myself. He's marrying Chloe. My sister is going to be his *wife*. "How's the wedding shaping up?" I asked brightly.

"Well . . . the answer is *fast*." Nate drew the breath through his teeth. "Your mom's efficiency is awesome, if not . . . downright terrifying."

I dipped my brush in the turps, aware that he hadn't exactly paid my mother a compliment. "Well, to be fair to her, three and a half months isn't long."

He blinked, perhaps at the unexpected sharpness in my tone. "Not long at all."

"But then, a short engagement's romantic," I pointed out. "And it's nice that you're getting married on Chloe's birthday."

"That was your mom's idea too."

"Really?" I smiled to myself at her manipulation.

Nate nodded. "Chloe and I had only gotten engaged a few hours before. We'd vaguely mentioned October, but then your mom suddenly said why didn't we get married on Chloe's birthday, as it fell on a Saturday; Chloe looked so thrilled I felt I couldn't say no—not that I *wanted* to say no," he added quickly. "I was just . . . taken aback."

"It'll make it easier to remember your wedding anniversary."

"That's true. And, as your mom pointed out, it's Fourth of July weekend, and that will make it easier for people coming from the States, as that Monday's a holiday, so . . ." He held up his hands in a gesture of surrender. "July third's . . . *great.*"

"Will your sisters be there?" I imagined all five of them, in a gang, outside the church, flinging fistfuls of rice.

"There's no *way* they'd miss it; they'll all be standing there, telling me what to do."

"It's going to be a big wedding, then."

"It looks like it. The guest list seems to be *huge,* but . . ." Nate shook his head.

"But what?"

"The idea of making such private vows in front of so many people . . ."

"Oh . . . you'll be fine: all you have to do is stand there and say 'I do.' "

We both laughed.

I decided that I didn't want to talk about the wedding anymore, so I steered the conversation to Florence and New York—we talked about what paintings we both loved in the Uffizi and the Frick; I asked Nate about his childhood, and he told me some more about growing up in Brooklyn with his sisters, about how he'd got the scar on his brow and about the dog he'd had when he was a boy. Then we discussed films and plays we'd both seen, books we'd read, and suddenly Nate was getting to his feet.

"Do you need to stretch your legs?" I asked him.

"No . . ."

"Let's have a break anyway." I put down my brush. "It must be at least an hour since we started."

Puzzlement furrowed Nate's brow, then he nodded at the clock on the wall behind me. "Ella. It's been two and a half."

"It can't be." I looked. It was. "I had *no* idea . . ."

"Well, we were talking a lot—like last time."

"Even so . . ." I turned back to him. "*How* can it be five to one?"

Nate shrugged. "Maybe we hit a time warp, or got sucked down a wormhole?"

"That's the only credible explanation." I put my palette on the worktable. My hand ached from holding it for so long. "Why didn't you *say* something? You must have been desperate for a break."

"No—I was quite . . . happy."

"But you haven't even had a cup of coffee—let alone a Hobnob."

"A what?"

"They're biscuits. Fancy one now?"

Nate smiled then shook his head. "Thanks, but I'm meeting Chloe for lunch."

I felt a piercing sensation, as though someone had plunged a skewer into my chest. I smiled at him. "Please give her my love. Say I'll call her tonight. So . . ." I untied my apron. "Is next Saturday okay?"

"That'll be fine."

Nate came over to look at the canvas. He was standing so close to me that I could almost feel the warmth of his body. "It's still in the early stages," I said as we looked at the broad lines and massed areas of flat colour. "But I've got down the basic structure of your face, and from next week you'll see yourself begin to . . ."

"Emerge?"

"Yes. Each time you'll recognise a little more of yourself until we get, well . . . the whole picture of you. Or as I see you."

"I wonder what you'll make of me."

I shrugged. "I don't know—I'm still working you out. But you're a good sitter."

"That's because I'm enjoying it."

I glanced at him, then smiled. "That's . . . great."

He turned back to the painting. After a moment, he said, "It's funny to think that I was dreading these sessions. Now, well . . . I find I look forward to them."

I felt a burst of euphoria. "Me too."

We went downstairs and I unhooked Nate's jacket, then opened the door. "So I'll see you next week, then. Ten-thirty again?"

"I'll be here."

I waited for him to leave, but for some reason he was still standing there, looking at me intently. My heart did a swallow dive.

"Ella?"

"Hmm?" Suddenly his eyes didn't look green at all. They looked quite dark.

"Ella?" he repeated gently.

"Yes?"

"Could I have my coat?"

"*Oh.*" I was still holding it—hugging it almost. "Sorry . . ." I laughed. "Here you go."

Nate slipped the jacket on, then leaned forward and once again kissed me on the cheek. "Ciao, Ella." He walked out of the house, then turned, smiling. "See you."

"See you," I echoed.

I closed the door then leaned against it, listening to his receding footsteps.

There's someone you like . . .

"Yes," I murmured.

You're very attracted to him.

"I am."

I can see it in your face.

"But he's engaged to my sister."

My euphoria shattered and gave way to dismay.

I wasn't falling for Nate, I reflected as I lay in bed the following morning. It was just a crush, a silly—no, in the circumstances, *insane*—infatuation. If I simply ignored it, it would soon pass. Once, when my mother was having yet another go at Chloe about Max, she'd told Chloe that she *shouldn't* have fallen in love with him. Chloe had retorted that she hadn't *chosen* to fall in love with him. "You could have chosen *not* to!" Mum had flung back.

I decided that Mum had been right. I would now make the deliberate, and rational, choice *not* to fall in love with my sister's husband-to-be. For the remaining sittings Nate and I would have a pleasant but purely professional relationship, after which we'd default to the friendly rapport expected of us as in-laws.

"Good." I swung my legs out of bed. "Got that settled."

As I pulled up the blind the alarm on my mobile sounded. Turning it off, I saw that another message had come in overnight from my father. With a sinking heart, I opened it.

Dear Ella, I hope you received my message of a fortnight ago.

"I did."

I realise that you may not wish to respond.

"I don't."

But this is to let you know the dates I'm going to be in London in case you do decide that you'd like to meet up. I'll be there for 4 days, from the 23rd of May.

I felt my pulse race.

It would mean so much to me if I could see you.

A wave of anger ran through me. "It would have meant so much to *me* if I could have seen *you* anytime in the last thirty years!"

In the meantime, here's my mobile phone number—and a photo. Sincerely, Your father.

"My *ex*-father," I muttered. At least he hadn't signed off as "Daddy" or "Dad."

I read the message six or seven times. Then, with a shaking hand, I opened the attachment.

I felt a sudden thud in my rib cage as I saw myself, aged about four, standing hand in hand on a beach somewhere with a man I knew instantly was my father. I was wearing a blue and white striped dress and was squinting into the late-afternoon sun, my short brown hair whipped by the breeze. My father, barefoot, in knee-length shorts and a casual shirt, was dark and tanned and powerfully built, with broad shoulders—a big, handsome man. In the hand that wasn't holding mine, he held a red spade, while behind us, on a yellow towel, were a picnic basket and a white sun hat. I had no idea where we were, but knew that the photo had been taken by my mother because in the foreground I could see her shadow stretching towards us across the pale sand.

I realised with a shock that this was the only photograph of my father I'd ever seen. He'd loved me enough to keep it; but sending it to me now was just an act of manipulation. I scrolled down to OPTIONS. DELETE?

I hesitated: then on his left hand I spotted his wedding ring gleaming in the sunshine. I exhaled, closed my eyes and touched YES . . .

I thought I'd feel relieved; instead, I felt upset—so much so that I then tried to retrieve the photo, but couldn't. I ran up to the studio and yanked open the bottom drawer of my desk, and from the back of it pulled out a large white envelope, the edges yellow with age. I lifted the flap and slid out the drawing of my father I'd done as a child—the one that I couldn't bring myself to throw away all those years ago. It was very much like him, I now saw. I must have been pleased with it because I'd signed it. And I was just trying to work out how old I would have been when I'd sketched it—nine? ten?—when I heard a car pulling up. I looked out of the window and saw Mike parking his BMW. Hastily, I put the drawing back in its envelope, returned it to my desk, then ran down and opened the door.

"Hi, Mike." I was glad to have the distraction of the sitting.

"Morning, Ella." He locked his car, then came in.

"Would you like a cup of coffee?"

"No. Thanks. I'm fine."

As he took off his jacket, I grimaced. "You forgot to wear the blue sweater."

He groaned. "Sorry—I've got so much on my mind."

"Of course, but the next sitting will be the last one, so I'll text you the day before to remind you about it, okay?"

"Sure . . ."

We went up to the studio. I got Mike's canvas out of the rack and set it on the easel. As I mixed the colours we chatted about the election, the date of which had at last been announced. "That must be a relief."

"It is," he answered wearily. He sat in the chair. "But it's going to be tough."

I squeezed a little Prussian blue onto my palette. "But you have a big majority, haven't you?"

"I do, but I can't take anything for granted."

Now Mike talked about the opinion polls and about how hard he found the door-to-door canvassing, having to persuade and cajole. "I feel like a Jehovah's Witness," he said ruefully. "Only less welcome."

"I don't know." I thought of Celine. "Some people are quite pleased to have the Jehovah's Witnesses turn up."

"Maybe . . . so who else are you painting at the moment?"

"A beautiful Frenchwoman—but it's been a battle, as she doesn't *want* to be painted." I imagined Celine and me, locked in combat over the canvas.

Mike looked puzzled. "Whyever not?"

"She says she finds sitting frustrating. Which in some ways of course it *is* but . . ." I shrugged, not wanting to add that I thought there was more to her resistance than that. "I'm also painting an extremely elegant Englishwoman who's in her eighties." I thought about how much I was looking forward to seeing Iris again; it wouldn't be for at least another week, as Sophia had phoned to say that her mother had a bad cold. "Oh, and I'm also painting my sister's fiancé." I felt my cheeks flush. "And I'm still working on the portrait of my mum." I nodded at her canvas, leaning against the wall. "It's almost finished now."

Mike turned to it. "She's beautiful. Her expression's interesting."

"What do you see?" I asked. I always wondered if others saw what I so wanted my pictures to reveal.

"She looks . . . guarded."

"She does look a bit guarded, that's true." I reached for the turps.

"I mean secretive," he mused. "As though she's hiding something."

"Oh . . ." I looked at the painting again. "Well . . . I don't see that." Now I regretted having asked Mike for his opinion—what did *he* know? "I don't do proper sittings with her," I explained. "She usually pops in for half an hour after she's been teaching at the English National Ballet School. She's going to be there tomorrow, so we'll do a bit more."

"So you're busy," Mike said.

"Pleasantly so, yes." I studied the tip of his nose, then added a highlight to its painted counterpart. "And I've just been commissioned to do a posthumous portrait."

"Really? They must be . . . tricky."

I picked up a smaller brush. "I'm about to find out. I've never done one before—I've always avoided them because they're rather sad and probably quite tricky, as you say. In fact, when I was first approached I said no."

"What made you change your mind?"

"I read a tribute to the person who'd died—her friends had each contributed a word or phrase that they felt encapsulated this girl. It . . . moved me. And for some reason I just don't seem able to stop thinking about her."

I felt the tension in the room tighten. "So who . . . was she? This girl?"

As I told Mike, he closed his eyes for a moment, then opened them again, as though he'd just been given bad news.

"There's been quite a bit about it in the press," I said. "You must have seen it."

The chair creaked as Mike turned away. "Yes . . ."

"It's so hard for her family, not least because they still don't know how it happened—or why she was cycling through Fulham Broadway at that time of day, given that she didn't live or work anywhere near there."

I thought of my first meeting with Grace's uncle, the day before. A quiet, silver-haired man in his mid-fifties, he'd come to my studio and talked to me about Grace for a couple of hours. He told me that she'd lived in Chiswick and had taught at a primary school in Bedford Park. He'd brought with him four photo albums—two that had been hers and two that belonged to her parents.

I'd looked at pictures of Grace on swings at age three, smiling gappily at five, riding her new bike at six, on a brown pony at eight, starting secondary school at eleven, atop Mount Snowdon at fourteen, arm in arm with friends in her graduation robes, and on a sunny day last September on the steps of her school, surrounded by the children she'd taught and loved.

"It was a hit-and-run," I said to Mike.

The corners of his mouth clenched. "They can't know that. The driver might have had no idea that he'd struck her."

"Surely he would have realised."

"Why do you say 'he'?" Mike snapped.

"Well . . ." The violence in his tone surprised me.

"How do you *know* it was a 'he'?" he demanded.

"I *don't,*" I conceded. My heart was thudding.

"Whoever it was . . ." Mike's sudden anger had vanished; now he just looked distressed. "They might very well *not* have known." He was blinking rapidly, as though trying to work something out. "Especially as it happened in the dark."

I exhaled. "That's true. The wing mirror might have just clipped her; and helmets don't always offer enough protection in a bad fall." Mike nodded, dismally. "But they're trying to enhance the CCTV; apparently, the images are very grainy and they don't have the license plate number, but there are things that they can do . . . Anyway," I dipped the brush in the white spirit, "that's my latest commission—Grace."

A mournful look came into Mike's eyes. "Grace . . ." he murmured.

I had no idea what to make of Mike's intensity. He was clearly already on edge, but he seemed . . . defensive. As I continued painting a tiny shiver ran through me. Perhaps he *did* know what had happened to Grace. After all, he often drove through Fulham Broadway and he had a black BMW. Perhaps it had been *his* car that had struck her but he'd had no idea at the time, only realising afterwards from the media coverage . . .

That would explain his turmoil. He'd be horrified at what he'd done, and he'd be dreading what the enhanced CCTV tape might reveal. He'd be in terror too at the thought of the newspaper headlines, given that he was an MP—and on a transport committee, a protector of cyclists. He'd be vilified for failing to stop. He might even face criminal charges. This could destroy his career, if not his life . . .

As my mind raced through this ugly scenario I remembered that Mike had cancelled his sittings at the end of January, a couple of days after Grace had died. The email he'd sent me saying he'd "suddenly got very busy" had been so incoherent that when I'd first read it I'd thought he must have been drunk. Now he was a shadow of the big, happy, self-confident man I'd started to paint less than four months ago. And he'd cried at a sad song on the radio. He was clearly under huge emotional strain. Was that why he'd seen what he had in my mother's face—because of what he himself was hiding?

"So . . . have you started the painting yet?"

"No." I felt awkward now, telling Mike about the commission, but he seemed to want to know about it. "First I need to get some feeling for who Grace was. I have some photos of her to work from." He flinched. "But I want the portrait to be more than just a good likeness; I want it to capture Grace's spirit. As I never met her, that isn't going to be easy."

"No," Mike agreed quietly. "It's going to be hard."

"I can only stay for half an hour," Mum announced when she arrived that afternoon. "I've *so* much to do. It's unending," she added with a curious blend of satisfaction and annoyance. She slipped off her coat and handed it to me. "The invitations have gone off to be printed. I've decided to enclose RSVP cards; people can be shockingly casual, even about weddings." I hung her coat up. "Will you help me address them?"

"Sure," I said as we went up the stairs. "I'll come over with my calligraphy pen." I pushed on the studio door. "So how many people are you inviting?"

"Two hundred and ten."

"Good God!"

"Well, there are people who've invited us to *their* children's weddings; and of course Nate has a very large family." Again I imagined his sisters, lined up like Russian dolls. "Chloe has a lot of friends," Mum went on, "plus she wants to invite some of her colleagues, so it's not hard to get up to that kind of figure." She went over to the mirror and checked her appearance. "Luckily we *can* accommodate that number, as the garden's so big." She opened her bag and took out her gold compact. "It's nice to make a bit of a statement."

"Is it?" I asked as she reapplied her lipstick.

"Yes." She snapped the compact shut. "It is." She put it back in her bag then glanced around the studio. "It's looking nice up here, Ella—less of a jumble."

"I've tidied up." I unhooked my apron and put it on. "Oh, well done," I added as Mum took off her cardigan. "You remembered to wear the silk shirt."

She walked over to the chair. "I'm amazed that I did, as I've *so* much to think about." She shook her head as if to stop it spinning; then she sat down, lifted her chin and laid her left hand on her chest.

My mother was still every inch the prima ballerina. She didn't just "sit" in a chair, she folded herself into it, ensuring that there was a graceful "line" to her body, that her limbs were positioned harmoniously and that her head was at an elegant angle to her neck.

"I'm *very* upset with the organist," she confided softly.

I adjusted the blinds. "Why's that?"

"He's trying to insist that we have Purcell's 'Trumpet Tune' but I've heard it at *so* many weddings."

I returned to the easel. "It's joyful, though."

Mum inclined her head. "That's true. And Chloe's wedding is going to be *very* joyful."

I felt the skewer turn in my heart. "It is." *For everyone except me*, I reflected, then I felt ashamed at the thought.

"But I'm putting my foot down about the Widor Toccata."

I picked up my palette. "That *is* overused. Look this way, will you?"

Mum turned her pale blue gaze on me. "But I've found a *wonderful* soprano. She's in the chorus at Covent Garden and her *voice* . . ." Mum closed her eyes in an attitude of ecstasy then slowly opened them. "We'll all be in floods. In fact, I may staple a tissue into each Order of Service."

"Good idea. I'm sure *I'll* need one," I added balefully. I dipped my brush in the light skin tone that I'd prepared. "So what's this wondrous soprano going to sing?"

" 'Ave Maria' after the first reading—the Bach-Gounod, not the Schubert—then 'Panis Angelicus' during the signing of the register; I *adore* both."

"Does Chloe?"

Mum shrugged. "She seems to be happy with *all* my ideas. She's being surprisingly easygoing about everything."

"That's lucky."

"It *is*—especially as I have so little time; I couldn't cope with any arguments, and you know how stubborn she can be." Mum tucked a stray wisp of hair behind her ear. "But she has yet to choose her dress. I thought *you* were helping her on that front, darling."

"I *am,*" I replied. "I'm going to a vintage wedding dress shop with her next week. She's going to try on a few dresses that we've seen on their website."

Mum was making tutting noises. "I *wish* she'd have something contemporary—I really don't want to see Chloe in yellowed lace."

"You won't, Mum." I began to work on her left hand. "These gowns are beautifully restored—and they're expensive; you'd better warn Roy that the one Chloe most likes the look of costs two thousand pounds."

Mum's eyes went round. "She could get an Amanda Wakeley for that."

"Something old—that's what she wants."

"Well, *I* shall be wearing something *new.*"

Now Mum told me about the outfit she'd ordered from Caroline Charles, the Philip Treacy "fascinator" that would adorn her head, the menus she was keen on but had yet to confirm with Chloe and Nate, the ice sculpture she was considering and whether I thought a peacock might be preferable to a swan. She talked about the hardwood flooring she'd ordered for the marquee and about the work

Roy was doing in the garden to get it looking "tip-top." Then she discussed the flowers.

"The church will already have flowers from the eleven o'clock service," she said as I painted a cream highlight onto the gold of her wedding ring. As I did this I suddenly wondered what Mum had done with her first wedding ring. Perhaps she'd flushed it away, or flung it into the sea. More likely, she'd kept it in a box inside another box inside a bag at the back of a drawer.

"That's good," I murmured. "Then you won't have to buy any flowers."

"It *isn't* good," Mum protested. "They might be hideous, and I *don't* want to find that we're lumbered with carnations and chrysanthemums. So I've asked the florist to strip them out, and we'll have tuberoses, pink peonies and green viburnum for the larger arrangements, with posies of sweet peas at the end of each pew. I *love* sweet peas . . ." Mum shivered with happiness, like a small child anticipating Christmas.

I found her excitement touching. It was as though it was *she* who was . . .

I dipped my brush in the zinc yellow. "Can I ask you something, Mum?"

"Yes."

"I've never asked you this before—or probably not since I was very young—but, what with Chloe getting married, I've been wondering . . ."

"Wondering what?" Mum asked serenely.

"Did *you* have a big wedding? The first time, I mean?" I suddenly imagined my mother standing at the altar with the entire corps de ballet fanned out behind her.

"No," she said after a moment.

"So . . . it was just . . . a small one, was it? But in church, presumably."

Mum blinked. "No."

"Didn't you want to get married in a church?"

"*I* did," she replied. "But, well . . . your father didn't *believe*. You know, it was such a *long* time ago and I really don't want to—"

I raised my hands in mock surrender. "Okay."

So Mum had got married in a register office both times. That would go a long way to explaining why she wanted to make such a "statement" with Chloe's wedding—she was turning this wedding into the big glamorous meringue-and-marquee number that she'd never had.

I dipped the brush in the pot of turps. "There's one other thing I wanted to ask you."

Mum suppressed an annoyed sigh. "What's that?"

"Did we go to the seaside somewhere—when I was about four?"

She inclined her head, like a bird suddenly aware of a predator. "Why do you ask?"

"Because . . . I recently had a memory of being on a beach somewhere. In a blue and white striped dress."

I held my breath as Mum considered the question; for a moment, I thought she would refuse to answer it. "We had a holiday in Wales," she answered slowly. "The summer before you were five. We went to Anglesey for three days. You *did* have a blue and white striped dress—I'm amazed that you remember it."

"So . . . that holiday must have been with my father. Is that right?" I added after a moment.

"Yes," she answered reluctantly. "*Now*, I'd just like to—"

"Three days for a holiday isn't very long," I interrupted before she could change the subject.

"Well . . ." I heard Mum swallow. "We didn't *have* long holidays."

"Oh. Why not?"

"Be*cause* . . . we couldn't." She brushed a bit of fluff off her skirt. "I was dancing principal roles, and so taking a fortnight—or even a week—off simply wasn't *possible.*"

"I see . . ."

"So we just took a few short breaks—where we could." I nodded, blankly. "Are you *all right*, Ella? You seem a little . . . intense."

I stared at her.

My father's sent me two emails and a photo. He'll be in London in a few weeks' time. He wants to see me but I know that would cause big problems for you, so I've been ignoring him, but it's making me feel confused and unhappy—plus I've fallen for Nate, which is also making me feel confused and unhappy. So, all in all, yes, I'm feeling a little . . . intense.

"I'm fine," I said.

Mum smiled. "*Good.* Now, I've got to find a jazz band—there's one that plays down by the river on Thursday evenings, so Roy and I are going to hear them this week. I've also been wondering about having an entertainer—a caricaturist would be amusing. What do you think, darling?"

"That would be fun."

"I wish *you'd* find someone."

"I don't know any caricaturists."

"I mean a *man*." Mum sighed, extravagantly. "I've always thought it a shame that you didn't settle down with David."

I picked up the tube of cadmium green. "I didn't want to." I unscrewed the cap.

"Why not?"

I squeezed too much onto the palette. "Because David was very nice, but it was terribly . . . cozy. I felt too young to be in the comfort zone for the rest of my life."

Mum shifted on the chair. "The comfort zone is preferable to many other, more hazardous zones, Ella. I hope you won't come to regret that decision."

"I know I won't—because a few weeks ago I bumped into David at the Chelsea Arts Club; he was with someone new, and I didn't mind. If you've *loved* someone I would think it would be hard to see them with anyone else."

"Very hard . . ." Mum agreed quietly.

I knew that she must be thinking of my father, because she'd seen *him* with someone else—the woman for whom he would eventually leave her. She'd once told me that she'd "come across them." Would *I* have been with her, I wondered now. Suddenly I felt sure that I *was*, because I had a vision of my father's startled face, and I saw that white skirt with its bold red flowers . . .

"Isn't there *some* nice man that you like?" Mum was asking me now.

"Er . . . no. There's no-one . . ."

My mother smoothed her hair, then put her hand back on her chest. "Now, what about *Nate*?"

It was as though I'd fallen down a manhole. "What do you mean?"

"I mean what about Nate's portrait? Sorry, darling, I've changed the subject—how's his painting coming? Do tell me."

I exhaled shakily, as though I'd committed a crime and had narrowly escaped detection. "It's going . . . fine." My heart rate slowed. "We've had two sittings." So only four more, I reflected with a pang. Odd to think that I'd once hoped to keep them to a bare minimum; now I wished I could have dozens more.

"So when will it be ready?"

"I'll aim to finish it by mid-June so that it has time to dry. Then Chloe can collect it the day before the wedding. I hope she'll like it."

"I'm sure she'll love it. I know you'll bring out Nate's intelligence and charm—and his *kindness*. He's a compassionate sort of man." Mum shook her head in bewilderment. "I still can't understand *how* you could have disliked him, Ella."

I accidentally smudged the line of Mum's hand. "I just . . . did."

"But you like him now?"

I know you're going to love *him!*

"I do." So Chloe *had* been right.

"And you're coming to the engagement party, aren't you? It's on May the first."

I frowned and began to fix Mom's hand. "Chloe told me about it, but I'm not sure . . ."

"Well, you'll have to let them know because it's a sit-down dinner for close friends and family—they're not having a big party because the wedding's so soon; Nate's having it at his flat."

"I know . . ." I wished I didn't have to go. It would be painful seeing him with Chloe. Surely I could think of some lie to get out of it . . .

Mum lifted her chin and the light poured over her face. "By the way, I presume you chat to Nate during the sittings."

"Ye-es." I adjusted the blind.

"Well, I don't want you to let on, should the subject arise, that Chloe's last boyfriend was married."

"I wouldn't dream of it. I don't discuss Chloe with Nate."

"Good. Because I've told her that it's better if he doesn't know."

"Why?" I returned to the easel. "It's got zero to do with him."

"Yes, but men can be . . . *funny* about things; it doesn't do to tell them everything." I wondered what sort of things Mum hadn't told Roy. "After all, they haven't known each other that long," she went on. "So I've advised her to say nothing about it until they've been married at least a year—or better still, not to tell him at all."

I picked a stray bristle off the canvas, smearing her cheek. "You know, Mum, I think it's for Chloe to decide what she does and doesn't tell her own fiancé."

"Well, I don't think that her association with Max is something that she should shout about."

I shrugged. "Nate would have to be a prig to care one way or another, and I don't think he is."

"Anyway, that's how *I* feel, and Chloe agrees." The chair creaked as Mum shifted her position. "But thank *God* she met Nate. I can't bear to think how unhappy she was before—thanks to Max's awful treatment of her."

I squeezed a little Naples yellow onto the palette. "Max wasn't 'awful' to Chloe, Mum. She said he treated her well. She was only unhappy because she couldn't *be* with him."

Mum laughed. "Of course she couldn't—the man was married!"

Mum was always so censorious about adultery, I reflected. But then, she knew only too well the damage it does. "In any case, he *didn't* treat her well—he stayed with his wife."

"Oh . . ." I was about to challenge my mother's somewhat skewed analysis of the situation but she was hurrying on.

"*Why* he stayed with her I really don't know. It's not as though they have children, so I assume it was because she earns a lot with those books of hers."

"I've *no* idea. Maybe he loved her—maybe he loved them *both*. Maybe he was just . . . *confused*."

"Confused?" Mum gave me a glacial stare. "Allowing men to be 'confused' gives them an excuse to just . . . string other women along, offering them *nothing*."

"Those 'other women' should keep away." A muscle at the corner of Mum's mouth clenched—she'd always loathed the idea that her daughter had been an 'other woman.' I pulled the brush through a rag. "But Chloe really fell for Max."

Mum sniffed. "Goodness knows *why*. He's not attractive—and he can't earn much, working for a charity."

"He doesn't just work for a charity, Mum—he runs Well-Spring, the international clean water charity; and he wasn't *un*attractive— just a bit unkempt."

"All right, what he does is worthwhile," she conceded grudgingly. "But that doesn't alter the fact that he should have left Chloe alone."

"She should have left *him* alone—I was appalled when she told me that she'd become involved with him. But she believed him when he told her that his marriage was on the rocks."

Mum smiled unctuously. "*So* much so that we now see him proudly posing with his wife in *Hello!*"

Mum had a point there. "So you saw that."

"I did—and it made me feel sick. But it also made me realise that I was *right* to give Chloe the guidance I gave her." Mum's lips had become a thin line. "Once she started talking about having his baby, I knew that things *couldn't* continue. Do you remember that, Ella?"

"Yes." I reached for the paint rag again. "*Not* a great idea."

"So I decided that it was time that Max's wife knew what was going on. I mean, there she was, writing detective fiction, while failing to detect that her own husband had been having a yearlong affair!"

I looked at Mum, aghast. "You weren't really going to tell Max's wife—were you?"

"I *was* . . ." She exhaled through her nose. "But Roy dissuaded me."

"Thank God! Chloe is a grown woman, Mum. You have to let her make her own mistakes—you've made *yours.*"

My mother stiffened. "What do you mean?"

"Well . . . just that *everyone* makes their own mistakes—even you, presumably," I added jokingly. "It would have been *dreadful* if you'd talked to Max's wife."

"I *know,*" she conceded tetchily. "But I was sorely tempted, because I felt that Chloe was on the verge of wrecking her *life.* I warned her that time was marching on, that it was quite clear Max was never going to leave Sylvia. Chloe had convinced herself that if she got pregnant, he would. So I told her she was deluded and that it would be . . ."

"Wrong?" I suggested.

The flanges of Mum's nostrils flared slightly. "Too big a risk. I was determined to protect her," she added quietly. "Just as I'd have protected you. Not that *you* would be stupid enough to fall for a man who isn't available."

"Hmm . . ."

"So I told Chloe, yet again, just what the realities of life *are* for a mistress." Mum's voice, normally so soft and low, had begun to rise. "I told her that she'd be forever waiting for him to call, and that she wouldn't be able to do anything with him openly and honestly. I said that her relationship with Max was *low.* She insisted they were in love. I told her that in that case, Max had to prove he loved her—by committing to her." Her pale cheeks were pink with gathering emotion. "I said, without that their relationship was besmirched—just a tarnished *fairy tale*," she added with bitter satisfaction. "Chloe finally recognised the truth of that and ended it—*at last.*" Mum inhaled through her nose, slowly, as though calming herself after some trauma.

"Mum," I said gently. "Why are you getting so worked up? It's all in the past now."

She blinked, as if waking from some disturbing dream. "Of course it is." She gave a little laugh. "Why am I even *talking* about it? Chloe's *not* with Max, she's with Nate; they're getting married and we're all *thrilled.*" She gave a little shudder of happiness. "Aren't we, Ella?"

"Yes. Yes, of course we are . . ."

Six

"Thanks for coming with me," Chloe said the following Thursday
evening. We were standing outside the Vintage Wedding Dress
Company in Covent Garden's Neal Street. She pressed the old-
fashioned brass bell. "It's good that they do evening appointments—
I don't feel I can take *any* time off during the day."

"So your nose is to the grindstone."

"It is—as are my cheeks, mouth and chin. I'm surprised I've still
got a *face*," she added, laughing, as the door was buzzed open and
she pushed on it.

"But you're enjoying the work?"

"Yes—and it's great to have responsibility. Oh. Hi." Chloe was
smiling at the woman walking towards us. "Are you Annie?"

"I am—you must be Chloe." Annie, the proprietor of the Vintage
Wedding Dress store, was about my age, slim, with short dark hair.
She was wearing a fifties circle skirt with a vibrant pattern of straw-
berries, and a bright yellow cashmere sweater.

"This is my sister, Ella," Chloe explained. "She's going to give me
her opinion on everything."

"Great." Annie smiled. "Come on in."

We followed her to the back of the shop. The walls were painted a restful pale green and were hung with framed sketches of wedding gowns by Balenciaga, Norman Hartnell and Dior. On the display stands were antique veils, vintage headdresses and exquisitely embroidered satin slippers. Beneath our feet the cream velvet carpet was voluptuously thick—a comforting surface for stressed-out brides.

The changing room was very big, with two carved mahogany chairs with blue velvet seats, like thrones. Hanging from the antique brass pegs were several wedding gowns, just visible inside their muslin bags, like cabbage white butterflies about to emerge from their chrysalises.

"I've brought out the ones we discussed on the phone," Annie told us. "So that's Gina here." She began to unzip the bag. "I've also pulled Greta, the slipper silk gown from the 1930s, and the sixties one that you liked, Jackie." She nodded at it. "It's by Lanvin—hence the price. There are also three others I thought you might try, including one designed by Marc Bohan before he went to work for Dior. Do you wear much vintage?" she asked Chloe.

"Quite a bit," Chloe answered. "I've always thought that if I ever got married I'd wear a vintage dress, in order to have something . . . original."

"Well, these are unique," Annie assured her.

"Where do you get them?" Chloe asked.

"I buy them at auction," Annie replied. "I get quite a few in New York—like this one." She gently pulled the "Gina" out of its bag. "It's by Will Steinman, which was a big name in America in the forties and fifties. And of course people bring dresses in to show me. I also have a friend who owns a vintage dress shop in Blackheath—Village Vintage."

"I've heard of it," said Chloe.

"This friend—in fact, I used to work for her—doesn't sell wedding gowns herself, so if she comes across a particularly lovely one she kindly sends it my way." Annie put her hand in her pocket and produced a pair of white cotton gloves, the kind Polly often wears. "So . . ." She pulled them on. "Let's make a start."

"Should *I* wear gloves?" Chloe asked.

"No—but could I ask if you're wearing much makeup?"

"Almost none," Chloe replied, "and I'll be very careful." She turned to me. "Will you come in with me, Ella?"

"Sure."

I sat in one of the throne chairs and Annie drew the calico curtain across, then went out. Chloe quickly got undressed. It was a long time since I'd seen her in just her bra and pants. I frowned.

"You've lost weight again, Chloe." She'd put it back on over the past year, but now you could see the jut of her hips.

She glanced anxiously at her reflection. "It must be the stress of the job—and of getting married of course, and well . . . everything really."

"I wish I could give you some of my pounds."

"You're not fat, Ella—just well built."

"I know; sometimes it's hard to believe that Mum ever gave birth to me!" I had the sturdiness and broad shoulders of my father, I'd realised since seeing that photograph. I saw myself standing beside him on the beach in Anglesey, my hand in his. Had he known then, as he'd smiled for my mother's camera, that he'd soon be leaving us? He probably had. Another good reason for not keeping the photo, I decided.

"I'm ready, Annie," Chloe called.

Annie parted the curtain and came in. She took the Gina dress off its hanger, and held it up, the silk swishing softly. Chloe stepped into it, gingerly, as though climbing into hot water.

Annie lifted the dress onto Chloe's shoulders, did up a few of the loop fastenings, then gently pulled it in at the back so that Chloe could see the fitted effect in the mirror.

"It's gorgeous," Chloe murmured after a moment. "But I'm too thin for it." Her hand went to her chest. "I don't have enough up here—and a dress like this needs to be . . . filled." She glanced at me. "In fact, it would suit *you,* Ella."

"I'm not the one getting married," I said—too sharply, I realised, as I saw Chloe blink at my tone. "You . . . could always stuff it with those chicken fillet things."

She shook her head. "That would make me feel fake; and your wedding day is surely one day in your life when you want to feel that you're being true to yourself."

"I agree," said Annie. "You *are* a bit slender for it." She undid the fastenings. "Let's try the Greta."

Chloe put the dress on. It looked much better than the Gina had, and the drape and gleam of the satin was lovely. Chloe didn't mind the low back, but the dress had clearly been made for someone tall, because even when she put on a pair of heels, the fabric pooled at her feet.

Next she tried on another fifties dress, Grace. It didn't suit her, but it made me think of Grace Clarke, whose portrait I had now begun. The photos that her uncle had lent me were good, but it was still going to be difficult to create the illusion of three dimensions out of the two-dimensional images. I decided to ask her uncle if there was any recent video footage of Grace that I might see.

Now Chloe was putting on the Jackie, which was made of thick shantung silk, which gave it a structured, architectural look. It was a beautiful dress, but, as Chloe had suspected, it was far too big.

Next she tried on another sixties dress, this one with a pleated skirt, then the Marc Bohan gown, which was a simple ivory tunic with a silvery lace overlay, like a cobweb; she then put on a 1980s duchesse silk dress with lace-trimmed, elbow-length sleeves. As Chloe looked at herself, she pulled a face.

Annie agreed. "It's not really you. It's very like Sarah Ferguson's wedding dress. That was way back in 1986, so I don't suppose you remember it."

"I don't," Chloe replied as she took the dress off.

"You did see it," I told her. "You'd just turned five. I remember it very well." I'd never forgotten the wedding, because of what my mother had told me that day.

"Are you sure you won't try on the Giselle?" Annie asked as she hung the dress up.

"I'm quite sure," Chloe replied. "I wouldn't want my dress to have *any* negative associations, and Giselle has a hard time of it on the wedding front."

Annie zipped up the bag. "Why? What happens to her?"

"She's an innocent girl," Chloe began, "who falls in love with this handsome huntsman Loys, who's been madly flirting with her. When Giselle finds out that Loys is really Duke Albrecht, and that he's engaged to Princess Bathilde, she goes insane with grief and grabs Albrecht's sword and stabs herself—"

"No," I interrupted. "She collapses because of her already frail health, *before* she can stab herself."

"Okay," Chloe conceded. "Anyway, she dies and then becomes a Wili—a ghost of a jilted bride—which is the only time she gets to wear a wedding dress, poor girl." I thought of Mum, in that poster, in her long tutu and veil. "Tell me," Chloe went on, "do you get to know the history of these dresses?"

"Sometimes," Annie replied. "In fact, I know the story behind *this* one . . ." Out of the last bag she took a 1950s gown with a ruffled silk tulle skirt and a heart-shaped satin bodice. The small bustle was topped with dainty blue flowers.

Chloe's face lit up. "It's *lovely.*"

Annie took the dress off its hanger. "It *is* exquisite, isn't it? I bought it from my next-door neighbour," she explained. "When I told her that I was setting up my own vintage wedding dress shop, she offered it to me. She'd kept it beautifully, but the red roses on the bustle had faded, so I replaced them with these forget-me-nots."

"Something blue," said Chloe happily as Annie held the dress out to her. She stepped into it and Annie pulled up the zipper. As Chloe looked at herself in the mirror her eyes widened with pleasure. "It's . . . perfect."

As I looked at Chloe's reflection I imagined Nate waiting at the altar, then turning and seeing her walking towards him in this glorious gown. I saw his face fill with delighted pride.

"Are you okay, Ella?" I heard Chloe ask. "You look a bit sad."

"I'm . . . just tired. But it's a *lovely* dress."

"It is," Annie murmured. "And it's a terrific fit."

Chloe turned to Annie. "So what's the story behind it?"

"The story is that it was never worn."

"Really?" asked Chloe. "Why not?" she added anxiously.

"My neighbour Pam told me she'd got engaged in 1958. She was twenty-four and still living at home, in a village near Sevenoaks. She saw the dress in Dickins and Jones—it cost thirty guineas which was a lot back then, but her parents wanted her to have her dream wedding so they bought it. Pam told me that she couldn't wait for her fiancé, Jack, to see her walk up the aisle in it. But a week before her big day Jack came to see her, and told her that he couldn't go through with it."

Chloe looked stricken, then she examined her reflection again, as if suddenly seeing the dress in a different light.

"Pam's parents tried to persuade Jack to change his mind, but he said he was sorry—he didn't want to get married. He said he had too many doubts. Her parents then realised that they had no choice but to cancel everything and let the guests know. So there was no wedding, and their relationship was over, because Pam told Jack she never wanted to see him again. Everything was ruined. She was distraught."

"*Poor* girl." Chloe had gone very pale. "I don't think I want the dress now, knowing this." I wondered what on earth had induced Annie to tell such a negative story. Didn't she *want* to sell it?

She held up her hand. "Wait, there's more. Because three years later—"

"She met someone else?" Chloe anticipated. "I hope she *did.*"

"Pam had moved to London by then, partly to get away from the memory of what had happened; she was walking to work down Regent Street one morning when she looked up, and in the crowd she spotted Jack, coming towards her. Her heart started to pound. She told me that she'd decided to walk straight past him, as though she'd never known him." That's what Mum would have done, I thought. "But some inner voice told her *not* to do that; so instead she called out his name, and he stopped, clearly shocked to see her again. So there they both were, in the middle of the pavement, with all these people weaving around them; and Pam asked him how he was, and he said fine, and he asked her how she was, and she said fine. And she was about to smile goodbye and walk on, when he asked her if she'd have time to get a cup of coffee with him. Pam hesitated, but then agreed. He rang her at work the next day and asked her if she'd have dinner with him one evening. To cut a long story short—"

"They got back together," Chloe murmured.

Annie nodded. "They were married a few weeks later, in a register office, with just two friends as witnesses. Pam wore a suit, but she kept her wedding dress because she'd been unable to part with it. So . . . that's why it was never worn. She didn't get her dream wedding, but she did have her happy ending—in fact, she said that she was happier with Jack because she believed she'd lost him."

"Was it hard for her to forgive him?" Chloe asked.

"She said it *wasn't,* because she still loved him—she'd never stopped."

"But why didn't he get in touch with her in the interim?"

"He'd desperately wanted to but didn't feel that he could—remember, she'd told him that she never wanted to see him again. But they were married for forty-five years and had two sons. So it *is* a happy story . . ."

"In the end," said Chloe quietly. As she gazed at her reflection, she frowned slightly as though struggling with something.

"Nate wouldn't do that to you," I said. "If that's what you're think-ing."

"I can put the dress on hold," Annie suggested. "If you're not sure."

Chloe looked at herself, steadily. "I *am* sure," she said resolutely. "I'm going to buy it right now."

I'd hoped that helping Chloe choose the dress in which she was to marry Nate might have an inhibiting effect on my emotions. It did-n't. They only intensified. In addition, I became prey to a kind of schizophrenia in which I looked forward to seeing Nate but at the same time dreaded it because it was impossible spending time with him in such an intimate way. I had to gaze at him professionally, when I longed to do so personally. I had to stroke his face onto the canvas as if it were just a technical exercise when it had already be-come a labour of love. I'd think of Guy Lennox, and imagine his frustration at having to look at Edith from behind his easel when he'd probably wanted nothing more than just to stride up to her and take her face in his hands.

In between sittings my mind would default to Nate, like a screen-saver. I'd open my eyes in the morning and there he'd be, just as he was when I closed them at night. I would wake with a feeling of eu-phoria, then as reality returned I'd feel sad and confused. And ashamed. I didn't even know whether it was Nate's own face I saw or the image of it that I was painting—they seemed to morph into one. I'd work on his portrait as a way of feeling close to him. I was in a state of exhilarated despair.

So as I waited for Nate to arrive for his fourth sitting, I decided to be reserved with him, in order to re-establish a distance between us. But although my mind was happy with this strategy, my body re-belled. Five minutes before he arrived my pulse began to race. It was as though all my nerve endings were attached to high-voltage wires.

The ring of the bell induced an adrenaline charge that was like an electric shock. As I opened the door to him my heart was pounding so hard that I was certain he'd see it beating. He smiled, and a sudden heat suffused my face. I felt my lips tingle and swell.

I'd never felt a physical longing like this for any man. As Nate followed me up the stairs, past my bedroom, the door of which was ajar, allowing a glimpse of bed, I imagined taking his hand and pulling him inside and putting my hand on the back of his head and drawing his mouth to mine and unbuttoning his shirt and—

What was I *thinking*? The man was marrying my *sister*! I felt a torrent of guilt and shame.

As we went into the studio I wished with all my heart that Chloe had *never* asked me to paint Nate. Then I could have gone on believing that he was a duplicitous creep rather than the decent and desirable man I now knew him to be.

As Nate sat in the chair, I remembered my resolve to be remote. So as we began the sitting I asked him how the project he was working on in Finland was going and what he thought of the Coalition. I told him I was looking forward to the engagement party that night—which was a lie, as I was dreading it and had been obsessing about how I could get out of it. I'd say I had a migraine; Chloe knew I got them sometimes . . .

I heard the chair creak. "Ella." Nate was looking puzzled. "Are you okay?"

"Sure. Why shouldn't I be?"

"No reason—you just seem a bit . . . subdued."

"Oh."

"Are you sure you're all right?"

"No . . . I mean, yes. I *am*—though I might be getting a migraine," I added. That would give me an excuse to skip the party.

Nate looked anxious. "Do you need an aspirin? A glass of water?"

"No, I'm *fine*, really . . . thanks . . ." I dipped the brush in the flesh tone. "I'm perfectly . . . okay, I'm . . ."

To *hell* with being reserved, I decided, furious with myself. Why shouldn't I chat to Nate, just enjoy being with him? I'd done nothing wrong, I reasoned, and I wasn't *going* to do anything wrong. Was I?

So we started talking about Nate's school days, and about mine, about his dog, Chopsy, and about the opera singer Raymond, who'd lived in the apartment below them and who used to get them free tickets for the Met. Then Nate talked about his first girlfriend, Suzanne, who he'd dated at Yale.

"Suze and I were together for two years—I was crazy about her." I felt a stab of jealousy. "After we graduated I wanted us to get an apartment together in New York, but she'd just gotten a news traineeship with NBC and said she didn't want a relationship. She said she needed to feel free, as she'd be spending a lot of time on assignment, with periods abroad, and so . . ." Nate drew his finger across his throat, dramatically.

"She ended it?"

He nodded. "It was hard."

I felt another shard of jealousy. "And . . . after Suze?"

He shrugged. "I had a few relationships, none of them long-lasting. I tended to date women who I knew I could never feel serious about."

"Why? Out of fear of committing yourself to anyone?"

He thought about it for a moment. "No. It was because I still hoped that it would work out with Suze. Whenever she was back in New York we'd see each other; we'd often email and phone; we kept on fanning the embers when we should have doused them. We often joked that we'd get it together one day. But then a couple of years ago Suze phoned to tell me that she was getting married to a guy she'd met three months before, and that she was very happy—so . . ." He gave a philosophical shrug. "*Finite la commedia.* Honey had been badgering me to come work with her in London, so it seemed a good time to accept."

"I see. It wasn't so much because your mum and sisters were hassling you to settle down."

"Well, they *were*. They'd been telling me for ages to forget Suze and just try to find someone I could *live* with, without expecting a great love or anything. And I'd just come round to their way of thinking when I met Chloe."

"At the Harbour Club?"

"Yes." Nate grinned. "In fact, she annoyed the hell out of me to start with, because she kept rushing onto my court to retrieve her balls, but then I realised what was going on and thought it was quite funny; we got to chatting in the bar afterwards . . ." He gave a bemused shrug. "Which is how we come to be where we are today. Chloe's . . . sweet."

"Oh, she *is*. She's lovely—and there's got to be some material in that story for your wedding speech. You can joke about her putting the ball in your court, or wanting to play doubles." Or doing all the running, I thought wryly. Chloe wasn't exactly shy when she set her sights on a man. I thought of how she'd met Max—right in front of his wife.

"She'd obviously had a bad time with her last boyfriend," I heard Nate say. "Not that she talks about it, but it's there, in your portrait of her. You can see it."

"He . . . just wouldn't commit to her," I said truthfully. "The usual story," I added casually. "But she's *so* happy to have met you."

"She does seem happy, yes." There was a silence. "Anyway . . . now you know all about my past."

"I'm disappointed that it isn't more lurid."

"Sorry." He smiled then shrugged. "C'mon now, Ella, it's your turn—what about yours?"

"Oh. Do I have to?"

"Sure you do. You can't just pry all this information out of your sitters without revealing anything about yourself."

"That's a fair point. Okay. Let's see . . ." I talked about Patrick, whom I'd dated at the Slade, and about the two or three brief relationships I'd had in my twenties, and then I told Nate about David.

"Two years is a long time to date," Nate remarked. "What happened?"

"Nothing. He was nice—and very talented. But though we liked each other, we weren't in love . . ."

"I see."

"I tend to date men that I'm not really in love with."

"Why? To make it easier when it ends?"

"Maybe." I knew the real reason, though I didn't want to discuss it with Nate. And suddenly I didn't want to talk about relationships anymore, because I didn't want to hear him tell me how adorable he found Chloe or how happy he was with her, so I steered the conversation back to the far safer topic of his family, then, as I re-drew the line of his left shoulder—I'd got the angle all wrong—Nate told me how much he liked Roy.

"Roy's a lovely man," I agreed proudly. "He'll be a *great* father-in-law," I added, to remind myself again of Nate's impending marriage.

"You've always called him 'Roy'?"

"Yes; I was five when I met him, so I could never bring myself to call him 'Dad,' if that's what you mean." Nate nodded. "Plus I knew that my own dad was out there somewhere . . . not that I had any idea where." Suddenly I wanted Nate to know my story. "Maybe Chloe's mentioned it."

"She said very little—only that you haven't seen your father since you were almost five."

"That's right. He'd run off to Australia with his girlfriend—not that I knew that until I was eleven."

"Where did you think he *was*—before that?"

I shrugged. "I had no idea. My mother would say only that he'd left us and it was best not to think about him. But I was convinced he was somewhere nearby. I kept imagining that I'd see him drive up in his big blue car, like he used to do when we lived in our flat."

I had a memory of how my mother used to stand by the sitting room window, looking down the street. Then I'd hear her call out, "Daddy's here!" and I'd run to her and we'd see him pulling up . . .

I heard the chair creak as Nate shifted. "You must have missed him a lot."

"I did—and of course I *did* think about him . . . all the time. Whenever I saw a car like his, I'd look to see if he was driving it. I'd search for his face in crowds and in the windows of passing buses and trains. I remember once, when I was ten, following this man around the supermarket because he looked like my father. But if I ever asked my mother where he was she'd give me the same answer—that he'd gone, and wasn't coming back. I remember panicking, thinking that he must be dead. Mum assured me that he was alive, but as we couldn't see him anymore it was best to put him out of our minds. Every time I asked her *why* we couldn't see him she'd make me feel that it was too painful for her to discuss—so I learned not to ask."

"Did *she* know where he was?"

"Yes . . ."

"Then why didn't she just . . . *tell* you?"

I rubbed a drip of paint off the corner of the canvas. "She said it had been to protect me from unnecessary hurt, that she thought it would feel like another rejection to know that he'd gone so far away—and she was right, because when she *did* eventually tell me, I was shocked and upset, because then I understood not only that he *wasn't* coming back, but that he'd never intended to."

"So . . . who was his girlfriend?"

"I don't know—I only know that she was Australian and her name was Frances. In fact, I didn't even know that until I was in my teens; my mother had only ever referred to her as 'the other woman.' But Frances must have had an amazing hold over my father for him to not just give up his wife and child for her, but let her take him to the other side of the world."

"Did Roy know all this?"

I shook my head. "Mum had concealed it from him too, because she was worried that if he knew, he'd tell me. She'd drawn a veil over her first marriage because of the awful way it ended. She'd been aware that there was this other woman, but when she actually saw them together it was a terrible shock; she said it was traumatic . . ."

"Even though she'd known about the affair?"

"Yes—she once told me that she'd found a hotel bill in his jacket pocket, and another time a love letter that Frances had written him. But I suppose actually seeing them together made it horribly *real*. Not long after he left, Mum had her fall. She said she was so upset that she missed her footing, so she seemed to blame my father for that too. In her darker moments she'd say that he hadn't just betrayed her, he'd *destroyed* her."

"Poor woman . . ."

"But she was very lucky, because a few months later she met Roy, who fell in love with her instantly, and she saw that with him she had the chance for a new start. That's why she wanted Roy to adopt me—in order to erase my father. So when I was eight I became Ella Graham."

"That must have felt . . . weird."

"It altered my whole sense of who I was; it took me years to get used to it." Now, as I squeezed some more paint onto the palette, I wondered how the adoption had worked. Did the natural father have to agree—especially where he'd been married to the child's mother? And was there any formal handover of paternal responsibility? I decided to ask Roy about this sometime.

I began to outline Nate's right arm. "Roy's been a wonderful father. Though it wasn't easy at the start . . . I remember my mother telling me she was having a baby with him—I was very upset. She then dropped several more bombshells, because she said that she and Roy would be getting married and we'd be moving to London, where we'd all live together in a place called 'Richmond': she said Roy would work in a hospital nearby and I'd go to a nice new school . . . even though I liked the school I was already at."

"So much change in your life," Nate murmured sympathetically.

"I told Mum I didn't *want* her to marry Roy and I didn't want there to be a new baby." I dipped the brush in the vermillion. "I said that we *couldn't* leave our flat, in case Dad came back and didn't know where we were. On the day of the move I had to be prised out of it, screaming. I would only agree to go once I'd been allowed to leave a note for him, saying where we'd gone—not that it would have been particularly legible, as my writing couldn't have been up to much at that age . . ."

"Poor little kid," Nate said, softly.

"So I hated Roy because I saw him as the cause of all this change. I used to cling to my mother to keep him away from her; if he spoke to me I wouldn't reply; I used to hide his shoes in the garden. I hated seeing his pictures and his books and told my mother that she should burn them on a big fire. But Roy was always wonderful to me. He told me that he understood why I felt cross; he said that *he'd* feel cross if he were me. But he added that perhaps I wouldn't feel so cross once I met the baby."

Now, as I mixed the colour for Nate's hair, I remembered being in the garden of the house we'd first lived in, in Richmond. Roy sat next to me on the bench and told me that the baby would be coming soon—in the next day or two. I started to cry. Then Roy told me there was no need to be upset, because the point was that someone was coming into the world who was going to love me. He said that was all I needed to know . . .

I looked up from the painting. "And Roy was right. Because when I saw Chloe for the first time my anger just . . . vanished. Roy would put her in my arms and I'd just gaze at her, and talk to her for hours, telling her all the things that I was going to show her when she was older. I almost fought with my mother to push the pram. In the mornings they'd find me asleep on the floor by her crib. And from then on I didn't mind Roy being in my life, because I understood that without him I wouldn't have had Chloe. But of course I still hoped . . ." My brush stopped. "I never stopped hoping . . ." I could hear the tick of the clock.

"To see your father again?" Nate asked softly.

I nodded. "But I found this increasingly hard to imagine because I was already forgetting what he looked like."

"Didn't you any have photos of him?"

I shook my head. "So I drew and painted him, almost obsessively, to try to remind myself." I thought of the faded drawing of him in my desk. "And I believed that if I did a really *good* picture of him—so that it was the *very* picture of him—it would somehow make him come back."

"Which is why you became a portrait painter."

I nodded. "It probably is. Because I was searching for this *one face*, hoping to see it again. I *kept on* hoping . . . even after I knew the truth." I felt my throat constrict. "I'd tell myself that I didn't want to see him." The unfinished face on the canvas had blurred. "But of course I did want to, I *did* . . ." To my horror, I started to cry.

I heard the chair creak, then footsteps; then I felt Nate's arms around my shoulders. A tear seeped into the corner of my mouth with a salty tang.

I was aware of the softness of Nate's sweater, of the gentle pressure of his arms, and of his breath, warm against my ear.

I closed my eyes for an instant, then pulled away, awkwardly. As I did so I saw that there was a red stain on Nate's chest. "I've got paint on you," I wailed. "From my brush. I'll fix it." I went to my worktable and tipped some white spirit onto a tissue; then I walked back over to Nate and without even thinking about it, slid my left hand under his sweater and gently rubbed at the wool with my right. "There . . ." I murmured. "It's gone."

I knew that if I looked at Nate I would want to kiss him, so I turned away; but he put out his hands, caught my face and stroked away my tears with his thumbs.

"I'm fine," I croaked. "I'm fine now. Thanks . . ." I went to the sink and started cleaning the brush, desperate to disguise my turmoil.

"Now I know why you seemed so subdued," I heard Nate say. "Your father must have been on your mind."

"He has been." I turned off the tap. "Very much so." I didn't tell Nate why, or that he himself had also been on my mind.

"Maybe you'll hear from him one day . . ."

I exhaled. "Maybe . . ."

"And what would you do if he *did* ever get in touch? Would you want to talk to him—see him?"

"See him?" I thought of how I spend my whole life seeing people—or trying to—in order to paint them. But would I want to see my father? I looked at Nate. "I . . . really don't know."

So much for being reserved, I thought grimly as I got ready for the party a few hours later. I'd bared my soul to Nate—impulsively telling him things I'd never even told Polly—and had ended up being held in his arms. Now I was going to have to go and make polite small talk with him at his engagement party.

The invitation was for eight o'clock but I was so anxious, I was running late. I couldn't decide what to wear and changed my outfit three times; then I made up my mind not to go; then I decided that I *would* go, and ended up walking because my front tyre was flat; then the bus didn't come and I didn't have enough money for a cab, because I'd forgotten to go to the cash machine. So by the time I turned in to Redcliffe Square it was a quarter past nine and I was feeling flustered and wretched.

Nate's flat was on the south side of the square in a big stuccoed house. In front, a huge magnolia was shedding its last petals. I rang the bell and an aproned caterer opened the door, took my coat, then offered me a glass of champagne from the tray on the hall table. I gratefully took it and swallowed two large, nerve-steadying sips. I was bracing myself to enter the room on my left, where the party was clearly in full swing, when Chloe came out into the hallway. I felt a stab of envy; the force of it startled me.

She beamed. "There you are, Ella!"

"I'm late," I mumbled. "Sorry."

"Never mind—come and join the party."

"Can I just take a moment? I'm a bit . . . stressed." I could hardly tell Chloe why. I had another sip of champagne and began to feel its sedative effects. I managed to smile. "You look lovely." Chloe was wearing a turquoise silk shift that skimmed her slight frame. She seemed so young, but now it struck me that she was just the age Mum had been when my father left—except that Mum'd had a five-year-old child. I thought again how unusual it was for an ambitious young dancer to jeopardise her career by having a baby. Perhaps her pregnancy was accidental, and that was the real reason she and my father'd had a register office wedding. What she'd said about his lack of religious belief had somehow rung false.

"Thanks," Chloe responded. "As she tucked a strand of hair behind her ear I saw something sparkle, and the skewer twisted again.

"Oh, show me your ring!"

Chloe held out her hand. A large marquise diamond winked and flashed. "Now I *really* feel engaged," she said, widening her eyes with mock anxiety. "We chose it a month ago but it needed to be made smaller so I collected it this morning while you were painting Nate. He's enjoying the sittings," she added as I followed her into the living room. Anxiously, I wondered whether Nate discussed them with her. "Not that he tells me *what* you two talk about." I exhaled with relief. "But he came back today reeking of turps—I teased him that he must have been doing some painting himself . . ." I prayed that he would never tell her the real reason.

There were about twenty people in the room, which was long and wide, with a deep bay window. On the white marble mantelpiece were a number of engagement cards and on the wall above it a large, semi-abstract seascape in boiling blues and greens. On the other side of the room was a pale gold damask sofa on which I instantly imagined Chloe and Nate curled up together.

At the garden end of the room I saw Nate, in a white shirt and jeans, chatting with his guests. Seeing me, he extricated himself and walked over to me. It was like one of the dreams I have of him in which his face slowly materialises out of a crowd of strangers and I have this sense of intense happiness and relief. Now though, knowing how powerfully I was drawn to him, I felt only pain and dismay.

"Ella," Nate said warmly.

I recalled the gentle pressure of his arms around my shoulders, the feel of his hands on my face.

I forced my features into a neutral smile. "Hi, Nate—sorry I'm late. What a great flat!" I turned to Chloe. "So is this where you'll live after the wedding?"

"That's the idea. Nate rents it, so when the lease is up we'll buy a place of our own; in fact, I like the streets where you are, Ella."

My heart plunged at the prospect of having Chloe and Nate living nearby—seeing them walking along hand in hand, or unloading their shopping from the car, or pushing a baby buggy . . .

"That would be great," I said, "though bear in mind it can be tricky living near the football stadium."

"True," Chloe said. "How often does Chelsea play at home?"

"Every other Saturday, but also during the week—the roads get *so* congested, and it's dreadfully noisy." I suddenly wished that she and Nate would go and live in New York—a scenario I'd dreaded when they'd first got engaged.

"Well, we'll see," she said. "There's no rush—is there, Nate?"

"No. No rush at all."

Suddenly Chloe's "old phone" ring tone drilled through the noise and chatter. She took her mobile out of her pocket and peered at the screen. She frowned. "I'm sorry . . . I'll just . . ." She went out into the hall, leaving Nate and me to chat.

So we talked about property prices in this part of London and about when interest rates might start to rise. Without the intimacy of the studio we were politely going through the conversational motions. This is how it'll have to be, I reflected, once the portrait's done.

Now one of the caterers came to speak to Nate; as I glanced around I saw that Chloe had returned and was talking to an old school friend of hers, Jo. I squeezed past them to talk to Mum and Roy, who were standing near the window. I caught snatches of party babble on the way.

—Wedding's not long now.

—So did he get down on bended knee?

—Capri's a lovely honeymoon destination.

—Actually, I asked him!

Mum was deep in conversation with another friend of Chloe's, Trish, and her husband, Don. Seeing me, Mum extended an elegant arm. She drew me to her while she continued to wax lyrical about Nate.

"He's *so* attractive," Trish agreed. "Obviously very steady . . . yes . . . perfect for Chloe—well, he'd be perfect for *any* woman really—but not as perfect as *you*," she added to Don with a laugh. Then Trish began telling Mum about the jazz band she and Don had hired for their wedding, and about the problems they'd had seating his divorced parents. As she and Mum began discussing the pros and cons of a formal receiving line I broke away to talk to Roy.

He smiled at me. "So how's our Number One girl?"

"Fine, thanks." I took another sip of champagne. "A bit wedding-weary, though," I confessed.

Roy sighed. "I know what you mean, but . . ." He fiddled with his bow tie. "I do hope you're pleased for Chloe, Ella."

I looked at him, shocked. "Of course I am. Why do you ask?"

A red stain had spread up Roy's neck. Did he *know*, I wondered. Had he seen it in my face, like Celine had? Did I have *I Heart Nate!* tattooed on my brow?

"Why are you asking?" I repeated nervously.

"Well . . ." Roy shifted his weight. "I thought you might not be entirely happy about her getting married."

"Why wouldn't I be?" My pulse began to race.

Roy ran a finger round his collar. He knew. He and Mum both knew. "Because it must be *hard* for you," he said, "seeing your mother and me *fussing* over your sister like this, not to mention spending such *vast* amounts on her, so I just hope . . ."

"Oh, I *see* . . ." I emitted a burst of relieved laughter. "You think

I'm *envious* of Chloe—because she's younger than me but is getting married."

"Well . . . I didn't really think that, but I want you to know that we'll push the boat out *just* as far for you. I've been saving for both you girls for years now."

I smiled up at him. He really was the most lovely man. "*Thank you,* Roy." I laid my hand on his arm. "But as I doubt it'll ever be needed for me, I hope you'll spend it on you and Mum."

He sipped his champagne. "You never know what the future holds, Ella. Anyway, it's good to know that you're happy for your sister."

"Of course I am!" I just wished that she were marrying anyone but Nate.

Now everyone was moving towards the wide wooden staircase that curved down to the basement.

"I think dinner is served," said Roy. "Very nice of Nate to do this."

"It is. But I'd like to wash my hands—I'll see you down there."

I went out into the hall and a caterer told me that the bathroom was at the top of the stairs. I walked up.

As I pushed on the door I saw a big claw-footed Victorian tub. On the rim were Chloe's shampoo and conditioner and some jewel-coloured glass tea-light holders. I tortured myself with visions of her and Nate enjoying a sensuous candlelit soak. Beside the basin, among Nate's shaving things, were Chloe's Cath Kidston wash bag, a pink toothbrush and a big tub of Elizabeth Arden body crème.

I *should* have pleaded a migraine, I reflected miserably as I turned on the tap. I lifted my eyes to the mirror, then looked away, unable to face myself. "I'm *not* in love," I whispered as I splashed water on my burning cheeks. "It *is* just a . . . crush—a silly, completely inappropriate, crush." I felt ashamed to acknowledge it, even to myself; I certainly didn't want anyone *else* to know about it. I resolved to keep my feelings concealed.

As I came out of the bathroom I saw that the door of the room next to it was ajar. Through the gap I could see Nate's green sweater lying on a chair, one arm dangling over the side, as though exhausted. Without thinking I pushed on the door, then stood there looking at the big sleigh bed, masochistically imagining Chloe and Nate spooned together in it, or lying face-to-face, their limbs plaited like rope.

On the chest of drawers I could see some photos in silver frames. I wanted to look at them—to know *more* about Nate—so, feeling like a trespasser, I went in.

There was a photo of a young couple—Nate's parents, presumably—leaning against a stone wall on a hillside, with Florence's Duomo rising above the buildings behind them. There was a close-up of a young woman on her wedding day—I guessed that it must be Maria, Nate's youngest sister, as he'd told me that she's the one to whom he's always been closest. There was a photo of Nate as a boy of eight or nine, perched on a sofa, cradling his dog like a baby. In a glass frame was a snap of Chloe and Nate at some black-tie dinner, her arm curved around the back of his chair. I felt another stab of jealousy.

I went out, pulled the door shut behind me, then ran downstairs.

The kitchen was very large, with a big conservatory dining room, the windows strung with little lights that twinkled in the gathering dusk. Everyone was finding their places at the trestle table.

I found my place card—written in Chloe's large, round hand—and was joined by a forty-ish woman with shoulder-length blonde hair and a slash of cyclamen lipstick.

"Hi," she said, smiling warmly. "I'm Nate's cousin. Honeysuckle."

I returned her smile. "That's a great name."

She laughed. "My father adored Fats Waller so I'm really 'Honeysuckle Rose,' but everyone calls me Honey or Hon."

I remembered my misunderstanding about "Honey" on the night of Chloe's party. I'd been furious at the idea that Nate might be two-timing Chloe; now a dark part of me *wanted* him to two-time her—with *me*!

"This is my husband, Andy." Honey indicated the sandy-haired man who was standing on my left.

I shook his outstretched hand. "I'm Ella—Chloe's sister."

"Ah—I've *heard* about you," Andy said. "You're painting Nate, aren't you?"

"That's right."

"Is he behaving himself in the sittings?" Honey asked as we all sat down.

"Of course he is." I saw Honey register my indignant tone. I felt my face flush. "I just mean that he keeps *very* still and he's . . . nice."

"Oh, Nate's a darling," Honey said as Andy poured us all some white wine. "We grew up together in New York; then my folks moved to London when I was twelve—hence my nearly English accent; Nate and I always got on well, and now we work together."

"He's told me a lot about you," I said. "Nice things," I added hastily. Then I remembered that Nate had said that Honey could be inquisitive. I'd have to be on my guard.

She smiled. "So . . . how long do the sittings take?" I explained. "And how well did you know him at the start?"

"I didn't know him—I'd only met him twice. But then, I don't usually know my sitters before I paint them."

Honey shook her head. "How bizarre—spending so much time closeted with a stranger." She laughed. "It must be like being on a blind date!"

I smiled. "In some ways, it is." Except that in Nate's case there'd been no possibility of the encounter ever developing into anything more. I felt a burst of anger with Chloe—for in asking me to paint Nate, she had, albeit unwittingly, put before me a feast that I could never touch. I felt like Tantalus, neck-deep in water that he could never drink, grasping at fruit that was always just out of reach.

I stole a glance at Nate, sitting on the other side of the conservatory, next to Chloe. I tried to work out what had happened between us this morning; then I told myself that there was nothing *to* work out. Seeing me upset, he'd instinctively comforted me. That was *all* there was to it. And yet . . .

Now Nate's friend James came and sat next to me with his wife, Kay; I already knew that James worked in London, for Citibank, had been at high school with Nate, and was to be his best man. James and Honey clearly knew each other, so as they struck up a conversation I chatted with Kay, who told me that she was going to school part-time, earning an art history degree.

The caterers brought in our starters but I was too stressed to eat. As I picked at my smoked trout I wondered how soon I'd be able to leave. My dinner companions were very pleasant but it was an effort to make small talk with them; thankfully, they seemed interested in portraiture, so at least I didn't have to scrape the mental barrel for things to say.

"Is there anyone you *wouldn't* want to paint?" Kay was asking me.

I lowered my fork. "I find young children difficult to paint, because their expressions are so fleeting. And I *don't* like painting women who've had plastic surgery—it's hard to deal with because it never looks . . . right. Last year I painted this fifty-something woman who'd clearly had her eyelids lifted; it just looked as though two stun grenades had gone off in her sockets. But I'm currently painting a woman of eighty-three who's had nothing done and is still very beautiful." I hoped that I'd soon be able to paint Iris again, not least because I longed to hear what had happened to Guy Lennox—his tragic story had got under my skin.

Now Kay was talking about self-portraits—Rembrandt's and Francis Bacon's and Lucian Freud's. "And there's a self-portrait by Dürer that I adore. It's *so* sexy," she added.

"You mean the Christ-like one?" I asked. "With the long curling hair?"

"Yes, *that* one—he's *gorgeous.*" She giggled. "I had a massive crush on him when I was a teenager because of that picture!"

I smiled in recognition. "Me too. It was as though he was *real*, not a two-dimensional image of himself that he'd painted five centuries before."

"So will Nate look as 'real' as that?" Honey wanted to know. "With women swooning over him hundreds of years hence?"

I smiled. "I'd like to think so. I'm certainly ambitious for his portrait."

"Ambitious?" Honey echoed. "In what way?"

"Well, a competent portrait just catches a likeness; a good portrait reveals aspects of the sitter's character; but a *great* portrait will show something about the sitter that they didn't even know themselves. That's what I hope to achieve with Nate's."

Andy raised his glass to me. "Then here's to a great portrait of Nate. He should have an official unveiling for it."

"Terrific idea," Honey said. "We'll all come see it—but I already know it'll be gorgeous, because he is." At that she caught Nate's eye and blew him a kiss.

Nate smiled back at her, then, as she turned to say something to her husband, Nate let his gaze rest, just for a few moments, on me. I flashed him a crooked smile then looked away, my face aflame. He's just checking that I'm not ill-at-ease among all these strangers, I told myself sternly. He's simply being a good host.

"Don't forget that little scar on his head," Honey was saying. "One of his sisters dropped him when he was a baby—I think it was Valentina."

"No." I lowered my glass. "It was Maria."

Honey glanced at me in surprise. "Was it? I was sure it was Valentina."

"No, Nate told me that Maria dropped him when he was four months old. She was six and had lifted him out of his cot because she wanted to cuddle him. They rushed him to the hospital and poor Maria was so upset that they had to buy her a big doll to make her stop crying. He said that she still can't bear to talk about it."

Honey nodded, slowly. "I'd . . . forgotten."

As our plates were taken away, Honey reminisced about Nate's father, Roberto. "Uncle Rob knew so many famous pianists," she said to Kay. "He worked with Ashkenazy, Horowitz, Martha Argerich and Alfred Brendel; and he was a terrific pianist himself—he used to give recitals in a local church, St. Thomas Aquinas."

"No, it was St. Vincent de Paul," I corrected her, without thinking.

Honey looked at me in surprise. "Was it?"

"Yes. At least . . . that's what Nate told me."

"Then . . . that must be right. You obviously take in what he says."

"I always take in what my sitters say; in order to paint them I have to get to know them. Don't I?" I added, then wished I hadn't.

Nate got to his feet and was chinking his glass. I assumed that he was about to make a speech, but he simply asked if some of us would pick up our wineglasses and swap places for dessert and coffee. Andy moved round, as did Kay, and a few moments later Mum came over and sat in Kay's chair. As I introduced her to everyone I realised that, like me, she'd had quite a bit to drink.

"So how are the wedding plans going?" James asked her pleasantly.

"Oh, *fine*," she answered with a smile. "We're sending the 'vitations out next week. That's going to be quite a job, as we've got a *huge* cast list."

Honey smiled. "I . . . think you mean guest list."

Mum looked puzzled. "Isn't that what I said?"

"Will there be any Italian elements?" Kay asked her.

"Yes. The soprano's going to sing some Rossini. And I'm thinking of releasing a pair of doves outside the church, to add a bit of *drama.*"

"Not that one wants *too* much drama at a wedding," Kay cautioned.

Mum heaved a tipsy sigh. "That's true. It's a pity we're not Catholic, like Nate; he and Chloe could've had a Nuptial Mass—

they're rather beautiful. But we'll *definitely* have those little bags of sugared almonds and I *do* want Chloe and Nate to smash a glass."

I had another sip of wine. "What's that about?"

"During the reception, the bride and groom smash a glass," Honey explained. "The number of fragments denote the number of years they'll be happily married—like in a Jewish wedding."

"That's right," said Mum as Chloe joined us. "Hello, darling." Chloe sat down next to her. "We're talking about the wedding, and I was *just* saying that I want you and Nate to smash a glass. I've *also* been wondering about confessi."

"Confessi?" Chloe smiled. "What have you got to confess, Mum? Come on—out with it!"

"Confetti," Mum corrected herself with a laugh. "I'm trying to make up my mind between delphin'm petals and hydrangea—*not* an easy decision."

Honey, clearly bored with the minutiae of the wedding preparations, was reminiscing about Nate. "He had this dog, Chopsy," she said to James. "He was one *ugly* little mutt, but Nate adored him."

"He wasn't ugly," I protested. "He looked very sweet. And he wasn't a mutt—he was a pedigree border terrier."

"Really?" said Honey. "Actually, you're *right*. I'd completely forgotten." She gave a bewildered laugh. "But how would *you* know what Nate's dog looked like?"

I could hardly admit that I'd been snooping in Nate's bedroom. "Nate described him to me," I replied truthfully. "I have a vivid image of him."

Honey nodded. "Ah."

Now as our coffee arrived Nate came and sat in the chair next to Honey's. I hardly dared look at him in case my face betrayed my emotions. I pressed my knees against the underside of the table to stop their trembling. How weird it was, that in the studio I could stare at him uninhibitedly—brazenly, even—but here I hardly dared throw him a glance!

Honey laid her hand on Nate's arm. I envied her the easy familiarity with which she was able to do this. "I was just telling everyone about Chopsy," she told him.

Nate grinned. "He was a *great* little dog."

"Why was he called Chopsy?" Chloe asked him. "Was it because he liked chops?"

"No, it was short for Chopin," I explained. "Nate's dad got him from a rescue centre. He'd come in half-starved, with cigarette burns on his legs—Chopsy, that is, not Nate's dad. Chopsy lived to fourteen, though he might have been as much as sixteen, as they weren't sure how old he was when they first got him."

"Oh," said Chloe. "I didn't know that."

I was suddenly aware of Honey's gaze, shrewd and knowing. "Well . . ." I stood up. "I'd better get home." I blew Mum a kiss, then turned to Nate. "Thanks, Nate," I said pleasantly. "It's been *lovely.*" He pushed back his chair, as if to show me out, but Chloe was already on her feet.

"I'll come up with you, Ella."

"Okay . . ." I lifted my hand to everyone. "I'll see you all at the wedding."

Mum smiled. "Not long now."

I followed Chloe up the stairs. "What a great evening," I said as we went into the hall. "I really enjoyed myself," I lied.

She handed me my coat and I put it on, then picked up my bag. "Ella . . . ?" As I saw her tortured expression, my heart plunged. She knew. How could she *not* know, when I'd jabbered on about Nate and Chopsy like that? So much for concealing my feelings—I'd drunk too much and had displayed them for all to see. "Ella . . . ?" Chloe said again.

"Yes?" She was looking at me so intently. "What?"

"I'm feeling rather . . . anxious and upset."

"Why?"

"I . . . think you *know* . . ."

"Know what?" I said innocently. *That I've fallen in love with your fiancé? Yes. I have. I didn't mean to. Please forgive me.* I braced myself for Chloe's censure. I deserved it.

She pursed her mouth. "That . . . getting married is . . . *scary.*"

"Oh." Relief flooded through me. "It *is* . . . I mean, it must be, but at least . . ." I fought down my emotions. "At least you've made a good choice. Nate's so . . . nice."

Chloe closed her eyes, then opened them. "I'm *so* glad you said that—he really *is*, isn't he? He's decent and hardworking, intelligent and kind. He's steady," she added earnestly. "That's important, isn't it? He's also very generous—and loyal. And he's attractive—did I say that?" I shook my head. "Well, he *is* attractive, very, and I know I'm just so *lucky.*" Her mouth quivered, then a tear splashed onto her cheek. "Sorry, Ella . . . I guess I'm just a bit overwrought."

I fumbled in my pocket and found some tissues. "That's very understandable . . ." I pulled a few out and Chloe pressed them to her eyes. "It's the emotion of it all."

She nodded, then regained her composure. "*So* . . ." She looked at me, her eyes wet. "How will you get home? Do you want me to call you a cab? I can wait with you until it arrives," she added, brightening suddenly. "We could sit here and chat."

"It's okay, Chloe; I'm going to walk—I need the air; and you ought to get back to your guests."

"You're right," she sighed. "So . . ." She flashed me a regretful smile. "I'll see you soon, Ella."

"Yes—and . . . please don't worry, darling." I bent and kissed her on the cheek.

As I went down the steps Chloe's words rang in my ears. She loved Nate so much that just the thought of it made her cry. She would soon marry him, and I would just have to be happy for her and view him in a different way.

When I got home I went up to the studio. I got out Nate's canvas, put it on the easel, picked up my palette and a flat brush and began to work on it. As I did I tried to understand why I was so drawn to

him. Was it because I'd hated him to start with and found the reali-
sation that I liked him exhilarating somehow? Was I competing with
Chloe? If so, I'd never competed with her before; I'd only felt pro-
tective towards her—I was six years older than her after all; never
had I felt even a flicker of interest in any of her previous boyfriends.
I was drawn to Nate, I realised, for the simple reason that I found
him so attractive and decent and easy to talk to—and yes, because I
sensed that he was drawn to me too.

I worked on his portrait for the better part of two hours; then,
satisfied with what I'd done, I cleaned the brushes and went to my
computer to check my emails before going to bed. I was exhausted.

There was a new enquiry, from a Mr. and Mrs. Berger, about
painting them to mark their silver wedding anniversary. That was
good news. There was also a message from Sophia, to say that her
mother had recovered from her cold, asking if we could arrange the
next sitting. I was glad. It would be good to see Iris again. I typed my
reply and as I pressed SEND another message arrived. It was from my
father.

> *Dear Ella, I've still had no word from you, but I continue to hope
> that you'll find it in your heart to see me, even if it's only for a few
> minutes. So this is to let you know where I'll be staying—at the
> Kensington Close Hotel in Wright's Lane. I'll be in touch again
> nearer the time, but for now I send you my sincerest wishes, and
> my love, your father, John.*

I stared at his message. *Hope . . . heart . . . love.* It was far too late
for him to be using words like that.

I scrolled down to "options." DELETE MESSAGE? I highlighted YES.
Then, without knowing why, I changed my mind. I pressed NO.

Seven

"Wasn't the party fun?" Mum asked the following Saturday morning. "I've been so busy this week I haven't had a chance to talk to you about it." We were sitting at the kitchen table in Richmond, having a cup of coffee before starting the invitations. Mum was in her dancewear, having already done the hour and a half of Pilates with which she starts each day. "I drank a little more than was wise. I didn't say anything *silly*, did I?"

"No—you just had a bit of trouble with the word 'confetti.' "

"Oh, yes." Mum rolled her eyes. "But it was a lovely evening—I liked Nate's friends." She moved the well-thumbed copies of *Brides* magazine, *You & Your Wedding* and *Perfect Wedding* to the end of the table. "You know he's in Finland at the moment?"

"I do—otherwise I'd be painting him right now." I wished I *were*, I reflected ruefully. I longed to see him again.

Through the French windows I could see Roy, at the very end of the garden, by Chloe's old wooden playhouse, toiling away in the long flower bed that skirted the lawn.

"I hope Nate won't have to do too much travelling," I heard Mum say.

I looked at the horse chestnut waving its white candles. "I think it goes with the job." I sipped my coffee. "What he does is look at companies with a view to buying them—at the moment he's putting together a leveraged bid for a liquid chemicals transport business in Helsinki. Its primary operations are in Scandinavia but they're expanding into Estonia, Latvia and Lithuania, so there's a lot of potential there."

Mum's brow furrowed. "You seem to know a lot about it, darling."

"Well . . . Nate talked about it—during one of his sittings."

She opened her glasses case. "It's sweet the way you pay so much attention to the people you paint—it must really put them at ease." She took out the spectacles, looping the mauve cord over her head. "And have you had a busy week?"

"No—the election threw everything into disarray. I couldn't paint my MP, Mike Johns, for obvious reasons. Another sitter, Celine, had to go to France to see a friend—she said it was very important—so she cancelled our sitting at the very last moment. Other than that I've been working on the posthumous portrait I'm doing—did I tell you about it?"

"You did." My mother shook her head. "That poor girl. And how's her picture coming?"

"Not well." I heaved a frustrated sigh. "It's just . . . flat. What I need is some close-up video footage of her, but there isn't any." I refilled my coffee cup. "Then I had another sitting with a lovely woman named Iris who's in her eighties." I'd hoped that Iris would continue the story about Guy Lennox, but an electrician had been there doing some re-wiring, so we'd only made small talk. I glanced at the garden again. "What's Roy doing?"

"He's planting lots of delphiniums, foxgloves and hollyhocks—they should flower just in time for July third. Then he's going to do some weeding—with last week's rain, the beds are like Papua New Guinea."

"I'll help him with that," I volunteered. "It's too much for him on his own. Or maybe Chloe could give him a hand—she's coming over today, isn't she?"

"No—she phoned first thing to say that she can't."

"Why not?"

"She said she needs to go into the office."

"I see. But however busy she is she should help you and Roy—I mean, this is all for *her*," I added crossly.

"*I'll* help Roy later," Mum said soothingly. She lifted her glasses onto her nose. "But you and I *must* get on with the invitations."

"Okay." I put my cup in the sink. "Let's start."

I went over to the large green box standing on the end of the kitchen table, lifted the lid and pulled out the first invitation. The card was so thick it could almost stand up unaided.

"Isn't the font elegant?" Mum said.

I looked at the flowing curlicues and extravagant swashes. "It's . . . a bit fancy for my tastes."

"Well, *I* love it. It took me ages to choose it."

"Didn't Chloe want to choose it?"

"No. She's left *all* the arrangements to me—except for the dress, which I've now seen, and I must say it's gorgeous." Mum took her glasses off. "Chloe told me she'd been a bit unsure about it, given its history, but I said there was no way Nate would try to get out of their wedding."

"I'm sure he wouldn't." Then I felt a stab of guilt for wishing that he *would*.

Mum put some printed sheets in front of me. "Here's *your* copy of the guest list. I want you to do A to M while I do N to Z. The addresses are all in *here* . . ." She thumped her Filofax onto the table.

I opened my backpack, got out my calligraphy pen and practised on a piece of scrap paper. *Nate, Nate, Nate, Nate.* I saw Mum peering at it, so then I wrote *Chloe, Chloe, Chloe, Chloe,* then *Nate & Chloe.* "It's fine," I said.

"Good." Mum unscrewed the top of her fountain pen, took an invitation out of the box, put her glasses on again, then began to write. I could hear the nib scratch across the card.

I inscribed an invitation to Mum's friend Joyce Allen and her husband, George; then I looked up their address, wrote it on the envelope and carefully blotted it. "There's the first one done." I slid it into the envelope.

Mum peered at it over her spectacles. "*Very* nice; don't seal them, will you—we'll be adding the accommodation list and RSVP cards afterwards. Right . . ." She turned back to her card. "Here's *my* first one." She inserted the invitation into the envelope then put it next to mine. I picked it up.

When I'd done my calligraphy course we studied graphology. I'd been sceptical at first, but studying my mother's writing convinced me that there must be something to it, as all her personality traits seemed to be there in the words she wrote and the way she wrote them. Her hand was forward-sloping, indicating ambition and drive; the words were evenly spaced and of a uniform height, denoting organisational ability and self-control; the I's were beautifully dotted, indicating a meticulous character. Now I noticed that the tops of her letters were perfectly closed. This, I recalled, pointed to a secretive nature.

"What are you doing?" Mum asked.

I put the envelope down. "Just admiring your writing."

"Thanks—it's not as elegant as yours of course, but it'll do. Now, shall we listen to the radio while we work?"

"Yes—in *fact* . . ." I looked at the clock. "I'm *on* the radio in five minutes' time. I'd completely forgotten." I told Mum about the BBC documentary I'd been interviewed for.

She went to the dresser and switched on the kitchen radio and we heard the tail end of *Travelling Light*.

"Now *Artists of the Portrait*," said the announcer, "in which our reporter, Clare Bridges, examines the fine art of painting people . . ."

We heard Clare talking about why it is that human beings have always sought to portray themselves, from the earliest scratchings at Lascaux to Marc Quinn's iconic bust, *Self,* carved out of eight pints of his own frozen blood. There were comments from Jonathan Yeo and June Mendoza and a rare clip of Lucian Freud. Then I heard my voice.

"I knew I wanted to be a painter from eight or nine."

Mum smiled as Clare back-announced me.

"I simply drew and painted all the time. Painting's always been, in a way, my solace . . ."

Mum glanced at me, and I thought I saw a flicker of guilt pass across her features.

"I like painting people who I feel are complex: I like seeing that fight going on in the face between the conflicting parts of someone's personality."

I realised that I often saw that fight going on in my mother's face—the glacial serenity beneath which I caught glimpses of the powerful struggle with her deeper emotions.

Now Clare was talking about the complex nature of the relationship between sitter and artist. I heard myself speak again.

"A portrait sitting is a very special space. It has an intimacy—painting another human being is an act of intimacy . . . I've never fallen for a human sitter, no . . ."

There was some discussion of the influence of the BP award, and of how portraiture, once seen as safe and conventional, has become almost cutting edge. Then the programme came to an end; I turned the radio off.

"That was fascinating," Mum said. "You spoke very well, Ella. But have you really never fallen in love with one of your sitters?"

"Never," I lied.

"Well, I hope you do someday, because it must be a wonderful way to meet someone—think of how well you get to *know* them—and they must get to know you very well too."

"Yes—depending on who it is, and how much I want to reveal

about myself . . ." I was walking on quicksand. "Now . . ." I peered resolutely at the invitation list. "Why are you inviting the Evans?"

"Because they're near neighbours, and because they asked us to Lara's wedding last year. In fact, they're about to become grandparents."

"Really? How old is Lara?"

"She must be . . ." Mum narrowed her eyes. "Twenty-four."

"She's having her family young, then."

"Twenty-four is young," Mum agreed. "Especially these days; I think it's better to wait."

"But . . ." I pressed the blotting paper down. "You had me when you were twenty-four."

Mum's pen froze. "That's true."

"And you were very ambitious—I could have ruined your career. I've always been surprised that you had me when you did—in fact, I've sometimes wondered whether you really . . . well, *intended* to have me."

Mum flushed. "Do you mean—were you an accident? Is that what you're asking me, Ella?"

I took another invitation. "Well, yes—it's unusual for young ballerinas to have babies, given how ruthlessly determined they have to be to succeed, isn't it? And you got married in a register office—so, lately, I've been thinking about it all, and wondering whether or not I was . . . planned."

"Oh, Ella." Mum reached for my hand. "I was so *happy* to be having a baby."

"But . . . weren't you worried that you'd be unable to get back to fitness afterwards?"

She shrugged. "I simply trusted that I would. As it turned out, I was onstage again within four months."

"So . . . presumably my father looked after me in the evenings, when you were performing."

"No." Mum picked up her pen. "He did very little in that respect."

"Why was that?"

"Well . . . he travelled a lot for his work. At that time he was building a school in Nottingham."

"But Nottingham's not far from Manchester."

"Even so, he'd quite often be away, and so I had babysitters for you—sometimes our upstairs neighbour, Penny, would help. And when I was on tour my mother would come and stay."

"I see. So Grandma would have been there in the flat with my father. That must have been awkward. Did they get on?"

Mum blinked. "Not really."

"Didn't he like her?"

"She didn't . . . like *him.*"

"Oh. Because she knew about his affair, I suppose." Mum nodded, grimly. "Well, that *would* have put a strain on the relationship." I began to write another invitation, to a friend of Chloe's, Eva Frost. I glanced at Mum. "What about *his* parents? I don't remember them at all—did we ever see them?"

Mum sighed. "They lived in Jersey and didn't come to the mainland very often. They weren't really . . . involved."

"Even though they had a grandchild?" She nodded. "How mean—not to make more of an effort."

"It was mean," Mum agreed feelingly.

"But we could have gone there—*did* we?"

"No . . . As I say, it was hard for me to take time off."

"I see. So I didn't do very well on the grandparent front, did I?"

My mother nodded regretfully. "That's true. You only had my mother, my father having died two years before you were born. As you know, he was called Gabriel, and I named you after him."

"And . . . remind me how you met *my* father."

At first I thought Mum wasn't going to answer; then she lowered her pen. "We met in 1973," she said. "I'd been with the company for two years and he came to a special fund-raising performance of *Cinderella.* I was the Winter Fairy and wore a costume that hung with 'icicles.' "

"How lovely." I imagined them tinkling as she danced. "So was my father interested in ballet?"

"Not particularly; he'd come along . . . with some other people. There was a cast and crew party afterwards to which some audience members were invited; your father and I were introduced, and we . . . just . . ."

"Fell in love?"

"Yes," Mum answered quietly.

"So you were, what, twenty-three?"

"I was. And he was twenty-nine."

"And was he artistic too?"

My mother's face tightened. "Yes. He did a lot of painting and draw-ing . . . so I imagine that's where you get it. Now," she said briskly, "we need to write the invitations for Nate's relations." The conversation about my father was clearly over. She pushed back her chair. "I've got their addresses on a separate list—if I can remember where I put it. Oh, I know . . ." She stood and went to the dresser, then opened a drawer. "It's in here." Pulling the list out, she studied it. "There's quite a gang of them coming. Nate's organising their accommodations—Chloe told me that he's paying for quite a lot of it too—he's terribly generous." Mum returned to the table. "Thank *God* she's made such a good choice. And she knows she has, because she keeps telling me how lucky she is. Yesterday I was on the phone with her and she suddenly reeled off a list of all his great qualities. It was very touching."

"That's just what she did with me, last week."

Mum smiled. "It's such a relief to see her so happy—and don't worry, Ella"—she laid her hand on mine—"I know that *you'll* find someone just as wonderful." *I already have,* I thought with a pang. Mum lifted her glasses onto her nose again, then peered at my pile of finished cards. "What letter are you up to?"

"G." I wrote an invitation for Chloe's godmother, Ruth Grant; and I was about to address the envelope when I put my pen down, unable to bear it any longer. "Mum . . . Can I tell you something?" My heart began to race.

She reached for another invitation. "Of course you can," she said absently. "Tell me anything you like, darling."

"Because there's something . . ." My voice trailed away.

She looked at me—her agate blue eyes magnified through the lenses of her spectacles. "What is it, Ella?" She blinked, then took the glasses off and let them dangle against her thin sternum. "Has something happened?"

"*Yes.* Something has."

"You're not in any trouble, are you?" She looked alarmed.

"No. But I have this . . . dilemma."

"Dilemma?" she echoed. "What dilemma?" I didn't answer. "Ella . . ." Mum put down her pen. "Would you please tell me what this is about?"

"All right . . ." I took a deep breath. "I've heard from my father."

My mother's cheeks instantly coloured, as though all the blood in her body had rushed to her face. "When?" she whispered. I told her, then explained how the contact had come about. She inhaled sharply, snatching the air through her nose. "I was appalled when I saw that piece in *The Times.*"

"I know you were, because you didn't say anything about it. I did ask the journalist to change it before the article was posted online, but he refused."

"I *immediately* worried that were your father to come across it he'd recognise you—and he *has.* So . . . what did he say?"

I'd already decided not to tell my mother that he was coming to London.

"He just wrote that he'd like to be in touch. He said there are things he wants to explain."

Mum's face spasmed with anger. "There's nothing *to* explain! You and I *both* know what happened, Ella. He deserted us when I was twenty-eight and you were only four—a little girl. A little girl who *adored* him! He was heartless."

"Well . . . if it's any comfort, he said that he feels very guilty. He wants to make amends."

My mother's eyes were round with contemptuous wonderment. "It's too *late* to make 'amends.' He made his choice—to abandon us and start a new life with . . . with . . ." She seemed unable to utter the name of the woman for whom my father had left her. "He has no *right* to get in touch now." Mum picked up her pen as though that concluded the conversation.

I could hear the hum of the fridge.

"Of course he has that right," I disagreed. "He's my father."

My mother's face flashed with renewed fury. "He *isn't* your father, Ella. He chose *not* to be." She nodded towards the garden. "*There's* your father."

I glanced through the French windows at Roy, in the far distance, his foot on the spade, bent over the gardens he was lovingly tending for Chloe's wedding. "Roy *is* my father," I agreed. "And he's been a wonderful one. But the man who brought me into the world, and who *was* my father, at least for the first few years of my life . . ." I felt my throat tighten. "That man now wants to be in touch."

Mum looked at me warily, her birdlike chest rising and falling. "So . . . what are you going to do?"

I shook my head. "I don't know. I feel torn, because a part of me *does* want to see him."

She blinked. "What do you mean—*see* him?"

"I mean . . . one day," I faltered. "If I *do* get in touch with him."

Mum stared at me. "Have you replied?"

"No. I've been in turmoil about it—so I've done nothing."

"Good." She laid down her pen. "I don't *want* you to reply."

"It isn't *up* to you, Mum—it's *me* he's contacted." She flinched. "But I felt that I *had* to discuss it with you—however painful that discussion might be—before coming to any decision."

My mother looked away. When she returned her gaze to me her pale blue eyes shone with unshed tears. "*Don't* answer him, Ella. I beg you not to."

"But it was all *so* long ago! Why are you *still* bitter about him?"

"Because of what he *did.*"

"Okay, so he left you." I threw up my hands, frustrated. "People get left every day, but they try to move on—*you* moved on; you've had a good life with Roy. So why can't you get over what happened with my father?"

"Because I . . . just . . . can't. *Please,* Ella, let it lie. No good will come of it."

I caught the note of warning in her voice. "What do you mean by that?" Mum didn't answer. "What are you trying to say?"

"Only that . . . if you *do* contact him it could cause a lot of unhappiness. He's decided to get in touch—no doubt because he's getting older now, and wants to be forgiven. But we don't *have* to forgive him, do we?"

"*I* can if *I* want to!"

Mum's eyes flickered with pain, then she picked up her pen. "We *must* get on with the invitations." Her voice had been calm, but as she took another card out of the box I saw that her hand was trembling.

"Mum," I said, more gently. "The invitations can wait. Because now that we're talking about my father, there are other things I want to ask you."

She started to write. "What things?" she said irritably. She was pressing on the pen so hard that her fingertips had gone red.

"Well . . . I've been having a lot of memories from that time coming up—memories that must have been triggered by my father's contact."

Her hand stopped. "So that's why you asked me about the holiday in Anglesey."

"Yes. In fact, he'd emailed me a photo of him and me standing on a beach. He's holding my hand . . ."

My mother exhaled sharply. "So that's how you knew about the blue and white striped dress."

"Yes. I was wearing it in the photo—otherwise I wouldn't have remembered it. But there are lots of things I *do* remember, and one particular memory is very confusing. I've been trying to work it out but I can't."

Mum was looking at me warily. "And what memory's that?"

"It's of you and him. You're walking along, with me in between you, holding your hands. It's a very clear, sunny day, and you're both swinging me up in the air, going, 'one, two, three, wheee.' And you're wearing this white skirt with big red flowers on it." My mother flinched. "But the reason I'm confused is because I would have been too young to remember it, because you can only swing children up like that when they're no more than two or three—yet I *can* recall it, vividly."

Don't let go, now . . .

My mother's already fair complexion had gone paler still.

Okay—let's do a big one.

"Why do I remember that, Mum?"

More, Daddy! More! More!

I could hear the hum of the fridge.

"All right," she answered at last. "I'll tell you. Then perhaps you'll understand why I feel as I do." She dropped her pen, then pushed the invitations aside and clasped her hands in front of her. "What you're remembering," she began softly, "is the day that I saw your father with his . . . with . . . his . . . *Frances.*"

This, then, was the "traumatic" encounter. So I *had* been there.

"She lived in Alderley Edge, a few miles to the south of Manchester, in a very nice house. She had money." Mum added it bitterly.

"What was our flat like?"

"It was very ordinary—it was part of a redbrick house on Moss Side, but it was convenient for the University Theatre, where the company was then based. And in September 1979, when you were almost five . . ." *So, well past the stage of being swung in the air,* I reflected. "It was a Saturday afternoon," Mum went on, relentlessly. "I'd been waiting for your father to arrive. He'd had to go to the office that morning. But we were due to have a picnic with him after lunch— the weather was wonderfully clear and sunny. By three o'clock he still hadn't turned up, and I had to be onstage that night—I was dancing *Giselle*—so there wasn't much time. I guessed that he must be with *her,* and I was . . . angry and *hurt.*" She looked at me beseechingly. "He'd done this to me *so* many times, and I couldn't stand just waiting for him, feeling wounded and disappointed. So I decided to go and find him."

"In order to do what? Confront him?"

She exhaled wearily. "I didn't know *what* I was going to do. There was a football match on—we could hear the roars from Old Trafford. I told you that we were going for a ride in the car; so I put you in the back and we drove to Alderley Edge."

"How did you know where she lived?"

"I just . . . did. Women are good at finding these things out, Ella. So I went past . . . the house." Mum stared straight ahead. "There was your father's blue car, in the drive." *So he wasn't even discreet about it,* I reflected dismally. "I parked about fifty feet away then sat there, sick with misery."

My heart contracted with pity. "How horrible for you, Mum."

"It was . . . *hell.* You kept chatting away in the back, asking me what we were doing—but I couldn't explain. I decided there was nothing that I *could* do—we'd simply have to go home. And I was about to start the car again when you suddenly said that you were hungry. There was a newsagent's a few yards behind, so we got out of the car and went in, and I bought you some chocolate. But as we were walking back to the car I looked up and, in the distance, I saw your father walking along with *her,* and . . ." My mother faltered. "With her, and . . ."

Ready, sweetie? One, two, three . . .

"And *what,* Mum?"

U-u-u-u-p she goes!

Mum's face was perfectly still—like a frozen waterfall. "And this little girl," she answered softly. "She was holding their hands. She was about three."

More, Daddy! More!

"They were swinging her up in the air, and they were all laughing. And then I understood . . ."

I tried to speak, but my mouth had gone dry. "She was his little girl?"

"Yes," Mum answered bleakly. "I'd had *no* idea—until then."

From outside came the silvery trill of a blackbird. "So . . . " My heart was banging in my chest. "You're saying that my father had a child with Frances? And that he'd never told you?"

"Never."

So this was why the encounter had been "traumatic."

"What a shock," I breathed.

"It was more than a shock. It hit me like a blow from a hammer." Mum was still staring ahead. "They hadn't spotted us, but by now I was in a panic, not knowing what to do. I decided that we had to leave before we were seen, so I hurried towards the car, but you kept trying to pull me in the opposite direction. I told you to come with me, but you refused. Then you turned and called out, 'Daddy! Daddy!' He glanced up. And when he saw us, he looked so . . ."

I saw my father's face, his mouth an O. "Startled," I whispered.

"Yes. He also looked ashamed and confused. I tried to hold you, but you wrenched your hand free and you ran towards him. I called you to come back but you wouldn't stop. I had no choice but to follow you, and so . . ." She blinked. "There I was, face-to-face with him, and her, and this . . . child."

"Frances had a child?" I echoed faintly, still trying to take it in.

Mum nodded. "He'd concealed her existence from me. I knew about the . . . relationship." I thought of the hotel bill that Mum had found in my father's pocket, and the love letter. "I tolerated it," Mum went on tonelessly, "because I believed it would end. But I had no idea that Frances had had . . ." Mum looked at me in bewilderment. "It didn't seem possible."

"Why not?"

"Because . . . John had told me that she was unable to have children—and she was ten years older than he was."

"Really?" I adjusted my mental image of the woman who'd so beguiled my father.

"So for her to have a child was the last thing I expected. She would have been forty-two when that baby was born."

"But . . . I still don't undertstand why you stayed with him. There he was having this long affair—an affair you knew all about, such that you even discussed with him your fears that the other woman might get pregnant? How horrible!"

Mum looked stricken. "It *was* horrible—it was *awful!*"

"Then why didn't you *divorce* him? You were young—and beautiful. You could have found someone else. Why didn't you leave him, Mum?"

Her blue-grey eyes shimmered, like melted ice. "Because I loved him," she answered softly. "I didn't *want* to leave him." She drew in her breath, slowly, as if in physical pain. "But . . . there we all were. And Frances looked at me with utter *hatred.*"

"But . . . why should *she* hate *you?*"

Mum gave a helpless shrug. "She just . . . did. Then you said, 'What are you doing, Daddy? Are you helping this lady?' And Frances gave you this awful stare that I've never forgotten."

"The skirt," I said quietly. "The white skirt with the big red flowers. It was *hers,* wasn't it? Not yours. *She* was wearing it."

Mum nodded. "Then she picked up the little girl and carried her inside. John looked at me furiously. And he told me he'd never forgive me."

"But . . . this all sounds the wrong way round—*you* were the wounded party."

"Yes," Mum said hotly. "I was!" She banged her hand down on the edge of the table. "I *was* the wounded party!" Her face crumpled as she struggled not to cry. "But I suppose he was confused and ashamed—his double life had been exposed." She dashed away a tear. "As I walked away with you, I felt as though my whole world was sliding off a cliff. Because there was a child, and I knew that this would change my life forever."

"But . . . you're telling me that I have a *sister.*" I stared at my mother. "What was her name?"

"Lydia," she answered after a moment.

"Lydia," I echoed blankly. "And you've never *told* me?" Mum didn't respond. I glanced into the garden. "Is *Roy* aware of this?"

She shook her head. "I knew he'd tell you—or make *me* tell you. And I didn't want you to know."

"But . . ." I felt anger and indignation rise up, corrosive and scalding, like magma. "What if I'd wanted to meet Lydia—or get to *know* her?"

A muscle at the corner of Mum's mouth twitched. "That's precisely what I wanted to avoid. Because if you had, then we would've had contact with John again, which was the *last* thing I wanted." Her hands were curled into fists. "I was determined to preserve the integrity and stability of *my* family."

"So you hid my sister's existence from me—all these years? How *could* you? How could you *do* that, Mum?"

She gave me a blinkless stare. "It surely must have occurred to you, Ella, that your father might have had other children?"

"Well . . . of *course*," I answered faintly. "I guessed that he'd probably had another family, in Australia—but that's an *abstract* thought. You're telling me that he had a child *here*, in the UK, just a few miles from where we lived—a child who was only two years younger than me, a child I'd actually *met* . . . and might have *gotten to know*?"

Mum smiled bitterly. "Oh, that would have been cosy. The daughters of the wife and mistress being playmates? Would *you* want that, Ella, if you were ever in the situation that *I* was suddenly in?"

I imagined myself in my mother's shoes. How devastating for her! "No," I conceded. "Of course I wouldn't. It would be very awkward, even today; and yes, thirty years ago it would have been . . ."

"*Unbearable*," Mum concluded. "You can imagine the gossip and speculation."

"All right." I exhaled, sharply. "Even so . . . the idea that you never, ever *mentioned* her to me, my God . . ."

"I *couldn't* . . ." She heaved an exasperated sigh. "If I *had*, then you might have wanted to contact her, which would have put us back in John's orbit, which, I repeat, I did *not* want."

I glared at Mum. "Everything's been about what *you've* wanted. What about me?"

She blinked, startled. "No, Ella. I *was* thinking of you. Because the point is not that your father got himself into that situation. The *real* point is that you were almost five years old by then, and your father had seemed devoted to you, but—"

"What do you mean 'seemed'?" I interrupted. "He was! He *was* devoted to me! That's why my memories of him are only happy ones. I remember him playing with me, and pushing me on the swings, and watching children's television with me, and taking me to the theatre to see you dance. I remember him putting me to bed, and reading to me, and doing painting with me; I remember him hugging me, and holding my hand . . ." My throat ached with a suppressed sob. "In *all* my memories of him, he's holding my hand!" I felt my eyes fill. "So don't tell me that he wasn't devoted to me—because he *was*!"

"You still don't understand," she said quietly. "You *still* haven't got there. So now I'm going to tell you."

"Tell me *what*?" I fumbled in my pocket for a tissue. "What are you going to tell me?"

"The truth," Mum answered bluntly. "I've never *wanted* to tell you the truth, Ella. I've sheltered you from it for thirty years. But now I will. Ella," she said quietly, "your father chose to be with this *other* child. He chose to spend his life with *her*, not with you." Tears glimmered in her eyes. "*That* is what I've never wanted you to know."

As my mother's words struck me, I imagined feeling my father's hand in mine, his grip firm and strong, then his fingers suddenly loosening, and letting go.

"But that's not *all* he did," I heard her say.

I stared at her. "What do you mean?"

Mom shuddered, as though she was suddenly cold. "That day, you and I walked back to the car, and I drove home. I was in shock—how I managed not to crash, I don't know. You were asking me why Daddy was playing with that little girl and who that lady was. I didn't answer—I simply didn't know how. Nor did I know how I'd be able to go onstage that night and dance, but I did; and *as* I danced I felt that Giselle's suffering was my own. Afterwards, everyone said it was the best performance of my life. What I couldn't have known was that it was to be the *last* performance of my life."

"The last . . . ?"

"At eleven, I got back to the flat. Your babysitter left, and I just lay on the bed, in the darkness, watching the headlights from passing cars strobe across the ceiling. After a while I heard the key turn in the front door—John was back. Despite what I'd discovered that day, my reaction was one of relief. He'd come *back.* I ran downstairs to greet him. But his face was white—he was trembling with emotion."

"What did he say?"

Mum was staring ahead now, reliving those moments. "He said that he couldn't stand it anymore. He said that he'd prevaricated for three years and it had driven him *mad.* He said that he was finally being forced to choose. I felt myself start to panic, but then he went wearily upstairs and I felt *so* relieved—he was going to bed. We would sleep, then work things out in the morning—I was certain every-thing would be all right, just as long as we stayed together. But when I went into the bedroom I saw him pulling his suitcase down from the top of the wardrobe; he began opening drawers and taking out his clothes and putting them into it. Then he looked at me . . . and he said . . ." Mum's voice caught ". . . that he'd decided to be with Frances. He said that he didn't want to lose her. He said he loved her . . . So this was the second hammer blow that day. I pleaded with him *not* to leave us, but he just kept on taking his things out of the drawers, dropping them into his case. Then he snapped the clasps shut, picked the case up and, without even glancing at me, went down the stairs."

My hand flew to my chest. "Didn't he say goodbye to me? Surely he wanted to say goodbye to *me*?"

"He *did* want to—but you were asleep and I wouldn't let him wake you. I didn't want you to know what was happening. So as I followed him down I told him that he'd *have* to come the next day, to reassure you. He didn't even answer. He opened the door and then, without a backward glance, he went down the steps." As my mother said this I remembered those steps—they were steep and black-tiled, and, in the rain, treacherously slippery. Mum exhaled. "I saw him throw his case into the back of the car. I called to him, but he didn't answer—it was as though he was sleepwalking. Then he got behind the wheel and I heard the ignition. Now the car was moving away. So I ran down the steps after him . . ." Mum shivered.

"That's when you fell," I said. "That's when you had your accident . . ."

"I was so distraught that as I reached the last step I slipped, and felt my foot twist. Then I was in agonising pain."

"Oh, Mum . . ."

She was shaking her head. "I must have screamed, because our neighbour, Penny, came running out. She called the ambulance, then stayed with you until my mother got there in the early hours. I'd broken my ankle—the surgeon who operated on it told me it was a very bad break—a 'complicated fracture.' So that was the *third* blow of the hammer on that terrible day, by the end of which I felt that everything in my life was . . . shattered." She laid her hand on mine. "But I consoled myself that I still had you. You were my only solace in those dark days, Ella."

"I remember how sad you were. You used to sit in the kitchen, for hours, barely speaking, or you'd lie on your bed, your face to the wall."

"I couldn't cope—I felt as though I'd been pushed into an abyss. What I would have done without my mother, I don't know. But it remained my belief that John would come back, because he'd always come back, and I'd always forgiven him—and I would have forgiven him again, *even then.*"

"Oh, Mummy . . ." Now I understood the depth of her feelings for my father.

"But this time there was no word from him. And when I at last felt composed enough to phone his office, his colleague Al said that John wasn't there. Al seemed embarrassed," Mum went on. "I presumed that this was because he knew John had left me." She pursed her lips. "But that wasn't the reason at all. It was because Al realised that I had no idea that John no longer *worked* there. When he told me this I was . . . stunned. I asked him *why* John had left—it was so humiliating having to ask him where my own—" Mum drew in her breath with a teary gasp. "Then I heard Al say, 'You don't *know*? That he's gone to Perth?' By now I was in turmoil, but desperately trying not to show it; so I asked him if John had gone there for work, adding that I knew he'd once done a project in Dundee. There was a pause. Then Al said, very quietly, 'Perth in Australia. He left ten days ago. He's gone there for good.' " Mum closed her eyes as if to shut out the memory.

"But . . . it takes *time* to emigrate," I protested. "All the bureaucracy—and the interviews."

"It takes a *lot* of time," Mum agreed. "So he would have known for at least eighteen months beforehand, probably more."

"But how had he managed to hide it from you?"

"I've *no* idea—but he did."

"He must have kept all the papers at work."

Mum shrugged. "But this is where he was *so* cynical, Ella." She looked at me bleakly. "He'd been planning it with *her,* all those months, while continuing to talk to me about everything that *we* were going to do; he'd talk about the lovely house we'd buy, and the life we'd live, the holidays we'd have, the three of us, when *all the time* . . ." Mum's lips quivered as she tried not to cry; then she looked at me with an air of victory. "*Now* do you understand why I feel as I do?"

"Yes," I said quietly.

"You were almost five," she said. "Now you're *thirty*-five. And your father says he'd like to make amends—as though he believes he can wipe the slate clean with a few friendly emails. I don't think he *can.* So . . ." Mum looked at me imploringly then she reached out her hand. "Are you going to answer him?" I didn't answer. "*Are you, Ella? Please tell me.*" I felt her fingers close around mine.

"No," I said after a moment. "I'm not."

"So that's that," I said to Polly, over lunch, a few days later. I'd already told her the bare bones of the story on the phone. Now, sitting in a quiet corner of the Kensington Café Rouge, I'd related it to her in more detail.

She sipped her mint tea. "So the memory that you'd had was of him swinging *Lydia* through the air; but you'd always thought it was you. What a *mess* your father got himself into."

I nodded bleakly. "I keep thinking of myself, age six, seven and eight, asking my mother when I'd see him, not knowing that he was on the other side of the world with his other family—his other little girl." The pain of this was so sharp that it was almost like a physical injury. The fact that Lydia had been born two years after me was an additional wound.

"It does make your mother's attitude easier to understand." Polly shook her head. "Even so, for her to have *kept* all this from you . . ."

"And now I feel confused, because on the one hand I'm angry with her for concealing something so . . . enormous, but on the other hand, I guess she was right. As a child I don't think I *could* have coped with knowing that my father had left me in order to live with his other child, thousands of miles away. It would have felt like the most terrible rejection—it feels like that now."

"But he didn't leave you in order to live with his other child, Ella. He left you in order to live with his girlfriend. It was your *mother* he was rejecting, not you."

"No, he was rejecting me too, because if he'd loved me enough, then no-one could have seduced him away from my mother. Instead he went to Australia, leaving behind complete heartbreak—a complicated fracture," I added bitterly.

Polly lowered her cup. "You said that Frances was Australian."

"She was—'was' being the operative word."

Polly looked puzzled. "What are you saying? That she's . . . ?"

I nodded. "Last night I Googled 'Frances Sharp'; the first thing to come up was her obituary."

"I see . . . that must have been a shock."

"It was—he'd said nothing about it." I reflected that my father had said nothing about himself in any of his emails . . . only that he hoped we'd meet. "It was in *The Western Australian,* from last December; it said that she'd been ill for some time. She was seventy-six—ten years older than my father."

"That's a big gap. So he must have really loved her."

"He clearly did. Mind you, Mum said the fact that she'd had money would have featured in his . . . calculations."

"Your mother probably would say that, whether or not it was true," Polly pointed out. "But what did Frances do, that she had an obituary?"

"She owned a winery near the Margaret River, south of Perth—it's called Blackwood Hills. I did a search on it and on its website it said Frances's parents had started it up in 1970 when that part of Australia was first being cultivated for wine. It explained that in 1979 she'd gone back to Australia to help them run it, and that she inherited it in 1992, on her father's death. The site briefly mentioned *my* father, but it was clear that the estate was managed primarily by Frances."

"So who runs it now? Lydia?"

"Yes. With her husband, Brett. There was a photo of them standing in a vineyard with the river in the background."

"Does she look like you?"

"She does." I shivered. "It was *weird,* Polly—recognising my own face in the face of a stranger."

"And . . . have you told your mother any of this?"

"No. Because now that I know what my father did I feel there's nothing more to say."

Polly lifted her spoon and stirred her tea. "A few weeks ago I said that perhaps there was another side to the story, that it might some-how be better than you thought—but it was worse."

"Yes, and the fact that he's only contacted me now that Frances has died is another mark against him. Perhaps he promised her he wouldn't look for me while she was alive," I added bitterly.

"But he didn't know where you *were* until he saw that piece in *The Times.*"

"I'm sure he *could* have found me, if he'd wanted to. So if I choose to reject him now, it's no more than he deserves."

"Would you want to get in touch with Lydia?"

I didn't answer for a moment. Then I said, "I'm still trying to get my head around the idea that she *exists*. It's like discovering that I've got another arm—I can't quite cope with it. But I can hardly contact her if I'm refusing to see him, so I guess the answer to your question has to be no."

Polly sighed. "It seems . . . sad."

"I suppose it does, but lots of people have half siblings they never get to see. At least my mother's finally told me everything."

"Well . . ." Polly grimaced. "Let's hope she *has.*" I glanced at her. "And presumably she's told Roy too?" I nodded. "What did he say?"

"Not very much—he was shocked. But he texted me afterwards to say he'd like to have lunch with me next week."

Polly nodded, then glanced at her watch. "We'd better go, Ella, or we'll miss our appointment." She waved at the waiter.

I opened my bag. "So we're having a pedicure?"

"We are," she said as the waiter brought the bill.

"Why did you ask me to have a pedicure with you when you've never wanted to have one with me before? In fact, I thought you never *had* professional pedicures, in case they cut your nails all wrong and put you out of work."

"*This* pedicure's different." Polly flashed me an enigmatic smile. "You'll see."

"You're being very mysterious," I said as we crossed Kensington Church Street. Turning onto Holland Street I remembered that this was where Iris had lived before she moved to her flat. I was looking forward to our sitting next Wednesday.

We passed a patisserie and an art gallery, then Polly stopped outside the last shop in the terrace. "We're here."

I read the sign. "Aqua Sheko?" Through the window I could see a row of large, clear tanks, in each of which was a shoal of tiny dark fish. "What *is* this? A sushi bar? We eat fish while we have our feet done?"

"No," she said mysteriously. "The fish eat *us*. My treat, by the way."

"Thanks," I said uncertainly.

We went in, and the proprietor, a young Chinese woman, took our shoes, then we sat while she washed and dried our feet.

"Okay," said Polly. "Up we go."

We climbed onto a green leather bench. Polly dipped her perfect feet into her tank and I shuddered as the fish swarmed towards them in a writhing black mass.

"Come and *get* it," Polly crooned at them.

"They're not baby piranha, are they, Pol?"

"Nope—they're tiny carp called 'Garra Rufa.' They don't even have teeth—they just suck." She nodded at my tank. "Your turn."

"Do I have to?"

"Yes—they're hungry."

I peered at the wriggling black shapes then, grimacing, lowered my feet into the cool water. The fish darted towards them and I felt their mouths dock against my skin. I shivered with distaste. "Ooh . . . It tickles. But . . . it's *okay*. In fact, it's quite nice."

"I thought you'd say that," said Polly. "In the wild they clean the scales of bigger fish, which is what two human feet look like to them. They'll nibble the dead skin off your soles and heels, then they'll go between your toes and around your nails."

"Yum."

"What's more, there's some hormone in their spit that's good for stress."

"I could certainly do with *that*."

I was surprised at how quickly I was able to forget about the fish as Polly and I sat there, quietly chatting, sipping green tea. Occasionally a passerby would stop and gawp at us through the window.

"Have you had much work, Pol?" I asked her.

"I did a shoot at the British Museum last week. I had to hold this Ming vase. It was worth thirty-two million pounds, so they had security guards there to make sure I didn't run off with it, and a thick mattress underneath, in case I dropped it, but luckily I've got very steady hands. And I've got a booking this Friday—I've got to run my hands up George Clooney's naked back."

"Sounds nice."

"No," Polly protested. "It's *dull*. These jobs always are. I've stroked Pierce Brosnan's chin, Sean Bean's chest, Jude Law's legs, David Beckham's pecs, Clive Owen's *face*," she listed in a sing-song. "It's *so* boring—especially when we have to do twenty-five re-takes." She stifled a yawn. "I'd love to *stop*. Or maybe not stop, because the money's quite good; but I'd like to do something *new* as well, something a bit more *stimulating*—not that I've any idea what."

A woman walked—or rather, wobbled—past the window, teetering along on five-inch platforms.

"See that?" I said to Polly. "*Why* do women wear big platforms? They're not even attractive—they're just clumpy and ugly . . . and dangerous."

"Well, originally they were very practical shoes, designed to lift the wearer out of all the muck and filth on eighteenth-century streets."

"I see . . ." I peered at "my" fish, which had now encircled my lower shins like feathery anklets. "So . . . have you had any luck on the man front?"

Polly cocked her head to one side. "There's a very nice divorced dad at Lola's school—we've chatted at drop-off a few times and I *think* he's interested. But if he asks me out I'm *not* going to tell him what I do. I want a man who's attracted to my face, not my feet," she announced firmly. "What about your love life?"

I thought of Nate. "Nothing."

"Are you still painting Nate?" Polly asked, as though she'd read my mind.

"Yes. We've got a couple more sittings—then that's it." *Only two more "dates with Nate,"* I reflected regretfully.

"Are you happy with his portrait?"

"It's . . . fine. In fact, I think it's going to be *more* than fine." The work I'd done to it after the engagement party had been good, despite the fact that I'd painted by electric light, and had had quite a lot to drink. But somehow I felt that I could see more of Nate's soul in it now.

"That's great." Polly sipped her tea. "I'm glad you came to like him, Ella—and it must have made him much easier to paint." I didn't tell her that it had made it infinitely harder. I'd never told her what I felt for Nate. There were times when I'd been tempted to, but I felt ashamed to admit my feelings, even to her. I suspected that Polly had guessed, but she was too tactful to say anything.

She took her feet out of her tank. "So how's it going with the wedding?"

"Oh . . . pretty well, I think. Despite last week's emotional upset, it all seems to be under control. Chloe's asked me to do a reading."

"That's nice—what are you going to read?"

"I don't know. She's still choosing."

Polly dried her toes. "It's nice of her to invite me and Lola."

"Well, she's known you all her life—and my parents want you to be there too, as do I. It's going to be a very big do."

"So how's Chloe feeling?"

"Pretty nervous." I thought of her tearful anxiety at the engagement party.

"That's normal," Polly remarked. "Remember how terrified I was before I married Ben?" I nodded. "Although . . . it was with good reason, now that I come to think about it. I knew, even as I made my vows, that I was making a mistake. It was the most awful feeling. But Chloe's happy?"

"She seems to be. She keeps saying how wonderful Nate is—in fact, she constantly eulogizes him and so—what's the matter, Pol?"

"Um . . . nothing."

"You were frowning—what were you thinking?"

"Well, I suppose I was thinking that—"

Suddenly I felt my phone vibrate. "Just a second, Pol. Sorry." I took the phone out of my pocket and peered at it.

"Oh God." Seeing my father's name, in light of what I'd recently learned about him, gave me a sick feeling. "I've another message from my father."

"Really? What does he say?"

I began to read it. "Just more of the same. He says that he understands my reticence, blah blah blah, but—oh, this is new, he refers to Mum. He says he hopes that she isn't discouraging me from responding to him. He says he hopes that I'll make my own decision, and that we'll meet when he's in London."

"Which will be when?"

"A week on Sunday . . ."

"Gosh—soon."

"Yes. And I *am* making my own decision about it, which is that I'm having nothing to do with him. What does he expect after what he . . . *oh.*"

Polly looked at me. "What?"

I stared at the screen. "He's spotted that I say on my website my studio's near to World's End."

"He's not planning to come round, is he?"

"No. He wouldn't know the address—I don't put it on the site. But he says that if he *doesn't* hear from me he'll go to a café on the King's Road every day of his stay. It's called Café de la Paix; he says he'll sit there between three and six on Monday and Tuesday afternoons, and between nine and twelve on the Wednesday morning, in the

hope I'll come. He says his flight back is at four on Wednesday afternoon."

"He's certainly determined," said Polly.

"He is."

"So . . . *will* you do that, Ella? Maybe you could?" she added ten-
tatively. "What do you think?"

I went to OPTIONS, then hit DELETE. "No."

Eight

"Haven't seen you for a while," said the taxi driver on the following Tuesday morning as he put my easel in the boot of his car. "You been okay?"

"Erm . . . more or less. And you?" I asked as I got in the back.

"Can't complain." He slid behind the wheel. "So we're off to Barnes again, are we?"

"Yes—to the same address on Castelnau, please."

He started the car and we drove away, passing the Harley-Davidson showroom, then The Wedding Shop with its displays of Wedgewood and Waterford. As we waited to turn left I gazed into the window of "Artiques," with its weird selection of fossils, crystals, shells, bleached animal skulls, sunburst mirrors and stuffed fish. On the walls were lots of frames containing huge mounted butter-flies in myriad hues of yellow, orange and blue.

As we pulled up to the light, the driver nodded at the railings. "Lots more flowers."

There were new bouquets, and two pink balloons bobbing on sil-ver ribbons. "That's because it's her birthday today."

The driver looked at me in the rearview mirror. "How do you know?"

"I was told—in fact, I'm painting her."

"Even though she's dead?"

"Yes. I'm doing it from photos."

"Right . . . I suppose that's easier."

"No—it's much harder."

As we drove on I thought about how unhappy I was with Grace's portrait. I spent the rest of the journey torturing myself with thoughts of how disappointed her family would feel when they finally saw it.

We turned into Celine's drive. I got out with my stuff, paid the driver, then pressed on the big brass bell. To my surprise the door was opened not by the housekeeper, but by Celine's husband—a tall, silver-haired man in a suit.

He beamed at me. "You must be Ella."

"I am, and you're Mr. Burke?"

"Do call me Victor—how *nice* to meet you. Let me get that." He took the easel, tucked it under his arm, then crossed the hall, pausing at the foot of the stairs. He put his hand on the newel post and looked up. "*Dar*-ling! Ella's here to *paint* you." He turned back to me. "She'll be down in a tick."

I followed Victor into the drawing room, where the dustsheets were already in place. He put the easel down and I opened it up and positioned it in its usual place. "So how's it going?" he asked as I got out my palette and brushes. "Could I have a peek?"

"Of course." I took the painting out of the canvas carrier and put it on the easel.

Victor rested his hands on his hips. "Yes . . ." He cocked his head to one side as he studied it. "It's definitely Celine."

"We've only had two sittings but the basic shapes are there, so now it's a matter of building up her face."

"I do hope you'll do her justice."

"I'll do my best. The sittings are going well," I added disingenu-

ously, then wondered if he had any idea what a nightmare his wife
had been.

"*Here* she is." Victor beamed at Celine as she came in. "Your portrait's *really* taking shape, darling."

"Good," she said absently. "Hello, Ella."

"Hi," I responded warmly. For all our difficulties, I had come to
like Celine and felt glad to see her.

Victor turned to me. "So today's, what, the eleventh of May? Celine's birthday is on the twelfth of June."

"The portrait will be finished at least a week before," I assured
him.

"Terrific. Now . . ." He glanced around the room. "Where will it
hang . . . ?"

Celine's face spasmed with alarm. "Not in *here*, Victor."

"Why not?" he asked.

"It's too . . . *public.*"

"Oh, I don't know . . ." He was eyeing the space above the mantelpiece. "I'd rather like it to go there—instead of the mirror."

"Absolutely not!" Celine looked appalled. "And if that's what
you're planning I won't do any more sittings!" Her vehemence took
me aback. I wondered if there was about to be a full-scale row.

"All right, *not* there," he placated her. "We can discuss it when it's
finished." He glanced at his watch. "I'm going to leave you both to it,
as I'm running late . . ." He straightened his yellow silk tie. "Bye,
darling." He bent to kiss Celine's cheek, but she turned her head and
he ended up kissing her ear. He gave a bemused shrug, then turned
to me. "Goodbye, Ella. *Very* nice to meet you."

"You too, Victor." He went out of the room then we heard his
shoes snap across the hall. The front door slammed.

Celine went over to the red velvet chair. "I'm sorry about that,"
she muttered as she sagged into it.

"Oh, don't worry." I tied on my apron. "Your husband's charming."

She put her bag down on the floor. "He is."

"He's obviously devoted to you."

"Yes." She said it wearily.

I began to squeeze out the paint, mixing yellow ochre with cadmium red to make the base for the skin tone. "And he's very good-looking."

She heaved an oddly regretful sigh. "That's true. My husband is charming, devoted and good-looking; he's hardworking, honourable and *very* generous. He's also wonderfully thoughtful," she added. "Oh—and he's a marvellous father."

I was reminded of Chloe's recitation of Nate's good qualities. "Well . . . then you're very fortunate."

Celine chewed on her lower lip. "Yes . . ."

"And will you have a birthday party? On the twelfth of June?"

She nodded. "Victor is giving me a dinner for forty friends."

I thinned the paint. "How lovely—where will it be?"

"At The Dorchester," she replied flatly.

"How fantastic." I selected a medium-size brush.

"Then we're going to Venice for four days. He's booked the Cipriani," she added without enthusiasm.

"Lucky you!"

"And for my present, he's taking me to Graff, where I'm to choose a diamond ring—four carats."

"Good God!" I wanted to laugh. "What an amazing husband you've got."

Celine looked at me bleakly. "He *is* amazing. Yes. *But* . . ." Suddenly her ring tone sounded. My heart sank as Celine fished her phone out of her bag, peered at the screen, then slid it open. *"Oui, chéri?"* She stood up.

Celine, I mouthed. *Please* . . .

She flashed me an imploring smile. "This is *very* important." She resumed the call. *"Il faut que je te parle. Oui, chéri. Je t'écoute . . ."*

As I watched her walk to the door, whispering endearments, I suddenly realised what Celine's situation must be. How slow I'd been! During the first two sittings I'd noticed that there was one caller to whom she expressed particular affection. The intense, covert nature of these conversations reminded me of how Chloe used to be when she was seeing Max. Celine was having an affair. That would explain why she didn't want to be painted. Victor had commissioned a portrait of her, but she was in love with someone else. It would also explain her irritability with Victor.

After four or five minutes she returned, looking slightly flushed, as though the call had affected her. "Sorry about that," she said as she crossed the carpet. "I'll put the phone on voice mail." She did so, then returned it to her bag. *"Alors . . ."* She sat down again. "Let's continue."

We chatted for a while, but Celine was clearly in an agitated mood. In her eyes was a kind of anxious longing that was painful to see.

My brush slapped across the canvas as I painted her dress—it was a pure mid-blue, like the blue of rosemary flowers. As I loaded the brush again I heard another deep sigh.

I looked up. "Are you okay, Celine?"

"Am I okay?" she repeated. "Well . . . I suppose it depends on what you mean by 'okay.' " I swapped the brush I'd been using for a finer one and began to outline her mouth. "I am in good health," she went on. "I'm not hungry or cold. I have comfortable accommodations, and clothes on my back, *but . . .*" Her eyes were suddenly bright with tears. "No," she whispered, fervently. "I am *not* okay."

"Celine . . ."

She fumbled in her sleeve, then pressed a tissue to her eyes. "Excuse me," she murmured.

"Don't . . . worry." I lowered my brush. "We'll wait until you feel . . . better."

"I am not *going* to feel better. I shall only feel worse."

"Is there anything *I* can do?"

"No. Thank you." She balled the tissue in her hand, clenching it so hard that her knuckles were white.

I wanted to ask her what the matter was but didn't feel that I could. In any case, I reflected, she was unlikely to tell me. I dipped the brush in the jar of turps and stirred it around.

"I want to leave my husband." I glanced at Celine, startled. "I want to leave Victor," she reiterated, desperately. "I've wanted to leave him for a long time, but now it's all coming to a head, because of my birthday. It's very difficult," she sobbed.

"Well . . . is there . . . anyone you can talk to about it?"

"I *have* just been talking about it—to my *friend*. That's why the call was so important."

"I see."

"And this friend of mine—Marcel." Her boyfriend, I decided. She sighed with frustration. "I . . . *love* Marcel." So I was right. "But . . ." Celine's voice fractured with emotion. "She will not *support* me!"

"Ah." *Marcelle.*

She sniffed. "She thinks I'm 'insane.' She told me so when I saw her in Paris last week, and she said it again just now. She says that if I leave Victor I will never ever find a man who will be as good to me as he has been."

"He does seem . . . very nice."

"He *is.* He's a wonderful husband. I know that I am *lucky* to have what I do, and that to be discontented in *any* way is horribly ungrateful, and *yet* . . ." Celine's mouth quivered. "I am *so* unhappy."

"Why?" I said impotently.

Celine looked at me, her eyes wet-lashed. "Isn't life supposed to *begin* at forty?" I remembered her saying this, with an odd bitterness, the first time we'd met. "Well, I feel that *my* life is going to *end* at forty."

"Why . . . should it?"

"Because . . ." She sniffed, then tugged another tissue out of her bag. "I've been with Victor since I was twenty-two. I'd known him for only a few months when I got pregnant. It was an accident," she went on. "I had *no* desire to have a baby at that stage of my life. But I couldn't bring myself to . . . *not* have it, and Victor was thrilled. He vowed to make me and our child *very* happy and I suppose I got carried away by his enthusiasm and his optimism." Celine pressed the crumpled tissue to her eyes. "So we got married and four months later I had Philippe; then not long after that Victor bought this house . . ." Her eyes had filled again. "Which is where I've been ever since!" She bit her lip. "But now I need to *leave.*"

"Does Victor know?"

"Yes—but he refuses to discuss it."

"Well . . . he clearly adores you."

"He does adore me! But he is *so* much older than me."

"Does that matter? After so long?"

"In some ways it doesn't. But the fact is, I got married *too young.* So whenever I meet a woman like you who has waited a long time to settle down I feel so . . . *envious.*"

"Envious?" I repeated, startled. "I thought you felt sorry for me."

Celine looked at me in bewilderment. "*No.* Women like you have had years of fun—changing lovers, changing jobs, changing apartments, changing cities, changing your very *selves*—and then you can *still* marry and have children—while I just have led the same existence for seventeen years. Much of it has been taken up with Philippe, who of course I adore; but he will soon be making his own way in the world. So now I want to live a *different* sort of life."

"I see . . ."

She blew her nose, then looked at me desolately. "There's no-one else—in case you thought that."

"No, no . . ." I lied.

"I've *never* had an affair." Celine said this not with pride, but with regret. "I wish I *had,*" she continued savagely. "Then I might feel less discontented now. But I've told Victor that I'm unhappy and that it's my wish to leave."

Poor man, I thought. "And . . . what did he say?"

She shook her head. "That he wants me to stay . . . that he can't live without me. He said that I'm having a crisis, because of turning forty; so I said, 'Yes, Victor, I *am* having a crisis because of turning forty—precisely—because I want to do *more* with my life! Then he said that he would retire early so that we can spend more time together, travel, perhaps learn new languages, take on new challenges."

"Then . . . why don't you take him up on that?"

"Because I want to do these things on my *own.*"

I felt a pang for poor Victor. "I see."

"I only ever meant to be in England for a year or two. After that it was my plan to travel to South America, Indonesia, or Africa. I got no farther than Barnes! And as my birthday has approached, I've been feeling so . . . *boxed in.*" I remembered how Celine had sat in the corner of the Knole sofa at the first sitting. *I am, as you say, boxed in.* "So now I want to try to get back some of the freedom I had when I was a very young woman—before I am an old one."

"How will you do that? Will you get a job?"

"I do want to work, yes; but first I intend to find an apartment, then take things from there. I've already started looking. I told Victor that, about a month ago. So what does he do?" Celine looked at me, clearly expecting an answer.

I shrugged, taken aback. "I don't know."

"*What* does Victor do?" she demanded again.

"I've no idea."

Celine was blinking at me furiously. "He commissions a *portrait* of me!"

"But . . . it's your birthday present."

"No! It *isn't.* It's a *trap!*"

"A trap?"

She leaned towards me. "Can't you *see?* He's trying to fix my image in this house. He's worried that I'll leave, so he's trying to pin me to the wall."

I nodded slowly. "I understand . . ."

"*That's* why he's so enthusiastic about the portrait. *That's* why he wants to put it there—right *there* . . ." Celine's left index finger jabbed at the mirror. "At the very heart of this house; I think he believes it'll work like magic—like *voodoo*—keeping me here, with *him*!"

"Do you still . . . love Victor?" I asked after a moment.

Celine gave a despairing shrug. "I am very *fond* of him, but I don't want to regret, when I'm on my deathbed, in perhaps *another* forty years, that I chose to remain in my safe, comfy box, with my safe, comfy husband. There . . ." She pressed the tissue to her eyes. "You asked me whether or not I am okay. *That* is the answer."

"You said you found the sittings frustrating—but I knew that wasn't the real reason why you didn't want to be painted. It was as though you were poised for flight."

She nodded bleakly. "I was. I still *am*."

"It'll take a lot of courage to do what you say you want to do. You may find you don't like it, but then you can't go back, because you've burned your—"

"Bridges," she concluded. "I know. Well . . . I'll take that risk. But seeing Victor get so excited about the portrait made me feel very upset. Then Marcelle phoned, so I told her about it, but she wasn't *sympa*. So I decided to tell you." She reached for another tissue. "I hope you don't mind."

"No. I'm glad you've told me, because at least now I understand what's been going on. But . . . what about counselling?"

"I've suggested it to Victor—if only so he should understand that I *mean* what I say. But he insists we don't have a problem. And the more I tell him that I want to leave, the more lavish his plans for my birthday become."

"I see . . ."

"I don't *want* a big, expensive party," Celine insisted, bleakly. "I don't want a diamond ring. I don't want to go to Venice—it's such a romantic destination that it feels quite wrong. In fact, I don't want to celebrate my birthday *at all*, because I feel *so* unhappy and unsettled that I think it would be dishonest. But Victor's been making all these arrangements as though nothing's amiss. So I'll be sitting there at the Dorchester, a month from now, feeling that I'm taking part in some lavish charade! I keep asking Victor to cancel it, but he refuses. So for weeks the pressure has been building up inside me and I feel like I'm going to go . . ." Her eyes widened. *"Boom!"*

"I'm . . . sorry," I said again, impotently. "I wish I could say more than that, Celine—but I can't."

"I know you can't. Still, I'm glad I've told you." She sighed. "And now we'd better get on." She rose and went to the mantelpiece, and checked her reflection in the mirror. Then she returned to the chair. "I must let you do your job."

Celine lifted her head, and resumed the pose.

As I waited for Mike Johns to arrive three days later, I thought about Celine. Our conversation had been going round and round in my head. Now I understood why she hadn't wanted to be painted and why she just couldn't sit still. I toyed with the idea of painting an open window into her portrait. Or a mounted butterfly in a gold frame.

Since her sitting I'd spent much of the time working on the picture of Grace—I had it on the easel now; and though it was almost finished, I could see that it still wasn't *her.* It caught a good likeness but conveyed little sense of who Grace had been. I bitterly regretted having accepted the commission, and imagined the disappointment of her family and friends.

Remembering the anguished conversation I'd had with Mike about Grace I decided I'd put her painting away before he arrived, and I was about to take it off the easel when the phone rang.

I picked up. "Hello?"

"*What* do you think of personalised champagne labels?"

My mother had clearly recovered from the emotional upset of the previous week and was once again fully focussed on the wedding preparations. But I had *not* recovered; I felt a bewildered distrust of her that was seeping into my soul like damp.

"Don't you think it would be nice?" I heard her say.

"I've no idea," I answered. "I didn't know you could personalise them."

"You can—and I think it would be rather fun for the bottles to say 'Chloe and Nate' with the date of the wedding. But Chloe's not keen—so I thought I'd discuss it with you."

"Why? It's not *my* wedding, it's hers; if Chloe doesn't like personalised champagne labels, I suggest you *don't* get them."

"All right," Mum said. "No need to snap."

"I didn't snap—I just told you what I think. If you don't want my opinion about something, don't ask me."

There was a frosty silence. "Ella—I hope you're not upset about the wedding." I bristled at my mother's solicitous tone. "You've been *quite* tetchy at times, darling, so it's crossed my mind that as you're older than Chloe you might not be entirely hap—"

"Of course I'm happy for her! As happy as I possibly *can* be," I added, more truthfully. "But . . . I'm still trying to get my head round what you told me about my father, and about Lydia, and so I'm *not* in the mood to discuss wedding trivia!"

"Of course . . . I'm sorry, darling." I heard my mother sigh. "I should show more understanding, because it *is* hard for you. I always knew it would be. Which is why I protected you from it for so long."

"You protected me?"

"Yes. Of course."

"You call concealing things of such huge personal significance 'protecting'?"

"I *do*. I'm not even sure that they *are* that significant. John and his daughter are of course your relatives, but they're relative *strangers*, in that you don't know them."

"Thanks to *you* I don't know them!"

"Thanks to *him*!" she flung back. I heard her inhale, as though trying to calm herself. "Ella," she went on quietly, "John and Lydia are *not* in your life. They live nine thousand miles and eight time zones away. Forget about them."

"How *can* I, when they're my own flesh and blood? Isn't blood supposed to be—"

"Blood is *not* thicker than water," she interjected. "If it were, your father could *never* have done what he did!" I had to acknowledge the inescapable truth of this. "Nor could Roy have done what *he* did," Mum added with an air of triumph, "which was to treat you as though you were *his*. He's never made the slightest difference between you and Chloe. You do realise that, don't you?"

"Of course I do. He's been wonderful to me." *How's our Number One girl?* "I've never said otherwise, and I love Roy, but—"

"Ella, I'm very worried," I heard Mum say. "Because you told me that you *weren't* going to contact John, but now I feel you're wavering. So let me say that *were* you to do so, it would be very hard for Roy— I hope you've thought about that."

"I have, of course I have, but . . . I'm *not* going to discuss it now." I remembered what Polly had said. "And I hope to God you haven't concealed anything *else*!" During the affronted silence that followed I glanced out the window and saw Mike's car pulling up. "But my sitter's arriving—I must go."

After I'd ended the call I had to take a moment to calm myself. I splashed cold water on my cheeks then went to the mirror. As I looked at my reflection I imagined Lydia's face transposed onto it.

Drrrrrrnnnnggggggg!

I ran downstairs and opened the door. "Hi, Mike." I was relieved to see that he looked a little less sombre than he had previously. "Congratulations, by the way."

"On what?" He touched his chest. "Finally remembering to wear the blue sweater?"

"No—though I *am* glad about that—I meant on the election. You won, didn't you?"

"Yes—that was a huge relief. It's been a tough time," he added as we went up the stairs. As I followed him into the studio I saw Mike stop. He'd seen the picture of Grace, still standing on my easel. He was staring at it.

"I'll just put that away," I said brightly; I wished I'd done it before. I quickly put it back in the canvas rack, then got out Mike's portrait. "Here's yours . . ." I placed it on the easel then tied on my apron while Mike put his briefcase down by the sofa; he sat in the chair. "Right . . ." I smiled at him. "This is our final sitting, so let's just go for it."

I began to paint Mike's sweater, then I worked on his hair, blending a touch of grey into the sideburns; then adding some blue into the shadows of his jaw. And all the time we chatted about the election and about how fraught it had been.

"I'm glad to be part of the coalition," he said.

"You've got a government job?"

"Yes—I was made a junior Transport Minister."

"How brilliant."

I asked Mike what he thought about the London mayor's bicycle-hire program, and about the proposed reintroduction of the Routemaster bus. And so the time passed.

I worked intently, enjoying the scent of the paint and the linseed. Then came the moment when I put in the very last thing I ever add to a portrait—the light in the eyes. That's when I feel like Pygmalion, having life breathed into his statue; because it's that little flick of white in each pupil that finally—*ping!*—brings a portrait *alive*.

"There." I took a few steps back. The touch of titanium white in Mike's pupils had given his portrait vitality. I put down my brush. "We're done."

Mike got to his feet, then stood beside me as we studied his canvas. "That's me," he said wonderingly. It was as though he was seeing the portrait for the first time.

"I hope your Parliamentary Association like it," I said. "Above all, I hope you do."

"I . . . do like it—but I look so *thin*." It was as though he hadn't realised how much weight he'd shed.

I nodded. "That was quite a challenge. Your weight loss changed so many things about you; it altered the planes of your face. I was worried that you'd appear less friendly than before, but I think you still look very approachable and warm and . . ."

"Sad," he said.

I gazed at the portrait. "A bit—thoughtful, perhaps."

"I look sad," he insisted softly. "That's what everyone will say."

My heart sank. He was unhappy with the picture. "If you're concerned about it, Mike, there are things I can do. I can tweak the corners of the eyes and mouth—less than a millimetre would lift your expression; but the truth is, I painted what I saw. And you *did* look pretty serious a lot of the time."

I now saw in the painting the air of tragedy that I'd noticed in Mike. I'd tried to avoid it but it had crept in. "It'll need at least a month to dry," I pointed out. "Then I'll take it to be framed but—"

"Could I see it?" he asked.

"The frame? Well . . . I go to Graham and Stone on the King's Road; I was going to suggest that you go and look at their mouldings—I could come with you, if you'd like—"

Mike was shaking his head. "I meant could I see the painting that was on the easel when I got here."

"Oh. Sure . . ." I kicked myself again for not having put it away before he arrived. If only Mum hadn't distracted me with her maddening phone call.

I took Mike's canvas down and laid it on the floor, face up, so that it wouldn't drip. Then I went to the rack, lifted out the painting of Grace and put it on the easel.

Beautiful, sparkling, funny, warm . . .

None of those qualities were evident in what I'd painted, I realised dismally.

Happy, loyal, brave, strong . . .

All I'd done was replicate her features.

I heard Mike exhale. "So is it finished?"

"It's as finished as it'll ever be. I've worked on it *so* much; I keep pushing the paint about, but I'm not happy with it. It's not . . ."

"*Real,*" Mike interjected softly. "It's as if you've painted a wax-work."

I realised that I didn't much like Mike's opinions about my portraits. I remembered what he'd had to say about Mum's—*it's as though she's hiding something.* Then I realised, with a jolt, that he'd been right.

I folded my arms as we stood side by side, studying the portrait. "The problem is that I never *met* Grace," I confessed. "So I have no memory of how she talked, or moved, or laughed—or how she felt about anything. If I'd been able to see some close-up video footage of her, that would have helped, but there isn't any—I've asked; and it's hard making someone look three-dimensional when you've only got two dimensions to go on."

Mike was still staring at the portrait. "It's lifelike," he said. "But not *alive.*"

"Exactly." I gave a frustrated sigh. "But I think it's as good as it gets. I'm going to have to accept that this portrait is *not* going to be my finest achievement." And I was about to put it back when, to my surprise, Mike lifted his hand to the canvas.

He pointed to the area below Grace's bottom lip. "She had a tiny scar," he said, quietly. "Just here. It only showed when she smiled; as you've painted her smiling, it needs to be there."

"Oh . . ."

"And her eyes aren't right." He put his head to one side. "The shape's correct, but they weren't such a pure blue—there was a lot of green in them, and the rim of the iris was a darker shade, like wet slate, which gave her gaze an intensity that you haven't caught. And she had this funny little dent, just here, on her forehead. It was tiny—smaller than a pinhead—but you could see it, if you were standing close enough—and there was a mole, just here, by her lip." He pointed to the place, his hand hovering over her face.

"I see . . ." I said, bewildered.

Mike continued to stare at the painting. "She was beautiful," he murmured. "She was really . . . beautiful. And if it weren't for me, she'd still be alive."

It was as though I'd been plunged into a bath of ice water. "What do you mean?" I stammered.

Mike blinked. "It's my fault that she died."

"But . . . *how?*" My heart was thudding in my rib cage.

He went to the sofa and sank down onto it. "My life's been hell," he said quietly. "It's been hell since January 20—since it happened. The *shock* of it . . . Then not being able to *talk* about it, all these months. Not being able to confide in anyone." He closed his eyes as if he was exhausted. "Let alone confess."

"Confess . . . ?" I echoed faintly. "Confess . . . *what?*"

Mike didn't at first respond. Then he heaved a sigh so profound it seemed to come from his very depths. "That her accident was *my* fault."

My heart plummeted. Why was he telling *me* this? If his had been the car that had hit Grace, then he should be telling the police. "Was it *your* car?" I asked after a moment. My mouth had dried: I found it hard to speak. "Was it *your* black BMW?"

Mike looked up at me in bewilderment. "*No.* I didn't knock her off her bike—that's not what I mean. I only meant that if it hadn't been for me, Grace wouldn't have been cycling through Fulham Broadway that morning."

"But . . . why *was* she?" Mike didn't reply. "Her uncle said that they think she must have been staying with someone—but they've no idea who, as that person hasn't come forward."

Mike closed his eyes. "She was staying with me."

I stared at him, dumbfounded. I'd been so taken aback by the turn the conversation had taken that my brain simply failed to keep up. "You were in love with Grace," I murmured wonderingly.

How else could he have known about the tiny scar under her lip, or be able to describe the precise blue of her eyes? How else could he have known about the little dent in her forehead that could only be seen by anyone standing very close to her, as he must have been? "You loved her," I reiterated softly.

"Yes," he said brokenly. "With all my heart, I did."

I sank into a chair. "And no-one knew?"

"No-one," he confirmed blankly. "Neither of us told a soul."

"That's why you cancelled the sittings." He nodded. And that's why he'd lost so much weight, and why he'd become upset when he'd talked about what had happened to Grace. That's why he'd wept when he heard "Tears in Heaven." "How did you know her, Mike?"

"She was a member of the London Cycling Campaign. Last September she and two others came to talk to the cross-party transport committee that I'm on. We discussed cycle lanes and whether there should be more red routes on busier roads, extra mirrors on lorries—all those issues. But I found it almost impossible to focus on anything other than Grace. She was so beautiful. It was as though there was a light on inside her—a sort of dancing light that spilled in all directions."

I glanced at the portrait; now it appeared all the more flat and dull.

"After that meeting I couldn't get her out of my mind; so I phoned her, and asked her if she'd have a drink with me sometime. To my delighted surprise, she said yes. We met again and realised that we were very drawn to each other." Mike looked at me. "Have you ever been with someone, Ella, and realised that it's just so incredibly easy—that there's this effortless rapport?"

"Yes. I have," I said ruefully.

"Then you'll know that it's just the most wonderful thing. And that's how it was with Grace and me. We simply loved each other's company." Mike clasped his hands in front of him. "Sarah and I had been unhappy for a long time—we'd been trying to decide whether to stay together or call it a day. Then I met Grace," he added with a kind of wonderment. "And I was happier than I've ever been in my adult life."

"I remember how happy you seemed—when you first came here, last December."

He nodded. "Now I'm still trying to take in the fact that I'll never see Grace again, or talk to her, or hear her laugh, or hold her . . ." His voice wobbled. "I haven't been able to talk to anyone about it; so I've felt completely . . . alone. I thought about going to a bereavement counsellor, but I was worried that it might get out—it would have ended up in the papers." He looked at me. "That's *not* why I'm telling you. I'm telling you because your painting isn't right, Ella—and I *need* it to be right."

"But . . . what actually *happened*? That morning?"

Mike put his hands on his knees, as if bracing himself against some impact. "Grace had stayed with me the night before. Sarah was in New York and wasn't due to return until Thursday morning—but early on Wednesday morning I saw that a text had come in from her, to say she was flying back a day early. I realised that she'd be home within two hours; I told Grace this, and she said she'd leave straightaway. I asked her to wait until it was light, but she said she wanted to go back to her flat so she could change. I urged her to be careful, because there'd been a hard frost. She told me she was always careful; then she put on her helmet and I kissed her goodbye . . ." Mike smiled. "It's not easy kissing someone when they're wearing a bicycle helmet, and we were laughing about it." He paused. "Sarah had texted that she didn't have her keys, so I waited until she arrived, at about nine, then set off for the House of Commons.

"As I drove up to the New King's Road I saw that the right-hand turn to Fulham Broadway was blocked off. I assumed this was because of road works and so didn't think anything of it as I followed the diversion. Then—I had London Radio on—I heard a report about a woman cyclist who'd been injured in a hit-and-run incident at Fulham Broadway. I immediately worried that it might have been Grace, so I called her on my Bluetooth, but she didn't reply. I told myself this was because she was in class, and to reassure myself I phoned her school, without saying who I was. They told me Grace hadn't arrived. By now I was in a panic. When I got to work I phoned the Chelsea and Westminster Hospital, as that's where anyone injured at Fulham Broadway is taken. But the nurse in the intensive care unit wouldn't confirm or deny that Grace was there; so then I knew that it *was* her."

"How terrible . . ."

Mike's eyes were wet with tears. "It was . . . *hell*. I had a meeting to go to, then a lunch; after that, there was a debate. I don't know how I got through that day. All I wanted to do was rush to the hospital, but I knew that I couldn't, even if I'd been free, because Grace's parents would be there. All I could do was to keep checking the news, which I did, every two or three minutes. By now there was a photo of Grace, and a brief biography of her on a number of news websites. And I was annoyed, because they'd all got her surname spelt wrong, without the E, and I was staring at it, furious that they couldn't get something as basic as that right, when the piece was suddenly updated to say that . . . that she'd . . ." Mike's head dropped to his hands.

"I'm so sorry, I breathed."

Mike looked up at me. "It was *my* fault. If Grace hadn't been with me, she wouldn't have been rushing away from my house in the icy darkness, because my wife was coming home. She wouldn't have been hit by a car, she wouldn't have struck her head on the kerb, and she wouldn't have been in hospital . . . *dying.*" He covered his eyes with his left hand. "*That's* why I feel responsible for what happened to Grace. And I've spent the last four months pretending that everything's normal, when my life's been a living hell. I hardly eat. I can't sleep. Work's been my only distraction from the pain and stress of a bereavement I can never admit to."

"Your wife doesn't know?"

Mike shook his head. "She thinks I'm like this because of the problems we've had." He let out his breath. "There's no-one in the world I can tell. When I realised you were going to *paint* Grace, I was . . . shocked. I wanted to talk to you about her then; I wanted to tell you everything I knew about her, but I bit my lip, because I was afraid. Yet when I saw the portrait just now, and realised how much is . . . *missing* from it, I knew I *had* to tell you, whatever the consequences."

I nodded slowly. "I won't say a thing, Mike."

"Please . . . don't."

"But her parents—they'd surely want to know; they need to understand why she was where she was."

"No. I couldn't face them. They'd say that I was a sleazy married man who'd messed about with their daughter. They'd blame me for her death. And I don't need them to do that, because I'm going to be blaming *myself,* for the rest of my life."

"Mike, you urged Grace to stay until it was light—she chose to leave. It's not your fault that she was knocked off her bike—in fact, that could have happened to her in broad daylight, in good conditions. She was just . . . unlucky. But didn't she even tell a best friend about you?"

"She simply told her closest friend that she'd started seeing someone called Mike, and that she was happy—which she was."

"Wouldn't your number have been on her mobile phone?"

"Her mobile was never found. It might have gone down a grating or been crushed by a van or lorry and the pieces swept up. But yes, my number was on it—and all my messages. Like I've got all her messages on mine." He put his hand into his pocket, pulled out his phone and looked at it. "I read them over and over again. And I listen to her voice mails to get that momentary illusion that she's still alive, and I . . ." He was pressing the buttons now, and I realised that he was going to play me Grace's voice messages. I didn't want to hear them.

"Mike. I really—"

"No, please . . . you *must.*" He handed me the phone, and my heart sank. Then, as I saw what was on the screen, it lifted again . . .

There was Grace. She was leaning against a kitchen counter, laughing into the lens. *Why are you filming me?* I heard her say. *Be-*

cause I'm nuts about you, Mike answered. Grace laughed, then picked up a bowl and offered it to him. *Then have a Brazil,* she giggled. *I hope this isn't going on YouTube,* she teased. *Certainly not,* Mike said. *It's so I can take my phone out from time to time during the day and look at you, and feel like I'm with you, because that's a wonderful feeling.*

Now, as Grace turned, I could see her profile; I could see the prominence of her cheekbones, the slight flare of her jaw, the curve and shape of her ear and the length and angle of her throat. *Smile, Grace* I heard Mike say. She turned back to the lens, smiled shyly and blew him a kiss. Then the screen went dark.

Mike got to his feet and picked up his briefcase. For a moment I thought he was going to leave. But now he was opening his case and pulling out a charger. He inserted the jack into his mobile, then handed the whole thing to me. "You can copy this onto your hard drive while I wait."

"Yes. I can. Of course I can. Thanks, Mike. *Thank you . . .*" I plugged the cable into my computer, opened a file, then downloaded the video and clicked on SAVE. *Saving . . .* Then I hit PLAY. There, enlarged to the full width of my screen, was Grace's living, breathing, moving, talking, laughing, smiling face. I could see everything I needed to see—the form and depth and mobility of her features and, most important, the life in them.

I looked at the portrait and knew what to do.

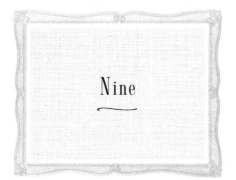

Nine

I spent most of Saturday engrossed in Grace's portrait—lost in the curves and shadows of her face, I replayed Mike's footage of her over and over again and wondered if he'd ever recover from the loss of his relationship with her; I wondered wether he'd ever be able to tell his wife—after fifteen years of marriage, perhaps he wished that he could. I wondered whether Mike would go to Grace's memorial service in September or if he'd feel he should stay away. Then I wondered what one word *he* would have chosen to encapsulate his feelings about her. As my brush moved across the canvas I thought about my mother and John; within twenty-four hours he'd be in London—the thought made me dizzy and anxious. I thought about Lydia, and Iris and Celine. And then my thoughts returned, as they always did, to Nate.

He'd messaged me earlier in the week to say he'd still be in Helsinki on Saturday, so wouldn't be able to make this week's sitting. I consoled myself with the thought that the delay would at least mean the portrait process would continue for longer. I even wondered about making deliberately slow progress in order to justify asking him for a few extra sittings, and then felt a tremor of shame at my selfishness.

On Sunday I woke late. Seeing how sunny it was I thought I'd go for a long walk—I'd been closeted too much in the studio lately. I meant to go up to Sloane Square and then back, but as I crossed the railway bridge I decided to turn down Lots Road and have a look at the auction house. *Previewing Now* announced the sandwich board on the pavement outside. I pushed the door open and entered the hangar-like building, crammed to the rafters, as usual, with a motley assortment of artefacts, antiques and household goods. I walked past the suites of modern leather furniture and the Persian carpets hanging on their rails. There was a huge rocking horse, a leather rhino, and a footstool upholstered in the British flag. In a glass case was also a rather lovely silver inkwell in the shape of a shell. I peered at it.

"That's George the Third," said a familiar voice. Whirling round, I saw Nate. I suddenly wished that I'd worn something prettier than my jeans and a T-shirt; why hadn't I made more of an effort with my hair and face? I felt my face flush with pleasure and surprise.

"What are *you* doing here?" I glanced round, half expecting to see Chloe amongst the people inspecting the lots.

He shrugged. "My apartment's only a few blocks away. I sometimes come here on Sunday mornings just to look—occasionally I buy something. Anyway, that inkwell . . ." He glanced at the catalogue in his hands. ". . . is London silver, circa 1810—estimate one hundred to one hundred and fifty pounds."

"So . . . is Chloe here?"

Nate shook his head. "She's gone to see your folks."

"Really? I haven't spoken to her for a bit." Again, I felt a rush of guilt. "I've been buried with work," I added lamely.

"I only got back from Helsinki last night, so she said that she'd let me off coming with her because she just wants to talk about wedding things with them. Anyway, I'm at a bit of a loose end." I nodded, unable to think of anything to say. "So . . . what are you doing now?"

"Erm . . . nothing much."

"Good—because I was just about to go and find myself some lunch. Will you join me?"

"Yes." I glanced down at my jeans. "As long it's not anywhere too smart."

He smiled. "You look great. So . . . where shall we go?"

"Megan's deli?" I suggested. "Though it gets busy on Sundays. Or we could just go down to the river, maybe . . ."

"Let's do that," Nate decided.

So Nate and I walked along Lots Road in the shadow of the power station. We turned onto the Thames Path and headed towards Albert Bridge and strolled along Cheyne Walk in the bright sunshine, past the barges and houseboats rocking on their moorings.

We sat on a bench and gazed across the river at Battersea Power Station and at the towers of Chelsea Harbour, watching the terns wheel and dive above the water. Then we walked on, talking of politics, and the weather, the price of groceries and the last movie we'd each seen.

"Is this place okay?" Nate said as we reached the Cheyne Walk Brasserie.

"Looks good."

We managed to get a corner table and sank onto the blue leather banquette.

"Would you like a glass of wine?" he asked.

"Yes—please."

"How about a bottle?"

"Oh, no—I couldn't manage a whole bottle."

"To share, I meant." He laughed. "With me."

"Oh—a much better idea."

Nate smiled. "It's funny seeing you outside of the studio. But I miss having you staring at me in that crazy way of yours."

"I don't stare on Sundays," I said as the wine arrived. "I give my eyeballs the day off. So . . ." I raised my glass. "Cheers."

He lifted his. *"Salut."*

Over the smoked salmon starter the conversation turned to Nate's father—I thought, with a rush of adrenaline, about my own father, who was perhaps even now landing in London, if he hadn't already done so.

"Ella." Nate lowered his glass. "Can I ask you something?"

"Of course."

"It's a little personal."

"Really? Like—what's my favourite colour? Well, if you must know, it's Phthalocyanine Turquoise, with Transparent Oxide Yellow coming a close second. What's yours?"

"Er . . . green. But that's not what I was going to ask. I was going to ask you something serious." I already knew. "Tell me to get lost if you want to, but how could your mom . . ." He paused, then shook his head. "How could she *not* have told you something so important?"

"Chloe's obviously told you what's happened."

"Yes . . ." Nate looked bewildered. "So . . . your father *did* contact you."

"He did. In fact, I have to confess that he'd already done so when I talked to you about him at the last sitting."

"Ah . . ."

"But I didn't tell you because . . . well, I was worried you might tell Chloe, who might have told Mum."

"I know how to keep secrets, Ella. But *now* I understand why you were so distressed . . . I . . . hated seeing you like that."

I realised that Nate *had* simply been consoling me when he held me in his arms that day. As my mother had correctly identified, he was a compassionate sort of man—and a tactile one too, not afraid to give someone a hug if they're feeling low. What a fool I'd been! I banished my dangerous, deluded and futile fantasy that his touch had ever meant anything more. "I've been discovering that there are all *sorts* of things my mother hasn't told me," I said. "Secrecy seems to be rather a habit with her."

"So do you think you'll want to be in touch with . . . John?" he asked. "And with your sister?"

My sister? "My sister" had only ever meant Chloe. Suddenly I realised it meant another woman too, a woman whom I'd met just once, for a few moments, when we were both very young children. I gave a helpless shrug. "I . . . don't *know*. I'm still really confused . . . so . . . I'd rather not talk about it, if that's okay." I heard the sharpness in my voice and felt myself blushing furiously.

"Of course," Nate murmured. "I didn't mean to intrude."

"You didn't—how could I possibly think you were intruding when I told you so much about it last time?" I reached for my wineglass. "But there's enough going on in the family at the moment, with the wedding, so I just want to . . . drop it all for now."

"I understand. Consider it dropped."

We ate our dessert, then the bill came.

I reached for my bag but Nate refused my offer to go Dutch.

"We're going Italian," he insisted. "So I wouldn't hear of it. Remember, I invited you."

"Thank you. I'm glad you did. It's been lovely."

As we left the restaurant I felt happy to think I'd had this extra time with Nate, and in this unexpected way. As we strolled back along the embankment, Nate's phone rang.

"Sorry, Ella. Okay if I take this call?"

"Sure." I hoped it wasn't Chloe. A call from Chloe would break the spell.

"Hi, Chloe," Nate said. "Yes . . . fine." Chloe's clear, slightly penetrating voice cut through the sunlit air. *I'm still in Richmond,* "I heard her say. *Where are you?* As Nate looked at me, I wondered whether he'd tell Chloe that he'd just had lunch with me. "Well, I've just bumped into Ella . . ." *How funny . . .* "Yes," he said. His face had flushed. *Give her my love.* "Will do . . . Okay. See you later, then, Chloe." *I'll see you later, Nate darling. I can't wait.*

. . .

Back at the house, there was a message from Roy on my voice mail asking me to call him. I did.

"I'm sorry I haven't been in touch with you about our lunch," he told me. "Work's been crazy, but I've got a few days off now. Would tomorrow be okay?"

"Yes—where shall we meet?"

"I thought somewhere close to you. How about that pub—the Chelsea Potter? It's halfway down the King's Road—I'm sure you know it."

"I do." It was dangerously close to the Café de la Paix. What if we encountered my father? "I'm . . . not sure about meeting there, Roy."

"Well . . . it would be convenient for us both, as I can just walk up to Sloane Square tube afterwards; but look, don't worry, we can go somewhere else. What about—?"

"It's okay," I said suddenly. "The Chelsea Potter's fine."

"Great. So I'll see you there at, what . . . one?"

"Could we make it half past twelve?" Then we'd easily be out by two-thirty, which would give me time to leave the danger zone before three o'clock.

"Half twelve it is, then," said Roy.

I went up to the King's Road an hour beforehand, as there were some things I needed to do. First I went into Graham and Stone and bought lots of oil paints, some canvas stretchers and a few brushes. I looked at frames, and decided that the Dutch Black with the brass scrolling at the corners would suit Mike's portrait. I took a photo of it to email to him. Then I went up to Waterstone's, as there was a new biography of Whistler that I wanted to buy. On the way there I passed the Café de la Paix. How strange to think that in three hours' time my father would be seated at one of the tables inside. I quickened my steps and walked on.

Maybe I should send him a text to say that I wouldn't be coming. I hadn't replied to any of his emails. To do so, if only to say that I didn't wish to see him, would have been to begin a dialogue with him that I just didn't want. Even so, I felt guilty at the thought of him wasting his time. But no—there was no need for me to feel guilty about *anything* vis-a-vis my father, I decided. If he chose to spend a few hours in a café on the King's Road, then that was his concern, not mine.

In Waterstone's I looked for the Whistler biography but couldn't find it. As the assistant went to see if there might be a copy in the stockroom I browsed through the novels on the tables; I'd just picked up the new Kate Atkinson when I noticed several piles of Sylvia Shaw's latest offering, *Dead Right.*

I read the back cover copy, with its gushing hyperbole: *Riveting . . .* Daily Mail; *Thrilling . . .* GQ; *It's Shaw good! . . .* Express. Then I studied the author's photo on the inside back flap. It was more flattering than the one in *Hello!* but she still looked rather grim and tight-lipped, as though she thought it inappropriate for someone who wrote about murder and mayhem to smile. I turned to the dedication page—*For Max*—and marvelled that she'd never known about her husband's affair. Or had she suspected Max was in love with another woman?

The bookshop assistant reappeared and told me they didn't have the Whistler in stock, so I ordered it, then briefly looked at the greeting cards. There was already a selection for Father's Day so I bought one to give Roy—*I've Got the World's Greatest Dad*—then left the shop, reflecting that I pretty much did. It was Roy who'd taken me to the park and taught me to ride a bike. It was Roy who'd helped me with my homework and who'd turned up to watch me in school hockey matches, concerts and plays. It was Roy who'd coped with the temperamental highs and lows of my teenage years, and who'd never failed to come out at two in the morning to get me safely home from parties and clubs. It was Roy who'd paid my art school fees and who'd lent me half the deposit to buy my house.

I stepped inside Chelsea Potter and there he was, waving at me.

I went to his table, greeted him with a kiss, then hung my carrier bag containing my new paints and brushes on the back of my chair.

As I sat down he asked me what I'd like to drink, then handed me a menu. I looked at it. "I'll just have soup, please."

"Have more than that, Ella."

"I'm not hungry, thanks; I'm a bit . . . stressed."

"Well, that's hardly surprising. Right . . . I'll go order." Roy went to the bar and returned with a pint of lager for him and a Diet Coke for me.

We sipped our drinks, then he lowered his glass. "Ella, I just wanted to talk to you," he said. "Because I felt it was important, firstly, that I should tell you, face-to-face, that I had *no* idea about . . . well, what you've at long last learned. If *I* had known, I'd have compelled your mother to tell you."

"Which is why she concealed it from you too. Mum's good at keeping secrets, isn't she?" I poked the island of ice in my drink. "I keep thinking that she should have been a spy, not a dancer."

Roy gave a hollow laugh. "I love your mother, Ella, but she's handled this *so* badly. I'm appalled at the degree to which she's . . . *manipulated* things."

I know how I want things to be. "Did you ever guess?" I asked him. "About Lydia, I mean?"

He shook his head. "I did once ask your mother whether she thought you might have any brothers or sisters in Australia. She replied that she didn't want to think about whether or not there were—which wasn't a lie, and wasn't the truth, as we now know. But the second, more important thing I wanted to say to you today was that I feel your mother's putting pressure on you *not* to reply to . . . to your . . ." He faltered.

"To John," I said gently.

"To John. Yes . . ." He cleared his throat, then paused before continuing. "She's insisting that you mustn't have anything to do with him—on *my* account. But I want you to know that if you do decide to contact . . . John, then I'd be . . . fine about it, Ella."

"But that would make you very unpopular with Mum."

His smile flickered. "So be it. You need to put your own feelings before hers—or mine." Roy fell silent while the barman brought my minestrone and his fish pie. "Anyway," he said when the barman had moved away, "I'll support you, Ella. In whatever you decide to do."

"Thanks, Roy. But I've given it a lot of thought." He glanced at me anxiously. "And I'm *not* going to get in touch with him."

Relief flickered across his features. "It's not long since you found out . . ." he said fairly. "Your feelings may change."

"I don't think they will. So I'm not going to answer his emails. And I'm certainly *not* going to see him."

"See him?"

"Yes." I picked up my spoon, even though I wasn't hungry. "I wouldn't see him even if he was in London right now. I wouldn't see him even if he was in *this* part of London, just a few minutes away from where we're sitting. I'd walk *right* past him, without giving him so much as a glance."

Roy looked surprised. "Well, he *isn't* here, Ella—but I think that for you to do that would be . . . *sad.*"

"*He* caused enough sadness, didn't he?" I began to eat my soup.

Roy studied my face a moment. Then he said, "People make mistakes, Ella."

"They do," I shot back, and heard the anger in my voice. "But what he did wasn't a 'mistake'—it was a calculated, cruel choice. That's why I can't forgive him."

"Well . . . please *try.* Not least because hanging on to the anger and pain will only hurt you, Ella."

We ate in silence for a while. Finally, I said, "Has Chloe said much about it to you?"

"She said she wasn't entirely surprised, but she was quite upset. I don't think she likes the idea of you having another sister any more than she ever liked the idea of you having another father. When she was about five and had worked everything out, she used to tell me as I was putting her to bed that she was afraid John would come to the house one day and take you away."

I laughed darkly. "An unlikely scenario, given that he was nine thousand miles away and not remotely interested in me."

"You don't know that he wasn't," Roy pointed out.

"I *do* know—because he never got in touch. It was as though I was suddenly . . . *nothing* to him." I pushed my soup bowl aside. "But now that we're talking about all of this, Roy, there's something I've long meant to ask you—about my adoption."

"Really? What did you want to know?"

"Whether, when you applied to adopt me, John had to give his consent."

"Let me think." Roy narrowed his eyes. "When your mother and I first saw our lawyer about it, he *did* say that John would have to agree to it, yes—presumably because his name would have been on your birth certificate. Your mum handled the application herself. All I had to do was to go along to the court one morning and satisfy the judge that I wasn't insane, didn't have a criminal record, was indeed married to your mother—she'd already submitted our marriage certificate—and that I was, as stated in the application, employed as a surgeon and would be able to provide for you. I do remember the judge asking your mum about John's whereabouts; she said she had no idea where he was."

"But that wasn't true. She knew that he was in Australia. She didn't tell the judge that?"

"No. If she had, I'd definitely have remembered it, as I didn't know that myself then—any more than you did."

"That's right. I only got *that* out of her when I was eleven."

"Well, as you say, your mother's good at keeping secrets."

"But . . . surely she *would've* had an address for him, because he had to have signed the divorce papers."

"Well . . . I'm not sure whether or not he did sign them. In cases of desertion the divorce is granted automatically, after two years, if neither side contests it, and I always had the impression that's what happened in their case." Roy heaved a bewildered sigh. "Your mother *may* have told our lawyer, privately, that John was in

Australia—I don't know. But the fact that she was able to say he'd made no contact for three years made adoption by me, as your stepfather, fairly straightforward. Why are you asking about it now?"

"It's been puzzling me, and I didn't want to ask Mum, because I don't want to talk to her about *any* of it now. I don't think *she* does either, since she's just carrying on as though everything's normal."

"She's probably blocked it all out—you know that's always been her way with anything she finds painful or unpleasant. She just slams down the mental shutters. And of course she's very preoccupied with the wedding, as am I. I want Chloe to have a really memorable day."

"I'm sure it will be." I thought again of Nate, standing at the altar, of his face when he saw Chloe . . . "Not long now."

Roy nodded. "The RSVPs are arriving thick and fast—everyone's coming."

"That's good. Mum must be pleased."

"Yes . . . Would you like a dessert, Ella?"

"No thanks. In fact—Yikes! It's half past two—I must go."

"Sure," Roy said, looking slightly surprised. "I'm glad we've had this chat."

"Me too—and thank you again for what you've said." As Roy went to the bar to pay I remembered what Polly had said. *He'll support you, Ella. I know he would.* She'd been right—but so had I, in predicting that he'd be upset. I was glad to know I wouldn't be exposing him to any more painful feelings.

Roy had to wait a few minutes to pay, so by the time we left the pub it had gone twenty to three. We hugged goodbye, then Roy walked towards Sloane Square and I went the other way, with a sick feeling gathering in my stomach at the thought of how close my father now was.

I tried to distract myself by thinking about work. I was going to see Iris again in two days' time. Then there'd be another sitting with Nate, on Saturday morning. Then I was going to do Celine's last three sittings over three days, as time was short—her birthday was rapidly approaching. I'd also spoken to the couple in Chichester—Mr. and Mrs. Berger. They wanted the portrait for their silver wedding celebration in late July so I was going down there in early June and get it done in a week. I was glad I'd bought the new paints—I was certainly going to need them.

I stopped dead. I'd left the paints at the pub. I'd put the bag on the back of my chair and had forgotten it when we left.

I ran back to the Chelsea Potter. The bag had already been handed in. I had to wait while someone went upstairs to the office to retrieve it, and by the time I left again, it was five to three. My father would be arriving. My heart banging, I began to walk down the road, fast—and there the café was, on my side, just a hundred yards or so ahead. What if he was there already and saw me go by? What if he rushed out and pleaded with me in the street? What had I been *thinking* in agreeing to have lunch within five minutes of where *he* was going to be? Had it been raining, I could have concealed myself behind an umbrella, but it was a bright, sunny day and I'd only have made myself more conspicuous.

Now the Café de la Paix was less than fifty yards away. I decided to cross to the other side of the road. I stopped at the kerb and waited for a number 22 bus to rumble past and was momentarily distracted by the sight, all the way up the back of it, of Polly's massively magnified thumb and forefinger, holding a memory card. Then I realised that crossing the road was hardly going to help: I'd be no less visible from the other side of the street.

I saw a taxi coming towards me, its carriage work gleaming like treacle in the sunshine. I hailed it, climbed in, then sank right back into the corner of the seat as we drove past Starbucks, Sweaty Betty and India Jane. Now we were within ten yards of Café de la Paix. With its full-length glass windows facing the street, it was as transparent as a fish tank.

I could see the barista making coffee, and a man of about sixty standing at the counter, but he was too tall and thin to be John. Waiting behind him were a couple of smoochy-looking teenagers. At a table in the window was a plump woman in a blue sleeveless dress, reading *The Independent*. Suddenly I felt heat flood my cheeks. For there, at the other window table, was my father. His face looked weathered and lined, but he was instantly recognisable from the photo he'd sent. He was still handsome, and broad-shouldered, though his hair was iron grey now, and swept back, giving him a leonine appearance. He was wearing a light suit over a white shirt.

By now we had drawn almost level with the café. I pressed myself farther back into the seat, desperately hoping he wouldn't see me through the taxi's quarter light window. There was a large *Thank You for Not Smoking* sticker on it, so I sunk right down so it would at least partly obscure me, and lifted my hand to the side of my face. Through my splayed fingers I could see that my father wasn't looking at the taxi at all; his eyes flickered over the passersby, his head turning from side to side. Now he'd spotted a dark-haired woman of about my age, but as he realized she wasn't me, he glanced away. I expected the taxi to crawl past the café, but to my dismay we suddenly stopped—there was a red light ahead. We were right outside now, the full length of the taxi reflected in the café's window. All that separated me from my father were two panes of glass. As I saw the anxiety on his face my heart contracted with pity. I imagined jumping out of the cab and going into the café.

How can I *not* do that, I asked myself miserably, when he's sitting there, *right* there, not ten feet away, looking for me? Then I thought of myself, age five, sitting at the window in our flat, looking for *him*. I'd sat there not just for a few hours, but for a year . . .

The traffic light changed. We began to move forward, quickly picking up speed, and my father was behind me now, as the taxi drove on.

"It's so nice to see you again." Iris smiled as she opened the door of her flat to me two days later. "This is our third sitting, isn't it?" she asked as I stepped inside.

"It is; we had a gap because you were out of London for a while, and then you were ill. But it doesn't matter," I added as I followed her down the hallway. "I once had a sitter who was so busy, her portrait took eighteen months to complete."

Iris gave me a rueful smile. "Given my age, I don't think we can risk it taking *that* long."

We went into the sitting room. "You look in fine fettle, Iris."

"I'm not doing *too* badly." She sat down on the sofa, leaning her cane against the arm. "Just this morning I was thinking that I've already outlived my mother by twenty years. But then, she'd been worn down by the war, and her life wasn't easy afterwards."

"What about your father? Did he reach a good age?" I put my equipment down.

Even as I asked the question I remembered that Iris hadn't told me anything about her father—she'd only mentioned her stepfather.

"My father died at thirty-seven," she replied evenly.

"So young . . ."

I wondered if Iris would explain what had happened to him, but she didn't seem to want to say anything more. Now, as I opened the easel, I inevitably thought about my own father. He'd be getting ready to leave London; he'd probably be making his way to the airport right now.

I got out my palette and began to mix the colours.

"Was I sitting like this?" Iris asked.

I looked at her, then at the canvas. "You were. But if you could just fold your right hand over your left—you've got your left over your right; and if you could lift your chin a little . . . and look *this* way . . . That's lovely."

As I began to paint we chatted about what was in the news. Then Iris told me that Sophia had gone to the Chelsea Flower Show that morning, but that she herself had always much preferred Hampton Court. She asked me whether I ever held exhibitions of my work.

"No. The Royal Society of Portrait Painters have an annual show and I might take part in that next year, otherwise I don't exhibit my work, because I'm painting on commission."

"You should have an exhibition of your own," she said.

"Well . . . maybe I will. I could ask a few of my more recent sitters to lend me their portraits; they could all come in the clothes that I'd painted them in. Would you come if I did that, Iris?"

"I'd be delighted to."

I could do it in September, I reflected. On my birthday. "I'll give it some thought," I said. Then I asked Iris about the paintings on her sitting room walls: there was a very fine Scottish landscape, a couple of beautifully executed botanical paintings and a geometric nude she told me was by Euan Uglow. But all I really wanted to talk about was the picture of the two little girls.

"Iris, I hope you don't mind my asking," I said at last. "But when I first came here you started telling me about the painting in your bedroom—the one by Guy Lennox?"

She nodded. "I remember, of course. But I didn't finish telling you the story, did I?"

"No, but I'd love to hear the end of it—if you're okay with telling me." It had occurred to me that she might have changed her mind for some reason.

"I'm happy to tell you—in fact, it was on my mind to do so. But I'm a little stiff today; would you mind fetching the painting for me?"

"Of course."

I put down my palette and brush then went out of the sitting room and along the hallway to Iris's room. There was the picture, in its place by her bed. I looked at it for a moment—captivated as before by the tenderness of the composition; then I lifted it off its hook, leaving a ghostly rectangle.

"Thank you," Iris said as I handed it to her. She placed it on her lap. "I can't recall where I was . . ."

I went back to my easel. "You told me that Guy Lennox was commissioned to paint a very rich man named Peter Loden, who

then started an affair with Guy's wife." I picked up the palette and
brush.

"That's right. It must have been dreadful for Guy. But—and *this*
was where I left off, I remember now—far worse was to come. Edith
told Guy that she wanted a divorce—that was a terrible enough blow,
but she also said that she was not prepared to admit to having committed adultery."

I began to paint Iris's hair. "I see."

"She argued that to have her name besmirched in a 'scandal'
would damage their two girls socially in years to come. Remember,
divorce was such a different thing all those years ago. It left a stain
on the life of everyone involved. Iris said that in order to protect the
girls *he* would have to be the adulterous party."

"Oh . . ."

"She added that if he didn't consent to it, she'd make sure he
never saw his daughters again. So, caught between a rock and a hard
place, Guy agreed."

"Oh, the poor man!"

"Poor man indeed," Iris agreed. "It must have been devastating
for him. But he went to a hotel somewhere on the south coast, where
he met a young woman who'd taken part in this kind of charade
before—for a fee, naturally. The chambermaid opened the door the
next morning to see them sitting up in bed together, and within
three months Edith had her divorce. But it turned out that Guy had
fallen on his sword for nothing. When, a short time later, Edith
married Peter Loden, she changed the girls' surname to Loden's.
Guy, outraged, went to court to contest it, at which point Edith carried out her earlier threat. She got an injunction, barring him from
having any contact with his children, who were then just over two
years, and twelve months."

I mixed a little more zinc white into the hair tone. "How was
Edith able to do this?"

"She made all sorts of charges against Guy—the main one being that he was mentally unstable, due to having been gassed during the war. And she must have convinced the judge, because the injunction was granted. For a period of five years Guy was not to contact, or attempt to contact, his children."

I lowered my brush. "How terrible."

"It was . . . *inhuman.* But he went on working—he needed the distraction of it almost more than the money. Three years later, in the summer of 1934, he was walking through St. James's Park. He was carrying his easel because he'd just been doing a sitting. As he approached the lake, he saw two little girls. He knew at once that they were his daughters. He stood and watched them for a while. They were playing with a red ball, and they had a dog with them, a Norfolk terrier called Bertie." I wondered whether Iris also knew the names of the girls but I didn't dare stop her to ask: I was suddenly desperate to learn what had happened.

She narrowed her eyes as she continued. "Their nanny was sitting on a bench nearby, knitting. Guy didn't at first know what to do. He didn't speak to the girls—not just because he was forbidden by law from doing so, but because it was clear that they had no idea who he was. He didn't want to frighten them, you see. So he spoke to the nanny: he explained that he was a portraitist and asked whether he might have her permission to paint this charming scene. Knowing exactly who he was, she agreed." Now I understood the nanny's puzzling expression in the picture—it was one of complicity. "So . . ." Iris shifted her position on the sofa a little. "Guy set up his easel a few yards away, and he painted the girls while they played, occasionally chatting to them. It was the first contact he'd had with his daughters for more than three years."

"How tragic," I murmured.

"It *was* tragic. He came to the park every morning for the next four days and continued to paint them. But when he arrived the fifth day, they weren't there. He later discovered that their mother had found out—the girls must have said something—and their visits to the park had been stopped. Guy Lennox never saw his children again." Her voice trembled.

"Not even when the injunction ended?"

"No. Because by then it was too late."

"Why? Didn't his daughters *want* to see him after so long?"

"No, that wasn't the reason." Iris shook her head. "In the summer of 1936 the Spanish Civil War started. In August of that year Guy joined the International Brigades and went to Spain. He survived fierce fighting near Madrid . . ." She gripped the painting in her lap. "But in March 1937 he was killed at Guadalajara." Tears shone in her eyes.

"Oh, that's so sad," I exclaimed. "*Now* I understand."

Iris looked up at me, sharply. "What do you understand?"

"Well . . . why the painting makes you feel so sad. It's a . . . heartbreaking story." Iris nodded slowly. "But you said that you bought the painting on an impulse, knowing nothing about it—not even who it was by; you obviously researched its background very thoroughly."

"I did. Most of it I learned in 1963 from my husband's friend Hugh, who took it to show to his uncle."

"You said his uncle had known Guy Lennox."

"Yes. He'd known him quite well. When Hugh brought the painting back and told me what his uncle had said about it, I was . . . shocked." She paused. "Then I took it back to the antiques shop where I'd bought it, and I asked the man there about the woman who'd sold it to him. He found her name and address in his purchase book and, as she lived close by, I went and knocked on her door. She was happy to talk to me and confirmed that she'd found the picture in her late brother's attic. He'd never married or had children, so she was clearing his house after he died."

"You said that he'd worked for Guy Lennox."

"That's right—he'd been his studio assistant. She told me that she'd thought the painting might have been by her brother, and since she already had a number of his paintings she'd decided to sell this one. When I told her what I had found out about it, she guessed that her brother had taken it to his own home after Guy's death."

"Would Guy have told him who the girls in the painting were?"

"Perhaps not—it was so very personal, wasn't it? But she thought it likely that her brother *had* known as the two men had got on well. She thought that it might have been his intention to try to give the picture to the girls. But then the war started and everything was in chaos, so it just stayed in his attic until he himself died."

"You went to so much trouble about that painting, Iris," I said impulsively.

"I did." She looked at me for a moment or two. It was an odd, penetrating sort of look and I suddenly realised that she must be tired and was hoping that I'd go. I glanced at my watch. It was ten past three. The sitting was over.

I began to pack up my easel and paints. "Thank you for telling me about it, Iris. I'm glad to have heard the story, sad though it is." I clipped her portrait into the canvas carrier, then gathered up the dustsheet. "So . . . is the same time next week okay for you?"

"Yes," she answered. "It's fine." She pushed herself to her feet. "I'll see you then, my dear."

I picked everything up and we walked to the door. I smiled good-bye, then went out, pulling the front door closed behind me. I walked to the elevator and pressed the button. I heard it begin to grind upwards, then clank to a halt. And I was about to pull back the grille, when my hand stopped. I turned and looked at Iris's front door; then, with a fluttering in my chest, I walked back down the corridor. I knocked on it.

After a moment or two I heard the chain being taken off. As she opened the door, Iris looked at me, expectantly.

"Iris," I said. "I've come back because I've been wondering who the girls in the painting were. And I've just realised who they were. They were Agnes and Iris, weren't they?"

She studied me for a moment, then nodded slowly. "Yes. They were."

"It's you in the painting—you and your sister. And Guy Lennox was your father."

"I was waiting for you to understand, Ella. I knew you would." She pulled back the door and I stepped inside.

"I was so absorbed in the story that I didn't . . . make the connection. Then it suddenly came to me with a little thud, here." I laid my hand on my chest. "And *that's* why the painting makes you feel so sad."

"Yes. That's why. Please come . . ." I set my easel and the canvas carrier down then followed Iris back to the sitting room. She sat down, propped her cane against the sofa, then picked up the painting. I sat down next to her and we held it between us. As I looked at it, I felt, like a sudden, unexpected blow, the intense sadness and yearning that lay behind it.

"So that's why you said you were 'shocked' when Hugh told you the story," I said.

"I *was* shocked," Iris responded softly, "because he'd said the name Edith Roche. I'd never known my mother had been an artist's model, or that she'd been married before. But she had. To Guy Lennox."

I lifted my finger to the darting figure of the younger girl, then glanced at Iris. "I can see now that it *could* be you, though it's hard to tell because she's painted in profile, and slightly blurred to give the impression of movement."

"That's why I didn't recognise myself—but then, I didn't expect to see myself in a portrait. Nor did I recognise Agnes." Iris pointed to the older figure. "Here her hair's long; when the war started she had it cut very short, which is how she always wore it after that. There *were* times, before I knew the truth about the picture, when I fancied the older girl *did* resemble Agnes, but I dismissed it as coincidence. And the nanny's features are painted in an impressionistic way—

added to which, this was a model for a larger picture, so Guy hadn't put in the detail he would have otherwise, had he been able to continue the painting."

"When I first came here, Iris, I asked you if you'd ever had your portrait painted. You replied that you had, but a long time ago. This is that portrait."

"Yes. And when I saw it for the first time in that shop I felt as though I'd been not just drawn to it, but almost *guided* to it. I had this overwhelming sense that I was connected to it. But I couldn't have known how or why."

"You said you showed it to your mother."

"I did—because I was staying with her at the time. She reacted to it negatively. I assumed that was because she'd thought I'd been extravagant, but I was wrong. It was because she knew at once what the picture was and who the artist had been. It must have made her feel guilty, because after that an enduring sadness seemed to descend on her."

"So you never knew, all that time, that Guy Lennox was your father?"

"Never." Iris paused. "Agnes and I were only babies when our parents separated. We had no idea, as we grew up, that the man we called 'Daddy' was really our stepfather. Or that our names had been changed from Lennox to Loden."

"But you must have asked your mother how she met your 'father.' "

"We did; she just told us they'd met at a party that Peter gave—which wasn't a lie." She shrugged. "But wasn't exactly the truth."

"What happened when you found out the truth? Did you ever confront your mother about it?"

"I couldn't say anything, never had the opportunity. Because she died a few months before I finally learned the truth. It was during the dreadful winter of 1963, when the country was snowbound. Agnes lived in Kent, and couldn't get up to London. I was in Yugoslavia. Our mother, who was already frail, caught pneumonia and died quite suddenly."

"So . . . she *never* talked about your father to either of you?"

"Never—not *even* when she saw this painting, which must have taken considerable self-control. But she'd concealed the true story for so long that I think she found it impossible to reveal." I thought of what my own mother had concealed from me and the pain at finally learning it. "But it's just as well," Iris went on. "Because if I *had* known while my mother was alive, I don't think I could have ever forgiven her. My sister still hasn't, nearly fifty years on."

"Did Agnes remember your father painting you both?"

"She did, because she was nearly six. Though of course she didn't know who he was. But she told me that's how she always remembers him—standing behind the easel, chatting to us and smiling. I have no recollection of him at all—though I'm sure it *was* some deeply buried memory that led me to notice the painting in the first place; I do remember feeling this instant sense of . . . *familiarity*." Iris sighed, then ran her fingers lightly across the painted image of her little brown dog. "I often think about how much my father must have missed us, and longed to be with us. He was deprived of us, as we were of him." She looked up. "But there are tears in your eyes, Ella. Don't cry." She put her hand on mine. "Please. I didn't mean to make you cry."

I fumbled for a tissue. "It's just so sad—to think how near you were to him."

Iris nodded. "We *were* near—and at the same time, so very far too. But my sister and I would give anything to have known him."

I thought of my own father, waiting for hours in that café, hoping to have the precious chance to know me. I felt my eyes fill again. "So now I know why this painting's priceless."

"It *is* priceless—to my sister and me. I asked Agnes whether she'd like to have it for a while, but she said she didn't want to—it upsets her too much. So I keep it close to me, beside my bed, and I look at it every day and try to imagine what my father was like. Agnes and I were fortunate in that we were able to visit Hugh's uncle. We talked to him about Guy and heard his recollections of him. We even looked at some photographs of him that he had, so that was at least some comfort."

"But . . . there must have been people who knew that Peter Loden wasn't your biological father."

"There were—but they wouldn't have discussed it in front of us. They probably assumed that we knew, or that we'd been told that our father had betrayed our mother and that's why we didn't see him anymore. Guy's name was simply never mentioned. But after I knew the truth I stopped referring to Peter Loden as my 'father.' "

"What happened to him?"

"He was a very busy, very powerful man." She gave a shrug. "He was always nice to Agnes and me, if rather remote: how much he ever thought about Guy Lennox and how he'd destroyed the life Guy treasured, I'll never know. But Peter lost everything after the war. I told you that he laid the first oil pipeline to Romania, didn't I?" I nodded. "When Romania became part of the Eastern Bloc, the pipeline was nationalised. My stepfather's losses were catastrophic. He had to give up his offices in the City. The house in Mayfair had to go . . ."

"You said that it was very grand."

"It was—it was a beautiful, elegant house. We lived there until 1940; then my sister and I were evacuated. In 1948 the house was sold and my mother and stepfather moved to a small house in Bayswater. Their later years were very hard. After he died in 1958, Agnes would come to town and help my mother, who was by then already quite frail. I'd spend time with my mother when I was back in London, but as I say, she never told me the truth. But then I chanced upon the painting and found out the truth—or perhaps it wasn't chance. Sometimes I even fancy that my father somehow guided me to it. It's a story I've told very few people, Ella. Only my two daughters and their families know it. And now you."

"I'm . . . so touched that you've shared it with me—but, why *have* you, Iris?"

"Because you're a portraitist just as he was—and because I saw that you were drawn to the painting; I think you sensed the intense longing that went into every brushstroke."

"I *did* sense that, yes. I did . . ." I felt my throat constrict. "But . . . I ought to go now." I didn't want to cry again in front of Iris, knowing it would distress her, or have to explain to her that my tears were prompted not just by her story, but by my own. I rose. "So . . . I'll see you next week."

"I look forward to it, my dear."

Iris came with me to the door. I picked up my easel, bag and the canvas carrier, smiled my goodbye, then left.

I didn't wait for the lift. Instead, I walked down the stairs, my mind filled with the image of my father, looking through the window of the café. I imagined his sorrow when he realised that I wasn't going to come. I thought of him waiting there yesterday, then going back this morning.

I left the building and hailed a cab. As it sped along Kensington High Street I saw the sign for my father's hotel, and was about to ask the driver to stop, when I realised it was useless. My father wouldn't be there. His flight was leaving in less than an hour. He'd be in Departures or making his way to the gate. I got out my phone and found his last message.

I hope you'll find it in your heart . . .

I hadn't. Now, because of Iris's painting, I felt that I could. I looked at his mobile number. Then, with no idea of what I would say or how I would even find the voice with which to say it, I began to dial: 07856 53944 . . . I pressed the last digit.

CALL?

I stared at the screen, my hand shaking. Guy Lennox hadn't abandoned his children. He'd fought to keep them, had sacrificed his good name to protect them, suffered injustice in his attempt to remain close to them. My father had simply left me, and had never looked back.

With a sinking feeling I realised that my mother, for all her bitterness, had been right. It *was* too late. I pressed the red button, then dropped the phone into my pocket.

I'd made my decision, I reasoned as I arrived home: my father was leaving. After all the agonising and tears, it was time to let things lie.

Which is what I would have done, but for the email that I received two days later . . .

It was Friday night, very late. I'd been to see a film with Polly, then we'd had a drink—I'd just gotten back home and was in the studio, thinking about my sitting with Nate, who was coming in the morning, when I heard an email drop into my in-box.

I went to the computer and saw that the message was from my father. I was filled with dismay. I didn't *want* to hear from him again. I'd made it clear that I didn't wish to have anything to do with him. What more could there be to say? For a moment I toyed with the idea of deleting his email without reading it. Then, with a sigh, I opened it. I was surprised to see that he'd written at length this time.

Dear Ella,

I'm very sorry we didn't get to see each other in London. I felt sad as the plane took off, but I consoled myself by deciding that I'd write to you on my return, so I could convey to you at least some of what I would have said, had we met.

First I'd have asked you about you—about your career, your friends. It would have felt strange having to ask my own daughter such basic questions, but I know so little about your life. Then I'd have told you a bit about me—in particular, that I was widowed six months ago and am still adjusting to that loss. I'd have told you that I live near a small coastal town called Busselton, not too far from Perth, on a winery that was started by my wife's parents, and to which it had always been her intention to return. I never entirely shared her enthusiasm for this plan, but in the end coming here be-

came a means by which to escape an intolerable situation, be-cause—as you know only too well—I'd made a dreadful mess of my personal life.

"I do know," I muttered. "I know the whole story."

When I first contacted you, Ella, I said that I wanted to try to explain. I hoped to be able to sit down with you and tell you in per-son why I behaved as I did all those years ago. I also wanted you to know that I did try to remain in touch, but all my airmails came back, unopened, with 'return to sender' written on them in your mother's neat hand.

I felt my breath catch.

I wrote to you many, many times, my darling daughter. In those letters I told you that I was living far away, but didn't say why, because you were too young to understand the circumstances that had led me here. I knew that your mum would have told you that I'd simply abandoned you both—and that, to my eternal shame, is true. But I wanted you to know that I still loved you, and missed you, and wished with all my heart that it had been possible for me to be with you.

Of *course* it would have been possible—if he hadn't run off with someone else!

I must say I didn't have my wife's blessing in any of this. She was very upset at what had happened.

I laughed sourly. *She* was upset?

Frances said that if I wanted to ease my conscience I should simply open a bank account for you that your mother could access. I did so, but your mum ignored my many requests for her to sign and re-turn to me the forms that I'd sent her. So then I began sending cheques, but she sent them all back.

Her pride wouldn't allow her to take his money. Perhaps her pride had also made her refuse to seek child support and alimony from him after they divorced. I read on.

Then I heard that your mother was leaving her flat—

What did he mean "her" flat? It was *their* flat.

I discovered this from my old colleague Al, with whom I'd stayed in touch. Al bumped into your mother in Manchester a couple of years after I'd gone to Australia. She told him that she'd recently married, and was moving to London. She mentioned she was no longer dancing—Al assumed this was because she was very obviously having another baby.

So my father knew nothing about her accident.

I was very glad to know that your mother had found happiness with someone else and I prayed that he'd be a good stepfather to you, Ella. But I still wanted to resume contact with your mother, not just because I intended to provide for you, but because it was my dearest wish to see you again one day. I hoped that you'd be able to come visit me when you were old enough, though I'd have to handle that very carefully with Frances, as she had found the whole situation so painful.

She'd found it painful? Having seduced my father away from his family and dragged him thousands of miles away from us?

So when Al wrote telling me that your mother was moving to London I wrote to the Northern Ballet Theatre asking them to forward to her a letter that I enclosed—but still I didn't hear from her. I placed an ad in The Stage, *with a box number, but she didn't respond. Your mother was clearly never going to forgive me for the way our relationship ended.*

Their "relationship"? What a weird way of putting it, I thought furiously.

I'm sure she must have told you how she and I met. It was after a performance of Cinderella, *in which she had danced the role of the Winter Fairy, in a beautiful sparkling tutu. Frances loved ballet and had bought special tickets that included an invitation to the cast party afterwards: so we went along . . .*

My father had gone to see *Cinderella* with *Frances?* Mum had said only that he'd been there with "a few other people." So *that* would explain why Frances had hated Mum—because she'd liked John too, but it was my mother who he fell in love with and who he married.

I'd gone to get Frances a glass of wine, and when I came back with it she was chatting to your mother; so Frances introduced us.

This all tallied with what Mum had told me.

She said, "Sue, this is my husband, John . . ."

I stared at the sentence.

And that's how it began.

It was as though the air had been punched out of my lungs.

This is probably hard for you to read, Ella, but it's important that I tell you the truth, which is that I never meant to become as deeply involved with your mother as I did. But she was captivating, and I was weak. By then Frances and I had been married five years. I loved her and I had never been unfaithful to her.

It was my mother who was the other woman . . .

I thought of the hotel bill that she had found in my father's pocket and of the love letter—it had been the love letter of a wife to her husband.

Now, without having ever meant to, I'd embarked on an affair. I'd try often to end it, but Sue would become so upset, and I couldn't bring myself to hurt her so deeply. But six months after we'd met I told her that it had to stop. It was then that she said she was pregnant.

I squeezed my eyes shut, then opened them again, and read on.

I didn't know what to do. I didn't want to hurt Frances—or lose her. I was also shocked—which you'll think is naïve; but I'd never imagined that Sue would risk her career by having a baby; she was young, and very ambitious, and ballet meant everything to her. She'd just started to dance principal roles. It was only then that I realised just how powerful her feelings for me were. She was willing to give up everything for me. I told her that I would never leave my wife. But Sue knew that Frances couldn't have children, and she must have believed that once I'd bonded with our baby, my love for Frances would fade.

Mum had me in order to get John to leave his wife. That's why she'd said she was "so happy" to be having a baby. Now I remembered her fury when Chloe had contemplated getting pregnant in order to force a commitment from Max. Mum knew, from her own experience, that to do so would be—how had she put it? "Too big a risk."

I read on.

Despite my huge anxiety, Ella, I was thrilled when you were born and immediately felt the most astonishing love for you. But your birth marked the start of a double life that was so stressful that I wondered at times how I'd survive it. In saying that, I'm not appealing for your sympathy; I'm just trying to explain how I ended up causing so much hurt.

So much, I reflected.

Your mother urged me to tell Frances the truth, but I refused to do so. I was terrified that Frances would leave me. I still loved her, you see. I loved all three of you—my wife, your mum, and you, my precious baby. I didn't know what to do. So, like many men in that situation, I did nothing. I'd visit Sue and you after work during the week and at weekends, wherever I could. I'd drive down West Street and I'd see your mother standing at the window of her flat, looking for me.

I remembered how she used to call out to me "Daddy's here!" Now I realised why she always referred to my father "arriving"; because he didn't *live* with us. So many of her elliptical remarks suddenly made sense.

You had no idea that your mum and I weren't like any other parents. I'd push you on the swings and take you swimming; I could easily have been spotted by someone that Frances and I knew, but I loved you so much that I was willing to take the risk: sometimes I'd take you to the theatre to see your mum dance. I'd read to you and paint and draw with you. I became so deeply attached to you that I decided many times that I would leave Frances. But then I'd agonise all over again, because I didn't want to lose her.

So instead he lost *me.*

Then Frances began to feel unwell. When she discovered that she was pregnant, it seemed a miracle, not just because she'd been told that it could never happen, but because by then she was forty-two. We were both so happy; but I was terrified to tell Sue. So I didn't.

Then in 1978 Frances began to plan for us to return to Australia. At that point my life became a true hell—because how could I go, when I had you? But how could I not go, when I had Lydia, who was by then eighteen months? At the thought of having to choose between my two families, I'd even contemplated killing myself— anything in order not to have to face up to such a hellish situation.

It was to be another year before things finally fell apart irretrievably. I'd promised Sue that I'd take you and her for a picnic—it was a beautiful Saturday in early September. But I couldn't get away and instead went for a walk with Frances and Lydia. Perhaps you know what happened next, Ella. Perhaps you even remember it.

"I do," I whispered. By now I felt only pity for my father.

Suddenly there you were, running towards me, looking so de-
lighted and surprised. I remember you chatting to me then peering
at Lydia with innocent curiosity. Your mother caught up with us,
clearly distressed. Frances was staring at you, Ella; then, as she
took in the situation, she gave your mother a look of utter loathing,
picked Lydia up, and walked into the house.

So the situation wasn't the wrong way round at all. Frances had
had every reason to hate my mother.

In that moment all the complexity of my life fell away. Awful
though it was, I felt the most intense relief that there were no secrets
now—only the terror of the decision that I would have to make. The
events of that day meant I would finally have to choose. So I
chose . . .

"To desert Mum and me."

. . . to stay with my wife. That choice has haunted me ever since. I
didn't know how to tell your mother. I didn't have the courage. So,
to my shame, I didn't. I just collected my things from her flat, and
left, because I knew no other way to do it.

"You ran away," I murmured.

So it's not hard to understand your mum's bitterness towards
me, or her determination to cut me out of her life. This of course
suited Frances. She forbade me from telling Lydia about you, be-
cause she didn't want our daughter contacting you in years to
come, for she was certain that would bring Sue back into our lives.
Lydia grew up knowing nothing about you, Ella. I wonder at what
stage of your life you were told about her. Perhaps you've known for
a long time.

"A *very* long time—three weeks!"

Lydia found out about you a year ago. It was only then that Frances, knowing how very ill she was, at last told her the story. Lydia said nothing about it to me at the time, but a month or so after her mother died, she told me that she wanted to find you. I felt a kind of euphoria, swiftly followed by dread, because I believed that you'd want nothing to do with me. Who could blame you if you didn't?

"Who could blame me?" I echoed dismally.

One day I happened to click on an article in The Times. *For a split second I was confused, because I thought I was looking at a photo of Lydia. Then I saw it was you, and I was . . . overcome. When I told Lydia, she was so excited that she wanted to email you herself, right away; but after we talked about it she agreed that she couldn't do that until you and I had re-established contact. I warned her that this very well might not happen, but told her I'd write to you, via your website. Yet when I sat down to do it, I found it impossible. I simply didn't know what I could say to you after so long, and having done what I did. The words simply wouldn't come.*

My emotions roiled; I didn't know what to feel.

Lydia insisted I should go to London: she was convinced you would agree to see me if you knew I was close by. So I booked my trip, then sent you my first message. There was no answer, so I emailed you again. Again, there was no answer from you. Lydia then said I should suggest a specific meeting place, near your studio, and she found the Café de la Paix online. So that's where I waited—I waited right up to the last minute, until I was in danger of missing my plane, but you chose not to come. Lydia's very sad about it, as am I.

"As am I," I echoed, and suddenly realised that I truly was.

Now I feel both better and worse—better, for having at least tried to see you, and worse, for having been rejected. Ella, when I first got in touch with you I wrote that I wanted to "make amends": but of course we both know that is something I can never do. All I can do is say how sorry I am for the pain and hurt I caused you; I only wish I'd been able to say this to you face-to-face.

With every loving wish,
Your father,
John

Ten

I read my father's email again and again. As I finally closed it, a wave of anger with my mother rose up. But then, to my surprise, it quickly subsided, leaving only an intense pity for her. She'd felt she had to conceal her true place in my father's life. Unhappy with the role she'd ended up in, she'd re-cast herself as the wronged wife, a role she'd played with such passionate sincerity that I'd never once questioned it. In fact, I almost admired her for having maintained the illusion for so long. She'd achieved this not so much through lies—though I now knew that she *had* lied—as through evasion and deflection. She'd always either refused to talk to me about her relationship with my father, on the basis that it was too painful for her to do so, or she'd cleverly equivocated. She'd avoided giving direct answers, responding instead with statements that weren't exactly lies, but weren't the truth. She'd suggested that what I'd innocently referred to as her "first marriage" hadn't taken place in church because my father wasn't a "believer," rather than admitting that they hadn't been married at all. She'd never spoken to me of her "divorce," but had let *me* refer to it without ever correcting me. She'd been truly masterful at allowing false impressions to stand.

I realised that my mother had never used the words "husband" or "wife"—she'd always referred to Frances as "the other woman"— which, in one sense of course Frances *was*.

Now I understood the real reason we hadn't taken proper holidays with my father—because he'd been unable to get away from his wife and other daughter for more than three days. I understood how my father had been able to hide his emigration papers from her, because they would have been sent to his home address. I understood why there'd been no child support or alimony, and no wedding photos— not, as my mother had suggested, because the photos had gotten lost in the move, but because there'd been no wedding to take photos *of*.

My mother had inverted the love triangle with tremendous sub- tlety and, at times, audacity.

That would have been cosy, wouldn't it—the daughters of the wife and the mistress being playmates! Would you really have wanted that, Ella . . . ?

I marvelled at her mental complexity. Or had she perhaps con- vinced herself that she *had* been married to my father, and this is what had enabled her to carry on the charade with such vehement commitment?

I was *the wounded party! I was!*

As I went wearily down the stairs to bed, I thought about my mother's apparent familiarity with the frustrations of being a mis- tress. It was here, I now realised, that she'd very nearly slipped up. How often she'd warned Chloe that married men "never" leave their wives! Why hadn't I realized how odd it was for her to say so, given that she, supposedly, *had* been left? Most of all I understood why Mum despised and even hated Max—not because he'd betrayed his wife, but because he'd *stayed* with his wife, just as John had chosen to stay with his.

He'd tell me about the lovely house we'd buy, the holidays we'd have and the life we'd lead—when all the time . . .

As I undressed, I realised that here was the real reason my

mother had always been so enormously censorious about adultery—because it hadn't worked out for *her*. Or was her indignation simply part of the performance, because it strengthened the impression that she herself had been a wronged wife?

As I got into bed, I struggled with a tide of new emotions. The fact that my father hadn't been married to my mother didn't make what he'd done any less inexcusable. He'd had two families and he had abandoned one of them—and that act of cowardice could never be swept away. But Polly had been right—there *had* been another side to the story. My father hadn't left us in a cold, calculated way, but in a blind panic. He was a weak man who'd got himself in a terrible mess. But he had *tried* to keep in touch—that he hadn't was one of my mother's few overt lies, a lie that had been essential to the damning case she'd built so systematically against him.

As I turned out the light I thought of my father's letters going out, then coming back to him, unopened. I went to sleep and dreamed of my mother, in her long, white tutu and bridal veil.

When I woke the next morning to the sound of Mum's voice I thought I was still dreaming.

"Ella?" I heard her say. "*El*-la. . . . ?" I'd slept fitfully and was so exhausted that I half expected to see her standing by my bed. "*Please* pick up, Ella—I need to talk to you."

I pushed back the duvet, then stumbled downstairs. As I picked up the phone the message machine clicked off, the red light flashing angrily.

"Thank goodness," said Mum. "I was worried that you weren't there. Ella? Answer me—*are* you there?"

"Yes. Yes I am . . ." Fury welled up inside me as I remembered her lies. Her deception. I longed to challenge her about it there and then, but every instinct warned me to wait, so I bit my lip. "What's the matter, Mum?"

"The matter is that Chloe's driving me *mad*."

"In what way?"

"She's being *so* interfering."

"Why shouldn't she interfere—it's *her* wedding."

"Yes—but I can't have her trying to alter everything at this late stage. She's unhappy with the cake—she wants it to have forget-me-nots on it to match the ones on her dress, not pink roses."

"Has it been iced yet?"

"No—but it means having to phone the cake shop to change the order, when I'm already *so* busy. Then she's being difficult about the menu—now she says she doesn't want *pot au chocolat,* she wants a tower of profiteroles."

"Well, why not? Or would you have to get planning permission for it?"

"Please don't be facetious, Ella. Worse, she won't make up her mind about the hymns, which means we can't get the Orders of Service printed. But one good thing, she *has* chosen your reading: it's 'The Good-Morrow' by John Donne. Oh, but she wants to change the crockery we're renting—I'd ordered the thin, plain white with a fluted edge, and suddenly she wants the pale blue with the gold rim. Having been *so* easy about everything, she's suddenly become terribly demanding."

"That must be hard for you—"

"It's infuriating—although, in *one* way it's a good sign, that she's now so involved; between you and me I think she had a little wobble a while ago—but then, brides often get jittery before the big day."

"You would know, Mum."

There was an icy silence. "What do you mean?"

"Well, only that you've been a bride, *twice,*" I said innocently. "So you would know."

"I can't *bear* wrangling with her," Mum went on smoothly. "Of course, your sister and I often rub each other up the wrong way—I suppose because in some ways we're rather alike."

"Oh, you are." For the first time, I realised how much Chloe's life had mirrored Mum's.

"Anyway, I hope she'll calm down and leave everything to me. Otherwise, this wedding will be a disaster."

"I'm sure it won't be." I glanced at the kitchen clock. "Mum, I have to go."

I quickly ended the call, realising that if I didn't, I'd be opening the door to Nate in my nightie. A part of me *wanted* to open the door to him like that. A part of me wanted to open the door to him stark naked. I groaned. Oh, God—I was truly losing my mind.

I went upstairs and had a cool shower, after which I didn't blow-dry my hair—I left it damp and unbrushed, my face bare of makeup. I put on a shapeless shift in a bilious shade of custard and chose a pair of hideous flat sandals that gave me fat calves. I wanted to make myself look, and feel, plain and frumpy in order to extinguish any sparks that had ever flared between Nate and me. But as I placed his canvas on my easel I felt the sparks crackle and glow.

It was as if the portrait *was* Nate—as though there'd somehow been a fusion of person and picture. I kissed the tip of my finger then placed it gently on his painted mouth. I suddenly decided that I wouldn't give the portrait to Chloe—I'd keep it, like Goya kept his portrait of the Duchess of Alba because he'd fallen in love with her and couldn't part with it.

Drrrrrrnnnnnggggg!

I took a deep breath, walked deliberately downstairs, then opened the door. There Nate stood, in jeans and a pale blue Polo shirt, the green sweater slung around his shoulders, as the day was already warm. I gave him the kind of neutral smile that I'd give the plumber or postman. "Hi there."

He smiled warmly in return and I felt my stomach flip-flop. "You look great," he said as he came inside.

"No I don't."

A look of surprise crossed his face. "You do," he insisted. "It's a . . . nice dress."

"It *isn't*," I protested, determined to make every moment with him difficult. "It's hideous. The colour's *vile* and the dress is completely shapeless."

Nate gave a bewildered shrug. "Then why are you wearing it?"

"Because . . ." I could hardly tell him the truth. "Because I'm going to be painting in it, so it doesn't matter."

"Well . . . I guess that makes sense." We went upstairs, into the space and light of the studio. I adjusted the blinds, re-arranged the screen, then tied on my apron. Nate pulled on the sweater, then came over to the easel and looked at the canvas. "You've done more to it since I was last here."

"I have—because time's getting short now. This is the penultimate sitting," I added cheerfully, as though I didn't mind a bit that the portrait process was almost over.

"And will the last one be next Saturday?"

I twisted my hair ruthlessly into a scrunchie. "The Saturday after, if that's okay, as I have to go to Chichester next week." I told Nate about the silver wedding portrait commission. "They need it very quickly. It's an emergency," I added seriously.

He grinned. "Do you charge more for emergency portraits?"

"I do. I have a 24-hour call-out, with an 0800 number."

"And flashing lights on your easel?"

I smiled. "Of course. Anyway . . ." I took the lid off the jar of turps. "Today I'll be working on your eyes, so I'm just going to come and stare right into them, if that's okay."

"Be my guest." I went over to Nate, put my hands on my knees and gazed into his eyes. I was so close to him that I could see my reflection in his pupils and, behind me, the square of the window, its sides curved across the convexity of his cornea.

He gave me a suspicious glance. "What are you muttering?"

"I'm counting your lashes. Now that you've distracted me, I'll have to start *all* over again. Okay . . ." I narrowed my eyes. "One, two, three, four . . ." I could smell the scent of his vetiver mingled with the faint tang of his sweat. I could feel his breath.

He smiled and his laughter lines deepened into small creases. "I can see myself," he said. "In your eyes."

"Well . . . that's what happens at this distance."

"Can you see yourself in mine?"

I looked into his pupils. "Yes," I answered. "I can . . . and my hair's a *mess.*" I pulled at my bangs. "Hey, don't blink. Okay . . . I think that's enough eyeballing." I went back to the easel and began to fill in his irises with tiny dots of lamp black and viridian green.

"I wonder how many times you look at the person while you're painting them," I heard Nate ask.

"Oh—*so* many." I wiped a drip off the back of my hand. "A portrait consists of many thousands of glances. You're a terrific sitter, Nate. I'm going to nominate you for a Golden Chair award."

He grinned. "So have you figured out exactly who I am yet?"

"Hmm . . . getting there."

"Let me know when you do, won't you? It's been driving me crazy."

"I hope you'll see it for yourself, in the portrait. And that you'll be happy with it."

"Are you happy with it?" he asked me.

"I *love* it," I said unthinkingly.

Nate smiled. "You love my portrait?"

"Yes . . ." I felt my face flush. "I mean . . . it's just that I feel a creative satisfaction with it. I think the composition's worked really well—having you looking straight out of the canvas, eye to eye with the viewer. It's dramatic, and engaging, and . . ."

"In your face?" Nate suggested, teasingly.

I smiled. "It's certainly very direct. I hope Chloe likes it."

"I'm sure she will." Nate's phone began to ring. He got it out of his pocket and peered at it. "That's Chloe now. Do you mind, Ella . . . ?"

The skewer turned again in my heart. "No problem. We'll have an early break."

"Hi, Chloe," he said as I went and filled the kettle. "No . . . you're not interrupting. Er . . . I do like profiteroles," I heard him say as I spooned coffee into the pot. "I'm *sure* Maria will have Claudia's bridesmaid's dress ready in time . . . no, I don't mind *what* colour the crockery is . . . we'll talk about the hymns—sure . . . I'll see you later." He closed the phone and put it back in his pocket. "Sorry—Chloe's getting all worked up about the wedding."

"She seems very happy."

"I think so."

"You must be too."

"I guess I am. It's pretty close now."

"Yes—so there's *no* getting out of it," I declared cheerfully as I handed him his coffee. "Not that you'd want to," I added hastily. I asked him when his sisters and mother would be arriving, and how long they'd be staying, and whether his friend James was looking forward to being best man.

"He can't wait—says he's already written the toast." Nate went back to the chair and sat down. "He says it's 'brilliant.' "

Once again at the easel, I picked up my tiniest brush and started to paint the fringe of Nate's eyelashes. Then I worked on the hollow at the base of his throat, on the swell and curve of his Adam's apple, on the blue shadow beneath his chin. We were in silence now, except for the rumble of traffic and the somehow incongruous trilling of a blackbird.

Finally, I put down my brush. "That's it, I think—for today."

Nate stood up and stretched, then he took off his sweater. As he did so his shirt rode up, revealing his abdomen, with its covering of dark, fine hair. I was almost felled by a wave of desire.

I put the palette on the table, took off my apron, then we went down the stairs. I opened the front door. "So . . . we're almost done now."

"Almost done," Nate echoed quietly. "*Ciao,* Ella." He bent and kissed my cheek. As his skin grazed mine it was all I could do not to put my arms round his neck and pull him to me.

Instead, I gave him a bright, impersonal smile. "Bye, Nate."

"*Ciao,*" he murmured. But he was still standing there.

"You've already said that."

"Have I? Oh . . ." He kissed me again. "And had I done that?" Heat spilled into my face. "Yes. You had."

"Ah. Sorry." His smile was crooked and rueful. "I got confused."

"Well, please . . . don't."

"I won't," he responded firmly. "I mustn't." To my despair, he kissed me a third time, and then he left.

"You've got that look on your face again," Celine remarked the following week. It was her final sitting.

"And what look's that?" I picked up my palette knife.

"A wistful look—as though you're thinking about someone . . . a man." I didn't reply. "I wish you'd tell me about him," she insisted. "After all, you know so much about me."

"There's nothing to tell." I put a few red-gold highlights in Celine's hair.

"But there *is* someone . . ."

"No. At least, no-one it could ever work out with."

"Why not? Is he otherwise engaged?"

"Yes. 'Engaged' being the operative word."

"Ah." She sighed. "That's hard."

"Yes." I put the palette knife down. "But there it is. Anyway . . . I've almost finished your portrait."

"You have?"

"Just one more thing to do . . ."

"I shall miss the sittings," Celine said. "I've come to enjoy them. I'm only sorry that I made it so difficult for you at the beginning."

"That's okay." I dipped my finest sable brush in the titanium white. "I'm sure it helped the painting to have had that initial . . . tension," I said carefully. Celine smiled. I studied her, then placed a touch of white in each eye. I stood back from the canvas. "That's it."

"Let me see." Celine came over to the easel and stared at the painting. "It's lovely," she said after a few moments. "Thank you, Ella."

I'd worried that Celine would look anxious and unhappy in the painting, but somehow, the woman whose image I'd painted looked calm and relaxed, though there was an air of determination about her.

She cocked her head and narrowed her eyes. "I look as though I'm about to get up and go somewhere. I think that's what people will say."

"Perhaps some will, but we all see different things in a painted face—it's extraordinarily subjective. Sometimes people see things in my portraits that I haven't even seen myself." I picked a stray bristle off the canvas. "It'll be a few weeks before it can be framed—I'll take care of that for you—but at least you'll be able to display it in the meantime."

She sucked on her lower lip. "I'm still not sure where; definitely not in *here*," she added wryly. I thought of her fury with Victor when he'd suggested that. "Maybe in the study," she mused. "In fact, if you wouldn't mind putting it in there now for me . . ."

"Sure—that'll be a good place for it to dry." I lifted the portrait off the easel and followed Celine across the hall with it, into the study, then laid it on a corner table.

"I hope Victor will like it," I told her, as we returned to the sitting room.

"I know he will."

"A portrait's a lovely thing to have and it will last for a long, long time." I began to pack up. "Barring fire, catastrophic flooding or nuclear attack, your portrait will *still* be being looked at in two or three hundred years, Celine."

She smiled. "Which rather puts forty years into perspective."

"It does. So . . ." I put the brushes in the box. "Are you looking forward to your birthday a bit more?"

"I *am*," she answered carefully. "Not least because I've reached a compromise with Victor. We *are* going to have the party, because it would be disappointing for our friends if we cancelled it."

I collapsed the easel. "Of course."

"But I've told him *not* to buy the diamond ring."

"I see."

"It's far too extravagant a gift when things between us are so . . . unsettled. Instead I've asked him if he'll make a donation to a charity."

"That's perfect," I said as I gathered up the dustsheets. I straightened up. "Any particular charity?"

"Yes. I was at a lunch a week ago," she said, "and sitting next to me was a man who runs an international clean water charity, WellSpring."

"Max Viner?"

"You know him?"

"I do—a little." I wasn't going to say how. "He's married to the crime writer Sylvia Shaw."

"*Was* married to her," Celine corrected me. "He told me that they separated two months ago and are divorcing."

"Really?" I wondered if Chloe knew.

"He talked about it briefly; he seemed sad, but said that it was quite mutual; it seems she's involved with her new publisher now."

"I see." The photo of Max standing proudly beside Sylvia at her book launch took on a different complexion . . .

"Anyway, I was very impressed with what he told me about the charity, and so having now talked to Max himself, Victor's agreed to make a donation that will fund forty new hand-dug wells in Angola and Mozambique."

"That's wonderful. What a marvelous birthday present!"

"Victor said he still wants to give me something for myself— something memorable, which is typically kind of him—but I can't think of anything."

"Well, I've decided that I'm going to do something for *my* birthday, Celine—it's in September. I want to have an exhibition of my recent portraits. I'll hire a gallery for a few days—I'd like to borrow your portrait back, if you'll lend it to me; and I'd love you to come, preferably wearing what I painted you in. Will you do that?"

She smiled. "I'd love to."

I'd come to think of my forthcoming week in Chichester as a working holiday, but it became clear from further telephone conversations with the Bergers that it was to be far more work than holiday, given that they now wanted the portrait to include their grown-up son and daughter, their three dogs and their two Siamese cats. I wasn't about to complain—a big group portrait like that would boost the bank balance; but it would be a challenge to do in a week, and I would also need a large canvas. I was just wondering how I'd transport it down there when Roy phoned to ask if he could give my number to a colleague who wanted to have his ten-year-old daughter sketched.

"Of course you can," I answered, cheered by the prospect of another commission. "I'll chat to him about the different options, so ask him to call me—thanks for that, Roy." Then I told him about my trip to Chichester.

"That's a big commission, then."

"It is—with a correspondingly big canvas; I don't know how I'll get it there."

"Surely you could buy the canvas in Chichester?"

"I could, but I have to prime it with emulsion first, which takes two days to dry, so I want to take one from London, already prepared. I'll have to hire a car, I suppose."

"You can borrow my car."

"Don't you need it?"

"I'm at the hospital only one day next week, and I'm sure your mother will lend me hers, or drop me there—it's not a problem."

"Well, if you're sure, that would be great."

So on Friday morning, I went to collect the car. "This is really kind of you," I said to Roy as he unlocked the garage. "You're saving me three hundred pounds."

He pulled back the green painted doors. "Glad to help my Number One girl." He went in and backed his silver Audi onto the drive. He got out, then handed me the keys. "Are you going to come in for a cup of something before you go?"

"Um . . ." I was worried that if I saw my mother, there might be a scene. "Is Mum here?" I asked, far too casually.

"No. She's gone to collect her wedding outfit—it was being altered."

"Right . . . well, I'll have a quick coffee, then."

We went into the house. It was the first time I'd been there since Mum had told me about my half-sister Lydia. I sat at the same place at the kitchen table and remembered seeing her eyes shimmering with tears, her face a mask of suffering.

I've never wanted to tell you the truth, Ella, but now I will.

She *hadn't* told me the truth—just her own twisted version of it.

What you're remembering is the day I saw your father with his . . . with his . . ."

Wife, I thought balefully.

"Are you all right, Ella?" Roy was frowning at me in concern. "You look a bit troubled."

"Oh . . . I'm fine." I was tempted to tell him about my father's last email, but it would have felt wrong to do so before I'd had a chance to confront Mum with it.

Roy filled the kettle. "I'll have to rent a tuxedo," he said as he got down two mugs. I suddenly wondered what I was going to wear—I'd have to buy something new. I saw myself in funereal black.

The French windows were open so I stood by them, looking out at the long, luxuriantly green lawn. Chloe's playhouse, long since turned into a toolshed, stood at the far end, next to the horse chestnut tree. I imagined the massive white tent that would soon dominate the garden with its awnings and ropes and gathered drapes. I

imagined all the guests drifting in and out of it in their formal suits
and dresses and hats, and the swarms of caterers, musicians and
entertainers, all presided over by my mother, with her glacial
charisma and ineffable poise.

"How do you think the garden's looking?" Roy asked.

"Wonderful. It will be a perfect place for a wedding."

"I'm doing it bit by bit, with endless mowing and sprinkling—I'm
praying there won't be a watering ban."

"Fingers crossed."

"And no freak high winds—we wouldn't want the marquee ending
up wrapped round the tree, would we?"

"That *would* be inconvenient. But it's going to be a huge event."

Roy set our mugs of coffee on the table. "It is," he said tonelessly.
"So far one hundred and *eighty* people are coming—and that's without all the replies in."

"Good God!"

He sat down then sighed. "It's *too much*. I tried to get your
mother to agree to half that number, but she said she wanted a wedding that everyone would remember—and that's what she's going to
get."

We've got a huge *cast list.*

"You'd think it was her *own* wedding that she was organising," he
added wryly.

I've also been wondering about confessi . . .

"Roy—" I said impulsively.

"Yes?"

I turned away from the garden and sat down opposite him. My
heart was thudding. "Roy, there's something I want to tell you, even
though I'm not sure that I should . . ."

He blinked. "Tell me what? Are you sure you're *okay,* Ella?"

"Yes—more or less, but . . ."

"But what?"

"It's just that . . ." I realised that I couldn't bring myself to tell
Roy what I knew—after all, my mother was his *wife:* he might not

want to hear it. And was it really my story to tell? ". . . that Max is getting divorced," I blurted.

"I saw that." Roy sipped his coffee. "In a newspaper—can't remember which one, but it was in the gossip column bit of it. His name leapt out at me."

"Does Chloe know?"

"Yes. I wasn't going to say anything to her of course, but then she mentioned it to me." He shrugged. "She said she felt fine about it."

"Well, that's . . . good."

"She said that she's looking forward to marrying Nate. Which is all as it should be," he concluded with an air of relief.

We drank the rest of our coffee in companionable silence, then I stood. "Well . . . I'd better get going. I said I'd be in Chichester by three, and I have to go and get my stuff first. Thanks again for the wheels. You're a lifesaver."

We went out to the front, I got in Roy's car, gave him a wave, then drove away.

At home, I got my equipment, my laptop and my suitcase, stowed everything in the back of the car, locked up the house, then set off towards the A3.

As I sped onto the motorway twenty minutes later I felt a surge of relief to be having a week out of London. It would provide a welcome respite from the wedding preparations. As the South Downs rose up in the distance, I felt myself begin to relax. Most of my recent commissions had been stressful in one way or another, so I was glad to have one that would be reasonably straightforward—dogs and cats allowing.

Frank and Marion Berger lived in Itchenor, very close to Chichester Harbour. I drove down their tree-lined lane, catching my breath at the sail-dotted water glinting in the distance. Then I saw the sign *The Oaks* and turned into the drive. The house was Edwardian, low and wide, flanked by a fuschia hedge that dripped with pink flowers. It was set in a large garden at the back of which was the turquoise glimmer of a pool.

As my wheels crunched over the gravel, the front door opened and the Bergers came out, followed by three black Labradors, who heralded my arrival with a volley of good-natured barks.

I parked where Mr. Berger indicated, got out, shook hands with him, then greeted his wife. They were much as I'd imagined— a pleasant-looking couple in their fifties. Marion was slim, with curly fair hair that was threaded with grey, and large hazel eyes—I already knew that she worked in the dean's office at Chichester Cathedral. Frank, a doctor, was tall and tanned. He looked comfortable in green corduroys and a short-sleeve blue-checked shirt.

"You'll be staying in the guest cottage," she explained as her husband helped me get my equipment out of the trunk. "That way you'll have privacy—but we hope you'll join us for meals."

"Thank you, I'd love that."

The cottage had an open-plan ground floor, on which I'd be able to put the easel if I needed to, and a prettily decorated bedroom and bathroom at the top of a narrow box staircase. From the bedroom window I had a clear view of the harbour—and in the distance, the shining expanse of the Solent.

Frank put my case down. "We've got Wi-Fi in here if you want to email. There's a radio, a small TV . . . lots of books." He nodded at the shelves. "But let's go and have a cup of tea now." I followed him back to the house.

"Have you any thoughts on where you'd like to be painted?" I asked them as we sat in the sunny kitchen.

"Perhaps in here?" Marion asked.

"Maybe." I looked around the room. I could paint them sitting at the table, with the children standing by the AGA. "Could I have a look at the rest of the house?"

They gave me a tour, first showing me the big blank wall in the dining room where the portrait would hang. Then we went into the sitting room.

"You could paint Frank and me standing on either side of the fireplace," Marion suggested, "with the children on the sofa."

I appraised the fireplace with its large over-mantel mirror. "Perhaps . . . but standing up all that time is going to be hard work for you; plus, it will look very formal—do you really want that?"

"No." Frank shook his head, as one of the cats came in through the open French windows. It began to wind itself in and out of his legs. "We want to look relaxed and casual, don't we, Katisha?" he crooned to the cat, scooping it up.

"Could we go outside?" I asked. I followed the Bergers through the garden doors onto the patio, where a second cat was sprawled on a low wall, blinking sleepily in the sunshine. The dogs ambled behind. "How about in the swimming pool?"

"Are you serious?" said Frank.

"I am. I once painted a family in their pool, and they loved it—it's on my website, you could have a look."

Marion grimaced. "I'm not sure I'd want to be painted in my swimsuit—but how about on the boat? It's moored in the harbour—you could put your easel on the pontoon."

"That would be tricky, with the movement of the water . . . and would the dogs and cats cooperate?"

"Ah. No," she said. "Forget that!" She laughed.

In the end, we decided that Marion and Frank would sit on the white wrought-iron garden bench on the lawn, the cats on their laps, their children lounging on the grass in front with the dogs. The harbour would be the portrait's background.

"That will be lovely," Marion sighed happily. "And how long will we sit for you each time?"

"If I'm to get the painting done in only a week, I'll need you to do three hours a day."

"That'll be fine," said Frank. "We've both taken the week off work for this—so we'll just chat . . . or look at the boats."

I started that afternoon. Tying the canvas to the easel because it was slightly breezy, I began to block in the main shapes with charcoal marks. It was a pleasure being in the sunshine, with the sound of the wind rustling through the trees and with the views of the fields rolling down to the sea.

The Bergers' children arrived from London that night—twins of twenty-three; Hannah, a pretty red-haired girl who was a graphic designer, and Henry, a tall boy with brown curls who worked in IT. They could only spare three days, so we agreed that I'd paint them first.

The week passed quickly because I was working so intensively. Sometimes thistledown would drift onto the canvas and I'd have to tweeze it off. Several times I had to extricate a ladybird or a mayfly from the paint, and I had to watch out for the dogs' wagging tails. Apart from these hazards, the composition flowed. It was a relief to have a break from the emotional intensity of painting a lone sitter, one on one.

I'd spend the afternoons working on the background landscape. At night I'd be so exhausted that I'd go to bed early and read: amongst the books on the shelf was a poetry anthology in which I found "The Good-Morrow." I'd forgotten how beautiful it is—a tender aubade in which, for the lovers, their "one little room" is an "everywhere."

I gave myself a few hours off one afternoon, drove into Chichester and visited the cathedral. On another afternoon I walked down to the beach and lay amongst the dunes beneath the blue bowl of the sky, watching the dinghies and surfboards rip past.

On my last night, after dinner, we drank champagne to celebrate the fact that the portrait was done. The Bergers would have it framed, locally, the week before their silver anniversary party.

Marion couldn't stop looking at the picture, propped against the wall. "It's full of warmth and happiness."

"That's because your family is," I told her. "I just paint what I see."

Afterwards, I went back to the cottage and sat by the bedroom window, watching the mid-summer sky turn from orange to crimson, to a deep indigo, against which the first stars were beginning to shine. I thought about Celine, who would be at the Dorchester now, mid-party. I wondered if she really would leave Victor and where her life would take her if she did; I wondered if Mike was coping, and how Iris was. Then I opened my laptop to check my emails: there was one from Chloe to say that Nate's final sitting would have to be postponed, as he'd had to go to Finland again. *I can't wait to see the portrait,* she'd added in a PS. I sent her a quick reply and was about to close my in-box when, instead, I clicked on CREATE, and in the TO: box I typed *John Sharp.*

Eleven

"So you had a good time?" Roy asked when I returned the car to him the following afternoon.

"I did. It was a wonderful break and they were really nice people." I handed him the keys. "I've filled the tank."

"That's thoughtful—thank you."

"It's the least I could do. So how's everything been here?"

"Oh . . . all right." He grimaced. "Actually, that's not true—there've been lots of squabbles."

"About what?"

"Oh, about the seating plan, inevitably, and the choice of hymns, and whether or not we should have fireworks—your mother wants them because it's July the fourth the next day, but I say absolutely *not*, as there won't be enough space to light them safely. There was a spat about whether the chairs should have white slipcovers—Chloe likes the idea but your mother doesn't . . . Anyway I'm glad you enjoyed your week away. What did you do in the evenings?"

"I listened to the radio or read. I had my laptop with me. In fact . . . there's something I wanted to tell you, Roy."

"And what's that?"

"Well . . ." My heart began to pound. "I've decided that I *do* want to get in touch with John." My stepfather's face flushed. "I'd been thinking about it," I admitted. "But then, last night, I decided to send him a short message; I just wanted to tell you about it, and say that I hope you're okay with it."

"Yes . . . yes, of course I am."

"Because, you see—"

"It's all right," he interrupted. "You don't have to explain."

"I feel I *do,* because I told you that I *wasn't* going to contact him and now I am."

Roy put up his hands. "You've changed your mind, Ella. That's fine."

"Yes . . . and there's a reason *why* I've changed it, which is that—"

"Ella," Roy said brusquely. "You're thirty-five years old. You don't have to justify getting in touch with . . . your . . ."

I felt my throat constrict. I didn't want to hurt this man. "I . . . just wanted to tell you that there are things I didn't know," I went on softly. "And now that I *do* know them, it's changed my view of what happened—at least in *some* ways," I hurried on, "because you see—"

"I don't want to talk about it," Roy said. "Do what you want to do, Ella, but please don't *tell* me." To my dismay his eyes glittered with tears.

I felt tears sting my own eyes. "But you said you'd *support* me."

"I did say that," he conceded quietly. "But . . . it's not easy." He drew in his breath. "The truth is, I've always dreaded this. I've dreaded it for nearly thirty years . . . I've read about how hard it is for adoptive parents when their children contact their birth parents—even when they've encouraged them to do so. Now I'm finding out just how hard."

"But you see, Mum never told me the whole story," I persisted. "And now I know it, and the point is that she's—" I froze.

Roy's eyes narrowed. "That she's what?" he asked.

Over his shoulder I saw Mum walking towards us, her arms outstretched. "*El*-la," she crooned.

"Don't say anything to her," I whispered. "Please."

Roy gave me a puzzled glance, but nodded.

"How lovely to *see* you, darling." Mum laid her palm on my cheek. It felt cold, and I shivered. "But what *were* you two talking about?" she added playfully. "You looked quite engrossed."

"I . . . was just telling Roy about Chichester."

"Did it go well?" Mum's ice blue eyes scanned my face. "You've got a little tan."

"Yes. I was painting outside."

"*En plein air*? How lovely. Now do come in and tell *me* about it too—I've just made a pot of coffee."

"No . . . thanks, Mum, but I need to get back. I've got things to sort out."

"That's a shame," she responded softly. "I was just about to email you to ask whether you'd come over next Sunday, to give Roy a hand in the garden. I've got a dress rehearsal with my students for their summer performance, so I have to be there most of the day, and there's a lot of last-minute planting to be done here. *Would* you be an angel and help Roy with it?"

"Yes—of course." It would give me another chance to talk to him alone.

The week passed quickly. I took Mike's portrait to be framed and in the dress shop opposite found an outfit to wear to the wedding. I went to Peter Jones and bought a hat and bag to match, then went upstairs to their wedding registry to order the soup tureen from Chloe and Nate's chosen dinner service. After that, I walked down to Waterstone's, collected the Whistler biography and bought the Everyman edition of John Donne's *The Complete English Poems* to read from in the church.

On my way home I passed the Café de la Paix. Impulsively, I went in, bought a latte, then, as a small act of atonement, I sat at the table where my father had, looking out. I got out my phone and read again his delighted reply to my email.

I spent the next couple of days working on the portrait of Grace, which, thanks to Mike's film of her, was now so much better than it had been. It had a real vibrancy and warmth. On Friday, I went back to paint Iris—she told me she had an idea about what I might put in the background of her portrait. Then on Saturday morning Nate came for his final sitting.

He was very quiet this time, which suited me. I was worried that if we talked, we'd inevitably flirt and banter, and that was a mine-field I desperately wished to avoid. But today there seemed to be an unspoken recognition by both of us that the bubble of exclusivity we'd been in was about to burst.

I dipped my finest brush in the titanium white, then put a tiny stroke onto Nate's pupils. It was like throwing a switch—his face was suddenly vital, radiant, *alive.*

I stood back from the canvas. "I think it's done."

Nate came over to the easel. But he barely glanced at the painting before saying, simply, that it was "very good."

I wiped my paint-spattered hands on a rag and smiled at him. "So . . . it's all over."

Nate nodded. "*Finite la commedia,*" he said.

I untied my apron, then we went down the stairs. I hoped that Nate wouldn't make the kind of lingering goodbye he'd made last time—the encounter had left me with a melancholy ache that wouldn't go away.

"Well . . ." I opened the front door. "Thanks for being such a *great* sitter."

He gave me a rueful smile. "Funny to think that you hated me when we started."

"Not *hated.*"

"All right, then—*loathed.*"

"Um . . . let's say 'didn't much like.' "

"Okay—I'm happy with that," he said judiciously.

"But it was all a misunderstanding."

"It *was* a misunderstanding."

"And . . . we're friends now, Nate. Aren't we?"

"We are. We ought to be," he added, "after twelve hours together—fifteen with our lunch," he added brightly.

"Exactly—I mean, that's more than a half day," I pointed out. Put that way, it didn't sound like very much. "Anyway . . . I look forward to the wedding." He nodded. "So . . ." I smiled. "I'll see you then, Nate."

"Yes," he agreed. "I'll see you then." The sittings, with their bittersweet intimacy, were over. "Bye, Ella." He kissed me, holding his cheek against mine for just a moment too long. Then he walked quickly away.

On Sunday, I put on some old clothes and then cycled down to Richmond. As I rode through Fulham Broadway I saw there were perhaps twenty new bouquets tied to the railings. I realised that it was sixth months to the day since the accident: Grace's family and friends must have been there earlier to mark the anniversary of her death. The yellow sign appealing for information was gone.

I cycled over Wandsworth Bridge, through Roehampton, then across Richmond Park to the house. In my basket were the card I'd bought for Roy and a big box of his favourite Belgian chocolates.

I locked up my bike by the garage, then hung my helmet on the handlebars. Mum's car wasn't in the drive—I felt relieved. I walked round the side of the house, and saw Roy at the end of the garden, surrounded by trays of plants. As I approached, he looked up and waved.

"Happy Father's Day." I gave him the chocolates and card.

"*Thank you,* Ella. You never forget. You always used to paint a card for me."

"I remember."

He sat on the bench that encircled the horse chestnut tree and took the cellophane off the chocolates. "I've kept them all, you know—your cards."

"You have?" I was surprised.

"Of course." He grinned. "I knew they'd be worth a fortune one day." He offered me a chocolate. "Dig in—before *we* dig in," he added with a baleful glance at all the plants. I took a caramel cream and nibbled on it, as Roy opened the card. *I've Got the World's Greatest Dad.* "That's . . . lovely," he said, his voice catching.

"Well, it's true. And what did Chloe give you?"

"Nothing—not that it matters. She's got enough on her mind."

"Is she coming over to help?"

"Not today—she did a bit yesterday while you were painting Nate. Now, you'd better put some wellies on—there are some in the playhouse—ditto gardening gloves."

"Don't worry—my hands are always covered in paint, so a bit of mud won't matter."

As I went into the playhouse I remembered how, when we were children, Chloe and I spent hours together in it. She used to have her toy oven in it and I'd sit hunched over a tiny table in her "café" eating pieces of plastic chocolate cake with rapturous relish.

I took a pair of Wellingtons outside, checked them for spiders, then pulled them on. "Right, I'm booted. What do I do?"

"We've got twenty white lavender bushes to plant." Roy pointed to them in their trays. "There are also twenty phlox, thirty Achillea, forty Acquilegia and twenty-five sedums. This side of the tent will be open—unless it's pouring—so I want the border to be a joy to behold."

I looked at the mass of delphiniums, peonies and acanthus. "It's already looking gorgeous."

"Well, this is the last lot to go in. Okay . . ." He handed me a small spade. "Let's make a start. Just follow the markers I've stuck in the ground—and don't impale yourself on the roses."

It had rained overnight, so at least the soil was easy to turn. I started at one end of the border, Roy at the other, and we worked towards the middle.

"We're doing well," he announced after an hour or so. He straightened, then ran his hand across his brow. "But let's stop for a bit of lunch. I'm starving."

"I'm glad you said that."

We left our boots outside and went into the kitchen. Roy washed his hands, opened the fridge and got out some ham and a bowl of salad while I set the table.

We didn't talk as we ate. Finally, however, Roy broke the silence. "I'm sorry I was a bit . . . touchy last week, Ella. When you spoke to me about John."

"It's okay. I didn't mean to upset you. But I wanted to tell you about it, because . . . well, it wasn't as it's always been portrayed."

Roy frowned. "What do you mean?"

At last I talked to Roy about my father's email. I told him about the many letters John had written to me when I was a child, about the ad he'd put in *The Stage* and the cheques he'd sent to Mum, about his attempts to open a bank account for me.

Roy sat very still until I'd finished. "This is very different from what your mother always told us."

I nodded. "She's always said that he behaved as though she and I never existed. And there's something else—something I've never known, or even guessed at." I told Roy what it was.

He didn't say anything for a few moments, as though he was trying to work something out. "Well . . ." he said at last. "Things that have puzzled me for years now make *sense.*"

"That's just what I thought when I found out. I was stunned—and yet somehow I wasn't. But I did feel as though I had to . . . re-think everything."

"During the adoption process, I do remember that your mother seemed keen for me not to see our marriage certificate."

"Because it would have said 'spinster' by her name rather than 'divorcee'?"

He looked at me. "She insisted on submitting it to the court herself. And she refused to talk about the way her marriage had ended. All she would tell me was that your father had abandoned you both to be with this 'other woman.' "

"You never guessed at the truth?"

"No . . ." Roy said, sadly. "Your mother was so *convincing*. And to be frank, I didn't *want* to talk about her relationship with John, because I knew how much she'd loved him and how much he'd hurt her. But . . ." He shook his head. "To think that you can live with someone for thirty years and not really *know* them." He gave a bewildered laugh. "And her near obsession with the horrors of adultery . . . All part of the charade, I suppose." He shrugged. "I really don't know what I feel. I think I mostly feel *sorry* for her."

"That was my reaction too, but I also feel *angry*."

"She's concealed so much from you, Ella. And she's outright lied to you. It's as though she's woven a web around her relationship with John—a tangled web," he added bleakly.

"Roy, the only reason I'm telling you all this is because I hope it'll help you understand why I've changed my mind about replying to John."

"Yes . . . I do understand," he said. "This does . . . change things."

"Roy—he was *here*."

He stared at me. "Here? In London?"

"Yes. He came to see me."

"You *met* him?"

"No, no—I didn't." I explained why.

"Are you saying that you went past that café, and actually *saw* him there but didn't go *in*?"

"That's right," I confessed faintly.

Roy closed his eyes. "*Poor* man . . ."

"All he wanted to do was sit with me for a few minutes, tell me that he was sorry. As I didn't give him the chance, he wrote to me, not realising that I'd never actually known the truth about him and Mum."

"And does it make what he did feel any . . . better?"

"Not much—but it does at least make it easier to understand. I no longer see him in the way Mum's always portrayed him—heartless and calculating; I see him as weak and confused."

Confused? Allowing men to be "confused" gives them an excuse to just . . . string other women along, offering them . . . nothing.

"And where does his wife feature in all this?"

"Nowhere now—she died last December. Then John began searching for me, and happened to see my name in *The Times.*" I shrugged. "The rest you know."

"So . . . you're in email contact with him now?"

"Yes. I explained to him that I hadn't known most of what he'd told me. I said that I didn't even know where he *was* until I was eleven."

"Did you say anything about your mother?"

"Very little. Just that she's 'fine.' I said that I have a sister who's about to get married. And I told him that I have a wonderful father, whose name is Roy." Roy flushed, then smiled. "You don't have to worry," I went on. "John's not going to become my *dad* again—even if I didn't have you. It's far too late for that. Plus, he lives nine thousand miles away. But . . . I'd just like to email him from time to time . . . if you're okay with it."

Roy hesitated, then said, "No. I'm not." My heart plunged. "Because I think you should do more."

"More? What do you mean—phone him? I've got his number— I suppose I *could* . . ."

"No. I mean you should go see him—see *them.* Your father. And your sister. If you can't afford it, I'll happily—"

"No, I *can* afford it—thanks. But . . . one step at a time," I added faintly. "It's all . . . so new to me."

"Of course." Roy nodded. "You need to build up to it—send some more emails. Look, are you going to *talk* to your mother about all of this?"

"I certainly am, but not until after the wedding, because it's going to be a very difficult and upsetting conversation. So please *don't* tell her that you know anything."

"I won't say anything to her," Roy promised.

The next few days passed quickly. I went to see a couple of art galleries with a view to renting one for a week in September, and decided on the Eastcote Gallery, halfway down the King's Road. I might get a little bit of press about the show, I reflected; it might even lead to a new commission or two; but most of all, it would be fun to get my sitters together and have a party.

There was space for about twenty portraits, so I began to contact everyone who'd sat for me during the past three years. To each I explained that I would personally collect the painting, insure it and safely return it.

I gave Celine the details when I went to collect her portrait to take to the framers.

"*Alors . . .*" She opened her diary. "Fifteenth of September . . ." She flicked over the pages. "That's a Wednesday." She wrote it down. "I shall be back by then." *Back from where,* I wondered. "At what time will it start?" she went on.

"It's going to be six-thirty to eight-thirty. I'll invite Victor too."

"Of course."

"So how was your birthday party?"

She smiled. "It was wonderful—Victor made a very nice speech, and Philippe said a few words. My friends and family were all there. It was a very happy occasion."

"I'm glad."

"And Victor is giving me the most *wonderful* present."

"Really? More than the gift to Well-Spring?"

"I couldn't think of anything I wanted, but yesterday Victor hit on a brilliant idea. He said that he'll give me a trip, lasting precisely forty days, during which I can go wherever in the world I'd like to go. And I'm going all on my now. I'm planning the itinerary."

"That sounds exciting."

"It will be *liberating.* I have friends in the States, in Argentina, in Cambodia, Kenya and Greece; I shall visit them all, with my round-the-world ticket, finishing my journey in Venice, where Victor and Philippe will meet me. We'll spend three days there before flying back to the UK, in time for Philippe's return to school."

"It'll be . . . fantastic." The doorbell rang. "Oops—that'll be my cab—I'd better get your portrait ready." The painting was still in the study, propped up on top of the desk. I carefully clipped it into the canvas carrier I'd brought with me, then went outside.

It was the usual driver, because I'd specifically asked for him. I set the painting carefully on the backseat, got in, then waved to Celine, who was standing in the doorway.

"Finished, is it?" The driver turned to look at it. "Beautiful," he breathed, then he glanced at Celine. "It's just like her." He started the car. "Now, don't forget—"

"I know. But if I painted you, you'd have to come to my studio, and sit for a total of twelve hours."

"Oh." He turned out of the drive. "Can't see myself doing that, to be honest—I do more than enough sitting in my cab. Couldn't you do it from photos, like that poor—"

"No," I interrupted firmly. "I paint only from life."

"They've found the car, by the way."

"Have they?"

"It wasn't a black BMW—it was a dark blue Range Rover; the number plate was so muddy, they hadn't been able to read it. Turned out the poor sod driving it had no idea. He hadn't even touched her, but he'd driven too close. He must have startled her. She skidded into a pothole and got thrown off."

"Oh, that's so tragic—"

"Actually, I'm not sure I *do* want to be painted," he added as we drove over Hammersmith Bridge. "Maybe you could just draw me."

"I could—in charcoal, or crayon, or pen and ink."

"So what does that cost, then?"

"Well . . . perhaps we could barter? I once painted my plumber in return for a boiler repair. So . . ."

"All right, then—I'll give you some free taxi rides . . . within central London, that is."

"Fair enough. And how many would you offer?"

"Um . . . would fifteen do it?"

"Fifteen would be perfect." He could help me collect some of the portraits for the party. "It's a deal."

On Saturday, the doctor colleague of Roy's brought his daughter for her sitting; she was a pretty, intelligent girl with long glossy dark hair, who told me she wanted to be a violinist. Her father stayed while I sketched her in red crayon on brown paper. On Tuesday I went back to Iris. Her portrait was very nearly done: in it, she looked distinguished and serene—and the background she'd chosen added depth and interest to the composition.

And suddenly, the wedding was only two days away.

On Thursday afternoon I cycled over to the house to write out all the place cards. In the drive was a big white van with *Pavillioned in Splendour* emblazoned on it; in the garden, a team of men were slotting steel poles together and unrolling expanses of white canvas.

Roy stood next to me as we watched the tent rise. "Well . . . it's all happening," he said. "And Nate's family have been arriving."

I glanced at him. "When will you meet them?"

"We're going to have a quick drink with Nate's mother tonight, then tomorrow your mum and I will have a quiet evening with Chloe—she wants to sleep in her old bedroom one last time."

"Of course—and how's she feeling?"

Roy shrugged. "Absolutely fine."

I turned and saw my mother walking towards us, shielding her eyes against the bright sunlight. She nodded at the men. "I hope they're being careful with the plants."

"I'm watching them like a hawk," Roy assured her. "I'm not going to let anyone trample my aquilegias."

"I'm very worried about smoking," Mum said. "I just *know* that Gareth Jones will light up—he's still on forty a day, according to Eleanor."

"Then I expect he will," I said.

"Let's hope he doesn't light up in church," Roy teased.

My mother ignored us as she considered the problem. "I think I'll tell everyone that smoking *is* allowed—but after-dinner cigars only: I'll get a big box of Romeo y Julieta."

Roy groaned. "That's another five hundred quid, then."

Mum looked at him reproachfully. "Let's not spoil the ship for a ha'porth of tar."

" 'Tar' being the operative word," he muttered.

She turned to me. "Ella, will you come and write the place cards now? I've got them all ready on the kitchen table."

"Sure." I followed her inside. Once there, she opened the box of gold-edged white cards, handed me the guest list, then I got out my calligraphy pen and set to work. "I feel like the official scribe."

"It's a great help that you're doing this," Mum told me. "It's all coming together very smoothly. We've got the church rehearsal in the morning."

"Do you need me for that?"

"No; it's really so the soprano can practice everything and so Chloe and Nate can go through their paces. Then tomorrow afternoon the caterers and I will lay the tables." She nibbled her lip. "You couldn't lend a hand with that, could you, Ella, darling?"

"No—I'm sorry, I can't: Chloe's coming then to see the portrait."

"Oh well, then." Mum shrugged. "She hasn't seen it yet?"

"No; she insisted she didn't want to see it until it was finished, so she's coming to the studio at three."

Mum smiled. "It'll be the moment of truth!"

. . .

At five past three the following afternoon the doorbell rang and I went quickly downstairs.

"Ella!" Chloe beamed at me, then turned to the elegantly dressed, white-haired woman standing beside her. "This is Nate's mother—Mrs. Rossi. She said she'd like to see the portrait too—I hope that's okay."

"Of course it is," I said. I held out my hand and Nate's mother shook it. "Hello, Mrs. Rossi."

"Please, call me Vittoria." Mrs. Rossi sounded very Italian, and was less frail than I'd imagined she'd be. She had pretty, mobile features and large, greenish-grey eyes that reminded me of Nate's.

"Nate looks like you," I said as I led them inside.

She nodded. "Sì—more than his papà."

"My studio's at the top of the house. I can bring the painting down if you'd—"

"No, no," she said. "I can go up." She followed Chloe and me up the stairs.

"Nate was a good sitter," I said to Vittoria as we reached the first landing. "He kept very still."

"Ah . . . well, he is a good boy."

We went into the studio. Vittoria smiled appreciatively at the paintings on the wall and remarked on the spaciousness of the room and the delicious scent of turpentine and paint.

"How was the rehearsal?" I asked Chloe.

"Fine. I think it'll all go very smoothly tomorrow. And are you happy with your reading?"

"Yes. I've been practising."

"That's good. So . . ." She clapped her hands together, beaming at me. "Let's see the portrait!" She turned to Vittoria. "This is very exciting, isn't it."

"It is exciting," Vittoria agreed.

I went to the rack, took out Nate's canvas and placed it on the easel. My heart was hammering.

Chloe and her future mother-in-law stood in front of the portrait, side by side.

In the silence that followed, I was aware of the muted roar of the traffic, and the distant urgent wail of a siren. After a few seconds had passed I began to think it would be nice if they said something. Of course, coming from Florence, Vittoria would have high standards, I reasoned; and while I wouldn't claim to be up there with Raphael or Leonardo, I was pretty sure I'd done a good job. But Vittoria and Chloe's continuing silence seemed only to confirm that they were disappointed. My heart sank.

Vittoria put her head to one side as she studied the picture. "*Piacevole,*" she said at last. *Pleasant,* I silently translated. She thinks the portrait is "pleasant." "*Molto piacevole,*" Vittoria added softly. "*È un buon ritratto*—a good portrait. Brava, Ella," she concluded and smiled at me.

But it was Chloe's reaction I craved. "I agree with Vittoria," she said, after a moment. "It's a . . . good portrait. Very good," she added firmly. "So . . . thank you, Ella. But . . . we have to go now."

I was bewildered and, I admit it, disappointed. "Won't you stay and have some tea?"

"Oh. No . . ." Chloe said. "I'm afraid we don't have time—I need to take Vittoria back to her hotel, then I have to collect things from my flat and drive over to Richmond. And of course I want to have an early night tonight. But I *thank* you," she said again, with a slightly stiff, dignified air, which wasn't like Chloe at all. *Wedding nerves,* I told myself. She turned to go.

"Aren't you going to *take* the portrait?" I asked her. "I thought you were going to give it to Nate tomorrow."

Chloe glanced at the painting again, then coloured. "Oh . . . no. I think I'll . . . wait."

"Until it's been framed?" I said.

"Yes. Yes . . . that's right."

"Fair enough." We went down the stairs. "So . . ." I opened the front door then smiled my goodbyes. "I'll see you both tomorrow."

"*A domani,*" Vittoria replied. She reached for my hand and squeezed it—as if to console me, it occurred to me; then she smiled brightly. "Brava, Ella. So nice to meet you—*arrivederci.*"

"*Arrivederci,*" I echoed. Then they left.

The next morning I woke early and lay in bed feeling not just depressed that this was Nate's wedding day, but weighed down—as though someone had left a pile of bricks on my chest. After a little while, I tried to distract myself by working—I finished the drawing of the doctor's daughter; I sent Chloe a text to wish her a "Happy Birthday"; then I looked at Nate's portrait, still on the easel.

Piacevole, I thought balefully. Vittoria's verdict made me feel a complete failure, and Chloe's response had been barely more enthusiastic.

I showered, did my hair and makeup and, having scrubbed the last traces of ingrained paint off my fingers, I polished my nails, then got dressed.

At 12:45 I heard Polly beep her horn—she'd offered to drive me to the wedding. I ran downstairs, opened the door, then waved as she parked her silver Golf.

She got out, opening the trunk so that I could put my hat inside. "Great dress," she said, with an appraising glance at my fitted silk shift with its deep ruffle across the front. "I love that lime green."

"Well . . . it's suitably bright and joyous." Not that I felt joyous in the slightest. "You look lovely, Pol." She was wearing a pink linen suit with flat silver sandals, through which her toes, tipped with candy pink polish, showed to perfection. I smiled at Lola, sitting in the back, in a sky blue linen dress, her long fair hair twisted into a bun. "And you look very grown-up, Lola."

"Eleven *is* quite grown-up," she pointed out gravely.

I went back into the house and fetched my bag and the book of poems, locked up, then, mindful of my seams, I lowered myself carefully onto the front seat of Polly's car.

She pulled on her driving gloves. "Gorgeous day for it," she remarked as we drove away.

While going through Putney, I told Polly about Chloe and Vittoria's visit.

"I bet they liked the portrait," she said.

"Um . . . I'm not sure they did."

She glanced at me. "What do you mean?"

"Well, Chloe said that it was very good."

"That's *fine,* then. I'm sure it's wonderful," she added loyally.

"But Nate's mother just said that it was *piacevole*—i.e., nice—as though she thought I hadn't done him justice."

"Look, Ella, she's his mum; she'd probably have said that if Michaelangelo himself had painted him."

"You've got a point. I'm probably being over-sensitive."

"You're entitled—you're an artist," she said, and laughed.

The traffic was surprisingly light, so we got to Richmond in good time. Polly parked outside the house, swapped her driving gloves for a pair of white lace ones, then all three of us got out. She opened the hatchback and passed me my hat.

"Let's have a quick look at the garden," I suggested.

The tent looked magnificent, the canvas a pristine white, the "ceiling" a lining of pale calico that spangled with tiny mirrors. The poles were swathed in cream voile and laced with long coils of summer jasmine. Bone china and lead crystal gleamed on the linen-covered tables, on each of which was a huge centrepiece of white belladonna lilies.

Polly gave a low whistle. "It's spectacular—isn't it, Lola?"

Lola nodded. "So many flowers . . ."

In front of each place setting was a gold-tasselled menu, and a silk mesh bag of pink and white sugared almonds.

Through the open side of the tent I saw four uniformed caterers crossing the lawn towards us, carrying a huge ice sculpture of a swan, anxiously supervised by my mother. They came in and lowered it onto the centre of the large side table from which the drinks were to be served.

Suddenly Mum looked up and saw us. "Polly!" she exclaimed softly. "And Lola—*you've* grown since I last saw you. And what a terrific outfit, Ella—you all look beautiful."

"So do you," said Polly. "It's all so . . . *wonderful,* Sue."

"Thank you." Mum gave Polly a gratified smile. "I must say I think the intensive planning's paid off."

"I thought you'd be helping Chloe get dressed," I said to her.

Mum gave an odd little laugh. "She insisted she didn't want me to. And she's got her hairdresser and makeup artist with her, so I thought I'd just leave them to it and get on with things here. But I'll walk to the church with Chloe and Roy."

I glanced at my watch. "I think *we'd* better go."

"We'll see you there," Polly said to Mum and reached for Lola's hand.

I put on my hat and we walked round the corner to St. Matthias. Nate was standing outside, looking so handsome in his morning suit and silver waistcoat that my heart contracted. Seeing me, he smiled, and my heart flooded with longing. I walked over and congratulated him, then introduced Polly and Lola.

"Great to meet you," he told them. "This is my best man, James," he added as James appeared, looking equally attractive in his morning dress.

I smiled at him. "I hear you've written a great toast."

"Oh, it's a humdinger." He clapped his hands, then rubbed them together. "I'm looking forward to it—after all, you've made me wait long enough for this day," he teased Nate, who smiled.

"You're certainly going to have a big audience," I said to James.

He nodded. "I'm told there'll be a huge crowd."

By now that crowd was beginning to materialise. Guests rounded the corner in knots of two and three, then congregated by the porch. A woman with a camcorder and a big black bag slung over her shoulder was filming us, while a man in a cream suit snapped away with a digital SLR camera. He took Nate and James aside to get a photo of them together.

"Shall we go in now?" I said to Polly.

"Yes, let's."

As we entered the church we could hear the organist playing "Jesu, Joy of Man's Desiring." I spotted Honeysuckle, wearing a black and white houndstooth suit and a wide-brimmed black hat, chatting to Kay, who was in a blue and white floral-patterned dress. I smiled at them and hoped that they'd both forgotten my intense behaviour at the engagement party. Honey's husband, Andy, who was an usher, handed Polly, Lola and me our Orders of Service, then we walked to the front of the church.

There were posies of sweet peas tied to the end of each pew; but as I saw the flowers on the altar I caught my breath—there was a tumbling mass of peonies, agapanthus, viburnum and tuberose—the overpowering scent of which brought to mind my mother's Fracas.

"Where should Lola and I sit, Ella?" Polly whispered.

"With me," I answered. "After twenty-nine years, you count as family."

So the three of us sat in the second pew on the left-hand side, leaving the front pew empty for my mother and Roy. The soprano, Katarina, was already sitting there, looking through her music folder. The sun sliced through the stained-glass windows, scattering coloured shards across the walls and floor.

Nate came and took his place at the front.

"Well," said Polly as she looked at him. "You did say he was attractive." She glanced at me. "You enjoyed painting him, didn't you?"

"I did," I replied neutrally.

"He looks very nervous," Lola observed.

"He does rather," Polly murmured.

Nate didn't look so much nervous as troubled, I reflected.

Across the aisle, a number of women, who I assumed to be Nate's sisters, were taking their places with their husbands and children; I could hear them chatting quietly in a mixture of Italian and English.

"—*che bella chiesa.*"

"—I am *so* jet-lagged."

"—*e che bei fiori.*"

"—*Sì—sono magnifici:* I wish I'd had lunch."

"—Mamma *dice che il ritratto è un disastro.*"

"Are those *all* his relations?" Polly asked wonderingly.

"I guess so," I said, once again trying to work out *why* his mother should think the portrait a *disastro*. It *wasn't* a disaster—it was a good, vibrant portrait. She and Chloe obviously hadn't liked the composition. And here his mother was, in an emerald green dress with a navy hat and shoes. As she stepped into her pew I smiled at her and she smiled back, then, having greeted her daughters, she fixed her gaze on the altar. I turned and glanced behind me. The central part of the church was now full.

A friend of Chloe's, in a beige silk dress, teetered past on six-inch black stilettos; for a moment she looked as though she might fall.

"She needs stabilisers," I whispered to Polly. "Or maybe a walker."

Polly nodded. "In the seventeenth century aristocrats used to wear heels so high that they'd have a servant on either side, holding them up as they walked along."

"How sensible . . ." I opened the book of poems.

Polly glanced at it. "Are you nervous?"

"Very. I haven't read anything in public since we were at school. By the way, how's the nice dad?"

"Just fine." Her eyes twinkled. "He's coming to lunch tomorrow."

"Have you dared to tell him what you do for a living yet?"

"I have, and it's not a problem. In *fact*—"

Suddenly the organ stopped and conversation subsided as the vicar, Reverend Hughes, stepped out onto the altar. He lifted his hands and we all stood.

"May the grace of our Lord Jesus Christ, the love of God and the fellowship of the Holy Spirit be with you all . . ."

"And also with you," we intoned.

I turned and saw, across the sea of hats, Chloe silhouetted against the west doors of the church, with Roy beside her—and behind her, Mum, who was making some last-minute adjustment to Chloe's dress. Then "Arrival of the Queen of Sheba" sounded, and Chloe stepped forward.

As she processed up the aisle on Roy's arm, my mother walked quickly up the left side of the church and slipped gracefully into the pew in front of us. Now Chloe was passing us, gloriously beautiful in her forget-me-not scattered tulle, a cream organza stole shimmering over her slender shoulders, her fair hair wound into a chignon and dressed with a single gardenia. She held a simple spray of white roses. Nate's niece Claudia, in a pale blue silk dress and matching ballet shoes, followed a few feet behind.

I glanced at Nate as Chloe approached. I'd imagined his delighted pride at this moment, but on his features I could see only anxiety. As Chloe drew level with him he smiled at her, but his smile didn't reach to his eyes. If Chloe noticed this, her face didn't betray it. As she turned to hand Claudia her flowers, she wore an expression of almost determined serenity. Claudia took the spray, then—her duty done—clambered happily into the third pew to sit with her parents, while Roy came and stood next to Mum.

As the Handel drew to a thundering close, I looked at Chloe's dress and felt glad to think that, fifty years after that cancelled wedding, its moment had finally come. Reverend Hughes let the last reverberations of the organ subside, then he welcomed us all to St. Matthias, to witness the marriage of Chloe and Nathan, to pray for God's blessing on them and to share their joy. Then he announced the first hymn—"Praise My Soul, the King of Heaven." As we sang it, Katarina's exquisite voice soared above us.

During the last verse I saw Nate lift his eyes to the altar. Chloe looked very solemn and quite pale. Then the hymn ended and we all sat down.

"And now the first reading," said Reverend Hughes, "which will be read by Chloe's sister, Gabriella."

My heart pounding, I stepped out of the pew and went up to the eagle-shaped lectern. I placed the book on it.

" 'The Good-Morrow,' " I said. "By John Donne." I lifted my head. The sea of faces before me was a blur. *"I wonder by my troth, what thou and I did, till we loved? Were we not wean'd till then?"* As I read on, I could feel Nate's gaze upon me, but was aware that Chloe was staring straight ahead. *"And now good-morrow to our waking souls, which watch not one another out of fear; for love all love of other sights controls, and makes one little room an everywhere . . ."* I paused. *"My face in thine eye, thine in mine appears . . ."* At that I felt Chloe turn and look at me. *"And true plain hearts do in the faces rest; where can we find two better hemispheres without sharp north, without declining west?"*

I read on to the end, then returned to the pew, my knees shaking.

Polly put her gloved hand on mine. "Well done," she whispered.

Now the vicar was declaring the gift of marriage to be a way of life made holy by God, and a sign of unity and loyalty that all should honour and uphold. "No-one," he went on, "should enter into it lightly or selfishly, but reverently and responsibly in the sight of almighty God." He lifted his hands. "First, I am required to ask, if there is anyone present who knows a reason why these persons may not lawfully marry, please declare it now." I glanced at my mother. Her jaw was tight with tension, but then, as no-one spoke, she relaxed.

The vicar looked at Chloe and Nate. "The vows you are about to take," he said intently, "are to be made in the presence of God, who is judge of all and knows all the secrets of our hearts; therefore, if either of you knows a reason why you cannot lawfully marry, declare it now."

There was a silence, then the vicar joined Nate and Chloe's hands. "Nathan," he said, "will you take Chloe to be your wife? Will you love her, comfort her, honour and protect her, and, forsaking all others, be faithful to her, as long as you both shall live?"

Nate didn't respond. I felt a sudden rush of hope, followed by a stab of shame. "I . . ." he began, then stopped. "I . . ." he faltered again, then exhaled, sharply, as though blowing out a candle. Then I heard him whisper, "I will."

The vicar turned to Chloe. "Chloe, will you take Nathan to be your husband? Will you love him, comfort him, honour and protect him, and, forsaking all others, be faithful to him as long as you both shall live?"

Now Chloe hesitated as well. I thought this was because Nate had hesitated, and she didn't want to look too eager, or to show that she had listened to the question carefully and was giving it her fullest consideration; but ten seconds passed, then fifteen, then twenty . . . The silence in the church thickened until it seemed to hum and throb. By now at least thirty seconds had gone by, and the pews were creaking as people shifted in their seats or craned their necks to see what was happening.

"Will you?" the vicar tried again. His face was crimson. Still Chloe didn't reply. She simply stood there, immobile, her head bowed. Suddenly her shoulders started to shake. She was giggling— *The emotion of the occasion must be making her hysterical,* I thought. Then I realised she wasn't giggling, she was crying.

The vicar, clearly used to brides weeping on their wedding day, ignored her tears. "Chloe, *will* you take Nathan to be your husband? Will you love him, comfort him, honour and protect him, and, forsaking all others, be faithful to him as long as you both shall live?"

Chloe drew in her breath, brokenly. There was a pause that seemed to stretch on forever. "No," she whispered.

There was a collective gasp. Mum's hand flew to her mouth.

"But . . . Chloe?" the vicar murmured. His face was beaded with sweat.

She looked at him imploringly, and her face crumpled. "I . . .

can't," she sobbed, quietly; then she glanced at Nate, who was staring at her, his jaw slack. She let go of his hand. "I'm . . . sorry."

Reverend Hughes whispered something to them both, and they nodded. I heard Chloe sniffle. Nate handed her a hanky, which she pressed to her eyes. The vicar cleared his throat, loudly, twice, and addressed us. "There will now be a slight change to the proceedings," he announced. "Miss Katarina Sopuchova will sing 'Ave Maria' while I repair to the sacristy with Chloe and Nate, to have a brief chat. Thank you all for your patience."

The organist played the opening bars of the Bach-Gounod as Katarina stepped out of the front pew and walked up the steps to the altar.

"*A-ve Ma-ri-a . . .*" she sang as Chloe and Nate followed the vicar. "*Gratia plena . . .*" Suddenly Chloe stopped and, to my surprise, beckoned to me to come with her.

"*Dominus tecum . . .*"

I stood up, stunned and uncertain, and so did Mum, but Roy whispered to her to sit down again. Reluctantly, she did.

"*Benedicta tu in mulierbus . . .*"

Numbly, I followed Chloe and Nate to the sacristy.

"*Et benedictus fructus . . .*"

On the table, the thick, leather-bound marriage register was open, awaiting Chloe and Nate's signatures. Chloe sat down, her cheeks gleaming with tears, while Nate sat next to her, staring at her in bewilderment.

"*. . . ventris tui, Iesus . . .*"

I closed the thick oak door and the singing faded.

"Chloe," said the vicar, looking at her. "Would you please tell us what this is about?" She didn't answer. He looked at Nate. "Do *you* know?"

Nate's face was the color of ashes. "I have *no* idea."

"Is it just wedding nerves?" Reverend Hughes asked my sister. She shook her head bleakly. "But yesterday, after the rehearsal, you told me you were looking *forward* to marrying Nate, and so . . ." He turned up his palms. "I don't understand."

Chloe ran the handkerchief under her eyes. "I'm sorry," she croaked. "I'm truly sorry. I should have called it off last night—or even this morning—but I didn't have the guts. I told myself that it was too *late,* and that I'd simply have to go through with it, decide what to do afterwards. But now that I'm here, and I have to say those words in front of all our friends and family, not to mention God, I just . . . *can't.*"

The vicar shook his head. "*Why* can't you, my dear?"

"Because . . . Because yesterday I . . . *discovered* something. I discovered that—"

Suddenly we heard footsteps, then the door swung open. Mum appeared, Roy just behind her.

"*Sancta Maria . . .*" we heard.

"Chloe!" Mum's eyes were blazing.

"*Sanc-ta Mar-i-a . . .*"

Roy shut the door.

"What are you *playing* at, Chloe?" Mum demanded hoarsely.

Chloe glared at her. "Would you please go away? You've done *enough* harm!"

Mum recoiled as though from a slap, then recovered her composure. "No," she said calmly. "I *won't* go away—not when this wedding has cost *forty thousand* pounds—"

"Don't, Sue," Roy interceded, but Mum ignored him.

"—and when I've *slaved* to make it an unforgettable day."

"Well, it certainly will be now," Roy said dismally.

"Whatever are you *thinking,* Chloe?" Mum persisted.

Chloe clutched the handkerchief. "I'll tell you exactly what I'm thinking," she retorted desperately. She blinked away a tear. "I'm thinking of how you've interfered, Mum, and manoeuvred, and . . . *manipulated.*"

Mum's lips pursed. "The word you should really be using here is 'helped,' and you clearly have *no* idea what—"

THE VERY PICTURE OF YOU

"Please, Mrs. Graham," Reverend Hughes interrupted. He turned
back to Chloe. "Chloe, can you *please* explain what's happened since
yesterday?"

"All right," she whispered bleakly. "I will." She shivered, then
said, "What's happened is that late last night I found out something
about my mother, something that, well . . . changes everything." At
that Roy emitted a low groan. "You see, I was once very happy with
someone," Chloe went on earnestly. She twisted the hanky in her
fingers. "His name is Max, and I loved him—and he loved me."

"Not enough!" Mum interjected.

Chloe ignored her. "But he was married."

Mum heaved an irritated sigh. "Don't *tell* everyone!"

"And my mother was *so* disapproving—as you've just seen. She
kept telling me that I had to stop seeing Max because he *wasn't* going
to leave his wife, and I was wasting my time, because it would never,
never, *ever* work out."

"It didn't!" Mum said triumphantly.

"No, it didn't," Chloe agreed miserably. Her eyes filled again.
"But it *would* have if you'd just left me *alone,* because now Max and
his wife have separated and are divorcing."

But Chloe had known this for weeks, I reflected; Roy had told me
that she'd been fine about it, so why would it bother her now?

Chloe looked at the vicar. "I'm not expecting you to approve of
any of this," she said quietly. "I'm just trying to explain . . ."

The reverend's brow furrowed. "So, you feel that your mother
stopped you from being with Max."

"She *did* stop me from being with him."

"How old were you then, Chloe?" he asked her.

"Twenty-seven—so, yes, more fool me for listening to her at that
age. But the point is, I *trusted* her, I believed she was acting only in
my best interests."

"I *was!*" Mum protested.

Chloe shook her head, grimly. "So I ended the relationship, and
it broke my heart. But then, last night, I discovered something about

my mother that made me realise she hadn't acted in my best interests at all."

Mum blanched. "Whatever are you talking about?" she asked, faintly.

Chloe stared at her coldly. Then she turned back to the vicar. "Over dinner last night, Mum and I had another argument. She said, yet again, how happy she was about the wedding, and how thankful she was that I'd 'seen the light' about my 'awful relationship' with Max—she was rude about him. I became very distressed. After she'd gone to bed Dad tried to calm me down. He knew how upset I was. He told me where this obsessive attitude of my mother's comes from. He said—and I'd never known this—that it was because she had a long affair with a married man—Ella's father, John." Mum looked at Roy, aghast. "Yet Mum's always told us that she was John's poor abandoned wife."

Mum sank onto a chair. "Roy, what have you *done*?" she breathed.

"What have *you* done, Sue?" he countered quietly. "In not being honest with us all these years? Ella learned it only very recently, from John, in an email. He had no idea that she didn't know. A few days ago, she told me. And last night *I* told Chloe." He closed his eyes. "And I wish I *hadn't.*"

"I'm *glad* you did," Chloe said hotly.

"But . . ." Reverend Hughes said in exasperation, "I still don't understand why this should have such a bearing on today."

Chloe looked at him desperately. "It's because last night everything fell into place. I finally understood *why* my mother had been *so* negative about Max—it was because my relationship with him reminded her of her own failed relationship with Ella's father—she was just transferring all her bitterness about *John* onto *Max.*"

"No!" Mum exclaimed. "I was trying to protect you."

"I was an adult," Chloe retorted. "I didn't *need* your protection; and now at last I realise how much damage your 'protection' has done. Not just because you stopped me from being with someone I loved, but because you've pushed and *pushed* for this wedding to happen."

Mum sniffed. "You didn't have to agree to it," she pointed out tartly.

Chloe stared at her. "That's true—but you're *so* persuasive, and Nate's a very *nice* man, and I was desperate to try and forget Max and move on, and so I allowed myself to get swept up by your plans, and I wish to God I hadn't," she wailed. "Because then there would have been enough time to avoid this . . . *mess* that I'm in now!" She buried her face in her hands.

"You've heard from Max again," Mum said quietly. "That's what this is about." Chloe nodded mutely. Mum's lips compressed. "When?"

Chloe swallowed. "On the night of the engagement party," she replied thickly. "He phoned to tell me that he and Sylvia had finally separated." I realised that was why Chloe had been so upset when she'd showed me out that night. "Max knew that I was engaged," she went on, "but he desperately wanted to see me again, before it was too late. So I did see him—it was the Sunday you were in Finland," she said to Nate. "Max and I only talked," she added. "Nothing else. *But* . . ." She clutched the hanky. "Seeing him again made me wish I *could* be with him." That's when Chloe had had her "wobble" about the wedding, I reflected. "I was terribly torn," she rushed on. "So I saw Max one more time—on that Sunday when you said you'd bumped into Ella, Nate. And I told him that it was all too late, because I'd made a commitment to you."

"You certainly *had,*" Mum said.

Chloe ignored her. "I thought about all Nate's good qualities," she went on. "I repeated them to myself over and over again. I told myself that I was very lucky to be with him."

The vicar looked perplexed. "You said that to me only yesterday, Chloe. After the rehearsal."

"I did. But there was a big problem that I didn't *know* about," Chloe said. "Because the thing is . . ." Suddenly the door opened and Nate's mother came in, with James and Honey. "The thing is," Chloe tried again. She turned up her palms. "Nate doesn't love me."

Mum gave a contemptuous snort. "Of course Nate loves you. He asked you to marry him."

"No." Chloe shook her head. "I asked *him*. We were in Quaglino's, celebrating my promotion—we'd had a lot to drink and I suddenly said, 'Why don't we get married?' I said it as a joke—we'd only known each other four months—but to my surprise he replied 'Okay—why don't we?' Then later that night, at the auction, we told you about it, Mum, and before we knew what was happening, you'd not only set the date, you'd made half the arrangements. You've controlled this wedding, Mum—you've controlled the whole show!"

"Why *shouldn't* you get married?" Mum retorted. "You're twenty-nine—Nate's nearly thirty-*seven*! And love isn't everything at the start of a marriage. Love *grows.*"

"That's what I told myself." Chloe sniffed. "But I knew I didn't feel for Nate a fraction of what I'd felt for Max."

"How can you say such hurtful things in front of Nate?" Mum demanded.

"The reason I can," Chloe answered calmly, "is because I know I'm *not* hurting him. And that's not just because, as I say, Nate doesn't love me. It's because Nate loves *someone else.* I had no idea until yesterday afternoon; it was only then that I realised that Nate loves . . ." She gave a bewildered laugh. "Nate loves . . ."

"Ella," Vittoria said. "Nate loves Ella." She looked at him. "Don't you, Nate? *Tu ami* Ella?" Nate didn't answer. My face flushed as everyone turned their gaze to me. "I saw it," Vittoria went on; "I saw it in the *ritratto*—the portrait; it's there, Nate, in your eyes, in the way you're looking at Ella as she paints you. I saw it at once. And I could see that Chloe had seen it too—but then, it's quite *unmistakable,* no-one could miss it." *I* had missed it, I realised. "And I felt very sad for Chloe," Vittoria continued. "I felt sad for you too, Nate, because I knew it would be a tragedy for you to marry Chloe when you were clearly in love with her sister. I couldn't say so though, because it was too late." She shrugged. "But you *do* love Ella."

Mum turned to me. "What have you done?" she demanded furiously. "Were you so jealous of Chloe, Ella, that you had to use the sittings to try to—"

"Ella's done nothing." It was the first time Nate had spoken and we all turned to him. "All she did was paint my portrait, and talk to me. But yes . . . yes, we got on . . . well."

Mum gave Nate a basilisk stare. "Then why were you going ahead with the wedding if it's *Ella* you love?"

"Because . . . I'm not a flake," Nate answered. "I wasn't about to cancel my wedding on the basis of spending a total of fifteen hours with Ella—especially as I had no idea what *she* thought of *me!*"

A silence fell, during which we could hear strains of "Panis Angelicus." Then Honey coughed lightly. "Sweetie, she's nuts about you." We all looked at Honey. "I didn't *tell* you that," Honey went on. "I didn't feel that I could, given you were about to marry Chloe. But I saw it, at the engagement party—in the close attention that she'd paid to everything you'd said to her, and in the little glances she'd throw you. I felt sorry for her because I knew she must be in pain." Honey turned to me. "But I don't feel sorry for you now, Ella. Because I think everything's going to be all right."

"Well . . ." said Reverend Hughes. "I assume that the upshot of this discussion is that Chloe and Nate are *not* going to be married."

"That's right," said Chloe quietly. She turned to look at Nate. He nodded in agreement, smiling a private little smile of encouragement at Chloe.

Mum's face crumpled. "There are one hundred and eighty-*nine* people out there." It was the "nine" that seemed to bother her.

Roy straightened his shoulders. "Well, then we need to tell them what's happening."

Roy spoke to Reverend Hughes, then we all went back into the church, where by now Katarina was halfway through Rossini's "Stabat Mater." The organist brought the piece to an end, and Katarina returned to the front pew, visibly breathless from her unexpectedly lengthy recital. Nate and Chloe sat in the front pew while I went back to my place beside Polly.

Reverend Hughes cleared his throat. "We're sorry to have kept you all waiting," he said. "But we've been having an important conversation, the conclusion of which is that Chloe and Nate have decided that they're *not* getting married." There were whispered exclamations as everyone reacted to this news. "They both recognise that marriage is too profound a commitment to make where there are doubts," the reverend went on evenly. "However, Roy has asked me to point out that today is Chloe's birthday, and he hopes you'll all come back to the house, as planned, to celebrate that instead."

Everyone was shifting in their pews, many were laughing, probably out of shock. "What *happened*?" Polly whispered to me as everyone stood to leave. "Did Chloe just get cold feet?"

"No," I murmured. "There's more to it that . . . I . . ." My voice trailed away.

"Are you okay, Ella?" Polly peered at me. "I know it's been a shock, but you look . . . dazed."

"Oh, I *am*!"

"Well, it's hardly surprising," Polly declared. "What an upset!"

"Yes . . . what an upset," I echoed happily as the pain and turmoil of the last few weeks finally subsided. As I stepped out into the bright sunshine, Vittoria came up to me. She put her hand on my arm, then smiled. "Now I can tell you what I *really* think of your portrait of Nate," she said quietly. "I think it is *fantastico*!" I wanted to kiss her, but simply gave her a grateful smile. Then I glanced at Honey, and wanted to kiss her too. Then I looked at Nate, and felt my heart soar. But I left him to walk to the house with Andy and James, who looked disappointed not to be making his toast. My mother walked stiffly beside Roy, trying to look dignified, but her face was white with shock and dismay.

When we reached the house, Mum didn't come to the garden with everyone else—instead, she opened the front door and went in, closing the door behind her: through the hall window I saw her walk slowly upstairs.

I went into the tent, where Roy was helping pour champagne. Next to him the ice swan was dripping into its tray. I went into the kitchen to help the bemused-looking caterers bring out the starters. Chloe was standing at the French windows, next to the large trolley on which the five-tiered wedding cake was standing, gazing at the guests milling in and out of the tent. As she picked up the phone on the dresser and began to dial, I knew instantly who she was calling. I knew too why she'd chosen the forget-me-not scattered dress—because she'd been drawn to its story of a love that had been ruptured and then restored.

Epilogue

September 15, 2010

I am at the Eastcote Gallery, on the King's Road, putting the finishing touches to my exhibition, which will open in five minutes' time. The twenty-five paintings are now nearly all hung on the white walls; most of them collected with the help of Rafael, the taxi driver, whose pen-and-ink portrait I am hanging next to that of David Walliams. There are the portraits of P. D. James, Cecilia Bartoli and, courtesy of the National Portrait Gallery, the Duchess of Cornwall. The biggest painting is the one of the Berger family, which takes up most of the back wall. There are also portraits of Polly and Lola, of Roy and Mum, of Celine, Mike, Chloe and a dozen more. Surrounded by their faces, I feel like the party has already begun.

The gallery assistant, Lucy, a pretty dark-haired woman a bit younger than me, is pouring the wine—just in time, as my first guest is arriving. Iris stands framed in the doorway, leaning lightly on her cane; she is wearing her blue suit and her lapis lazuli beads. "Ella."

She smiles as I cross the pale wooden floor to greet her. "Many happy returns! And congratulations!"

"Thank you, Iris. I'm glad you're the first—this was your idea, remember."

She nods. "I do." She looks around. "What lovely paintings— I shall enjoy looking at them, and meeting the people behind them. But do first satisfy my vanity and tell me where *I* am."

"You're over here, on the other side of that screen." I take her to her portrait, which I collected from the framer only yesterday; we study it for a few moments.

Iris tilts her head and narrows her eyes. "I like it. I feel that it's . . . me."

"I'm glad."

"I loved being painted," she says. "It gave me the chance to really think about who I *am* and how I've lived my life. And I didn't cry, did I?"

"No, you didn't. *I* did, though."

"You did," says Iris thoughtfully. "And I'm just so glad that in our last sitting you chose to tell me why."

Lucy brings us both a glass of wine. She looks at Iris, then at the canvas. "I love your portrait. You look so . . . distinguished."

"Thank you," Iris smiles.

"But what's this?" Lucy points to the corner of a painting that is included in the background of the larger portrait.

"A fragment of a painting that's very precious to me," Iris explains. "It's of my sister and me when we were children."

Lucy peers more closely. "So that little girl chasing the dog—is that you?"

"It is. I wanted my new portrait to contain my old one, so my younger self and my older self could be brought together."

"I like that idea!" Lucy exclaims. "So who painted you as a child?"

"My father," Iris replies. "Guy Lennox."

"Oh, I've heard of him," the younger woman says. "So it's a way of having him in your portrait with you?"

"Exactly." Iris smiles again.

Lucy glances at the door. "Here are some more people; 'scuse me, I'm on drinks duty."

In comes Polly, with Lola, who's gripping a silver balloon. Polly smiles broadly. "Happy birthday, Ella!" She kisses me, then I introduce her and Lola to Iris, and Polly takes off her jacket to reveal the same green T-shirt she's wearing in her portrait. "I'm afraid Lola's too big for the yellow dress she wore when you drew her but she's put on something similar."

Lola ties the balloon to the back of a chair, then goes to look at her red crayon drawing, which I've hung next to that of the doctor's daughter.

Lucy brings Polly a glass of wine, and Polly sips it. "This is nice—what is it? Prosecco?"

"No. It's sparkling chardonnay from the Blackwood Hills estate in Western Australia."

She smiles. "So it's from John?"

"It is. I told him about the exhibition—and he and Lydia kindly sent me six crates."

"How nice," Iris says. "You told me that you might be going to see him."

"I am going to," I say. "Next month. I'm spending a week there."

"Will you go alone?" Iris asks.

"No. Nate's coming with me."

Polly glances around. "Where is Nate?"

"He's on his way from the airport. He should be here soon. Oh, here's Chloe!"

Chloe hugs me, then hands me a shiny blue gift bag. "Happy birthday, Sis."

"Thanks—let me get you a drink."

"Just half a glass," she says as Polly and Lola chat with Iris. "I can't stay long. Max's giving a talk about the charity at the Wellcome Trust. He sends his apologies," she adds as we walk to the drinks table. "He'd love to have been here."

"That's a shame—but never mind." I hand Chloe a glass of wine.

She sips it, looking around. "So where am I? I hope you've hung me next to someone I *like.*"

"You're next to Cecilia Bartoli."

"Oh, that's nice—perhaps her portrait will sing to mine; but not 'Ave Maria' or 'Panis Angelicus.'" Chloe grimaces. "I don't think I want to hear either *ever* again." We laugh, then walk over to her painting and study it. "I *do* look a bit grim," she remarks.

"Well, you were suffering."

"I was," Chloe agrees quietly. "I wanted to be with Max so much that I thought I'd go *mad.* I look quite mad," she adds cheerily.

"You do a bit—I didn't want to paint you like this, remember?"

"I know you didn't—I insisted on it. But you know, Ella, I've been thinking that I *would* like you to paint me again."

"I'd love to. I could paint you and Max together—gratis, of course. After all, I owe you a picture," I add with a nod at my por-trait of Nate—which, under the circumstances, Chloe decided not to keep.

She grins. "Okay, then—it's a deal. Maybe we could sit for you when you're back from Australia," she adds happily. "Oh, here's Dad."

Roy's wearing the same tweed jacket and grey bow tie that I painted him in two years ago. "What a nice sight—my two beautiful girls!" He beams at us.

"Hi, Dad," Chloe says.

Roy kisses us both. "Happy birthday, Ella." He glances around. "This is rather fun. So where's my portrait?"

I smile. "That's what everyone asks first." I lead Roy to it and he stands right next to it.

"Spot the difference!" he challenges.

"Well . . ." Chloe narrows her eyes. "Your hair's quite a bit greyer. And you're a tad thicker round the middle . . ."

"All *right,*" he says good-naturedly. "I asked for that. But this is a very jolly idea, Ella." He looks round at all the other portraits. "I imagine your subjects chatting with one another after we've all gone. Ah . . . and there's your mother," he says with a glance at her painting.

"Is she going to come?" I ask him. "She wouldn't commit herself when I asked her yesterday."

"I'm not sure," he answers, a little vaguely.

"So how are things?" I ask it quietly.

"We're still . . . building bridges, I think the expression is."

"That *is* the expression," Chloe concurs. "She's hardly speaking to me, though."

"Well . . . she'll just have to get over it," Roy tells her. "Give her time."

I think of the ruined wedding and of how undone Mum was by Chloe's accusations—Roy said she didn't leave the house for over a week. When the tent was down and the rental chairs and silverware all returned, I braced myself for a confrontation and visited.

"You kept my father's letters from me—dozens of them," I told her. "And you lied to me—about him, and about Lydia—you've lied for years."

She'd pursed her lips. "He abandoned us, Ella, so he had no *right* to contact us. And sometimes a lie can be a *kindness*. I was protecting you."

"No, you weren't, Mum. You were protecting yourself. Your relationship with John hadn't worked out, so you wanted nothing to do with him; and I understand that, truly I do. But that meant depriving me of the chance to be in touch with my father. Don't you think I should at least have known that he still cared for me, even if he couldn't live with me anymore?"

"*He* was the one who did the depriving," she'd insisted. "He chose *them,* Ella, over us. You can take an indulgent view of John, if you wish to, but I *can't*. Let's not forget that his behaviour led to my accident."

"He didn't even know that it had *happened,* Mum—you can't blame him because you slipped on those steps." I'd told her that I intended to visit John in October.

She'd looked away for a moment. Then she murmured, "Poor Roy."

"Roy's happy for me to go," I pointed out.

"Well . . . go if you must," she'd said, tartly. "But please don't tell me about it."

"All right. You and I need to reach some kind of reconciliation, though. It would be easier for that to happen if I felt you regretted the way you've handled things."

"I regret having caused you any unhappiness ever," Mum answered, which I suddenly realised was as much of an apology from her as I was ever going to get. With that, she'd got up from the table and gone into her studio to put her body through its daily ritual of stretching and twisting . . .

Now Roy takes a glass of wine from Lucy and smiles his thanks. "Everything will settle down," he assures Chloe and me. "Hopefully it will happen well before your mother's sixtieth birthday in November—we'll want to have a nice party for her. How's Max, Chloe?"

"He's fine. I'm meeting him later."

"I hope you realise there's no money in the kitty for a big wedding if he ever pops the question." Roy says it with mock seriousness.

She grins. "A big wedding is the last thing either of us would ever want. If it does happen, we'll get married in a register office, with two witnesses—maybe you and Nate," she suggests to me with a laugh. "I *like* Nate," she adds. "But I've always loved Max. And it's screamingly obvious who Nate loves." She nods at Nate's portrait.

I hug her and as Chloe smiles at me, I think of the conversation that I had with her two days after the wedding fiasco.

"Couldn't you *see* it, Ella?" she'd asked me wonderingly as we sat together in her flat, sharing tea and a super-indulgent cake.

"No," I'd answered. "I missed it completely. Perhaps because I was so close to the portrait. But now I know why you reacted the way you did when you first saw it."

She shook her head. "It was a . . . shock. I felt so humiliated and upset—especially as Nate's *mother* was there. I knew that Vittoria had noticed it, and I was trying not to let her see that *I'd* noticed it too—but I knew she had and that she was desperately trying to pretend she hadn't. We both were. It was in every line and brushstroke. And I was standing there thinking that no-one must *ever* see that painting, which was why I didn't take it with me—I didn't *want* it. I thought I'd have to burn it like Churchill's wife burned the portrait of him she didn't like."

"But Chloe . . . if you knew Nate was in love with me, why did you go ahead with the wedding?"

She'd thrown up her hands. "Because it was less than twenty-four hours away! And because I was such a coward. As I left the studio I consoled myself by thinking that perhaps you'd painted Nate badly, and just made him look like he was in love with you, when he wasn't. Then I convinced myself that it was some fantasy *you* had that he was in love with you, and that you'd projected that onto the portrait. I couldn't face up to the truth, because that would have meant cancelling the wedding and I couldn't bear the thought of the embarrassment of it. Or Mum's reaction when I did."

"And then Dad told you about Mum and my father."

"It . . . knocked me for six. I was awake all night, trying to work everything out, remembering everything Mum had said over the years and putting it in that new context; and I realised what she'd been trying to do; I even thought that she'd been motivated by jealousy of me—that she'd been unable to have the love of her life, because he was married, and so she didn't want *me* to have mine. I was so confused! My thoughts were . . . all over the place. But as the sun came up my only thought was that I *had* to go through with the wedding—what a fool I'd look if I backed out at the very last second! But as I stood there, at the altar, the words simply wouldn't come . . ."

Chloe looks at her watch, then sips the last of her wine. "I've gotta go or I'll be late for Max." She kisses me on the cheek. "Bye, Ella. Bye, Dad."

"Bye-bye, my girl," he replies; then he chats with Polly and Lola and looks at their portraits. All three of them are laughing and light-hearted. The gallery is filling up; my sitters are comparing notes with one another.

"—She's really caught your smile."

"—not sure about my hair."

"—hard work sitting, isn't it?"

"—a bit like therapy really."

"—feel I know a lot more about myself."

I feel a light tap on my shoulder and turn. I smile. "How nice to see you, Mike! I wasn't sure you'd come."

"No—it's good to be here. I've even remembered to wear the blue sweater." He looks as though he's put on a little weight.

I point to his portrait. "There you are," I say.

But Mike is distracted by the painting of Grace. We walk over to her portrait instead. "I would never have asked Grace's parents if I could borrow it," I said, "but her uncle saw my show listed in *Time Out* and phoned to say that her family would be happy for her painting to be included. I told them I'd be delighted."

Mike and I stand in front of the canvas. Grace has one hand under her chin, and is smiling. "You've caught her inner light," Mike says.

"If I have, it's thanks to you." I glance at him. "Did you go to the memorial service?"

He nods. "It was held at her school. They put your painting at the front of the stage. I overheard her parents talking to someone about it; they said they find it very comforting."

"Well . . . I'm really . . . I'm glad. And I hope you're okay, Mike."

"I'm . . . fine. Sarah and I have separated now . . . so . . ." He shrugs. "I keep busy. Distract myself. That's all one can do."

"Let's get you a glass of wine." We go over to the table. "Lucy," I say, "this is—"

"Mike Johns," she interrupts with a smile that lights up her face. "You don't need to introduce him to me, Ella. I know who he is— that's the nice thing about this exhibition, no introductions needed, just match the person to their picture. Hello, Mike," They shake hands. "I'm Lucy. I work at the gallery."

I leave Mike chatting to Lucy as I see Celine arriving, in her blue linen dress, with Victor. She looks very tan, and her hair is short. "Happy birthday, Ella!"

"Thanks," I say. "It's terrific to see you. I'm sorry you weren't there when I collected your portrait. But you look great." She is still glowing from her trip.

"So how old are you today?" Celine asks me.

"Thirty-six."

"Wait till you get to forty," she says. "Forty is . . . easy."

Victor smiles. "It's so long ago for me that I can't remember," he teases us.

"How was Venice?" I ask them.

"Wonderful," they say in unison, then look at each other and laugh. "And now . . . back to real life," Celine tells me. "I'm going to re-train—as a French teacher. There's a course I can start in January."

"It sounds ideal."

"So . . . can I see my portrait?" She looks around. "Ah—*there* it is."

We walk towards it, but before we reach it, Celine is distracted by another painting. "And there *you* are, Ella," she says. "So you've painted yourself too."

I nod. "Last month. I hadn't done a self-portrait for over twenty-five years."

"It's lovely. You look . . . peaceful. And this handsome man here, next to you." Celine has stopped in front of Nate's portrait. "Well . . . he's in love, isn't he? Lock, stock and barrel." She laughs, then turns to me. "Of course—that was slow of me. He's in love with *you*. I hope that you're equally smitten with him, Ella."

"I am, actually."

"Is this the man you told me about? The one who was otherwise engaged?"

"Yes. But things are different now."

Celine smiles. *"Très bien!"*

Now I overhear Polly chatting to Iris. "I've been Helena Bonham Carter's hands," she's explaining. "And Joan Collins's once, which was ridiculous as she's ages older than I am." Then I hear her telling Iris about her new boyfriend, the nice dad at Lola's school. "He's a publisher," she explains. "And I'm going to do a book for him."

"About what?" Iris asks.

"It'll be a cultural history of footwear from the earliest Bronze Age shoe to the present day. It'll be small, but beautifully illustrated and full of fascinating facts. We'll sell it in shoe shops. I'm enjoying the research, aren't I, Lola?"

I see the journalist Clare arrive, then just behind her Honey comes in with Andy, James and Kay. They get drinks, then chat with me.

"So we get to see Nate's portrait at last," Andy says as he looks at it. He puts his head to one side. "It's very striking, Ella. But is it a 'great' portrait?"

"I don't know . . . I can only say that I'm happy with it. *Very* happy," I add, as I see Nate standing in the doorway. He makes his way through the throng towards me, and suddenly I want to cry with simple joy.

"You told us that a 'great' portrait reveals something about the sitter that they didn't even know themselves," Andy is saying. "So what was it that Nate didn't know?" He smiles. "That he was in love with the woman who was painting him."

And now Nate is by my side. "I *did* know that," he says. He slides his arm round my waist. "I knew it from the start."

As Nate pulls me to him, I recall the night of the wedding. We'd kept our distance, but when everyone had drifted away, he'd come to find me. I was sitting on the bench by the horse chestnut tree.

He'd sat down next to me and had taken my hand. Then he'd just held it in both of his. "It's nice to be able to do this," he'd said quietly. "I've wanted to for so long."

"But then why . . ." I'd heaved a sigh. "*Why* did you . . . ?"

"Go ahead with the wedding?" I'd nodded. "Well . . . because I didn't know what you felt for *me*. And because I thought that Chloe was committed to marrying me and I believed that to have pulled out would have destroyed her, and the wheels of the wedding were turning *so* fast—it was like this . . . juggernaut, powering on."

"Thanks to Mum," I said balefully.

"Yes."

"Well . . . she wanted fireworks," I said. "And she got them. But did you really feel that Chloe was in *love* with you?"

"She seemed . . . glad to be with me. There were two or three weeks when she became quite remote—now I know why; but then she was suddenly full on with the wedding again, really involved with all the arrangements, constantly telling me how great everything was and how happy we were going to be. But now I know that she was just trying to convince herself."

"Were you in love with her?"

"I really . . . liked her," he answered. "I was . . . charmed by her. We'd gotten engaged in such a rush—almost by accident; I panicked at first, but then I told myself that I was thirty-six years old—why *not* get married? So I persuaded myself that I could be happy with her. But then I got to know you, Ella. And I fell in love with you. I was in agony, not knowing what to do, and not being able to tell you how I felt because it would have made me look *so* bad. But you must have realised how attracted to you I was."

"I . . . did."

"But you gave me no indication."

"How could I? You were marrying my sister! I wasn't going to wreck her happiness—or risk her having another breakdown like she had over Max. Added to which you and I had spent so little *time* together. Less than a day."

"Well . . ." Nate turned to me. "We've got all the time we need now." So we sat side by side, under the tree, just looking at each other. Nate smiled. "What are you doing? Counting my eyelashes?"

"No. I already know how many you've got. One hundred and sixty-two on the upper lid . . ."

"Really?"

"And seventy-four on the lower—but don't worry, that's perfectly normal."

"Good. You had me worried there."

We were still gazing at each other. "I can see myself," I said.

"Your face in my eye . . ." he murmured.

"Thine in mine appears."

Nate touched his lips against mine. I felt my insides dissolve. "You kiss with your eyes open," he said.

"That's because I don't want to stop looking at you, Nate." His lips touched mine again, his hands cradling my face.

In the gallery, Nate greets his friends. "Honey!" he exclaims above the party chatter. "Andy. Kay. James. Great to see you all."

I slide my arm around him. "You're here," I murmur happily.

"Of course I am." Nate kisses me. "Happy birthday, Ella."

"We were just talking about your painting," Kay says . She looks at Nate, then at his portrait. "It's the very picture of you."

"It is," Honey says as she studies it. "You've really . . . *captured* him, Ella."

Nate kisses me again. "She has."

Author's Note

The Very Picture of You is a work of fiction, but the inspiration for the story of Guy Lennox was reading about the sale at auction of a picture by the portraitist Sir Herbert Gunn. Called *Design for a Group Portrait,* it was painted in 1929 and was of Sir Herbert's three children, from whom, following his divorce, he had been estranged. I also wish to acknowledge that I have taken one or two liberties with the history of the Northern Ballet Theatre, now Northern Ballet, whose production of *Giselle* was in 1978, not 1979.

The following books were a useful resource during the research and writing of the book:

Northern Ballet Theatre: 40 Years in the Making, published by
  Biskit Ltd.

Portraiture: Facing the Subject, edited by Joanna Woodall,
  published by Manchester University Press

Portraiture by Richard Brilliant, published by Reaktion Books

Painting People by Charlotte Mullins, published by Thames and Hudson

A Face to the World by Laura Cumming, published by HarperPress

Changing Face: Contemporary Portraiture by Peter Monkman, published by Watts Gallery

Acknowledgments

I am indebted to the portrait painters Jonathan Yeo, June Mendoza, Nick Offer, Fanny Rush, Paul Benney and David Noakes, who kindly shared with me their insights into the art of portraiture. Any inaccuracies are entirely my own. I'd also like to thank Rodney Baldwin, of the art supplies shop Green and Stone; Amanda Wright, for giving me the lowdown on life as a hand and foot model; and Shani Blich, for correcting my Italian. Heartfelt thanks to my brilliant agents, Clare Conville and Jake Smith-Bosanquet, and to everyone at Conville and Walsh. At Bantam Dell, I'm eternally grateful, once more, to my brilliant editor, Kate Miciak, and to Loyale Coles, Randall Klein, Evan Camfield and Sharon Propson. In the U.K. I'm indebted to Sarah Ritherdon, and to Lynne Drew, Hana Osman, Laura Mell and all at HarperCollins. My gratitude, also, to my friends Rachel Hore, Louise Clairmonte and Eliana Howarth, who kindly read the manuscript, and encouraged me along the way. Finally I'd like to thank my family, who were unendingly supportive and tolerant during the writing process. So huge thanks and love go, as ever, to Greg, to our children, Alice and Edmund, and to my stepsons, Freddie and George.

ABOUT THE TYPE

The text of this book was set in Filosofia. It was designed in 1996 by Zuzana Licko, who created it for digital typesetting as an interpretation of the sixteenth-century typeface Bodoni. Filosofia, an example of Licko's unusual font designs, has classical proportions with a strong vertical feeling, softened by rounded droplike serifs. She has designed many typefaces and is the cofounder of *Emigre* magazine, where many of them first appeared. Born in Bratislava, Czechoslovakia, Licko came to the United States in 1968. She studied graphic communications at the University of California at Berkeley, graduating in 1984.